AGENTS OF SYMPATHY

As riveting as today's terrible headlines, Frank O'Neill's first novel is a breathless thriller which effortlessly spans continents in the deadly and always uncertain arena of international espionage.

From North Africa where passions and politics ride high and any moment can see the touchpaper of insurrection ignited, to the cold safety of Geneva, the race is on to stop the Russians from destroying the fragile Western alliance carefully set up in a crucial third-world country. Giovanni Sidgewick Stears, an Italian-American investment consultant to rich Arabs and part-time CIA agent, is enmeshed in this delicate power balance. And he knows that any brash movement, whether it be in the Arab slums of Paris or the drug docks of Marseilles could set the whole world alight, on a time-switch to destruction. A time-switch that was constantly being quickened by treachery and betrayals.

AGENTS OF SYMPATHY has already won warm praise and drawn comparisons with the masters of the genre, le Carré and Ambler.

About the Author

Frank O'Neill is a native of Charleston, South Carolina. He was born in 1943 and educated in Switzerland and Oxford University, and after a spell in the wine trade, became a journalist. He has lived in Geneva, Paris and Washington D.C. and now makes his home in Atlanta, South Carolina. He is at work on his second novel, set in East Germany.

'O'Neill's sharp descriptions of Geneva, Paris and North Africa evoke the right mood for treason, murder and heroism'

Booklist

'Readers could not but become involved in AGENTS OF SYMPATHY'

The Listener

'Each of the book's distinctive characters is developed with painstaking detail'

Publishers Weekly

AGENTS OF
SYMPATHY

Frank O'Neill

CORONET BOOKS
Hodder and Stoughton

Copyright © Frank O'Neill 1985

First published in Great Britain in 1985 by
Hodder and Stoughton Limited

Coronet edition 1987

British Library C.I.P.

O'Neill, Frank
Agents of sympathy.
I. Title
813'.54[F]   PS3565.N495

ISBN 0 340 40280 6

Printed and bound in Great Britain for
Hodder and Stoughton Paperbacks, a
division of Hodder and Stoughton Ltd.,
Mill Road, Dunton Green, Sevenoaks,
Kent (Editorial Office: 47 Bedford
Square, London, WC1B 3DP) by
Richard Clay Ltd.,
Bungay, Suffolk.

To my wife Ramona, with love

Now we are come to the place I told you of,
Where you will see the wretched people
Who have lost the good of reason.

—**Dante**,
The Inferno

Prologue

Seen from the Mediterranean, in the early morning light, the city of al-Tabek can look like a sugar-white birthday cake with green candles all around. The gardens, each with its cypress or oleander, in every crevice of its terraced hillside, give the city its characteristic look of horizontal white and vertical green. Al-Tabek is the capital of Berbia, and Berbia is the backwater of North Africa, so the silhouette of al-Tabek is not to any great extent broken up by billboard, apartment complex, skyscraper, or hotel. Just below the royal palace it is true, the Hilton stands broad-shouldered as a bouncer. Well below it, eating up a salt marsh untouched since Carthaginian times, are the cranes and earth-piles of the newly negotiated United States naval base. The Kingdom of Berbia is conservative, pro-Western, and poor.

Poor. It is not much of a cake close up. The narrow white streets are stained with dung of goat and ass, and far from being serene, it is extremely noisy – Arab music wails from radios, motor scooters howl in low gear. It is hot, airless, steep, smelling alternately of sewage and exhaust. The gardens, all enclosed, cannot be seen from the street. These are facts of life.

The city resembles a hotel taken over by disaster victims. Al-Tabek is the refuge of last resort – the refuge of coastal peasant driven out of mechanized vineyard, of Tuareg nomad destitute from drought, of ragtag families wandering in from the guerrilla war in the south. It has the bazaars with merchants drinking coffee at their stalls; it has the veiled ladies slipping down its streets; but,

1

aside from one cool, watered terrace with French shops and a grand hotel, all seems precarious. The solid white squares are choked with shantytowns. Too many streets are full of lean, dull-eyed young men. There is a great, foul camp outside the docks, and the day-labor gate is mobbed each morning. Crowds collect fast, and the French-uniformed police go down the streets in Jeeps – in some quarters their rare forays resemble military expeditions. A smell of charcoal, urine, sickness, and cheap food challenges the coffee and hibiscus. Al-Tabek floats nervously on a formless human flood.

The man entered the square and walked around it to the café. He sat at the outermost table, though the rest were empty, facing the street where he had come from. He was a young man, a sharp dark-skinned Arab in Western clothes, cheap and shiny but smart enough in this square. The square was making a last stand. Slum surrounded it on three sides. The café seats were cracked. The shop signs sagged. The man had entered from the slum.

The waiter brought him coffee and looked at him without expression. Then he went back into the café and shut the door. He locked it. The man was controlling his breathing but sweat ran down his face. The coffee sat untouched. From time to time he looked very quickly up the street in front of him, but he listened without ceasing towards the street he had come from. Nothing. Only four minutes to wait. He had lost them. And why not? A man alone can lose a mob.

It was afternoon. Two streets away, the black-robed muezzin mounted the fifteenth circle of stairs of the minaret. He emerged and stood blinking, crowlike, in the glare. Below him, al-Tabek lay open to the muezzin and the sun. Far out at sea, a freighter pointed like an arrow to the port. But the muezzin never looked that way, now, for there was the naval base, the foul nest of the American infidels, the enemies of God. The muezzin, his eyes now equal to the glare, looked down. From one of the mean streets below the mosque's white walls, a faint sharp sound of shouting and of riot separated itself from the city's noise. The muezzin nodded. A mob of men, two or three dozen of the city's lowest class, roamed the streets, gathering adherents as it went. They shouted and brandished clubs and knives. But there was something tentative about the sound, as though the object of their rage were not at hand.

The muezzin reached into his robes. He drew out a small black coffer like a holy book. From its edge he gently drew a silver wand. He touched the coffer to his mouth as though in devotion and said, "I am here."

Down near the mob, but not of it, a thin young man in dock laborer's clothes lounged on a motor scooter, a radio to his ear. He moved it quickly to his mouth and said, "We have lost him. You were too long climbing the stairs. He must be running still."

"I will look."

The voice came back. "The traitor is in the Square al-Habiq. I see him plain. He is at the café there. It may be that he expects help. It is but four streets from you. You must go . . ."

"I know the way. Tell me if he leaves. But I think he will not."

"God go with you."

The young man kicked the scooter into gear. He rode towards the mob, his face contorted into a sudden rage. He yelled, "I have seen the pig we seek. He mocks us in the Square al-Habiq. Follow me, brothers! We will destroy him yet."

When there were two minutes to wait, the man at the café heard them. They were chanting now, the final word rising in a howl. There seemed more than when he had escaped them, more than had been at the meeting of the Brothers of Islam. He could hear them moving to and fro in the warren of streets, but it was impossible to tell whether they were making for the square or not. He doubted it. One does not hide in squares. In two minutes, Hussein, his CIA colleague, would be here. Thirty seconds to tell him and then easy to hide. But tell him what? That cover was blown. The meeting had been a setup, a trap, a well-planned denunciation before an already rabid mob.

And now he saw them. This was his first moment of fear. His denunciation had been a long second of disbelief in the dim, smoke-stained back room piled with sacks, behind the bazaar where the radical Brothers of Islam met. The image of the Mullah Ibrahim – face like a starved horse, black, fat eyes, the heavy gold ring on the outstretched finger – was engraved on his memory. The Mullah Ibrahim had drawn sudden breath at the end of his weekly rambling diatribe against Americans, spies, fornicators, Zionists, unveiled women, and the King, and with a look of hatred and wild joy had turned on him, pointing, accusing, dossier-perfect, giving the date of his recruitment, the fact, accurate for a change, that it was the Americans he served. Denunciation was nothing rare among the Brothers, and that had given him his chance. For the denounced – of fornication, of spying in some general way, of trading with the Jews – would whine, or plead, or even bellow their innocence, while he in a second, less, faster than the unsuspecting door guards could react, hurled the nearest thing, a broken floor tile, to the middle of the room and in the eye-blink while the Brothers winced, waiting for the explosion, or simply gaped, he rushed, feinting, kicking – one guard in the groin – down the short passage through the grocer's shop into the bazaar. A man alone can lose a mob. He knew the city. He was good. Tell Hussein to close the network, then vanish, sink. He would even survive, he thought. It could be done.

But the mob came into the square like police dogs to a throat. The leaders ran silent, straight. Their weapons were not brandished but deadly, at their sides. He had been quite wrong. They had not blundered into him, they had known that he was there. They came straight

4

toward him. He saw the hard faces, the slum fanatics, the hooligan puritans, the cropped heads, the unthinking eyes, the motor scooters at the side, the bludgeons and the knives and knew himself alone against both intelligence and brute.

And now he ran. The street before him led uphill. He heard the motor scooters behind him whine, but three steps marked the entrance of the square, and that would slow them down at least. He leaped them. He forced himself to plan, to think. A quarter of a mile away were better streets, police. A man could lose a mob, but not one guided, steered. He could outrun a man, perhaps, but not a motorcycle. If they had known he was there, there could be others circling him, around the corner. He could be trapped already. He did not understand. The Brothers of Islam were extremely dangerous but extremely crude. He was the professional.

That was a blind alley. He had almost taken it. The leaders had surged past the motor scooters at the steps, but the machines were over them now, whining up the hill, not powerful, not fast even, but faster than a man.

The muezzin, who saw with the eye of God, was pleased. The little figures of the faithful were close, very close, a few doorways' width behind the hireling, the apostate, the spy. It was good that they were, for the devil was already near the Godless streets of cars and infidels and police where the faithful could only hide and wait. But then the muezzin saw and understood and knew that God's judgment was ever ready and very close. The devil would meet his death on earth in the fires of hell. He spoke again into the radio, speaking twice before the rider on the motor scooter heard him.

"Let him run as he runs. God awaits him. But do not let him turn, and be ready to cut him off. The way is blocked."

The man heard the motor noise drop back. It puzzled him, but only one small sector in his brain still thought – his being was concentrated in his spine and his lungs,

5

and his eyes saw only the street ahead. Too late to dodge, to turn. His hope lay in meters – *broken pavement there, I could have stumbled, died* – a few hundred, now – *less, I know that doorway, it's around one more turn* – led from the warren of mean streets to traffic, plane trees, sun, life, police. He could not look back. The motor noise came back, gaining again. No chanting behind him now – breath as hard as his but firm, unflagging. His panting wind received but did not note a rich warm smell of tar burning in the air. With sudden hope he heard a car horn, traffic at a light. He ran harder. One more bend. Then he heard the motor noise beside him. He looked in horror, looked into the rider's face two meters away – Ali, the boy from the docks. He flinched. He almost stumbled. But it was over now.

But it was not. His tiny, unbelieving brain saw Ali smile, ride on, like an evening promenader acknowledging a friend. He couldn't think about it. And now, thirty meters, all straight. He could see the plane trees, the cars. Already, surely, they could not kill him here.

He saw the road machines when he was almost on them – the asphalt truck warmly reeking, the rolling machine, the flames. They did not quite block the mouth of the alley. There was a gap and in the gap was Ali, a tire iron in his hand. Ali smiled again. He slowed, just a little, just to understand the smile.

The first blow hit him then – a plank between the shoulder blades. Falling headlong, he actually ran faster a few steps. Then he fell. A crowbar struck his back. He crawled. He crawled right up to the asphalt truck. Something struck his head, driving his face into the stone. He felt a blade but did not quite know where. His vision was narrow and bordered with black. His legs had left his body. Then nothing hit him. Perhaps they went away. No, they had not gone away. Ali, his friend, who had smiled at him, was standing beside the asphalt truck, just above him. He was pulling a lever on the side. Perhaps this was where Ali worked. He thought about it.

Perhaps he could raise his head. The rich, warm smell became intense. He looked. He saw Ali step aside. He wondered why. He saw the thick, smoking flood slide to the ground and sweep toward him. He understood. He didn't care. He didn't care until it bathed his face and he arched and twisted like a spider on a burning log.

The muezzin watched from on high. The Koran strictly forbade the torture of prisoners, pain for pain's sake. This was not such. Spies were all about. This was exemplary punishment of a traitor by the faithful of God. Did not the Koran say, *He who breaks with the Messenger and follows a path other than that of the believers, him we shall consign to roast in Gehenna?* He bethought himself. It was the time. He straightened and drew in full breath. He looked to the sky. His voice, trained, beautiful, flowed out. The call to prayer rose over the rooftops like a bird.

Part One

1

Between the pâtés and the Bries, Persephone Salfield experienced a moment of pure pleasure in the vicinity of the olive salad. This was not, for her, a common occurrence. She had a degree from Vassar, no child, a husband who would actually have been influential but for the last election, a totally renovated house on Capitol Hill with an ingenious skylight, some satisfactions, a great many interests, and a triumph or two, but actual pleasure was rare. This one made her want to stretch her back. It was a combination, she thought, of time and weather and Saturday morning. At 10 A.M. Neam's was all but empty. The mushrooms looked like butter; the lettuce looked like lawns. Georgetown would be eighteenth century for another hour. The traffic between here and Capitol Hill had been light and even amiable. And best of all was her party this evening. She looked forward to it with a perfect equilibrium of confidence and ambition. Old friends and desirable friends and not only that. A lion had accepted, one of the biggest and fiercest of the diminished Left. This in turn told her that even if Mason was no longer with the White House, he was nonetheless senior aide, administrative assistant, to the only liberal on the House Armed Services Committee: their life had not crumbled, they had set a scaffolding under adversity, they stood perhaps higher among the Left defeated than among the Left in power, chance still pointed like a compass needle. This gave her a lightness and an energy indistinguishable from sex. So when she heard her name called, and turned to see Susannah

Bolling weighing her Belgian endive, she turned upon her a smile so rapturous that the other started in a small surprise before she smiled herself. Susannah, a little older, had fallen equally on her feet. Her husband was administrative assistant to a liberal senator of national name. They lived in Georgetown, where Persephone only shopped.

Susannah, in fact, minutely underlined it. "So nice to be here early," she said. "So nice to have Neam's in the neighborhood. How's Mason liking it in the Rayburn Building? Not too depressed?" She reached the meat counter.

Persephone made herself laugh, which was really not difficult, for she was happy still. "Oh, no," she said. "Feeling very creative. Very together. We're out from under the rubble." She smiled. "Absolutely."

It might not be true – since the election Mason had been miserable, frightened, and getting fat – but it would do for now.

Susannah shifted her head by forty-five degrees. "No, no. Not beef. We don't eat beef. Maybe lamb, but only if the eggplant's good. It is? Your smallest leg, then, and boned. You're going to enjoy Jonathan Snead," she said. "So glad you're going to know him."

Where the hell, thought Persephone, *did she get my guest list?* "Oh, I know," she said. "He is fun, isn't he? But I think it matters a great deal more that he's one of the ones who are really doing something – even with things as they are."

Jonathan Snead was her lion.

"He told us he wanted to meet you," Susannah said. "In fact we ought to have you all at our house soon. He's not the only one you ought to know. Don't count on his little girl. She's dreary. No. No veal. See you soon, then." Her espadrilles whispered on the floor toward the mineral water. *Bitch!* murmured Persephone; but she was happy still.

On his way home, Mason Salfield felt a qualm. This was in spite of the weather and the place. His walk home

12

gave him, usually, a daily sustenance – a single, small, much-needed compensation for his removal from the staff of the National Security Council and his lodgement on the staff of the Armed Services Committee. He lived close by at Lexington Place. Daily, when he left the Rayburn Building, the Capitol would enfold him in its grave, maternal arms – he was close still, very close, to the center, to the source. Before the Supreme Court building, his rather pudgy shoulders would take on a motion combative and intent – he devoted a daily ten seconds to scoring old betrayals, old success. At A Street he entered, like a warm, stale bath, the knowledge of the excellence of his manner of life. Here were the clever renovations, bow window gardens and solar roofs that showed forth the inventiveness, the resourcefulness, the sheer healthfulness of his kind. And here, interspersed among them were the People, the mixed blocks. Mason and Persephone lived right among the People – here, to prove it, was the Museum of African Art. He lived not only extremely well; he lived in harmony with everything he thought. He walked these blocks with a quiet smile of self-delight on his veal-colored face. But at Stanton Square, when he thought of this evening's party, he met the qualm.

The qualm bore the likeness of Jonathan Snead. Jonathan Snead, the scourge of the CIA, represented the trembling ground that lay between a triumph and an overreach or, equally, between the liberal parks and the radical jungles. On the whole, this was just the territory that Mason knew himself to use best. He could slip into the jungle, make some friends, forge an alliance, extend the frontier, and then, at the scent of a real wild beast, scurry back to liberalism through invisible gates. He was a frontiersman, a scout. That was fine so long as beasts smelled like beasts. Mason reminded himself that his nose was good.

While they waited for their first guests, Persephone said, "Do we know anything special about Berbia? That's what everybody's going to talk about, and I don't see why

13

Larry and Angela should steal the show. And you know they'll try. I didn't want to have them, but Julia Drew asked me to as a favor. Couldn't you have found me a Berbian?"

Mason said, "The only Berbians in Washington are embassy people, and they kiss ass with the Administration."

"I met somebody who had a Berbian cabdriver. He said the King was worse than the Shah."

"Well, I wasn't in the cab," said Mason. "Yes, I do know something special. We've been debating Berbia for a month. How's this? The Berbian mullahs don't want the base, and some of them are willing to declare solidarity with Khomeini. UCAAM sent a mission and found that out. Only friendly congressmen have the report."

"Well, why should they want the shitty base? What's Ucam?"

"United Clergy Against American Militarism. What are those?"

"Ground lamb in vine leaves."

Mason ate one with an oily, sucking sound.

"Stop it. You've left a hole in the plate, and I went all the way to Georgetown for those. Anyway, you've been gaining weight ever since the election. It's very unhealthy. You should direct your anger outwards."

"I do. Larry and Angela won't have heard about the mullahs. State didn't get a report."

The living room had a deep bay window. They had glassed in the bay and filled it with plants – moss, foliage, and a canopy of trees. The evening light came in aqueous and cool. The furniture was either low and squashy or soft leather and stainless steel. On the black lacquer dining table the food was set out in woven baskets from mainland China. The baskets looked like newly crusted bread. Along the walls, on lacquered stands, was excellent pottery, gray and rust. Persephone worked at the Hirshhorn and her eye was good. They had two

14

salaries and spent them on the house. There was an abstract print of Chairman Mao, who would have detested it. Mason and Persephone stood close together and not at all relaxed. They played with glasses of white wine.

"Who have you been talking to?" Persephone said. "Susannah Bolling knew the whole guest list."

"She couldn't have."

"She knew about Jonathan Snead."

"Did she?" said Mason. The qualm returned.

When the best guests were there, Larry and Angela Monkton arrived with a Berbian mullah. Larry was with State and they had returned from a posting in al-Tabek nine months before.

"You won't mind, will you?" said Angela. "Ibrahim's such an old friend. Larry and I knew him in al-Tabek. He's very important in the opposition now, and we thought you'd like to meet someone who really knows. He called us. State wasn't going to give him a visa, but Larry was able to tip off the ACLU and they began to raise a fuss and the Administration chickened out. We're almost the only people he trusts in Washington. It's wonderful. He's here to testify before an interdenominational committee of all the major churches."

Persephone smiled quite nicely. Although Angela had blond hair and no makeup, she wore an Arab dress. The Mullah was thin, not old, and his head combined the features of a weasel and a starved horse. He took no notice of Persephone at all. In his black robes, he looked just like the mullahs on the evening news. All three refused wine. "Do you have some yogurt?" said Angela, but Persephone did not choose to hear.

The Mullah was wonderful. The best guests who gathered around him smiled kindly in greeting to an ally, to a friend. They were met by a flat, black, obsidian glare that pushed them one pace backward and knocked their eyes to the floor. When the holy man spoke, his

15

head stretched forward as though being pulled from his neck, and the big gold ring on his outstretched finger flashed.

"No," he said. "My hope is small. It is not for hope that I come, and I do assure you it is not to beg. It is perhaps you who should beg. I have come that you should know that what you do is an abomination in the eyes of God – that you may turn from your foul alliance with our King, from your killing, from your spies. With our brothers in Iran you were blind. You will be blind to us."

The youngest girl there, with a silver necklace, said, "You must hate us so." She was beautiful and guileless, and she wrung her hands. The holy man took the offering, though he did not look at her.

"And it is good that we hate you. It is very good. It is good that we hate Satan and all that he does."

Mason Salfield had not meant to be near the Mullah at all – Persephone was glaring at him. But he obscurely felt himself to be the home team and he bravely said, "An Administration's hardly a country, of course. There's tremendous sympathy here for the Berbian opposition. The Administration props up the King as an American puppet, but people are beginning to see that he's an oppressive colonial relic with no future. We're just as much against Administration policy as you are. It's not America."

The Mullah knocked him flat. "And for twenty-seven years it is not America? Our pretty little King takes tanks from Eisenhower and jets from Kennedy. And Mr. Johnson sends him instructors for the army and the air force, and for the torturers, too. And Mr. Nixon sends him ships. And Mr. Carter reads him a little sermon, but he also sends him aid. And now that the power of the faithful makes the King shake on his throne, you come with your base and your fleet and your helicopters and make him happy again. But it is never America. No."

16

The Mullah was a great success. There was a group around Angela and Larry to discuss what he meant.

This was why, when Jonathan Snead arrived, Persephone kissed him. In sober fact, she felt that to kiss the cheek of the man who had as good as killed four CIA agents in the last three months was a little melodramatic, even Sicilian, but it extinguished the Mullah and it was undeniably, of sorts, a thrill. This, although the cheek she kissed was angled away from her and quite unresponsive so it was a little like kissing a side of beef. Jonathan Snead was looking straight at Mason, who was looking queasily at his wife. It had been his hope that Snead could be presented as one who would anxiously seek Mason out but whose wholehearted welcome was by no means sure. And here was Persephone behaving like the Traviata. Mason attempted damage control. He went up to his guest and took his hand, thus removing him from his wife, and greeted him while turning, thus addressing the room.

"You must be Jonathan," he said. "And I'm very pleased to meet you. I don't know how we didn't meet on the McGovern committees. We've so many friends in common."

But Jonathan Snead stood fixed and looked slowly around the room. "We have some here," he said. "Hello, Larry. Hello, George. Hello, Julia."

Even Persephone realized that the scent of her lion made her party uneasily shift and sidle. For George and Larry answered but dropped their eyes, and only Persephone's old school friend, Julia Drew, who did educational things for the PLO and had trained herself to adjust to violence, forthrightly grinned and said, "Hello, Jonathan, dear. How's tricks?"

She was the most striking woman in the room – a beacon of red hair over flawless skin, and a runner's body in a Halston dress. She quite eclipsed Persephone, and she was responsible, besides, for Angela and Larry and

17

the Mullah, too. Nonetheless, *Bless, you Julia*, thought Persephone.

For this lion was carnivorous, no doubt of that at all, and the mode of this gathering was vegetarian. Jonathan Snead had first begun to matter in the McGovern campaign – and so had half those present. He had had a role in Chicago in 1968 – and so had a few. He had played an honorable part in the boarding party that had leaped from the smoldering pinnace of the Left onto the Carter ship of state – and Persephone's party could have filled a lifeboat there. His specialty by then was foreign policy, and he had served usefully under the U. S. ambassador to the United Nations. He had edited, for a time, a counter-foreign policy magazine, *Free Planet*. Thus, when Jonathan Snead later became director of Free Information, then a mildly querulous McGovernite group calling for the discontinuation of American intelligence gathering and the release of all classified information, it had seemed no more than his entitled share of the general burrowing into tax-exempt foundations, the Civil Service, and the Congressional staffs.

But while his peers grew three-piece suits, Jonathan Snead grew claws and teeth. Free Information had become the brazen trumpet broadcasting, with extraordinary fidelity, the names, addresses, operations, and codes of the CIA's best-covered agents in whatever sectors were, at the time, most exposed and sensitive. The rest was left to the locals. In Iraq, an agent had been shot in a steam bath. In Ankara, another had been blown to pieces in his garden. In Surinam, the supposed director of the American Library had been found in a garbage can, and his mutilations had probably been received while he was alive. One might have no choice but to admire Snead's courage, one might know in one's heart of hearts that it was sentimental to waste sympathy on agents of the CIA, but, still, around Snead there was a scent of blood on which Persephone's guests quite genuinely choked.

18

It was a vibrant odor, nonethless. Nobody could deny that since the election, while the Left in general had burrowed deeper, had stayed very still, had clung grimly to jobs once seen as modest stepping-stones, Snead had hardly broken stride. Free Information had funds, a legal staff, skills, success, and tax exemption. It effectively savaged the foreign policy of a right-wing Administration. One might prefer to reject Jonathan Snead – but did one have the right?

On the other hand, if one had a public job, did one dare accept him?

And Mason Salfield, seeing his qualm take flesh, seeing approval of his harboring of Jonathan Snead in a gathering of the respectable Left hang trembling in the balance, intuitively grasped this and said, "How are we going to stop the Administration from getting us into a new Lebanon in Berbia?"

Jonathan Snead, whose face was thin and whose cheeks were as vertical as the sides of a ship, achieved a smile in the small space between them and said, "You tell me. You're with the Armed Services Committee."

And Mason smiled – not only socially but because it had worked. One could not disagree with outrage over a positive American military presence in a corrupt monarchy with an increasingly publicized guerrilla war. Besides, Mason had the pleasant certainty that no one present had access to any more privileged information on the nation's Berbian policy than he himself – mullahs didn't get security briefings. Of Mason's knowledge, the interesting part was classified, of course, and that had to be treated with care. Privileged information was the currency of Washington, but his position was not strong enough to allow him to be seen spending it profligately. He calculated. He was among friends, like-thinkers. A moral person ineluctably was forced from time to time to savage the policies he officially enacted. The moment of tension was safely past. Eyes looked at him invitingly. Larry and Angela had their own circle around their mullah. He'd be damned if he'd let them, in his own house, steal the scene.

He chose a morsel with care. He said, "Do you know how much support King Fahd has? We had to authorize a supplementary weapons shipment and this one was secret. The CIA was all over it. Topline tactical weapons, latest issue NATO. And you know what it was for? The palace regiment. He wants them to have stuff the rest of the army doesn't have. That's the only force he trusts. We're backing a king who can only count on one regiment! It's wonderful."

"It's sickening!" Persephone said.

"That's very interesting," said Johnathan Snead. "Armoured personnel carriers, weren't they?"

"Oh, a lot more than that," said Mason. "AR-15's. M-79 grenade launchers. Scatter-shot mortars. All sorts of stuff."

"Yes, of course," said Snead. "I remember hearing something about that. Where did you get it?"

"It came in DIS. Don't quote me, though."

He meant the Defense Intelligence Summary.

"Of course not," said Snead.

Larry and Angela stuck fast to their mullah and kept their mullah at a distance from Jonathan Snead. They had known Snead since 1972, but he had placed himself, for the time being, a little outside the bravest safe interpretation of showing one's independence from one's job. Particularly since Steven Lutrick, a quasi-elder at State whom Larry had not expected to find here, had joined the group, though his eyes seemed mainly upon Julia Drew. And if one had – who knew? – the possible Khomeini of a future Berbia tamed and eating out of one's hand, it was folly not to show it off.

Angela explained, "Islam's not a bit reactionary, you see. It's not like our churches at all. When you really understand it, you find that in some cases it's more progressive than socialism."

20

Julia Drew, of Palestinians for Peace, demurred. "That's so naive. In Saudi Arabia it's the imams who keep the people chained under an oppressive feudal monarchy."

The Mullah reached up his ringed hand as though to ward off evil and advanced his face toward Julia's. "The Saudi King is an American whore like the King of Berbia, and the Saudi imams are his household pimps. Mecca itself is in thrall to the American beast, yes, as much as al-Tabek. The true Islam in Riyadh hides itself. The true Islam knows the King for the Satan that he is."

"It's all the West, you see," said Angela vaguely.

"That's such balls," said Julia pleasantly. "The Saudis and Khomeini are two sides of the same camel-driver. George Habbash is worth ten of them."

And drew holy lightning.

"You speak blasphemy," said the Mullah. "And you blaspheme from ignorance. Why do you speak when you know nothing? You wear a harlot's dress. You have a harlot's tongue. No doubt you have a harlot's mind."

He turned his back. The Mullah was terrific.

Steven Lutrick came to Julia's aid. His heavy lenses and his snowy collar inclined beside her. He touched her arm with the manner at once of an English butler and an expensive family doctor and led her to a puffy seat under the jowls of Chairman Mao. His manner did not disguise that he was the oldest there, that this was somewhat, for him, a children's party – his own daughter had been at Madeira with Persephone and Julia. He had attained that condition of permanence in Washington where his ideology was as little noticed or questioned as the architecture of Memorial Bridge. But to Julia he did not condescend.

He took her by the arm again in a manner that aspired to avuncularity and failed. But Julia softened nicely. He was quite high on the Middle Eastern desk at State.

He said, "I wouldn't necessarily buy George Habbash, but in general I think you're absolutely right. It's sad.

Our policies consist of apologizing for the Storm Troopers in Israel to the bucolics on the Gulf. The Palestinians are the future and we ignore them. It's frustrating."

Julia's manner was absolutely down to earth. She had learned it in Virginia as a fox-hunting miss and she thought it suited the ambience of the PLO.

She said, "That's so clever of you, Steven. Are you thinking of doing anything about it, by any chance?"

He said, "At Palestinians for Peace . . . you're not just the receptionist now, are you? That's become a little bit of a blind, hasn't it?" His arm added, *You ought to be in pictures*, but she ignored that and answered, "Well, you know, we're not AT&T. But, yeah, you could say the guys there, with me, they talk and they listen. I'm the American. There's a lot they need me for. I can go where I please."

He profoundly paused. She profoundly waited.

He said, "That's precisely what I mean, Julia. That's exactly it."

She looked impressed.

"There is a growing body of serious people who feel as we do. I am not talking about malcontents and snitches but about men and women of authority and expertise who also happen to have private consciences and convictions. In State, in CIA, in the UN delegation, even in DOD. We execute the official policies, but meanwhile we lay the foundations for the policies of the future – which are often almost the opposite. It's a question of time. People need to learn that the violence, as they call it, of the PLO is only relative and anyway is caused by transient historical circumstances. Israel is doing that for us. And, besides, of course, we have no right to try and impose our values everywhere. That's obvious.

"What we need most of all is clear lines of communication with Palestinian power centers. It's not that easy. Look at how they martyred poor Andy Young. And these lines must be kept distinct from the occasional clumsy efforts of the Administration to 'talk to the PLO.' Much of this can be done best by CIA. My old school friend Jason

Witham is head of CIA in Cairo and he's first-rate. But we need contacts in Washington too, and this is such a goldfish bowl. Now, your group is very moderate, very open, very educational. What I'm asking, Julia, is this: would you be willing – I'm perfectly certain you'd be able – to act with me as an interface" – the arm joyously concurred – "between men and women of individual conscience here and in Palestine? It would be so easy. I know your family. We both live in Georgetown. My place in Virginia isn't far from theirs. We could meet in contexts that would be absolutely nonspecific. It could be so important."

Julia lightly patted his knee. "Steven, darling, of course I can. No trouble at all and really quite fun. You just tell us about anything particularly nasty the Administration has up its sleeve, and we'll help the right people here make the breakthroughs and all that." Steven Lutrick looked pained. "Or whatever it is you really want. Now, stop looking so soulful or people will think you're propositioning me and I've turned you down. You'd ruin my reputation. Now would you please get me a glass of Mason's cheap white wine."

Julia went over to Persephone, who was alone for a moment. She stood comfortably beside her.

"Well, Persy," she said. "What's up? I mean really up. I don't see enough of you."

Persephone made a small, uncertain gesture and a little smile. She was shorter than Julia and much less vivid and the fact that their coloring was the same made them look like two birds of identical species of which Persephone was the drab little hen. She nibbled on a vine leaf.

"It's not so bad," she said. "We really did OK. Oh, shit, it's awful. I thought Mason was going to be an under-secretary of state. I really did. Funny, isn't it? Do you know how old some of the people he works with are?"

Julia made a consoling sound.

"Twenty-four. Goddamn little babies. Makes me feel like Eleanor Roosevelt. You know what could have been worse? Things were going so well that Mason wanted to have a baby and somehow I had sense enough to wait until the election. Christ, wouldn't that have been something? Come with me and get some wine."

They walked slowly toward the carafes.

"Do you know how many staffers there are on the Hill? Seven thousand two hundred and twenty-seven. Do you know how many administrative aides there are? Five hundred and thirty-five. Mason's a wreck. He's fat and unhappy and he doesn't know what to do. He's not making as much and we're getting in debt. And he's even worried about his job. He only got it because he used to be with the National Security Council and his congressman's looking for an excuse to give it to one of his old chums. Thank God I've got the Hirshhorn. And our friends are worse off than us. And nothing's going to get better for two years, if it does then. Why did that bitch bring that Arab? I was looking forward to tonight, I wish you hadn't asked me to have them, Julia. And I don't like Jonathan Snead. I wanted to have him. It was my idea, but I don't like him. His eyes are too small. And his skin's cold. I wish he hadn't come."

They were in the kitchen door now. Julia had slowly led them there. She looked surprised and even shocked.

She said, "Oh, no, Persy. He's *it*. He's what you need. I mean, who cares about his skin? I mean, you don't have to go to bed with him, do you?"

Persephone smiled and elegantly shuddered. "No," she said.

At a moment when Angela was so fulsomely interpreting the Mullah that the Mullah was in fact alone, Julia went quickly to him. She spoke in Arabic, quietly and fast. "I am she," she said. "Welcome."

The Mullah, now, spoke soberly and tersely. His manner was composed.

24

"You are as you were described," he said.

"Good," said Julia. "This has to be quick. It was complicated to have you brought here. Are the Monktons being useful?"

"Yes. I had forgotten how tiresome they are."

"Was the agent without problems? I know he was killed."

"Yes. I denounced him as agreed and the religious louts killed him. I had one of our people there to guide them. It was easy. I believe they roasted him in asphalt, the poor fellow. The Brothers of Islam are the best weapon of Berbia's Baath party. The PLO doesn't give us enough credit. I am now the only infiltrator. The CIA man would have discovered me. He was good. But not yet and now not ever."

"Do you think you can manage with the committee tomorrow?"

"Did I convince your friends tonight?"

Julia richly, quietly laughed.

"Then I shall convince the committee tomorrow. I shall be the holy fool. I shall be what a raving mullah should be. Young woman, I wager my life for the PLO daily that I can persuade Arab fanatics that I am a great religious leader. I can surely get support from a committee of American churchmen."

"Very good," said Julia. "But before long we shall have to talk. And you can't be around the Monktons forever. I have a house in the country, near here. A way will be found to get you out there. I will call you."

He said seriously, "Good. I was not very gallant to you. It seemed necessary. I am sorry."

Julia said in English and a funny accent, "Come up and see me sometime."

The Mullah looked puzzled.

"You don't understand that, do you?" And again in Arabic, with irony. "The Peace be unto you, then."

Ibrahim for the first time smiled.

"And unto you the Peace," he said.

25

Late in the evening, when Mason thought he was alone, eating, he found Jonathan Snead by his side. His guest had approached silently from behind and then had stood there, arms crossed. Mason was so surprised that some flakes of pastry escaped from his lips and, in unsolicited testimonial to their lightness, floated down like snow. Snead watched them with neutral eyes. Mason realized that of his guests only Jonathan Snead and Julia Drew were left.

"Good party," said Snead. "Useful. Broad base."

Hugely and casually, Mason swallowed the rest. "Thanks," he said. "Glad you came. I thought we ought to get together. Fill your glass?"

"No, thank you. I don't do that."

Julia and Persephone joined them.

Snead said, "I'm glad we agree about Berbia."

Mason gestured seriously, hopelessly. "Doesn't everyone?" he said.

"But you're in a position to do something about it."

Mason, who was not falsely modest, faced it straight. "A certain amount, of course. My congressman listens to me, obviously. You could say that when he voted last week against selling King Fahd the Cobras, that was really my vote. But look at the committee. My congressman's one against eleven, and at best he's with three against nine. I can deal a little, but not much. It's depressing."

"That wasn't quite what I meant," said Snead. "I know you don't count on the committee. I was thinking about access. We know you see the DIS. Now your man would get the DIAB too, wouldn't he? At least the parts of them that deal with sectors the committee is concerned with." He meant the Defense Intelligence Agency Bulletin.

"Yes," said Mason. "He does." He realized that he had used the tone of someone asking for money and he said it again more brightly. "Of course he does."

Snead now kept his eyes steadily upon him. Mason decided he did not like that.

Snead said, "It's so difficult for those of us who are trying to do anything about Berbia. We're working in the dark. You could change that."

And Mason, feeling that the floor had turned vertical while he wasn't watching, actually stepped backwards and vehemently shook his head. He said, "No. No. That's much too dangerous. I don't even see that stuff." Which was worse, a stupid lie, and he changed it quickly. "At least, only a little of it. My congressman doesn't give me full access."

Snead went on pleasantly, "Well, he wouldn't, would he? You're not one of his old friends. He doesn't count on you much. But you could see those reports, Mason. I'm sure you could. You're the administrative aide. You must have the keys. I suppose you can work a Xerox. Stay late at the office, Mason. Work a little harder. That impresses people."

Mason saw Persephone standing open-mouthed, a full ashtray frozen in her hand. He suddenly remembered Julia Drew and found that she was perched on the back of a chair, watching the three of them with benign interest. He tasted the vine leaves in the back of his throat.

He said firmly, "No." But Snead went on without pausing.

"You can't imagine how it would help. The DIS would have reports of where King Fahd's troops are on any given day. Where his helicopters are. Think how many lives that would save. The DIAB would tell us what Fahd's doing with his new weapons – training schedules . . . when they're operational. I'm very interested in that. I want to stop a feudal reactionary from murdering his own people. We're on the same side, Mason. The Administration doesn't own that information. The People own it. Don't you want to help?"

Mason said quickly, "Of course I do. Yes. But it's just too dangerous. You don't realize what could happen to me."

Snead took a step forward. He said, "The fact is,

Mason, I do know. In my next newsletter – it comes out next week – I'll put in what you *were* able to tell me about the clandestine weapons shipment and the King's regiment. And I'll accredit it to you properly. That was classified information. And I'll accredit some things to you that came from sources who have turned out to be better friends than you. Julia will confirm you said it all."

Julia smiled brightly. Persephone looked at her with wide eyes.

"Oh, Julia!" she breathed.

"Well, I'd have to, wouldn't I, darling? I couldn't tell a lie."

"You'll never get a job in Washington again. You know that, of course. And Justice is getting ugly about that kind of thing. There's no one to protect you. You know that too. So let's not argue anymore.

"Now listen carefully. From now on, you will eat lunch alone every Wednesday at one o'clock at the cafeteria of the National Gallery. It gets crowded there. People share tables. Sometimes you'll end up with somebody else's napkin. On it will be written what we need for that week. Often, there may be nothing. You will have brought the material from the last week. It will be under your tray. And you'll leave. Just leave. It's that simple. We'll stay out of each other's way from now on. It's better like that." He looked around the room with its wineglasses and ashtrays and broken cheese. "I won't be able to reciprocate," he said.

Julia and Jonathan walked a hundred yards together, towards their cars. Soul music came from the unrestored house a block down the street, and black teenagers clustered in the lamplight on its stoop.

Julia said, "You can't have all of him. You couldn't have done it without me. We want some of him, too."

Snead said flatly, "There will be a quid pro quo."

Julia said, "I mean it. We're in this one together."

Snead's car was closer. He unlocked it. He said, "This

is not part of our joint operation. This is not *Lyusi*. This is straight KGB. You'll get something. Don't worry."

He did not offer to walk her past the teenagers on the stoop. She watched him drive away.

"Toad!" she said.

2

Giovanni Sidgewick Stears, whose name since Choate
had been Wop among Wasps, looked to the mountains
for solace. Beyond the carnations in the silver vase,
beyond the restaurant window, beyond the traffic policeman in his music box by the bridge, beyond the lake, the
Mont Blanc gleamed flawless and remote upon Geneva.
He smelled for a moment the high mountains, the chilled
electric air. Then, again, he smelled cigar. To his right,
the hard mountains; to his left, the soft jowls of Hajji
Melouf; in between, the gauzy veil from Hajji's Havana.

Hajji's eyes were upon his face, soft brown orbs of an
anxious spaniel. But the master Hajji adored was money,
and his anxiety was for the one perfect investment,
tirelessly trailed and never quite retrieved.

Hajji said, "But dollars, Mr. Stears? Is that wise? Is that
safe? For years and years in our family everything was
dollars. When the war was finished my father went to his
father and pointed under the bed where the box of gold
sovereigns was and he said, 'Father, that is old-fashioned
merchant ways.' No longer. No more gold. No more
spices. Now we buy dollars. With dollars we shall buy
Fords. 'Father,' he says, 'the man with dollars lives in
America even while he drinks coffee in al-Tabek.' Damn
right, Mr. Stears! And so we did. And God smiled on us,
Mr. Stears, you know how much. Am I in the bazaar! Hell
no! I am in Geneva. I am in New York. I am in Cannes.
Seven daughters, Mr. Stears, in English school. All swell.
We sell Fords, then trucks, and then tractors and even
planes. We love America."

Actually, Hajji was not so bad. In the depths of that enormous, worried face there could suddenly come a sly little shine of humour – even, and this was unusual in an Arab – humor if not exactly for himself than at least for his circumstances. So he slightly smiled at Hajji and said, "And then? And then?"

"And then America shut its eyes. For ten years the dollar is less and less. My friends say, 'Buy Swiss francs. Buy a nice chalet in Gstaad. Buy gold. Buy German stocks. Buy a fine house in London.' But my father says, 'America only blinks.' Mr. Stears, I know men who were small men once who now laugh at me with their francs and their gold. So finally, when my dollars were trash blown in the wind, I sell them and buy not so damn many francs. And now, you, who are advising me for two years only, say, "Sell those francs for trash and buy American.' For today the dollar is up. A woman has a new hairdo. For a day she is pretty. Mr. Stears, I trusted."

And this was not a game. Hajji's eyes mourned softly, and not for cash alone. They mourned for an act of cruelty, for a pointless breach of faith, for the wanton spoiling of a harmonious structure, for the theft of a harmless dream. It was at such moments that Wop would discover for an instant that he intensely liked his Arabs. *They don't know what an abstraction is*, he thought. *Their money's like children. It's a damn dangerous thing to deal with trust.*

He said, "America remains the world's strongest economy. The change in political direction three years ago is fundamental, though we still do not know how sweeping. The recovery of the dollar is, I am convinced, a major event of long-term significance, not just a trick of interest rates. If you have less than fifty percent of your assets in dollar holdings you are missing the main action. And there will be action. I do not know whether the bull market will take three months or nine months to reassert itself, but reassert itself it will and you can afford to wait. With certain exceptions, I do not like the American

31

blue chips over the long term – they're overmature companies for the most part, but, as you well know, there are secondary stocks with solid earnings records that will give you a net return of twenty-five percent if we diversify sensibly. I'm speaking of growth industries. I don't like zero-sum games. I also like certain American real estate for the short term, and if it's carefully chosen. In fact, I find the dollar part of your portfolio easy and I like it that we're beginning from scratch. It's the other part that interests me."

And we've damn near thrown it away, he thought. Outside on the Quai des Bergues Alfa-Romeo followed Mercedes-Benz past banks and jewellers. On the Persian carpet, the dessert cart coasted down upon them. Hajji followed it with thoughtful eyes. *We had the strongest system there ever was and we threw it away in our sleep. It's not the Russians – those poor, grim bastards were a joke once. These people thought we hung the moon and now we beg them for nickels.*

He said, "We should divide non-dollar holdings between Europe and the Middle East. Your European holdings are pretty good as they are, though I'm nervous in the long term about German automobile stocks, and the Swiss pharmaceuticals may be overbought. It's becoming a political game to beat up on them. Let us talk about the Middle East."

He had calculated once that there were fifty thousand good men in the Northeastern states who could read a ticker tape and five who could read an Arab face. Four and himself. Hajji's face looked thoughtful and minutely sad. *He's going to start playing games. He's going to lie to me. Even Hajji. Hajji too.*

He felt for a grip. He said, "I'm very glad, you know, that we got you out of gold at seven-fifty."

And Hajji – this was interesting – preferring to play it straight said, in double gratitude, "Oh, Mr. Stears, that was swell. That was so fine. For the first time in so long I enjoyed the privilege of laughing a little bit myself. Do you suppose I might, after all, have one of those delicious little crème brulées?"

The waiter bowed. The tiny pot was gently placed in front of the huge brown face. The cigar smoked on alone.

"Which gives us," Wop said, "good funds for Middle Eastern investment because I would not care to return to gold right now."

And again, as at the touch of a switch, the face turned muddy and soft.

"The Middle East is a very difficult and dangerous place," said Hajji.

"Which is precisely why we keep out of the Gulf. I agree. Kuwait, Saudi Arabia, the Emirates, all have the political imponderables that I detest. Good for short-term gains, but not long investment. But your own region, the Mahgreb, Tunisia, Berbia, even Algeria – a region where your knowledge, Mr. Melouf, supplements mine – has stable governments by and large, decent growth, a middle class. You know all this. You made your money in Berbia."

"Made it, Mr. Stears, yes."

"And keep much of it there still. And why not? A sound banking system. No currency control."

Hajji now remembered the poor cigar and, swallowing the crème brulée, relit it very carefully. *How beastly it all must taste*, thought Wop.

"Mr. Stears," he said, "you wanted to see me for a general review and I willingly flew up from Cannes. But not for that. Do anything you want with my dollars and my marks and my francs. I may question you but I trust you perfectly. And what am I but a poor merchant from the bazaar?" This was so funny that Hajji brilliantly smiled, but melancholy was close behind. "But I have an instruction for you. Sell all my Berbian holdings in mineral rights, government bonds, and real estate. Sell also half my equivalent holdings in Tunisia. Transfer the proceeds from the Middle East. Sell with no noise and with speed."

33

In the five seconds of silence that he allowed himself, Wop thought three things. *He hates this. He's the third this month. I think we need a tape of this.* He reached into his pocket and nervously removed a pen, thus activating a recorder.

"Why?" he said.

"The war. It is bad. It stinks. You think I want to end up like an Iranian?"

Hajji's face was now so closed that the features looked incidental, stuck on, as on a death mask. Wop himself wore an American's innocent question. They sat at the table, two statues of pretense.

"The war," said Wop, "has been going on since you were a child. You once sold trucks to the rebels yourself, I think. It never changes much. What has changed is that the King now has solid American support. You should be more confident, not less."

"Mr. Stears," said Hajji, "when America fights openly beside you it is time to kiss your wife good-bye and buy your grave. All the world knows this but you."

Hajji nodded, ponderous, pious, and prudent as a *Times* editorialist with a free lunch. *Times* editorialists do not become the richest dealers of the Barbary Coast.

Wop shrugged. "There will be losses. That is a major liquidation for that market. But I see your reasoning. You want a low-risk, low-activity portfolio for your retirement years." What Hajji would never reveal to questioning he might reveal from pique. "You will want to liquidate the shipping interests as well. The days have passed for small Arab shipping lines with general cargo ships – they don't compete with the American high-tech lines."

"No. Those I keep." He had left Hajji not an inch behind. Hajji smiled, the smooth unwrinkled face not far beyond its prime. "They will be an old man's retirement toys." But his eyes were still sad.

It was one of Wop's very best skills to know when, once in a hundred times, to approach an Arab straight, direct, head-on – the nobly ingenuous Western friend. He laid, literally, his hands on the table and said, "What? Mr. Melouf, what?"

But Hajji slowly shook his head. "No, Mr. Stears. I would truly like to talk to you, but you have other clients. I see I did not impress you with melodramatic phrases from a nationalist paper, but it is not so wrong as you think. I wish it were not so. America slept too long. I will buy your dollars, but believe me, Mr. Stears, you are outside the game."

He refused Hajji's offered ride – leather and cigar smoke of a big Mercedes-Benz brought a foretaste of queasiness as much of mind as stomach. His office was a kilometer away, along the Rhône embankment. He looked down into the current. Swift green cold cleansed him of Arabia. Geneva might be the Arabs' favorite city, almost their Bloomingdale's, but it was resistant to their touch as the emeralds, like the Rhône, the diamonds, like the mountains, the sapphires, like the lake, that glowed on velvet pillows in the ship windows behind his back. *If I did this in Cairo, I would rot,* he thought. Brown Arab eyes, rich secrets, corrupt, beseeching trust, wealth caressed by stomach and by loins, these dissolved his substance. Giovanni Stears, Boston wop, nephew of a New England banker and a Tuscan count, loved order, structure, place.

He did not take them for granted. He had grown up in the sad ruin of a father's ineffectual half treason. Sidgewick Stears, expatriate poet, in photographs the figure always just behind the Fitzgeralds or Dali or Sylvia Beach, had made of pre-war fascism a snobbish and elegant toy. In the war, the fun turned ugly – refuge in Vichy France, waspish satires of FDR translated and published in Berlin. Wop's boyhood had been spent in a flimsy half-fugitive exile until his second exile to the boarding schools of England old and New. The tragedy was that his parents were sweet – a pretty, silly girl who had somehow nonetheless made a kindly home against

35

the odds of total irresponsibilty and utter waste, and a father whose appalling public views had never once extended to an act of actual cruelty. From them, Wop learned the love of color, money, love, wit, grace, and from their lives the knowledge of the swiftness of corruption. Geneva pleased him. Not necessary to imagine, here, wealth as a fabric of debauch, of a whore's gown, a catamite's chamber, a life's wreck. Here fabulous wealth, the strength of nations, crystallized quintessentially into jewels, clockwork, markets, gold – at worst, a white Ferrari.

Then, abruptly, he began to walk along the Quai. *You are letting Hajji get you down*, he thought. *Hajji and Berbia. You love dark eyes when they are Marie-Sophie's. Now, what was I to do? Pick up her watch? Yes, quite. And her house this evening. Well, good. Must take her some chocolates. No, she's on a diet. Better flowers. She liked the irises. Well, get them after work.*

His office was above a bank. That it was a bank was not immediately apparent. Across the river, a hundred meters away, were the three giant banks, the fortresses of Swiss financial power. On that side, money was majestic. On this side, money was chic. A bright brass plate said, LEVANTINE COMMERICAL CREDIT BANK. In the lobby was an Aubusson carpet, pale peach with green cornucopiae. On the carpet were six Louis XVI desks, scattered artfully around, and at the desks, four sleek young men in pin-stripes and two young women in tailored suits. Three desks had clients. The clients were without exception Arab, two North Africans in Western suits and one superb Gulf sheikh in flowing, blinding white. Wop smiled at pretty Emanuelle alone behind her desk. A soft susurration compounded of French and Arabic, reassurance and advice, drifted like incense throughout the room. He waited for the elevator. It came. It had been redecorated last year, for some reason, as a sedan chair.

Giovanni S. Stears – Investment Counseling. If his mother

had not named him so, he would have made it up. The Arabs loved it. It was cosmopolitan, and those who judged their status by the houses they had away from home trusted that. It allowed him to dress for Wall Street out of Savile Row and yet never intimidate, never offend. Giovanni Stears could be at home on the Riviera, which was fortunate because he liked the Riviera. Change it to Williston Sidgewick Stears, let us say, and he could have barely gone there. Williston Stears, who happened to exist, in Providence, as Wop's own cousin, could never have done this job. His name allowed him even to decorate his office as he liked. No peach color here. *Giovanni* handled that. His room was big and light, open to all the lake, a lacquered desk with a Persian silver vase, a single Bokhara glowing like a ruby on the wall. It particularly pleased him that even the television face of the securities and markets computer in the corner, the best tool of his trade, did not look out of place. In the anteroom sat his secretary, Mademoiselle Bonvin, Marie, his typist, and Serge, his confidential clerk. One could have handled the work, at a pinch, but numbers impressed his clients.

Mademoiselle Bonvin looked reproachfully from her desk. "Husein ben-Barak called. He wished to know if he should sell Canadian wheat. Monsieur Joseph Samal called. He cannot play tennis. Madame Marie-Sophie de Segonzac" – this one syllable by distasteful syllable – "desired you not to forget her watch. So important. You are later than you said you would be. Monsieur Stears."

Mademoiselle Bonvin was stately, sixty, and slim. She was the spitting image of the matron at the English school he had attended before Choate. He nodded.

Serge said, in English, "Nothing much. The lira's taking a beating again. Dollar's steady. Zurich is off a little bit and Paris is up. New York's about to open."

Serge was a young man who was going to New York for an apprenticeship in the fall. He was gradually buying American clothes and today he looked like a combination of a Southern senator and a blues trombonist. The language of the office, otherwise, was French.

Wop said, "Let me have the Melouf file back – also the Radwan and Belebek files. Tell ben-Barak he can keep his wheat for now. Then leave me alone. I shall not exist, my dears, until four o'clock. Serge, there is nothing special anyone should buy or sell today unless they need the exercise. You can tell them that."

He went into his office and shut the door. He sat behind his desk and looked first upon the lake – a noble old paddle steamer, white and autocratic as a swan, was crossing it – and then at his Persian vase. He smiled in slight, familiar pleasure. Then he turned to his files. These three were the files of North Africans of wide connection who had instructed him to sell prosperous interests in the stable and pro-capital Kingdom of Berbia. He looked for the common factor he already knew. The interests to be sold were long-term investments or concessions of rare metals in the rich fields on the border of the Spanish Sahara. He knew the tears of blood that had been shed, the thousands of dollars of his own time taken, in one case a daughter married off, in order that these concessions should first have been made. Any interests kept were short-term trading interests to do with transport or imports of machines.

He crossed to the computer. He perched on the skeletal bronze stool before it woke it into life. The New York Exchange opening appeared, orderly sweeps of figures marching across the screen. His fingers, composed as a pianist's, played the keys. He sat in rapt attention. He loved to work at it, thus, his mind lancing out to seize this, that market from the world. He was the sorcerer with the genie at his call. He did not go through any standard list. Every answer raised another question in his mind, instantly and fully answered. Any fool could make the genie speak. Few knew what to ask. He stopped.

He typed a new set of numbers on the keys. The screen

went dark, then flickered and came back. The words LINE SECURE flashed and vanished. He tapped again. LINE SCRAMBLED, then, ENTER PERSONAL CODE. He did so. He was now directly wired to the communications computer bank in Brussels, of central office, Europe, CIA.

To his surprise a message leaped, unbidden, to the screen. He read.

PRIORITY 1. NORTH AFRICA. CENTRAL NETWORK. BERBIA. MOST URGENT DISCONTINUE ALL COMMUNICATION THIS NETWORK. ASSUME ALL IDENTITIES KNOWN. FIELD AGENT KNOWN LIQUIDATED. PENETRATION OF RADICAL RELIGIOUS GROUPS TERMINATED. REPORT TO EMBASSY BERN IN PERSON TOMORROW 1300 HOURS FOR DAMAGE CONTROL. MESSAGE ENDS. 043874.

The last was the day's confirmation code.

The message vanished. Wop looked into the void behind it.

"Christ," he said. "A blackout. Now."

3

Wop took the morning express to Bern. Pleasantly nourished on croissants and coffee, he sat in his compartment, luxurious, alone. He spread the *Herald Tribune* wide. From his gray lapel rose the faintest, sweetest trace of the perfume of Marie-Sophie's closet where it had spent the night. He breathed it with gratitude and pleasure and then with quick, acid, self-dislike. He was already positioning himself in front of the CIA. Wop's relationship to his real Americans was, even he knew, unnecessarily complex. It seemed to him suddenly that to present oneself before one's superiors bathed in one's lady-love's scent was just the sort of thing a Giovanni would cheaply do and a Williston would gracefully avoid. He wished that he had changed. In penance, he thought of duty.

Berbia, he wondered. *What the hell was up?* It was not his habit to ask himself questions the answers to which he couldn't guess and would anyway soon know. He did not bother with how the network had been blown, but why. It was not a common occurrence anywhere, and Berbia was Western turf – of all North Africa his smallest worry. And stable. And not too explosive as the Third World went. With a smart little cookie of a uniformed King. Fahd might be a libertine but he was no fool – ran the army himself. The base, of course, ten years negotiated and finally won, had the Reds in a flap, and Libya, Algeria, and the PLO too. But that was known, allowed for, and well worth the heat. He considered the known sources of trouble. Guerrilla war in the south, spilling

40

over from the Spanish Sahara – sponsored by Algeria and now Libya, too. Heating up but still contained. Then the mullahs didn't like their Westernized King – champagne at the palace, film stars in Cannes – now they longed for some fun and games like Khomeini's. It was a pity that Fahd's father had been a virtual saint and that the Berbian monarchy had a pious tradition – sooner or later there could be trouble from that. Then some leftish pan-Arab types, pro-commies admiring the PLO. Berbia had a sizable displaced population and it was known that this element was spreading through the good offices of the KGB. A nasty mixture, not to be ignored, and the PLO, now prowling the Middle East for a new Lebanon, had the nose for weakness of a hungry shark. But it was also inchoate, not congealed. And not enough. Not enough to send Hajji running, and his friends. They were tough traders, not skittish sheikhs. If they ran, something ugly chased them. He could not see it.

He could not see it, but he had no doubt whatsoever that it was there. In the five years that Wop had been a specialist of sorts on the Middle East it had become his abiding certainty that he knew almost nothing worthwhile about it. Men, he could judge. Men of money he could judge very well indeed. His knowledge of the intelligence, the wisdom, of individuals in the Middle East gave him small, steady lights in the darkness. If Hajji ran, a bear was coming. He hoped, without much confidence, that his superiors had it in their sights.

A farm swung past the train, a long stone barn with a grove of poplars standing sociably around it and the small mansarded manor house behind. Wop read his paper in small bits, watching the countryside between. Soon the land tilted up and the vineyards began. He was in, he always thought here, the most civilized landscape in the world. To the right was the lake, framed by its mountains, the most splendidly audacious piece of landscaping in the garden of the grandest châtelaine there ever was. Along it were coral pink and ivory villas punctuated by towns with toy wharves and mellow grand hotels with dowagers and willows. A landscape of capitalism golden as afternoon. But not unbalanced. Across the track the hillside rose in well-groomed terraces of ripening vines. Villages of sweet stone houses, cars, a church nestled in the dimples of the hill. Let us have a good hand for Voltaire, here. And banks. Above, the vineyards narrowed into scree, then boulders, fir trees, meadows, cliffs, the stately and unsullied Alps, then snow. In life, Wop thought, one could ask only for the frameworks as a gift, and this was as graceful a framework as there could ever be. This was a garden, not an accident; an achievement, not a chance; a virtue, not a gift. It seemed to Wop essentially right that the poor tortured lands, the peoples of ignorance and generals and blood and drought, should be given a helping hand and a guiding hand, but that the same hand could decently guard against them too.

He walked quickly through gray, Gothic Bern. The U. S. embassy, by contrast, was a neat, clean, modest, low, retiring place like the nicest sort of lying-in home for unmarried mothers. *Your neutrality is safe with us*, it said. But Wop walked in briskly striding, conscious of – even though he automatically laughed at – a slight awkward pleasure that this was not only his embassy but that he was an agent, an official of it and, more, in fact, than the young Marine, its guard. He sniffed at his lapel. Really, the scent was not too strong.

Jason Witham said, "Whatever our critics say, we learn from past mistakes."

He smiled charmingly. The smile made clear that the second-in-command, North African section, was no gray functionary, but just as civilized a fellow as those who thought the CIA a joke. No one responded. Jason Witham made a small gesture with his well-kept hand, dismissing either the jokelet or his four dull colleagues. He continued.

"The mistake being, of course, Iran. There are super-ficial similarities. Iran was intended as our surrogate in the Persian Gulf. Berbia is our presence in a North Africa dominated by Algeria and, much worse, Libya. The prime object of our policy toward Berbia has been to support the government in the guerrilla war against the Popular Liberation Front in the Spanish Sahara – that is to say, against Algerian and Libyan surrogates – thus retaining pro-Western control of major deposits of strate-gic metals in the northern Sahara as well as preventing a demoralizing military defeat for the government. Our second objective was to use this support as a lever to gain acceptance of a major naval and air base – our only base on Arab soil. Both of these objectives have been accom-plished. The government is at least holding its own in the war, and the base is in early preparation. There will shortly be U.S. power in North Africa. The Russian presence in Libya and Algeria will be bracketed between Egypt in the east and ourselves in the west. This will also seal the region against any adventurous amibitions of the PLO, though the likelihood of that has, in my opinion, been exaggerated. So far, so good – but that is just where we remember Iran."

Wop suddenly felt misgivings. This was very good, acknowledging mistakes, learning. Very good. But the intelligent face, the firm, well-modulated voice, the Brooks Brothers suit, were all too perfectly designed for orthodoxies. He had the uneasy suspicion – it was like talking to a respectable economist, it was like talking to the Ambassador, he thought – that he was seeing the birth of a new certainty, just the tip of it, that would destroy them all in due time.

Jason Witham briskly, dispassionately, went on. "The Iranian revolution came from below, where our contacts were not good. We did not predict it and the CIA bears partial responsibility for the worst American foreign policy debacle in a decade. That will never happen again. In particular, it will not happen in Berbia. For two years we have carefully infiltrated the potential trouble spots of Berbian society. That is to say, principally, the guerrilla forces themselves, the Islamic extremists who are linked to Libya, and the left wing, which is supported by Algeria. At the same time, Berbian expatriates in Paris have been penetrated by a network responsible to McNaughton, here. This complements Stear's partial surveillance of the financial transactions of wealthier Berbians."

Wop and Michael McNaughton warily acknowledged each other across the table. McNaughton, in his late fifties Wop supposed, looked, grumbled, smoked, coughed, and wore a stretched tweed coat all in the movie image of an aging reporter. Among the gray pin-stripes, he was a representative of the rougher classes. He and Wop were the odd men out, here, but McNaughton made it gruffly obvious that he considered Wop a decorative amateur and worse, not better, than the Ivy League.

"This," Jason Witham continued, "necessitated a considerable network of Arab agents. It is this network that appears to have disintegrated. Henry Peckham here, as chief of covert operations in al-Tabek, will brief you on this."

It was, Wop thought, a remarkable property of the CIA to be capable of discussing anything from nuclear holocaust to back-alley murder in the tones of trust officers of a particularly reputable bank. Henry Peckham was the aggressive youngster who would demonstrate the bank's new blood. His hair was blond and his face was even.

"I think that what we have here is a firestorm-type situation without any smoke to go with it."

He paused a moment to let his formulation penetrate. Henry Peckham had the trick of talking while barely opening his teeth, except to pounce on a word from behind and bite off its tail.

"We had developed three nonconnected networks

44

joined only at control level. One, geographically dispar-
ate, is assigned to penetrate the Popular Front and
operates out of Aiun in Spanish Sahara. The status of that
network is unknown, but we are currently regarding it an
nonoperative. The two remaining networks concentrated on insurgency-type organizations primarily in
al-Tabek, namely the Brothers of Islam and the Baath
Socialist Party, both illegal. These were steady-state
surveillance operations with some disinformation component. We had agents at the lower planning levels of
both organizations, reporting through intermediaries to
control. These operatives had been in place for more than
two years and both were professionals. The operative
penetrating the Brothers of Islam was originally recruited
as an anti-Nasser Egyptian. Surveying the Baath organization was a native Berbian. Two days ago, Abdul, the
Egyptian, was beaten to death by a mob in a back alley of
al-Tabek. We do not know the circumstances, but the
mob seems to have been made up of Brothers of Islam
sympathizers and they appear to have shouted death-to-
the-spy-type slogans. We can therefore assume that our
agent was publicly identified in circumstances unknown.
We were notified yesterday by a source in the al-Tabek
police that the body of our agent surveying the Baath
Party was pulled from the harbor the night before. This
was an apparent drowning, and we have no clue to the
circumstances of this death. Both of their intermediaries
have vanished, but this may be elective. If it is, they are
instructed to surface after five days. Please note that these
agents were in no way operationally connected below
control level and that neither had, in the immediate past,
received instructions or communicated information of an
extraordinary nature. Any questions at this time?"

Wop decided it was time to speak, if only for relief from
Peckham's voice. He said, in his mildest tones, "It would
be nice, of course, to know that they *had* reported
recently. Informationwise."

But he was not to get away with it.

"That, of course, is the next item," said Peckham. "Any *other* questions? OK. Background. The objectives of the two groups are what you would expect. Both begin with the overthrow of the monarchy. Both are maximally anti-Western. Both regard the U.S. base as a primary target. The Baath movement is overtly pro-Russian, militantly Third World. It wants a secular, socialist society, distribution of wealth, etc. It has strong operating ties to the PLO. Since Lebanon, the PLO has vastly increased the aid it gives to the Baath, and it probably regards the Baath in Berbia as one of its likelier cat's-paws. Remember that Fahd always opposed the PLO and took none of its refugees. Those boys want his ass. Organized strength probably about two thousand but a high level of sympathy among the floating labor populations, especially around the docks. They also supply manpower, weapons, urban troops, and communications to the Popular Liberation Front in the desert. Primary suppliers are Algeria and the Soviet Union. PLO operatives function as trainers. I will brief you on operations later.

"The Brothers of Islam are overtly influenced by Khomeini, but they antedate him. They began in Egypt where they still exist under tight control. The people who murdered Sadat are a spin-off. Historywise, they were not significant in Western North Africa until three or four years ago. Primary supplier is Ghadaffi's Libya. Anti-Communist, but much more anti-Western and supported by the KGB on the sly. No overt PLO contact, minimal covert. Organized strength about three thousand, including a third of the mullahs. However, the Brothers have a high level of support among the poorer population in al-Tabek and the villages, and also among the marginal merchant component which is nongratified by the Westernization of the economy. Are you with me?"

McNaughton rumbled, "Jesus, Henry. I've been there for three years."

46

Henry Peckham paused, flushed, and said, "OK. OK. I know this is a current-scenario-oriented group. But the background matters, guys. OK. Operations and support. Both groups have shown a steady increase in resources over the last eighteen months – which happens to coincide both with the Lebanon War and the finalizing of the base. Which is more significant is negatively established. Probably equal. In the Baath case, the funds come directly from the KGB via Algeria and the weapons are Warsaw Pact issue. There is also a suspicion of funds from higher Berbian economic levels which we can't explain. The weapons are light arms plus some antitank and mortar stuff. It comes in through the docks. As I said, the docks are heavily pro-Baath and our people estimate the government captures thirty percent of it. No more. More of it is coming in than seems to be used. A lot of it goes to the guerrillas, but our people were positive that a lot more was being cached. They were negatively able to penetrate the cache operation. The Baath organization primarily engages the police and assassinates landowners and political figures. Forty-three in the last year. They are a major pain in the ass, but at this time they are primarily a marginal arms-supply source for the guerrillas. If the cache theory is correct, they are probably building up to a higher level. We have some reason to believe that this indicates an eruption into full-scale urban guerrilla war in the next eighteen months."

Jason Witham said, "Fahd, of course, has a damn good army." He said it firmly. Wop groaned to himself.

"Check. We're watching it but we don't see frontal destabilization. OK. The Brothers of Islam. They have growing resources, too, but it's harder to trace. We can trace Ghadaffi's money, but that's not all of it. A good deal seems to be internal. We know that some of the radical mullahs are channeling mainstream religious funds to them. There are also some eternal funds coming in from the West – more about that later. Operations. Armswise, they're much less sophisticated than the

47

Baath. They have about sixty trained guerrillas and demolition men – we have names for about half of them – and they're very good at crowd control and communications. Mainly, they're hysterically xenophobic thugs. They identify people as pro-Western, or as spies, or as fornicators if they can't think of anything else, and they beat them up or kill them. Two new things. They began a campaign against Berbians working on the American base construction. They've killed a couple so far and beat up some more. We think they may overplay their hand here. There's high-level unemployment in al-Tabek. They've also started an active campaign for converts in the army. Some success is predictable, here, but our analysis of Islamic tradition in Berbia negatively suggests the likelihood of large-scale defections to militant extremism. Berbia's not the Gulf and it's not Iran either. Now the Western funds – the Brothers have recently come up with a more sophisticated-type publicity operation which we would have predicted to be beyond their means. They're reaching out to left-wing religious groups abroad saying, basically, that the King's corrupt and they're the holy guys. You may not believe this, but some American churches are considering support."

"I believe it perfectly," murmured Wop. "I believe it most of all." More aloud, he said, "Does this overview come from information brought in by the agents who got murdered?"

"Primarily, affirmative. Exclusively, negative."

"But it's still pretty historical, isn't it? What was the *last* thing they brought in? Or almost the last? Could we have that?"

Jason Witham looked at him, blandly askance. "I should imagine we are coming to that, Stears," he said. Jason had never yet managed to say *Giovanni* and rarely sank to *Wop* – neither, at any rate, was going to run this meeting.

Harry Peckham, equal to equal, addressed himself exclusively to Jason Witham.

"Check. Now there's a timing factor here. The

Brothers had two regular weekly meetings. A religious observance on Friday, of course – all of them were meant to attend that – and a looser meeting two days before it. That was the organizationally important one and it was held in a semisecret room behind a shop. Some of the members were usually at that – any member could be ordered to be there. Our agent attended as often as he nonsuspiciously could, and made contact with his intermediary, usually at a café, on a varying schedule after it. Our agent was apparently exposed in the course of one of these meetings and liquidated immediately thereafter. Consequently, the last contact was never made – or if it was, the intermediary has, as I said, vanished. There is no specific pattern in the last three contacts. One new Brother was admitted. Crosschecking reveals a previous involvement in the Baath organization – this is unusual but not unknown, especially among younger men. The Brothers crow over it when it happens. There is a continuing nonspecific suggestion that the Brothers were tilting away from religious fundamentalism toward increased anti-Americanism and direct political action, and that this connects to the rise in dominance of a mullah known as Ibrahim. We don't know anything about Ibrahim except that he came from outside al-Tabek. Also, he wears a big gold ring. But, I repeat, that's non-specific. They seem to have gotten a relatively large infusion of money from a nonprevious source. Namely, it wasn't brought in by the mullahs, it didn't come from the normal shakedown operations, and it didn't come through the Bank of Valletta, which is how Ghadaffi's money gets in. Abdul thought it was Berbian money or money that was very well laundered in Berbia, but that's all we know. He was working on it, but he was not, repeat not, instructed to push his cover on this. That's all. Nothing on the Baath."

McNaughton looked up quickly from his ashtray's Tartarean depths. He said, "How much nothing? You guys scenting a blackout yet?"

"Legitimate question. Negative. Not yet. We've had blank periods before. The Baath is to some extent nonautonomous. Sometimes they're told to cool it for a while. Sometimes that comes before a change of tactics. Not always."

Wop said, "How much money? What *kind* of channel? What *kind* of source?"

"Not available. Almost certainly in excess of $250,000, which is considerable for the Brothers. Adbul learned of its existence in general terms. He was working on channels and sources. I told you that."

"It would have been nice to know," said Wop. Through the window he could see just the white peaks of the Bernese Oberland fit like saw teeth into the pale blue sky. The problem was not urgent there, either. Henry Peckham sat down.

Jason Witham sat back in his chair. He looked pleasantly, quizzically around and then briefly held up his hands as though cupping a generous sphere.

"Thank you, Henry," he said. "The primary question, then, is this. Are we dealing with a specific, technical network failure or with a more grandiose deterioration of the Berbian climate? Henry's briefing, I think, suggests the first. The Berbian situation is by all data fundamentally stable, and a radical change would go along with much darker signs and portents than we have here. I am going to ask Stears and McNaughton whether this is paralleled in their areas of expertise. Michael? What about the expatriates?"

The difference, thought Wop, was remarkable. Peckham, who at rest looked abrasive and informed, turned into something closer and closer to a television screen the more he lectured, browbeat, quoted facts. When McNaughton opened his mouth a heap of old laundry became a rich, impressive presence. The presence first shifted heavily on its chair, then patted a briefcase.

"I've got sixty pages here," McNaughton said, "of who met who. And most of it doesn't mean a crap. Most

50

of *them* don't mean a crap. We can sort them into factions and levels and run it through a computer and you know what? We come up with a bigger load of garbage than we put in. Four Berbians can set up a meeting and talk for four hours about money and guns and it doesn't mean a damn thing – they could be talking about the Irish sweepstakes for all I care. Then, when you think that all you've got to worry about is a bunch of deadbeats, the bastards blow up a banker and send a boatload of Soviet rockets into Berbia all in the same week. Partly it's that there are real tough guys hiding among the deadbeats, and sometimes they surface. You all know that. What you all forget is that it's chance and combination for them, too. The KGB's in it and they're good, but they're not ten feet tall. The tough guys are good but their resources are limited. *When* the KGB want action, *when* the professionals are available, *when* they can come up with opportunities, *when* the combinations work, then the lid goes off. Apparent activity doesn't always mean anything and results can be an accident. So you look for the ebb and flow, the pattern of contact, changes, the movement of money if you can find it. Big if. I've got expatriates of eight countries to watch and not very many men, and I don't trust all the ones I've got. You may be interested to know that the KGB has four times as many men as I've got doing the same thing – and I'm in a friendly capital.

"So McNaughton's bitching. OK. What have I got? Not a lot, but a little. I'm seeing a lot more meetings between Baath exiles and PLO nasties than I used to. I agree with Jason that the PLO may not have enough punch left to take over a country, but I wouldn't bet my shirt on it, either. Remember, if the PLO can use the Baath, the KGB can use the PLO. They none of them like each other, but it just happens that Berbia is a big plum for all three – stop the base, get a new homeland, get into power. So it bears watching. And remember this – there are a lot of PLO tough guys sitting around with orders to be good boys in the countries that took them in. This may sound simpleminded, but those boys are getting bored. Their status is slipping. I don't like bored terrorists. And I don't know what I'm looking for. I do know the Palestinians owe Fahd absolutely nothing and that makes me edgy. Obviously, we look for the KGB too, but we haven't found it yet.

"What else? Mainly a feeling. Overtly, the rightist religious groups are increasing their activity and the Baath is cooling down a little. Could be deceptive. Give you an example. Three fundamentalist toughs got reinfiltrated back to Berbia a month or so ago to head up the new business about destabilizing the army that Henry told you about. Glad to have it confirmed, Henry. They went in a boat owned by an Algerian operating out of Marseilles. That Algerian is a Communist and under orders from the Baath. That's one incident. There are more like it. OK. So what have we got? Divided loyalty? Anything for a dollar? An alliance? Or is the Baath beginning to run the Brothers? I grant you I don't know how they'd do it. And maybe we've got the KGB and the PLO running the Baath. And I'm not swearing to any of it. You ask me what it all means, Jason, and I'll tell you that's your business."

Jason nodded, a connoisseur. "Interesting analysis, Michael. Conjecture, of course, as you say, but then we can't all deal with hard fact. Now, Stears, do you have any news from the world of fashion?"

And as Wop gave them his little offering, his three rich clients, he reminded himself that the CIA receives each day enough hard fact to fill a telephone book, that it monitors radios over all the world, that it can pick up electronically a telephone conversation between a janitor in Odessa and his friend in Tomsk, that the spy satellites can photograph the face of a Russian private in a field in the Ukraine. He knew that the American intelligence agencies publish more than ten secret factual summaries a day, some of more than fifty pages. We drown in fact. In fact is our ignorance. And here he came with his three fat Arabs, his little bit of gossip, his whiff of fear.

So he ended it laboriously, not eloquently at all, saying, "It seems to me that too many straws are moving. I trust these men. I trust their acumen. Jason, I'm damned if I know what's up. But I think that something is and – damn it, I'll say it – I think something's shifted at the center."

Which, except for a flicker of McNaughton's eye, fell not only on silence but on embarrassment itself. We are serious men and we are embarrassed for colleagues who shoot off their mouths.

But Jason Witham, a leader, was tolerant, judicious. "Us tigers get pretty close to our work here, Stears. Right now we're looking at the problems, at the rough edges, so that's what we see. Back off a little bit and it starts to change. Now I told you, and we're damn serious about this, we're never going to be caught with our eyes shut again. But the CIA doesn't run screaming to mama every time somebody sneezes. Look at Berbia. Look at it whole. Well-established monarchy. Competent King. First-rate armed forces – army officers trained in France, air force trained in the U.S. Nicely growing multi-based economy. Sound middle class. There aren't the gaps, Stears, there aren't the fissures there were in Iran, or that we worry about in Saudi Arabia. We don't need to run off saying the sky is falling, we need to replace our network and find out how it was penetrated in the first place."

And Wop nodded, for Witham was right. He was inarguably right. Wop nodded heavily. Jason nodded lightly in return, amiable and effortless victor. He had devoured Wop's poor little reservation at a gulp and it seemed gratifyingly unlikely that others would come forward.

He went on briskly. "Now. Confession time. I had instructions up my sleeve before I came here. The primary purpose of this meeting was to uncover anything known to any of you that would fundamentally change our understanding of the situation. And we have decided that there is nothing. We are treating this as a low-level penetration of a network, possibly caused by ineptitude on the part of the agent himself. The surrounding circumstances are basically benign. However, there is no denying that we are temporarily blind to an important element in what I shall gracelessly call the unstable underbelly of Berbian society. I hope I have made it clear that policy since Iran specifically does not look kindly on blindness in such sectors. To be a little plainer, gentlemen, we are not going to say to Washington, 'Sorry, guys, but we've lost the Brothers.'

"As we all well know, to infiltrate another operative into this level of the Brothers of Islam would take a minimum of two years. I do not propose to have, for two years, a hole in my sector big enough for a congressman to stick his head through. Therefore, we shall improvise. We shall work with what we have. We shall work with McNaughton and Stears."

It must be remarkably easy, Wop thought later, *to get known for sangfroid.* The truth was, he hadn't even wanted to jump. By the time he fully saw, Witham had rolled smoothly by.

"We are, of course, aware that to change a network's operations introduces a moment of potential danger. In Libya, in Syria, we would not consider it. But in friendly circumstances, I think we can be a little bold. Basically, Stears, McNaughton, you will move a little from passive to active. McNaughton, I want you to develop a plan to infiltrate expatriate groups returning to Berbia and to maintain surveillance there through the expatriate network. Let me have a scenario in two weeks. Stears, your instructions are a little more sensitive and represent, in fact, a promotion in the Agency. I want you to use your established contacts to move into an active search for the internal-funding channels of Baath. I also want you to use any means in your power to identify any sympathizers they may have in the upper levels of Berbian society. You will not push beyond your cover, but I expect you to push to its limit. I see no reason for you to prepare a scenario – you will have to handle each contact as it comes. My experience, and it is a long experience, is that agents who are asked to change objective invariably act as though the Agency had played them a personal foul. Let me tell you that I have taken the plan up the line and it is considered economical of resources, workable, and sound."

4

By unspoken bidding, while Henry Peckham remained with his chief, Wop and McNaughton were dismissed. By rule, each left the embassy alone. By necessity, both went to the railroad station. By the clock, it was time for lunch and early for a train. Wop settled into an oak-lined booth in the first-class buffet. By the time he had the menu, and had looked up from it, McNaughton filled the door, looking like a bear who expects things to go wrong. He looked first irritably and decisively away from Wop, as if that much had gone wrong already, and then walked heavily over. When he sat down, Wop felt squeezed within the ample booth.

McNaughton said, "Anybody watching us knows where we've been already. And nobody is watching us."

Wop nodded. "With the possible exception, of course, of our chief."

McNaughton weightily said, "Yeah. Our chief. This place got sandwiches?"

"You should have the shrimp curry," said Wop. "It happens to be the best in Switzerland."

McNaughton grunted. Then he said, "Peckham seems to have his data straight. Good presentation, you ask me."

McNaughton rooted in his pocket and brought forth a shapeless pack of Gauloises.

"You agree with him about the army? The destabilization stuff? Not much risk there?"

Wop said, with no emphasis at all, "Well, it is not really data, is it, that the loyalty of the Berbian army is traditionally a personal loyalty to the King and that that loyalty itself is earned by the King's traditional stature as the spiritual head of Islam in Berbia and that this present King's interpretation of his faith is to some degree heterodox, consisting as it does of booze and starlets."

McNaughton looked at him through smoke.

"Right, Stears, you got it. That ain't data. Not data at all."

The waiter stood beside them. Wop spoke to him at length in German, which McNaughton did not know. He said, "The curry comes with Bombay duck and popadum and I have told him to bring sliced apple on the side. A Fendant would go nicely with it."

McNaughton looked at him, this time in dismay.

"Jesus, Stears, I said a sandwich, not a Bombay duck. A ham sandwich. And a beer."

"You are missing," said Wop, "the best thing in Bern. What kind of beer?"

"Drinking beer. Draft, for God's sake."

Wop consulted the waiter minutely on the choice of a half of Fendant for himself. McNaughton resettled into a resigned distaste.

Wop resumed with dispassion, removing a crumb from his cuff as he spoke.

"It is also not data, I imagine, that one of the constants of Berbian history has been the emergence of marabouts, or militant holy men, in all periods of royal decadence, and that one of Berbia's three great heroes is one marabout, Lyusi, who led an extremely successful revolt against the somewhat worldly Sultan Mulay Ismail, who dabbled with Western alliances. Sixteenth century."

McNaughton's eyes, he noticed, did not take part in the theme of rumpled tweed – no genial, boozy blear. They were a scientist's eyes.

"Or that the heart and center of every Berbian village is the *siyyid*, the tomb of a saint, that the saint's descendants are usually the guys who run the village, and that, in short, the potential power of religious revivalism in

Berbia is an explosive charge laid straight through the center. Billy Graham, by comparison, is simply a joke."

McNaughton said, "They call it Jerry Falwell, now. You're out of date. Yeah, right. That's not data, either."

"My three fat cats, of course, grew up knowing all this. And there's one other thing that's not data. And I don't know what it's worth. One of my rich Arabs looks like Sidney Greenstreet, but I do not think he has ever drunk a glass of wine and his forename is Hajji, which, as you well know, signifies that he has personally made a pilgrimage to Mecca. I don't have Peckham's advantages, you see. I don't know anything."

McNaughton looked at him and held his eye. "Stears," he said, "I had always thought you were an asshole."

"No," said Wop. "Just an Italian."

McNaughton coughed gently into his smoke. "That wasn't an apology. What you looked like is the fellow club member of someone in upper brass who got you a special-assignment intelligence job because you're so goddamned smart. Half the fuckups in the Company come from guys like Peckham. And those fuckups fall on the heads of Intelligence guys like me who work at one job for twelve years in one city and one in a hundred of those fuckups gets you killed. So if I didn't like the look of you, that's why."

It was curious, thought Wop, who had been recruited at Boodle's Club in London by an old school friend from Yale, that he felt neither resentment nor unease. He felt, in fact, a pleasant deference and an unexpected warmth. He said, "Should we cooperate? Our contexts are not totally watertight, you know. Some of my people don't necessarily go all the way with the King. And aren't some of your expatriates professional types?"

McNaughton shook his head in grand dismay. "Christ no. You work on yours, I'll work on mine. If I want your reports I'll know where to get them. Unauthorized collaboration gets you all snarled up every goddamned time. Don't even think about it."

The waiter came back, bearing on upraised hand a tray with, for McNaughton, a stein and a plate, and, for Wop, two casseroles, a spirit lamp, a dewy bottle, and a choir of relish plates.

"You really should have had this," Wop said mildly.

McNaughton said, "I'll live." He moved his ashtray cosily near his plate.

"So," said Wop, "what happened? What happened in al-Tabek?"

McNaughton ate in silence. He finished half his beer before he spoke. "Jason Witham, as it happens, Stears, is not a fool. He is buying the official line on Berbia and we are not. We are right in thinking, at least, that he is wrong. That does not mean, as I believe you now think, that Witham is always wrong and that we have our personal right answer for everything. There is, in fact, nothing in what we have said that excludes the likelihood that what happened in al-Tabek was a fortuitous event, a low-level penetration of cover on a local scale. It is, from Witham's point of view, the most convenient analysis, but it is also the most likely one. We both have difficult but feasible assignments that maybe we shouldn't have been given, but which, with luck and skills, we can accomplish. It is not up to us to develop a personal scenario for what could have happened out of our sectors in al-Tabek."

"I still," said Wop, "have my suspicions."

"Suspicions without base," McNaughton said, "are luxuries."

On the train, although they were alone in a compartment, they did not speak for some time. McNaughton read from his briefcase, holding papers, Wop saw with mild surprise, delicately and neatly. Wop, who carried most of the files in his office in his head, considered them slowly, one by one. Fribourg and its station had swung past the unslowing train before McNaughton spoke.

He said, "Occurs to me I was maybe a little brusque

59

back there about collaboration. Didn't mean to shoot you down personally."

Wop said, sincerely, "Hell, don't worry. You're right, anyway. It's usually a lousy idea. Just a thought."

And McNaughton said, "Good. Because so long as you think it's a lousy idea, I have little of it to suggest. Private collaboration. It's enthusiastic official collaborators give me the shakes. OK?"

Stears saw the intense blue eyes briefly upon him. He said, "Shoot."

"Organizationally, we're screwed up, you and me."

Stears nodded. They were. In operations, they were part of the Middle Eastern Department of the CIA. By residence, they were part of Western Europe.

McNaughton went on. "So you know what happens to your reports. They go to Bern, because that's your station. Then they go in triplicate, one to Western Europe, in Brussels, one to Middle East, in Cairo – that's Jason Witham – and one to Virginia. OK. Now suppose one of your reports becomes the basis of an operational directive to me, drawn up by Jason Whitham. That directive goes from him in Cairo to Paris, with a copy to Virginia, to me. Stears, it's an operational goldfish bowl. It's the worst collaboration in the world. Jason's not a fool, but the first thing in his mind is to look good. Now he might be a cagey bastard all by himself, but if he has to make decisions with the whole goddamned Company looking on, he's going to make the one that makes him look like a hotshot. Does that suggest anything to you?"

"What it suggests," said Wop, looking serenely out of the window, "is that he will show the world what a team he's made out of us. He might even do this at the expense of instructing us to integrate our operations in ways that might be inappropriate. Because our operations, as I said, are not watertight. Because there will be expatriates who show up in the money markets. Because there will be moneymen who hang around the political boys in London and Paris."

McNaughton, for the first time, minutely smiled. "Right, Stears. Right again. So what do we do?"

"We could always doctor our reports a little. If we found a case that looked like that we could fuzz it up. Not give Witham quite enough to let fly with a directive so the whole world would know. We would have to stay in very careful touch with each other. That's dangerous. It's also impermissible. The Company's canned people for a great deal less. But on the other hand we would be operating in our own way, at our own rhythm, that is, for results – and not in Witham's way, which just might possibly, once in a while, be for appearances."

McNaughton sighed. "OK. You got it. I wouldn't do this for every jerk off the street. I think you may have some sense, is all. You know my cover details?"

"Oh yes. James Donnelly, Ph.D. Jamie Donnelly. The pro-Arab writer. I need a telephone, though."

McNaughton gave him a card. He took it with sudden reservation. It was the concrete evidence that he had agreed to – had himself somehow initiated – an unauthorized collaboration between agents whose covers were wholly without connection. He tried to think of an act more heinous. A date with Andropov, perhaps. He quickly cursed his own doubts of Witham and then cursed Witham for causing them.

They were on the Trans Europ Express to Lausanne, where Wop would change for Geneva and McNaughton stay on for Paris. No clickings or screeches or clangs on the Trans Europ Express – it raced along as over a carpet, its whistle was polite, and it spoke with discreet pneumatic sighs of automatic doors and windows.

Wop suddenly and pensively said, "Do you like your Arabs?"

The McNaughton he asked was to some extent an unfamiliar one, as though a charcoal rendering of a night-desk city editor had become the pencil sketch of a professor of English with a penchant for Sterne.

McNaughton laughed slightly, out loud, without a cough.

61

"Do I like juvenile, witless, violent, self-indulgent, grown-up delinquents who'd start World War III to get rid of an oil minister they didn't like? Yeah, I do. From time to time I like them pretty much. How about you?"

"Do I like anxious, greedy, smug, duplicitous parasites who scuttle out of their own countries like rats at the first sign of trouble? Yes. I find myself able to like them a lot. Why?"

"Because they don't try to seem better than they are. That's even at the bottom, even at the root, even in front of God. Allah never asked for perfection. For belief, yes, and he gave them a snarled up bunch of rules to keep, but not perfection. Nothing impossible. They pretty much like themselves. It's catching. That's about it."

"Yes," said Wop. "That's about it."

"They lose it when they turn commie."

"Yeah. They're straight-through bastards then."

The train said, "The next stop will be Lausanne. Thank you." It said in English; it said it in French; it said it in German and Dutch. It used a different voice each time. In English, the train was a debutante.

Wop took his briefcase down from the rack. He said, with warmth behind the conventional phrase, "I'll be in touch."

To which McNaughton, not raising his head, firmly and bleakly said, "Not much."

And Wop, in silence, turned his back and opened the compartment door.

McNaughton said, "Stears?" Wop turned. "Are you a racing man?"

Wop said, surprised, "Yes. I am."

McNaughton said, "I thought you might be. If this thing's ever over, be my guest in Paris and we'll have a day at Longchamps."

And then as Wop walked out, he called after him, "You may think doctoring reports is easy. It's not. Don't screw up."

5

She was in the garden. He saw that a half kilometer away from the road along the lake. For Marie-Sophie's house was on a promontory, just beyond the first detached village outside the Geneva sprawl; a gray stone wall surrounded it on three sides and dropped into the lake, one spreading willow rose above the wall, the house was on a little mount; and the whole expensively assured its owner that the pocket handkerchief lawn was a geographical feature and the suburban villa an estate. She was leaning on the wall, her back to him, looking into the lake. There was a family of ducks there and, when she got home from work, she gave them bread.

He got out of his car to open the big iron gate. The autoroute between Geneva and Lausanne, a quarter of a mile inland, thundered with rush-hour traffic like a drum. Felipe, her Spanish gardener, who looked disconcertingly like an aging bank teller dressed for a day outdoors, hurried up to help.

"Madame la Comtesse is in the garden, Monsieur Stears," he said.

Marie-Sophie never used the title since the divorce, but Felipe was a Spaniard and a snob.

"I will join Madame there," said Wop. "You need not announce me. Did you spray the roses? The fly was getting bad."

It had become his job to "speak to the gardener." Wordlessly, Felipe swept his hand to the rosebeds. They gleamed and dribbled with moisture and gave off a faint and poisonous smell.

"Good," said Wop. "It was none too soon."

She heard his footsteps on the lawn, he could see that by the softening of her body, but she did not turn, and he sat down on the wall beside her, as she meant him to, facing her, and kissed her.

"Mm," she said. "How was Bern? You look tired, my dear." She put her hand over his so that he felt equally her warm hand and the cold stone wall.

"Not so bad," he said. And lied, "That client is difficult, though. Felipe sprayed the roses."

"I know. It stinks. So does the dining room. The windows were open, the fool. We shall have dinner on the terrace. We are lucky it is warm. Do you know," she said, her dark eyes looking solemnly, seriously, down into the water, "the little ducks are almost grown now. I think their parents will soon drive them out. I shall miss them."

Under the wall, the water sighed and gurgled. Across the lake, the ramparts of the French Alps began to darken and grow heavy in the evening light. On the wall, beside him, Wop Stears, Middle Eastern expert, felt the light body, and breathed the scent, of his Moroccan mistress, Marie-Sophie, perhaps his love.

They walked up the lawn when the lights in the drawing room – in an un-Swiss fashion they had been lit before her maid went home – began to glow palely through the French windows.

"I have no idea," said Marie-Sophie, "what Marcella has left us. But you have been here an hour without a drink, poor man, so please make us both one while I go and see."

He went to the pantry and made a Campari for her and a martini for himself. In the kitchen, before the blue Delft counter, she was standing in front of an oblong wrapped in foil. He stood behind her, his hand on her waist.

"Cold fish," she said, snuggling. "No. *Ferat* wrapped for baking. Better. And, good, she left the oven on. Thank you, my dear." They spoke in French but she

64

called him "My deah" in English. "This will take twenty minutes. There's cucumber salad. Go wander."

At this time he never sat. He liked to stroll around the house, coming up short in front of an object here and there. "Having lunch with Marie-Sophie," he called it. For the record of her lunch hours – she always shopped, she never ate – was on the walls and tables, and quite often on her body, but never on her ribs. She spent, he told her, like a drunken sailor. *No, no*, she would argue, *just like a rich, vulgar Arab*. Poor girl, he thought. If it were just that simple!

For her house was beautiful, in perfect, no, *brilliant*, taste, and quite awry. He had walked into the dining room. One long wall had been done by Moroccan artisans in a mosaic gloriously derived from the Alhambra. The floor was cool, blue marble. The table, the sideboard, the chairs, were the most correct, most tailored Directoire. One stood, at first, in awe. The Directoire, the very spirit of France, the West, floated, piece by piece in limpid, cool Arabian space. It was superb. But if you looked too long, it floated too much. It floated like Salvador Dali. He finished his drink and drifted toward the pantry, to the tray. He looked into the kitchen. She was bent a little over the cutting board, mincing herbs with the childlike deliberation of the careful but inexpert cook.

She was the daughter of the richest banker in Rabat, Hassan ben-Sayis, a man equally proud of his corsair ancestors and his French library. For an Arab to have called his daughter born in 1950 by a French name, Marie-Sophie, was either craven obsequiousness to the precarious ruling power, or splendid defiance of vulgar nationalism, or overprecious whimsy. Certainly not the first, thought Wop, and probably both the other. So she had grown up in a huge cool house speaking Arabic to a score of servants and French to Papa and Maman and later to Cher Monsieur Camus and even Monsieur Malraux, too.

Her father's acquaintance was as distinguished as his wine, which – he was always a devout Muslim – was served only to guests. The French were honored guests, the King, a trusted friend. It was young Arabs, the fierce, heroic students, the freedom fighters, the Algerians – or, her father, said, the louts – who represented the enemy, bombs, death. Marie-Sophie, grew up in fear of her generation. A friend of her father's was shot twenty-five times in his own house in front of his wife and children. She saw her own father that day. He called her to his study – the room where he was not her wonderful, warm Papa but a stately, sad figure in a Paris white suit. He told her that his friend had died a martyr. She gravely thought. She asked, to what? To French Islam, he said. To something that might have been.

At fourteen they packed her off to Paris. This was just in time for her to be installed in school at the height of the anti-Arab backlash. The school was in Fontainebleau, a gray house among beech trees in a small, damp park. She slept in a dormitory of seven girls, all French, one a *colon's* daughter. They were never truly mean to her. Out of pure form, to keep the side up, Angélique, the *colon's* daughter, used at first to ask her where her bombs were, whom she had murdered lately; but it was too silly to keep up – Marie-Sophie was generous and sweet. She was *la petite arabe*, an outsider, somewhat sponged off, but confided in, and mysteriously credited with unspecified sexual wisdom and power. She used to lie in her frilled white bed, among the Franks, watching through the windows the alien beech trees dip in winter, and think of her body as dark as chocolate, spicy as cumin, rich as blood. It terrified her. It had always seemed so light.

It was a secular school – her father would never have sent her to the Christian nuns. She learned to ride. She learned to dress. Later she learned which regiments, which embassies, which merchant banks, were inhabited by the most eligible young men. She learned so well that even Angélique forgot all but her first name. Her skin became a permanent, perfect suntan from Cap d'Antibes. She became French. She became beautiful.

She persuaded her reluctant father to send her to the Sorbonne. Here she suddenly again met Arabs. They excited and confused her. One day, in a steamy student café, she was approached by a dark-haired young man with luminous black eyes. He talked to her, appreciated her. He bought her coffee. He asked her name. He looked in puzzlement, then anger. *"Tu es donc arabe?"* he said. She nodded. He looked her up and down with spiteful care. *"Jolie petite française,"* he said and walked away. He was getting his raincoat from the peg when something seemed to strike him. He came back. "Your father is also a traitor," he quietly said.

So she dated Frenchmen. She first slept with Philippe, and when she – in some things, still a high-born Arab girl – made it clear that this would not long go on outside of marriage, he braved his family and married her. He was the Comte de Segonzac. He was little older than she, athletic and with soft brown eyes, well read, original, and lazy. He was perfectly content to return to the hideous family château near Bordeaux, produce excellent but not actually famous wine, co-exist with Gran'mère and Maman, and let her socially sink or swim. She sank. Gran'mère and Maman regarded an Arab daughter-in-law as a creature out of the zoo, tolerable only because it spoke French, spoke little of that, and came with a huge endowment. Bordeaux, more than any other region of France, was full of the most vengeful and Arab-hating ex-*colons*. They were not won over like Angélique. She was all but ostracized. But in their bedroom things were not so bad. Philippe loved her, she thought, and was even whimsically proud of her oddness. It was slightly fun to be the Comtesse de Segonzac. They went to bed early and slept late and she used whatever she possessed of the richness her schoolmates had assumed in her. Her baby was born.

That was the disaster. It had never occurred to her that French babies were baptized into little Christians. If it had occurred to her, she would never have known that she cared. She had not read the Koran in seven years. She saw the family leave for Mass on Sunday without a thought. But it seemed to her suddenly that her daughter would not be hers, that the blood of blue sea and white city, her own father's blood, would die in her little veins and be replaced by a gray and sour liquid of France. She protested. She was simply annihilated. Philippe looked insulted. Gran'mère made it plain that she was not going to see her own flesh and blood sire a domestic brood of little heathen Arabs. The child was baptized, held by its grandmother. She was christened Joséphine. It was as though Marie-Sophie had unmasked at last. She was now not *la petite arabe* but *cette arabe*, with venom.

Things went from bad to worse. It became clear that Phillipe had begun to have affairs. The bedroom ceased to be a refuge. She came to spend most of the day, now, in a special corner of the château's huge, hot terrace, playing with Joséphine when she could get her, otherwise reading magazines. Their flat vineyards were spread out below her like a map, but the work in them meant nothing to her for no one had ever troubled to explain it. At mealtimes, in the dark dining room, it was forgotten that she never spoke. Maman would from time to time note piously that of course she would never now serve pork. Marie-Sophie stuck it out for five years. Finally – after Philippe had embarked on a particularly flagrant fling with a visiting Napa Valley girl oenologist, pneumatically busty and straight out of *Playboy*, and had announced that he was going to move her into the château for further studies – she had enough, gathered up Joséphine, and left. In spite of the spirited intervention of the local priest, Phillippe had so far overplayed his hand that the French courts let her keep her daughter. She was divorced.

The name of France now made her shudder. But, other

than Arabic, French was her only language and French manners were all she knew. Arabs frightened her. Ever impressionable, she had somehow absorbed the image that she was descended from a race of dishwashers and murderers – her father, perhaps, the sole exception.

Geneva beckoned. It was French but not France. It had schools for Joséphine. All sorts of people lived there, accepted more or less. It had good shops. It had a blue lake with a white fountain. It had even defied the horrible Catholic Church. Her father sadly supported her choice and gave her another small fortune – her dowry was gone. She bought a pretty villa by the lake. She lived alone with Joséphine, less lonely than she had been for years. She was twenty-eight.

She said, *"Oh, merde!"* He had heard the oven door swing open. This was a common sequence. He slowly completed his second circuit of the house, his second drink, and ended in the kitchen. She was standing over the spread-out foil, hands on her hips, bent slightly over, and laughing, embarrassed.

"It's stuck," she said. "It's stuck to the sheet. Oh, shit. I always do this with fish. We shall have to scrape it off onto the plates and since the dining room stinks with poison, we can take it outside and share it with the bugs. Will you choose the wine? I don't know why I don't have Marcella stay."

Marcella, Wop thought, had the easiest job in town. Madame had coffee and a peach for breakfast. Madame neglected lunch in town. Madame finished dinner herself. She employed a cook, he supposed, by reflex.

Actually, the terrace was nice. They sat at the stone table, close together, lit by two small hurricane-candle lamps and the bright yellow windows from the house. The lake was sown with filaments of light reflected from the village. At the limit of hearing was the music from the harbor café. Marie-Sophie, so French by daylight, migrated south by night. By candlelight, he had noticed, some women glittered and some women glowed. Marie-

Sophie glowed. Her black hair vanished into the darkness, but her black eyes, the pupils dilated, shone; when she raised them to look at him he could fall out of his chair, straight in. Her soft lower lip moved gently as she talked, making her mouth seem tentative, making her younger than her years. She had been talking about Joséphine's boarding school.

She said indignantly, "They think that we are all alike! They had her in a dormitory with two cowlike little things from Saudi Arabia who were sent there so their fathers could say they had their daughters in Switzerland. What kind of stimulus is that? She will learn to gawp about with big vacant eyes, just so, and talk about her mother's jewels. I will not have it. I had her moved to a room where there are two Swiss girls, so she will keep her feet on the ground, and a French girl so she will learn to defend herself, and an American girl so she might possibly learn English. You must talk to her in English too. Was I not right, Giovanni?"

Wop said solemnly, "They teach them splendid morals, the Saudis do. Much better than yours."

"Savages! Butchering that poor little girl because she slept with a man. They are disgusting."

"Yes," he said. "You were quite right. What do you know about Berbia?"

"Serious?" she said.

"Yes, please." He asked her, quite often now, questions about the region, not for her detailed knowledge, which was uneven at best, but for her increasing confidence in taking Western received opinions at its proper value – which was usually, he thought, nil. Also because it gave her patent pleasure.

She put her feet in his lap. They had finished dinner.

"I was never there," she said. "But Daddy often was. I should say it is more like Morocco than anywhere else, but much, much more primitive, a little like Libya in the old days. Al-Tabek is not Casablanca or Rabat, but like some much smaller place – Agadir, perhaps, or Tangier.

Foreigners do not realize that because the King has built sophisticated places for his friends to play in and the French built a very grand hotel. What I want to say, I think, is this: the people of Casablanca or Rabat are as much city people as those of Geneva or Milan – different, but as much – and that is not so in al-Tabek. The common people of al-Tabek are for the most part very close to the country, and to the very far country, and they are very simple and primitive and mostly Berber, not Arab. And I do not know if you know what that means, my dear, for I suspect that the most simple person you have ever met is a skiing guide in St. Moritz."

He spread his hands apart, in half-acquiescence, around her feet, and slightly smiled.

"It will try to tell you so you understand. My father's servants. The less important ones, and the gardeners, came from small villages. In our house they wore clean white robes and they carried trays of pretty china very quietly and they polished the French furniture so that it shone and they always opened the doors at the right moment and they made the house very – civilized. But, Giovanni, they were not there. Their faces were closed, asleep, year after year. Their voices were like someone muttering in bed. They were trustworthy, we could count on them, but only, I think, because they made no connection between themselves and what was around them. They lived in the city world as if in a dream and if they had woken up I do not know what would have been there. Now that is most of al-Tabek and almost all of Berbia – much of Morocco and Tunisia, of course, too, but we have some real cities. You bankers and diplomats who deal with places like Berbia and Kuwait and the Yemen are holding the skin of a soap bubble and you know nothing of what is inside it. One day it may go *poof* in the night – just like your Iran and Libya. I do know this: I know very little of these people and you know nothing, clever as you are."

He nodded, pleased. Her intelligence was a part of his

delight in her, a heightening of her body, her kindness, her grace. To find a woman's mind asexual he had always thought the meanest ingratitude. That was part of it. He also knew that if he rejected Henry Peckham's worst inanities it was in some part through her. It was through her that he had learned to put a value on the Arab crescent and to accept the Arab world as a precarious and at least somewhat grand achievement. He carried always in his head, now, how fragile it was – how easily it could be shaken, how easily debased. There was a great deal to be said for taking your work to bed.

She went on. "There is also something more specific that I know from the agency."

She worked for the International Red Cross. He had guided her to the job – it dealt with famine relief, and they liked "Third World" people in those bureaus now. She was not entirely happy there. Her boss, an old-fashioned Belgian socialist, was given to telling her acidly that the price of her usual wardrobe would stop a medium-sized famine in its tracks. But she was conscientious, and somewhat enthusiastic, and it was better for her than sitting all day by the lake.

"Things are worse there than people are saying. We think that we will have to classify the southern half as a famine area later this year and that means it is quite bad. It is not so much the drought, it seems. It is the guerrillas. It appears that they are getting more of their supplies from outside now, and they are beginning to destroy the peasants' cattle, often just for the sake of doing so. That means the peasants either starve or move to the slums in al-Tabek, and what the government will do with them, I cannot think."

"That is very interesting," he said slowly.

Though he could find his watch in the dark of her bedroom as easily as he could find her waist in bed, her room still gave him a pleasure of its own like an outer body of Marie-Sophie that he first sank into before

72

sinking into her. One of the many failings of marriage, he thought, was a single, denatured bedroom. He had undressed first. He lay between her sheets bordered with yards of foamy lace that made him feel like a prizefighter, a coal heaver; improbably, terrifically, male. She crossed and recrossed the room, sat at her dressing table, her arms behind her neck in a gesture that he loved, skilled and vulnerable, undoing her pearls. She stood up and unhooked her bra, the shoulder straps sliding down her arms in an inanimate caress that made his own hands ache and, stopped suddenly as by a thought, turned and said, "I never thanked you for getting my watch, Giovanni. It was sweet of you."

It still brought his heart to his throat that such a gorgeous prize would come so trustingly to him. The bra was between her hands like a lace butterfly. Her skin was just dark enough that her loins and breasts were never emphasized by the silly summer bleach of a bikini. He couldn't take his eyes off her; how could her breasts be familiar as his pillow and as deep and explorable as a landscape? She saw his eyes and smiled.

He said, "I'm sure you'll make it up to me."

And he laughed with delight when his serious Marie-Sophie threw one stocking over a chair in a satirical arabesque, and missed. He couldn't take his eyes off her. He could have described her loins, her thighs, as well as he could her face, her rings, but her body still kept a hierarchy of wonder, as graceful as modesty, and familiarity never wore into routine. He turned on his side toward her and threw the cover back. Her skin-warmed scent first enveloped him and then her limbs and mouth, fire and velvet. He shivered and glowed.

He lay in the darkness, looking through the window past her face at the dark mass of mountains, darker than the night. Her unsleeping breath was gentle. After love, before sleep, she was as soft as a bird.

She said softly, "Giovanni?"

"Yes."

73

"I never know how much I need you until you come back. You were only gone for a day and it made no difference to my day that you were gone, but when I heard the gate open for you this evening I said to myself, 'Well, now it's all right,' and I hadn't even known that anything was wrong and I don't think I've felt that way since I was a little girl. I just want you to know that. You don't have to say anything."

And he didn't; he cradled her waist more closely and gently kissed her neck. He did not go to sleep quickly. By the time he did so, her even breathing made a small, warm circle on his chest.

Part Two

6

Jennifer Carrabis, who lived with Jonathan Snead, woke this and every Saturday with vague dread. Jonathan still slept beside her, naked under the sheet. She woke with the memory of his body on hers, but she had no impulse to snuggle up beside him. She knew that any moment in the next quarter hour his eyes would snap wide open and without moving a muscle he would be fully awake, not drowsy, not affectionate, and that he would have their whole day's program ready in his head, and that, still without moving – certainly not toward her – he would recite the program to her in an unquestioning and uninflected voice. They spent all Saturday together. That, at least, used to send a warm pleasure down her body as she lay there waiting for him to wake. But she lay this morning with depression like a small headache pulling at her brow, and, because his face was toward her, covered herself with the sheet. It now made her strangely uncomfortable that those uncompromising eyes should open on her thin breasts. She still took a great, quiet, and even wondering pride in being the woman of one of the authentic heroes of the American left – Jonathan was truly greater than a Panther or a Weatherman – but in her wraithlike body and her young girl's mind she had begun dryly and dismally to wish that it gave her greater pleasure, greater warmth. She was nineteen.

The eyes opened. Her heart unaccountably sank. He said, "We'll go shopping in Georgetown this morning. We'll go to the bookstore and the record shop. You can get your things at the pharmacy. We'll probably have lunch with a man from the *Post*. Then we'll go to Roosevelt Island in the afternoon."

She said, "I don't have to go to the pharmacy, Jonathan." She obscurely disliked it that he made her get her things from a particular pharmacist at People's Drug on Wisconsin while they shopped together. She disliked the pharmacist. He had sly eyes.

He said without a change of tone, "Yes, you do. You don't want to get pregnant, do you? That is what we'll do." And then, with a rare and sudden warmth that actually lifted the ache from her brow, "We'll buy that Pavarotti record for you."

She had been wanting it for a month. She was free, now, to get up and make coffee before she took her shower.

Jonathan Snead woke each Saturday with care. This was the day of contacts, the day of possible mistakes. He felt that every moment, from opening his eyes on through the day, should be carried out with care, with forethought, at an even pace. He heard the shower start and pictured, without great pleasure, the skinny little rabbit in it. She would be ten minutes. He had that long to himself. He rehearsed the probabilities. If he was not wrong, North Africa, specifically Berbia, was now the first concern. That would be in "Michael's" message, not often as an order – as an officer, no longer merely an agent, of the KGB, he was largely above that now – but as an expression of priorities. The rest was up to him. How to milk his sources, to tailor each approach, to balance what information was most valuable, what information the source could most accurately give, what would not risk a refusal so final that it could not be bullied, wheedled, threatened away – this was his skill, his craft. The danger, at any given contact, was very small. Most small mistakes could be, melodrama aside, contained. But the small degree of danger was endlessly repeated and was cumulative to some extent. He had the sense, now, of a net stretching behind him through increasing years, not buried in time but there to snag suddenly on some forgotten dead detail and bind him tight. He blessed his foresight, his brilliance, in insisting on a cover that was itself flagrantly subversive. His superiors had thought him deranged. The argument had gone, he believed, straight up to Moscow Center. But it was genius. Not only – this was simple – would nobody conceive of a buried agent using a cover that shouted from the rooftops, but also – and this was what Moscow simply could not bring itself to understand – his subversive status almost perfectly protected him. American security was by now emasculated enough, God knew – the FBI director, William Webster himself had said, after repeated Congressional harassment, that the FBI was "practically out of the domestic security field" – but even here an ordinary citizen might just perhaps come under some suspicion, be surveilled. But a known subversive was tacitly protected by the courts, by the press, by a demoralized FBI. Once he had thought himself surveilled and had guessed that his dossier was on the sort of list that the Privacy Act, Section E (7), so loved of federal judges, had ordered destroyed. A word to the press and the agent's head had rolled. He seriously doubted that he was followed now at all. And, if he was, the girl made most of the contacts. Thank God even for a dwindling supply of star-struck little radicals. And lucky, too, he thought, her brains aren't any bigger than her tits.

He brought his thoughts back to the problems of the day. Berbia pointed toward Nelson Aldrytch. Too much did. The old man was his star source and he was driving him toward a crisis. Still, it could be handled. Aldrytch had psychologically gone too far for sudden confession. He did not think that Aldrytch would kill himself before his wife died, and that was apparently some months away. He would have to let up on him a little then. There was Mason Salfield, now, but he was new, untried. It was uncertain yet what he could do, but he seemed weak, pompous, and hungry and he would, sooner or later, do whatever he could. He would start him off easily. He made a careful division between those contacts, usually instantly identifiable, who could be led, then tricked, then forced inexorably into open treason, and those from whom only sparse crumbs of indiscretion – simply, really, the rent on their liberal status – could be drawn. Salfield was one of the first kind.

The shower dwindled, stopped. He swung out of bed and padded through the room. It was a spare, boxlike space, without molding, with iron windowframes flush with the wall. The furniture was in no way poor – it was light colored, mostly of the kind called "Scandinavian" – but it made little contact with the room and might just have been put there for storage. It was very neat. The brightest, rowdiest element was his clothes and Jennifer's, jeans and shirts, thrown over the back of an office chair. He picked up the clothes as he passed. The room achieved, then, complete neutrality, as though with relief. It was one of a thousand rooms in a sprawling neighbourhood of spare and sensible apartments, 1950s bastard Bauhaus and melancholy as parking signs, around 6th Street in South West Washington. His neighbours were teachers, civil servants, less glamorous staffers from Capitol Hill. There were underpriviliged young trees outside. He stood in the pullman kitchen. The last falling drops made spreading ripples in the coffeepot. He poured a cup. Their clothes were under his arm. The wadded jeans were harsh on his naked skin. Snead preferred not to wear jeans, but they were much the best dress for sniffing the air of the liberal Georgetown nightspots on Friday night, the night that people both drank and talked about their work. He decided that they would wear them also today. Jennifer came from the bathroom, dried and flushed.

"Put them back on," he said. But his tone was not harsh.

They parked the Volvo in Georgetown, on Q Street. Jennifer was happy. Each Saturday, at different stores, they shopped for books. Third World Books downtown, was, she knew, the one she ought to like. Here they looked at books on peasant communes, Cuban progress, CIA plots, liberation, and the wise and wonderful essays of Professor Herbert Marcuse. She read them and talked about them, especially Marcuse. She really did. But in the Georgetown shop, where there was level after level of little low-ceilinged, paneled rooms, she could wander through Astrology and Health Foods and Indoor Plants and feel warm and curious and not at all alone. Sometimes she would even wander off without Jonathan for an ice cream on the sidewalk outside. She saw Jonathan go into Foreign Classics. He always looked at what no one else did.

He loitered before the shelves but he moved between them briskly. Bookstores gave him no pleasure. To begin with they reminded him of his childhood, of the poorest days when his father, the ex-professor, supported them on the part-time salary of a bookstore clerk. His father, even before the purge, had given forth a sour sense of failure as some men give forth sweat. Too undistinguished an academic to stand forth proudly as the Marxist he was, too undistinguished to find a place at any university where he could possibly have survived as one, he had anxiously taught at a small Midwestern campus and dealt as well as he could with the reputation of being "left-wing." The Knights of Columbus began the agitation. By 1956 leftist teachers were in trouble throughout the state. William Snead was fired in spite of a humiliating recantation. Four years later he got a job in an elementary school. To Jonathan Snead, the bright smell of a new-printed book was the very mildew of poverty and failure.

He found books to be ridiculous, besides. These shelves were full of babbling. How many novels! How many matings! How many "dilemmas"! Why all the

81

fuss? Get it right once and then be quiet! And the essays, the nonfiction, were mostly trash. History and politics were of some polemical value – Jonathan Snead respected ideas as tools – but the rest of it, the impressions, the "memoirs," the self-aggrandizement, the pointless criticisms of the silly novels, the photo books of rich men's toys, were things he could quite easily bring himself to hate. Well, there it was, the Flaubert that he hated more than most. He reached eagerly for *Salammbô* and turned the pages. He did not read French.

For the illegal agent, the moment of maximum danger is the physical meeting with another agent and the transfer of documents between them. This is when a stakeout pounces. This is when guilt is irrefutable. This is when two surveillance operations can come together, clinch. This is when a whole network can explode. The danger can be much reduced by dead drops – leaving-places where the agents never meet. The dead drops themselves can fail – children can find them, bums pick up cigarette packs with microfilm inside. They are totally defenseless to anyone else who may know that they are there. They are rigid and clumsy if rarely serviced, dangerous if too frequently. The two systems can be combined. A dead drop, or, better, one of the several dead drops on a schedule may be used to set an arbitary time for direct meeting or a warning not to come. This Saturday was the Georgetown bookstore, Flaubert, fourth title by alphabet, page number 26, the day of the month. It was clear.

They went on to the Podium, the record shop. On Wisconsin Avenue, the postindustrial society over-flowed the sidewalks and brought the automobile age to a clogged halt. In the Design Store, the payrolls of leftist foundations bought ironstone dishes from neutral Finland. In Britche's Clothing, radical lawyers, past thirty-five and quite respectable, were fitted with business suits of British cloth cut with a luxurious panache that itself made the subtlest, most backhanded of counterculture costume statements. Johann Sebastian Bach, a prisoner of the Podium, breathed God's own Lutheran music over Transcendental Meditators, biorhythm fetishists, and aging Maoists. The time was long past when Jonathan Snead would play with ironic counterpoints between his engaged purposes and the world he lived in – to do so notoriously led to slow insanity – but still, Wisconsin Avenue on a Saturday morning made him lick his chops. It was heartening to play against a Main Enemy with the defensive disciplines of a children's party. He thought with momentary, scornful anger of the Soviet citizens, even KGB men, who had defected, apparently, for just this trash.

Jennifer bought her Pavarotti – the singer on the record cover dressed as a barker with a drum to celebrate the frenzied overexposure of his glorious voice. The Podium was the cut-out dead drop. Since the book in the bookstore could conceivably, by sheer ill-luck, be tampered with or sold, the simplest, most urgent message – it would be "do not meet me on any account" – would also be conveyed by removing the price tag, thirty minutes before contact time, of the record whose title was highest in the alphabet in the small shelf of foreign poetry recitation. If the message was even worse – *vanish* – the cellophane cover was to be removed. Nothing is perfect. Even this record, even the putatively unpriced voice of Jean Cocteau, could conceivably be sold that very minute. But it was not likely. It was not so.

Jennifer said, "I don't need to get my pills at that pharmacy, Jonathan. I don't need them till the middle of next week anyway."

He felt her stiffen and begin to hang back like a puppy that sees it's going to the vet. It worried him. *What is it that scares her? Could she really be catching on?* It wasn't all that easy, every single Saturday, to find something at the prescription counter she had to buy. This week, at least, was birth control pills, which were to some degree

83

inarguable. In a sense it wouldn't matter if she did catch on. She was a thoroughgoing little socialist – wouldn't stick at spying for the Soviets at all. Wouldn't mind tossing a bomb, most likely, if it didn't hurt any birds or bunny rabbits. But, on the other hand, his safety would be diminished by a definite and dangerous degree if she knew anything. She'd be putty to counterespionage. He'd throw her out first and begin again. His thoughts drifted, as now and again they did, with wistful lust to the hard, comely body and steel-trap mind of Julia Drew of Palestinians for Peace. Pity she was totally unmanageable.

He said, "You forgot them altogether last time. I'm not letting you do that again. We'll get them right now."

And he didn't even slow his pace, pushing through the clogged sidewalk. But she did and suddenly there were bodies between them. He stood still and waited. She came up. She looked him in the face and said, "All right, Jonathan, but not at that pharmacy."

He could hardly conceive of a blank refusal, but it frightened him because he didn't know what to do if she gave him one. His impulse was to slap her full force on the face – it had worked before on another matter, but that had been in the apartment and she had cried for half an hour first. Here he couldn't risk it. So he did the next best thing and took her fondly by the neck and found the nerve and pinched it so her face went rigid and she drew in her breath in a shocked and wondering sort of way and he looked her calmly in the eye and said, "I think it's better that we get them there." Then he let go of her and she stood beside him like an automaton and walked when he did.

It wasn't that she was scared. It wasn't even that she minded being used. She was pretty sure that Free Information and the magazine were somehow only about half of what Jonathan was, and she guessed that most of what they did together had to do with things she didn't know about. She didn't care if it put her in danger.

She'd die for the Revolution. She really would. But going each Saturday to the pharmacist with slinky eyes and knowing smile to ask for, half the time, something intimate for her body – the body that she wanted to share with Jonathan – and then having the package taken from her and given back opened at the apartment made her perfectly sure, once a week, that he didn't care a thing for her and didn't even have the imagination to know that she would know. If he would explain this one thing, she'd do it gladly. That was all she meant. And now she was frightened, too, and hurt and sick.

But she stood in line and made sure she'd be served by the nasty little man and not the pretty black girl her own age who was his assistant. He looked like someone who was meant to be a dwarf but had grown most of the way after all. He had a dwarf's secret movements. She stood, looking at an ugly white basin behind the glass on the shelf. Then it was her turn. He looked at her hard but Jonathan hadn't given her an empty box this week to get refilled and she told him what she wanted and after a moment he went behind the counter and came back with a small white package. He hadn't had time to wrap it but she really didn't care anymore. She paid for it and walked back through the garden hoses and the shaving cream and the bug sprays and the corn plasters. Jonathan was on the street in the crowd outside and she gave it to him and he dropped it in the shopping bag.

He read it in the men's room at Nathan's restaurant while they waited for the man from the *Post*. It was written on a small sheet folded up where the drug specifications would normally be. It read:

It is to be regarded as inevitable that the Main Enemy will make every attempt to rebuild his networks in Berbia. This must not take place outside the knowledge of our intelligence. The enemy will not immediately reduplicate his past efforts – apart from the probability of our penetration he will know that it would take too long. It is probable that he will attempt to extend other networks that already exist. You should, therefore, press for information regarding increased CIA activity in neighboring countries or increased urgency of general Arab-directed intelligence gathering. Specifically, we have known for some years of a highly effective CIA surveillance of Arab expatriates in foreign capitals, especially Paris, which we have never been able to satisfactorily penetrate. Information on this would be of the highest priority.

He tore it up and flushed it down the toilet. He went back to the table, through the smell of lasagne and good coffee. The reporter was there. He was only a minor reporter – a young man on the foreign desk referred to Snead by Steven Lutrick at State for off-the-record background. That was good. Lutrick was developing nicely. He was not under control so far, just an agent of sympathy, but sooner or later he would do something indiscreet enough to be controlled thereafter. He remembered: he should find out precisely what Lutrick had said to Julia at the Salfied thing. The reporter wanted some background on the CIA in Chile. Jonathan Snead was sure he could help. He greeted him warmly.

7

The car was old and faded but it was a good English Rover and it smelled of leather and dog. The dog got out first, a gray-muzzled golden retriever with a delicate way of setting its feet to the ground. He turned and waited for his master. His master was clearly of the American Establishment. He was not in business clothes – this was Saturday – and he wore an old check shirt, a pair of Zeiss binoculars, tan trousers, and scarred Topsiders. He did not need to be in business clothes. He could have been the authenticating figure on the cover of the catalogue of the best gunsmith or tacklemaker in the land. His hair was graying and his eyes were blue. He was an edge over six feet tall and he had the face of an autocratic but amiable horse. In the concrete parking lot off the George Washington Memorial Parkway, by the causeway to Roosevelt Island in the Potomac, among the Datsuns and Winnebagos, he looked like an English fly rod on a drugstore shelf.

His name was Nelson Aldrytch. He was a member of the National Intelligence Advisory Board, the small group of men from outside government that takes precedence over all but the National Security Council in the management and direction of the nation's intelligence. He had served under six presidents and he had been a friend of three. He had once nearly been attorney general. He was a partner in the firm of Aldrytch, Mathews, and Smythe, discreet and formidable even among Washington law firms. He was on the board of Princeton, the National Wildlife Foundation, the Save the Children Federation, and a vestryman of St. Alban's Episcopal Church. He felt himself to be as close to hell as it is possible to be on Earth. He was a traitor and he loved his country. It was to be assumed that he was going to watch the birds. It was his desperate and occasionally realized hope that that would be all the truth.

The dog followed him, gravely, not needing to be called. Roosevelt Island, the green stand of wilderness a mile long and a third as wide in the middle of a city river, stood before him in the heavy, drying foliage that comes before the fall. Only the dogwoods, under the margin of the tall trees, had just begun to turn. He walked onto the causeway. As he crossed it and approached the woods, his figure became more at one with his surroundings, less alone.

He loved wild places and his life had taken him to them. This unholy afternoon was a twisted link in a chain whose fairer ones were bacon-smelling mornings on the Allagash beneath the spruce when the beached canoes floated in the mist, summer climbs in the Alps through the smell of wild meadow hay, the whirr of chukar grouse in the high plains autumn. He had not hunted for years. His soul had softened, mellowed since his son's death, he supposed, since the Tet Offensive. He preferred to look. He liked it so; and yet he knew that his former, hard, hunting, young man's self would never have been taken by the trap he lay in. At the mouth of the woods he actually stopped, unable to go on. This place was tainted like a slaughterhouse by a score of other such afternoons. The dog turned and waited for him anxiously, as though knowing that this place was not what it seemed. *Well, why not prison?* At this very place the thought rose weekly to his mind. *Could it really be worse than this?* And three slow paces farther on the answer was waiting with a grin: *You're damn right it could be, Nelson. It could be a whole lot worse.* He had known poor Mitchell, well, and Martha.

A drilling in the oak above him made him raise his

forgotten binoculars. A pileated woodpecker, of course; he had raised them only in salutation. He followed the path. This was the marshy margin. In the spring, spiky yellow lizards' tails with vine-shaped leaves marked the border of the path, and bolletes grew in the shade; now the berries were beginning to harden, and soon a few migratory mallards would join the native wood duck. The path turned inland through ferns and beeches. He saw the spiderwebs in the unsunned hollows. The dog sniffed there and even gave an aged pretense of hunting. Raccoon, most likely. Sooner than he expected he was at the Roosevelt Monument.

This, in particular, always gave him a special twinge of shame; a double one, in fact, since he was beginning to see even shame as a luxury. Its stone stability reminded him of a world he vaguely knew as a boy. It was a world of sureness and of duty, he liked to think, the antithesis of the world of exquisite conscience on which he had floated into hell. He tried to think of Theodore running in the middle of the night to a Red journalist to spill his country's secrets out of the fear that, if he didn't, the Marines might land in Angola. Well, 1975 was not 1912, he supposed, but in Jonathan Snead he sure as hell had picked a bully pulpit. He literally shook himself, and the dog looked at him, perturbed. *Come on*, he thought. *Get on with it. Be a man, at least.*

The dead drop was a hundred yards from the monument down a side path in a cavity under the roots of an oak. He paused a moment to see if anyone was following. No. Fortune smiled on treason. He was alone. It could not be seen from the path. The receptacle was a pill bottle – a good choice, earth colored, imperishable, waterproof, small. It would not betray them. Them. He stooped down and scooped it up. He breathed the sharp smell of root and earth. Last week it had been empty. It sometimes was so. He held it a while before he opened it. *Ah, no. This time we have a paper. Well. What now?*

You will meet me at 4:00 P.M. precisely at the southern point of the island under the second span of the Roosevelt Bridge. If you are followed it will be assumed to be intentional. Destroy.

This was unprecedented. Never before in their collaboration had Snead ordered or even allowed a personal meeting. Quite right, of course. In Aldrytch the former intelligence professional now all at once ousted the wounded naturalist. Even to his own lingering horror, he was acutely interested. The Soviet machine was running at full blast, that he knew well, but why, all of a sudden, this? It would have to be something without past reference, urgent, and complex. He walked on and found a hollow in the woods to wait. Forty-five minutes. He called the dog. The dog, happy to see the improvement in his master, gladly came.

Jonathan Snead, from the shadow of the bridge piling, saw Aldrytch pick his way down the unused path with a woodsman's ease and quiet. The simmering anger that Aldrytch filled him with bubbled and turned sour in his chest. It seemed to him a personal insult that this duped, degraded, pathetic old aristocrat should come to his doom looking like a vacationer in a genteel Maine resort. And, wonderful, with a bird dog! He warned himself to let personal dislike have no part in his dealings. But soon he was personally pleased, though professionally dismayed, to see that close up the old man looked pretty bad – falling cheeks, a stoop now, and a less certain eye. Outside of newspaper photographs, he had not seen him for a year.

He stepped out of the shadow. Aldrytch had already seen him but now he stopped, silent, ten feet away. The dog looked rigidly at Snead. It crossed Snead's mind, and was rejected, that it might be vicious, some kind of trick.

He said, "Are you alone?"

Aldrytch nodded.

"You'd better be." He waited deliberately to let Aldrytch's unease grow.

He said, "You don't have much left in Berbia, do you?"

Aldrytch neither spoke nor moved.

Snead felt a bubble rising again inside him. "You shouldn't do it anymore, building bases, moving troops in, taking over, on the offensive. You're too toothless. You've got nothing left. You're feeble. It's our game now." He fought the bubble down. He should have handled this by message. No one but Aldrytch caused this in him, or even the desire for it.

Aldrytch said, "Did we meet for conversation?"

He was uneasy and yet suddenly elated. He had recognized his control all along as a professional. The entrapment had been very nicely done. He had gone to Snead, then editor of *Free Planet*, a journal of foreign affairs, with anguished good intentions to leak the news, and stop Ford and Kissinger's appalling plan to send troops in force to Angola, presenting Congress with a *fait accompli* and the inarguable necessity of sending more to protect those sent first. Snead had handled it very well: even on short notice the recording was undetectable, the manner was just right, and the subsequent requests, from a like-thinker, from an ally, for secret information closer and closer to the bone were beautifully judged. He was tied hand and foot with magnetic tape. Aldrytch the man was dying in the merciless trap, but Aldrytch the professional had recognized at least that there would be no folly, no mistakes.

But this was a degeneration, and he was pleased and scared. He had not seen Snead for a year, and an edge of hysteria seemed to be working toward the skin. It wasn't only in this outburst. He had lost weight. Standing in the shadow, he had been tense without cause. His eyes seemed at once harder and less strong. It seemed of a piece with the power he served. For the last two years, the Soviet Union had given the appearance of a machine being run at unremitting full throttle. He wondered what pressures Snead was under. Still, none of this was any surprise. Illegal agents do not last forever, and agents against their own countries last less well than most. With rare exceptions, ten years was it, and then they cracked or were retired. By that timetable, Snead was perhaps half-finished. But only half. He was now also most dangerous. He still said nothing.

And Snead, at last controlled, resumed, "I'm changing your priorities. El Salvador is of secondary importance now. North Africa is the area of primary interest. How do you intend to rebuild your networks in Berbia?"

Aldrytch said, "I can't answer that. DCI has not reported to FIAB yet." He meant Director of Central Intelligence and the Foreign Intelligence Advisory Board.

"When will he report?"

"We are scheduled for a two-hour meeting on Wednesday. I assume that it will be on the agenda. There will certainly be questions."

Snead said, "Of course there will be. You will have to make sure of it. But we may have to take quick action on some of this so you had better create a climate for questions and not ask too many yourself. We are assuming that you will extend networks that are already in place – in Morocco, say, or special-purpose networks surveilling Arabs in general. We need to know which. We need to know how they are rated for effectiveness. We need to know which officers' assignments will be changed. We need to know any changes of cover. You understand?"

"The FIAB does not deal with individual officers' names. What you're asking for is dangerous."

Snead shrugged. "Order an investigation. Find out how Berbia got blown. Order up competency-evaluation reports. That's what you're for. You can do it. One more thing. You've got a network in Paris surveilling Arab expatriates. It's a good one. I want to know everything about that. Changes of plan. Names, covers. Get it. As far as we can tell, that's your best one in the region and you'll probably use it."

Aldrytch said, "Let me be sure that I understand you. You want me to go in, initiate an investigation in extraordinary detail, pass the results to you, and sit there while your people effect some kind of immediate response which you have not defined to me. I cannot contain that. That is not even professional unless I know in advance the parameters of the action you people intend to take. Unless I have become expendable. Have I?"

Snead said, "No. No. We won't trash you unless you make us. You can have three weeks for the details if that's what you need. But I need the outline next week. We need to know where to get people in place. What covers to watch for. Names can come a little later. When the time comes we'll tell you what we're going to do to the extent we think you need to know. Make your drop at this time next week. I may have instructions for you or I may not."

Aldrytch said, "I see. May I assume that that is all?"

And Snead moved several steps closer, quickly, so that Aldrytch thought, with dismay that even surprised him, *He's going to take hold of me.* But the dog growled, quietly but from its chest, and Snead stopped at once.

He said, "Not quite all. No. We're going to be needing a lot from you in the next few months, maybe during the next year. More than before. Some of it may push you pretty hard. If you do your best and your cover blows we'll give you all the resources that we can to contain it. You'll probably get out without a trial. If you try to cheat us we'll make it worse than it is. They won't even give you bail. You'll be in prison when your wife dies of cancer. I promise that. Do you understand, Mr. Aldrytch?"

"I understand."

He turned abruptly, back up the thinly traced path. At least he would not wait to be dismissed. It surprised him that he felt so little. The whole interview could have taken place half a mile away. The truth was that what was uppermost in his mind was the formidable problem of how to manage the FIAB meeting. He knew in advance that if he did it well enough, he would have a secret measure of unholy pride. Shame and fear were not dead, of course, no fear of that at all. They were so much the companions of his life that he did not always notice them. Except at their own special address that he visited once a day. They lived at four o'clock in the morning.

8

Bartolomeo Pompini came from time to time into Stears's life like a fish nuzzling one's legs in murky water. That it was slippery was felt at once; that it had teeth was only guessed; perhaps it was venomous. It was Italian.

It was also an investment counselor, a double kinship doubly undesired. Pompini lived at the limit of the respectable and foraged farther out. Not precisely crime, Stears thought, not actually Mafia; just the business of clients who left minority shareholders wailing in every court in Europe, clients of almost operatic crookedness – Chianti made of bulls' blood, snails made of sheep's lungs – clients with darker connections still, to Malta, to Libya, to Damascus, to God knew where. Of the last, Stears knew less than he would have liked. Pompini treated him as his Society friend. When he wanted to move up, he nuzzled Stears. Stears sometimes requited. Pompini had uses. If a client's aspirations turned out to be gamier than Stears could face, he did not have to be insulted and jilted, he could be given a date with Pompini. Investment counselors in the Arab trade cannot entirely ignore the rogues' gallery.

And so today. Pompini had the lacquered and melancholy look of gentlemen travelers in old posters of ocean liners, doglike devotion in the mustache and a gleam in the eye.

He said, "It is nice that I can come to you, Stears, you know. Your clients aren't stuffy." He made a face comically stiff and then took a cigarette from a gold case. It would be Turkish.

"Aren't they, now?" said Stears. It was Pompini's special offense to suggest that not only were they both Italian, not only were they in the same trade, but that both, really and truly now, worked for crooks. He could fix the first at least. No Giovanni for Pompini. With Pompini he was Williston and Stears.

"You know what I mean, old chap. Now this man, he is perfectly, he is absolutely clean." Pompini turned his palms up. They were clean. "He makes espresso pots. He packages ice cream. Is that bad?"

Stears looked down the New England steeple of his hands, enjoying it.

Pompini went on. "And do Arabs drink coffee? Do Arabs eat ice cream?"

Stears nodded.

"So he wants backing for the Arab world. Exports. Distribution. Everyone makes money."

Stears said, "At last count Geneva had fifty-seven banks."

"He made a mistake once. I wouldn't hide it from you. He had bad friends. With a bank, that's endless trouble."

Stears said, "Is he out yet?"

Such bad taste made Pompini sad. He said, "Old chap." And then, "But you have people he could easily work with. A small consortium. In Iran in the old days I had a client . . ."

Stears said, "Not a chance." Pompini stopped.

"I sell skill. I sell knowledge. I also sell respectability. An Arab who comes to me, Pompini, knows one thing: he will never be made a fool of, he will never look bad."

"Yes," said Pompini. And his eye became vague and wandered the wall and settled on a new painting there, an early Kokoschka got with more luck than money.

"That's very nice," he said.

It was. Pompini knew paintings. He shrugged. "I just wondered," he said.

Which should have been the end of it, but wasn't.

For on the way out Pompini took his arm and said,

"There is something else. Quite different. I have been approached by three men. All Berbians. Two of them I do not know much about. One is Amal Khannafi. Do not tell me you do not know of that family."

"Of course I know them." Khannafi was one of the great trading names of Berbia. Not a spot on it.

"I think, frankly, that they are out of my league. But for that reason, especially, I do not want to just walk away. I would like to refer them. To you, my friend and compatriot, to you."

Stears said, "Khannafi should be all right."

"Of course, of course! That's just what I mean. The tops!" He took a card from his pocket and passed it so quickly over that Stears hesitated a moment. It was as though it were hot.

"Their card. See? Khannafi, just as I said." Pompini, now, was all but hanging from Stears's sleeve. "They are in Geneva for a few days. Can I say that you will call them? You will at least do that?"

"Yes," said Stears. "I will call. Why should I not? Good day."

And he sounded brusque, but he was not. He was puzzled. For three things were odd. Pompini would have known that Stears would reject his convict. There was no reason in the world that a Khannafi would approach Pompini and even less, if one did, that Pompini would give him to Stears.

And one thing odder yet, so odd that it had taken him time even to see it.

Pompini was scared stiff.

He was to go to the hotel. They were at the President, which fit – an expense-account baroque caravansary for the wandering rich with no ties to the old Geneva. It had little conference rooms. He knew them well.

But he was sent up to the tenth floor, their suite, and Pompini was just enough on his mind that he left the lobby behind him with regret. The corridor was empty.

97

And, afterward, leaving richer by $35,000 – his commission on $3.5 million of bearer bonds – he almost felt a fool.

Almost, because it made no sense. Two men, not three. Amal Khannafi, about thirty years old, had modeled himself, perhaps, on a successful Monte Carlo pimp. He had the expression, fatuous and sly, the butter-smooth expensive skin, the silver tweed suit, and the gold Rolex, the weight of which could have given him his exercise. A spoiled son of a new-rich trading family and inconceivable as the leader of anything beyond a raid on Gucci's. The real leader must be the other, with the Nixon jowl, Hussein Yamadi, presented as the lawyer, neat, hard, watchful, and as personable as a ball-point pen.

Not at all the sort of man to imagine that he needed Stears to buy a block of bonds with ready money.

They were a Berbian export-import firm, it seemed, based in Paris, or at least were soon to be one, or at least would buy one. Their money was in the Bank of Malta. They would park it in bonds until their investment, which would be very soon.

Paying Stears, therefore, much more in commission than the bonds would yield. The bearer bonds, the most anonymous instruments available, would be bought on Stears's account, into which the Maltese money would simultaneously vanish.

He had clients who laundered their money more often than their underwear. He almost shrugged. But Malta, in debt to Libya, is where Ghadaffi's money, for terror, for fraud, enters the West.

And one thing more: he understood Pompini now and that made no sense at all.

What could there be in a suite at the President – white suede walls, a view of the lake – what could there be in a spoiled young puppy and his dubious mentor to make him wish never to be there again? Nothing. Not the room. Not them. But there had been the trace of an absent third in a sudden, fearful, and then relieved glance of Khannafi's eyes at an empty chair and in Yamadi's luxurious amusement when he saw it. It was like a scent, of sweat or gun oil in a frilly bedroom, that smelled of the incongruous, perhaps the trap.

Which was all very foolish. It had been a profitable morning and he need have nothing more to do with them.

The next day, Yamadi called. Stears was to sell the bearer bonds on settlement in five days' time and buy a second package to the identical value and hold these for future sale against an investment. He was then to report.

He had made $70,000 now and he wished he had made none of it. He had developed a fine nose for the clients with whom one ended up by scrambling out of trouble. He knew just what he wanted to do with these people. He wanted to introduce them to Pompini.

Three days later, Stears ended lunch with Joseph Samal, a lunch repeated once a month, part business, part social, wholly agreeable, and hardly Arabic at all. Samal was a Lebanese Catholic, an early and serene expatriate from the old Beirut of tolerance and head-waiters. They arranged for tennis on the weekend. It was quarter of two. Stears took the lemon from his coffee, looked around the restaurant, and saw without enthusiasm Yamadi and Khannafi and a third man's back. It was the day he was to report. He had made the sale.

He gestured to Samal and said, "Clients of mine. I should stop by their table."

And thought that Samal looked at him as though meeting him in a hotel corridor with a good friend's wife.

He said, "Hussein Yamadi is your client?"

"Young Khannafi is the client. Yamadi is his lawyer, though I should guess he calls the shots."

Samal now looked alarmed and reserved at once. One does not lightly question one's friends' affairs. He said,

"Lawyer? Is that what Yamadi is now?" And then, "Does it pay well?"

"So far ridiculously well."

"Well, so much the better. Tennis on Saturday at two, I think. I will meet you at the club."

They had not seen him. He stopped beside Yamadi. There was little sense of partners and none of friends. Khannafi had a bottle of wine, apparently to himself. His eyes were on his foie gras. No one spoke. Stears greeted them. The third man looked sharply up.

Stears said, "Everything is in order, as of this morning. I will send you the confirmations, but I thought you would like to know."

He remembered only with effort what he was there to say. For in the third man was the presence in the room, was Khannafi's eyes, was Pompini's fear.

Not a ruffian, not a thug, not even a cold-eyed bodyguard.

Yamadi said, "Mr. Stears, this is our partner, Hussein Khamal. Hussein, this is Mr. Stears, of whom you have heard."

Khamal looked at him slowly. The delicacy of the face was feminine, but it was carved out of stone. The hair was dense and black and curled. Feminine, but not a trace of woman, or even boy. It was like a stone angel. That was also in the eye.

Khamal said merely, "I am sure we are fortunate to have found you, Mr. Stears." But Stears felt both naked and alone, for the eye was not only enveloping; it was utterly without humanity, or impurity, or mercy, or weakness, or doubt. They were eyes to see at the moment of one's death.

It passed. Khamal looked down. Yamadi said, "It is good of you to have been so prompt." Three rich Arabs at a snowy tablecloth with flowers. The headwaiter passed and bowed to Stears. He took his leave.

He woke in the night with a vague memory of cold and

100

fear. He was alone, until a faint warmth upon his back recalled Marie-Sophie, from whom he had rolled away. He moved gently back. Perhaps it had concerned Yamadi's people, for he had suddenly remembered a detail from the first meeting at the hotel. He had spoken first in Arabic. Though his accent was not good, he usually did so; few Westerners did and it had an effect. Yamadi had switched quickly into English, but the two men had been surprised and there had been a sentence or two of Arabic. There is one language throughout the Arab world, but many idioms and accents. Stears, though no expert, could recognize some.

Khannafi, certainly a Berbian, spoke like one. Yamadi, claiming to be one, did not. Not North African at all. Yamadi's accent was from the Eastern Mediterranean. From Palestine. Any Arab would hear this instantly. Few Westerners would.

His neck tensed on the pillow and made Marie-Sophie stir in her sleep. It was four o'clock. He was wide awake.

At the end of the second set, Stears gathered up the balls and walked to the net. They were 4–6, 6–4. Around them, racquets conversed in the measured rhythms of weekend tennis. The club, at the edge of Geneva, by the lake, and a mile or so from Marie-Sophie's villa, was cleaned and polished by money – bright grass, ocher courts, white shirts, and sapphire lake.

He said, "That's a draw. Another?"

Joseph Samal's shirt was open to the third button. The hair of his chest was damp and gray.

"Two's enough. I smoke too much."

He was aging, thought Wop, and found that it saddened him.

And today not only aging but nervous and uncertain, too. They sat on the veranda, watching the courts and talking little. Wop ordered lemonade. Marie-Sophie had evening guests for drinks. A doubles match ended on the nearest court. It would soon be time to go. He said so.

Samal said, "Your client Yamadi? – have you known him long?"

"A week or two at most. Have you?"

"I have never known him. I had a friend who did. He hanged himself."

"Not because he knew Yamadi? He's not that tiresome."

His smile was not returned.

"I suppose not. This was in Beirut. Yamadi was his client at the end but he had many others. He was a man somewhat like yourself, at least in your line of business. I have to say that this was at the end of the good time in Beirut when the PLO first came, and he was not the only man to take his own life."

"Then there would be no connection."

"As I said, probably not. There is one thing more. I said he hanged himself, which is what the police said, and maybe that was true. But while he was hanging himself, he was smoking cigarettes."

Wop looked at him.

"Yes. And not just one cigarette. Many. And he put them out all up and down his back. It is a terrible thing, this craving for nicotine, but, in my opinion, Yamadi might be worse."

He heard it less through his ears than through his spine. He looked at the lake, meditating disbelief, and then asked simply, "Why? Why did it happen? Do you know?"

"No, Giovanni, I do not know. A lot of odd horrors began to be seen in Beirut then, like stray rats before a plague. But I know that my friend had been puzzled by Yamadi and by what he had asked him to do. Perhaps he had tried to find out something. Perhaps it was not Yamadi at all. But you have no need of this, Giovanni. It is not your world."

He was a bad host. Marie-Sophie's guests chattered and eddied. He wandered from group to group, standing distracted on their outskirts. He called Marie-Sophie's friend Madeleine "Marguerite," though he knew her well. He caught Marie-Sophie looking at him with a puzzled frown.

He was thinking of Witham.

He had been manipulated. He had been tricked.

He was not a Company professional. Certainly not career. He was barely paid. His limited recruitment, by the fireplace of a London club, had seemed a lark. That was until he reflected much later that the old school friend who did it had known that he would not refuse and had touched every key learned through long friendship to make sure. Over Wop Stears hung his father's disgrace, wartime apostasy, near treason. He had never wholly overcome his boyhood of mean exile, in Vichy France, in neutral Switzerland. None of this attached to Wop, of course, Williston Stear's boy shouldn't suffer, should he? Not at Choate, not at Yale, not in the middle of the night. So, while the firelight flickered on brass in Palmerston's old club, his friend had lightly offered redemption. He had been recruited by a pro with care.

And with limits. His cover was real. It was not even cover. He was absolutely, definitely, an investment counselor in business on his own account. Only his clients' secrets were the Company's.

Witham had cheated. It was no part of Stear's covenant to "move into a more active surveillance" – he wasn't meant to be active at all. It was not part of it to be involved with monsters of the deep, certainly not when they had been identified as monsters. Witham's casual instruction could ruin his business. Worse – and this, the recurrent boyhood nightmare, made him sweat – it could get him thrown out of the country.

He would not consider Beirut. Nor the eyes at lunch.

He could easily quit. *Williston's boy, you know.*

He passed someone a plate of olives, as an ashtray.

He found himself listening for the waiter's footsteps

outside in the corridor of the President as though they were the proof of a normal world. Yamadi talked. Khamal looked. Khannafi gazed into the air.

There was now an atmosphere of queasy intimacy. He was their man. He was Khamal's, and through no action of Khamal's whatever. Khamal gave off intimidation like a secretion, a sticky wash from which Stears tried to break free.

Yamadi said, "Happily, we are now at the point where we can move toward our main purpose. You handled the preliminary business with efficiency, Mr. Stears, and it is our decision that you will continue to act for us."

Because it was a trial of will to ask questions at all, Wop said abruptly, "How did you hear of me?"

Yamadi answered without expression, "A certain Bartolomeo Pompini was under contract to us, and when he became unsatisfactory we required him to find a replacement quickly. He recommended you. He said you were a luxurious, stateless bourgeois with no loyalties and dependent on the goodwill of the Swiss. The business we are concerned with is the purchase of an export-import firm in Paris."

It did not help at all that Yamadi's meaning appeared on Khamal's face. He saw himself reflected there, timorous and weak, smiling hopefully at insult and threat.

"You will buy it and we will buy it from you. Your commission will be quite small, I think. We have given you a lot already. Is that not reasonable?"

He pushed himself to it again. "I shall require, of course, to know more about your business to serve you effectively. What kind of export-import? Specifically, between where and where? Mr. Khannafi is a Berbian, of course. As you all are."

That was damn close, he thought, and it appalled him that he almost flinched at a sudden cloud in Khamal's eye.

But Yamadi said smoothly, "Not at all, Mr. Stears. All you need to know is the name of the firm we have chosen and the price that we have agreed to pay, and that you will have before you leave. You will then only have to go to Paris to consummate the deal. You will not refer to our names there. They would not know them."

As Stears left, Yamadi said, "This is by no means the end, Mr. Stears. There will be more business. We expect that it will be soon."

Paris, then. He salvaged what satisfaction he could from the thought that Yamadi would pay for his ticket to call upon McNaughton. It was time.

He took an early flight. He read the Geneva paper, *La Suisse*, at the airport, standing between the watch boutique and the caviar counter. The oil ministers were meeting in Lausanne. The West German deficit was down. On the inner pages, there would be a horse show this year at Coppet. That might be fun. The body of an Italian national, Bartolomeo Pompini, a consultant, had been recovered from the river. Suicide was suspected. His papers had been revoked. He was to have left Switzerland in thirty days.

At ten past two McNaughton walked slowly out of the Place de la Concorde onto the wooded walk beside the Champs-Elysées. At two-fifteen, Wop Stears, walking from the Crillon, intercepted him at right angles. Surprise of two American, two friends! They walked toward the Rond-Point. Ledoyen, the most pointlessly expensive restaurant in France, lurked in the forest.

"What you are going to say," said Stears, "is that there's no linkup. There's nothing."

"Yeah. I could say that. What about this outfit you just bought?"

"It's small. It's poor. It's going downhill. It's a warehouse and a little office over in Clichy. They handle ball bearings and things like that. Two or three salesmen. I dealt with the owner, Michelet. He's certainly French. He's late middle-aged and he looks sick. I'd say he's perfectly clean, doesn't have a clue what he's dealing with, and is delighted to get out of it. You find anything about him?"

"Not a thing. You're right."

Wop had called the meeting. He had set the place. McNaughton lived nowhere near here. Wop was weary of taking both the risk and the pupil's role. It gave him a small, unworthy pleasure that he had brought McNaughton up from Montmartre so that their walk should end at the Avenue Montaigne, where he would buy Marie-Sophie a dress.

"Then what do they want with it?"

"It's export-import. Covers a lot."

Wop said, "You don't understand. A business has a life of its own. People don't realize that. It's hard to change. You can take a respectable, mediocre little outfit like Michelet's and turn it into something else, but it takes time. Or it takes a ruckus. These people are very quiet. They don't want a ruckus. And I can't prove this, but I don't think they have any time."

It was extraordinary how completely McNaughton assumed the role of Donnelly. There was no possibility of doubt that Stears was walking with a down-at-the-heels, self-important, probably alcoholic, and scrounging American intellectual of the fourth or fifth rank. He found patronage creeping into his voice. It was he who was out of place. Perhaps he was a respectable relative.

"This guy in Geneva. You think they did it? You think they made him do it?"

"I have no idea. If the paper said the police wanted him out, then they did want him out. Maybe that's why he was scared. Maybe that's why they got rid of him. Maybe it's not them at all. But, McNaughton, Pompinis don't kill themselves. Not if there's a choice."

And he had a spasm of sorrow and pity for Pompini, with his rococo deals and his paintings and his cigarettes, who must all at once have realized that the fox den held a pack of wolves.

106

"And the other guy? In Beirut? You think it happened?"

"I'm sure it happened. But there's no link."

"And you're straight about the accents?"

"Yes."

"I guess you'd know. Well, Stears, you know what? You got yourself the PLO. Maybe Ghadaffi, but I'd say the PLO. Maybe both. The one does not exclude the other. Now all you have to do is tell me what they want."

"The only possible point of the export-import is the transfer of something to somewhere on a regular basis. The only link we have to Berbia is Khannafi."

"Who you have down as a jerk. It could mean nothing. He could be a radical groupie. He could be a hanger-on."

"Yes. But this is what I think. I believe that Khannafi is frightened. And I believe that he is too stupid to realize how frightened he should be."

"What would they have on him?"

"God knows."

"But what you're saying is, picking on the Khannafis would not be easy, and if that's what they're doing then it must be Berbia."

"That is what I had thought, yes."

"And the connection between their funding and whatever they do is now so tangled that it would be known only to you."

"That is right. And I, you see, have just read about Pompini."

"They tossed him in the river to get your attention?"

"Yes."

It seemed to Wop that McNaughton's shoulders bowed as at the onset of a familiar pain.

"That is quite tough, Stears. That is quite tough."

They crossed the Avenue Winston Churchill and back under the trees. The chestnut leaves were heavy and edged with gold. They passed the Grand Palais. Lovers and horses, exhibited within, flew on posters through Chagall's sky.

Stears said, "What worries me is that they need me for quite a limited purpose, and that purpose will soon be achieved and that they will disappear and I will never see them again. Of course, the Company could keep them in sight, but that means organization and that means Witham. What do you think?"

"I think these guys are good. I think Witham would order heavy-duty surveillance. I think they'd spot it and go to ground. And I think they would know who the link was."

"That was my suspicion too. So I will not go public unless I am about to lose them and I will try as hard as I can to make them need me. And if they come to Paris I will make it necessary for them to tell me where. So that you will know."

McNaughton said, "Thanks, Stears. They'd be fun to know." And then looked at him with the clear blue eyes that led a slumming existence in the bleary face. "I don't want to act as though you're stupid, but do you know what kind of people these are?"

Wop said, "Yes. I'm going into Valentino's now and I don't think it's your kind of place."

And this time, once again, it was worse. The white suite itself was taking on a subtle sluttishness – sweet aftershave absorbed into the walls, marks of heel or ash or food on silk. He wondered how many degrees of nastiness he had still to know there. Khamal's manner now was as to a prostitute whom he had leisurely sodomized the day before and who would come quickly again to his bell. If Pompini's corpse had been in the middle of the floor it would not have been more evident. It was all quite polite, of course.

He gave Yamadi the papers. Yamadi looked them over. Stears was given instructions to open an account in Geneva in the warehouse's name, to sell the bonds again and deposit the cash.

"That is surely more money than you will need for

operations, at least at first," Stears said, "and that account bears no interest. Should I not do something else?"

Yamadi folded his arms. "No, Mr. Stears, you should not. We have confidence in our business and we have decided on an immediate expansion. The Marseilles market appeals to us. We have decided that Michelet et Cie., which you have been so good as to acquire for us, will immediately purchase a firm in the Marseilles area. We have even found such a firm, Mr. Stears, for in business speed is all. You will not even have to go there. The owner is here already. Not actually in Geneva, for he finds crossing borders tiresome, but in Annemasse on the French side. You have an appointment with him there this afternoon. You should take him cash, which you will withdraw as treasurer of Michelet et Cie. from the new account which you opened this morning. It is a little irregular, but the Swiss know you well. You have a reputation – unlike poor Pompini, who disappointed us greatly, I fear. The owner's name is Claudio Araggio, a Corsican gentleman, but he is something of a prankster and he is registered at the hotel there as Dupont."

He stopped abruptly, allowing a time for protest while Khamal lay back on the sofa and looked Stears in the face.

Stears said, "When shall I come back with the papers?"

Khamal smiled. "When we call you, Mr. Stears. Exactly then."

It was to be the airport, the next morning. They were leaving. He had lain awake much of the night. Their departure, their simple absence, seemed to lift from him a morbific ulcer: of danger, of fear, of knowledge of his own fear, of pretended obsequiousness, of obsequiousness unpretended. They were probably finished with him. He could easily let them go. A slightly obtuse report to Witham, putting them in with much else, and his job was done.

They were buying watches. They were the sort of

people who buy watches duty free on the vague assumption that they must be cheating someone. Yamadi looked at the papers while the girl delicately wrapped the gold bracelet around Khannafi's wrist.

Yamadi said, "Very good, Mr. Stears. Perhaps this is farewell. And perhaps we will need you again."

He pushed himself to it and said, "I assume that I can find you at Michelet et Cie."

Yamadi looked at him mildly. "Perhaps you could, Mr. Stears. Perhaps. But why would you want to? We have no pending business."

Stears looked both eager and afraid, which was not difficult. He said, "I am not without contacts in Paris. Your business will need further expansion, surely. I might hear something to our mutual advantage. I assume you would be interested?"

Yamadi's face came close. The eyes, like a watchful rodent's, felt his. Yamadi's breath was of Sen-Sen. He said, "If the advantage were to us, Mr. Stears, then yes. For the rest, I would not have employed you if I had thought you stupid. I hope you have an imagination too."

Their flight was called. His last sight of them was Khannafi looking fatuously at his new gold watch. It had a stopwatch, the time in all major cities, an alarm, and the phases of the moon. Khamal spoke to him sharply. He followed to the gate.

The mist lifted from Geneva as he drove from the airport. He had the sense of an uncleanness departed beyond the mountains. *Fanciful, that,* he thought, *but still . . .*

He was to meet Marie-Sophie at lunchtime, in the old town, in a gallery. French eighteenth-century oils. There was one, after the school of Fragonard: a landscape of beeches and rotundas and afternoon, a girl in a tempestuous skirt floating on a swing above a lute and a kiss. Marie-Sophie wore a peach silk dress that flowed across her waist.

110

"I like it very much, Giovanni," she said, "but it's terribly expensive and I suppose it's a bit silly."

She looked at him, expecting dismissal.

"Buy it," he said. "It's the least silly thing I've seen all week."

9

The writer James Donnelly, in whom lived and worked the CIA deep-cover officer Michael McNaughton, spent his evenings in the Arab cafés of Paris. James Donnelly was a big, blustering, falsely genial Irish-American in whom a boozily Catholic anti-Jewishness vied with tatterdermalion "Third World" enthusiasms, shabby anti-Americanism, and a stale Irish romance with violence. He was the very model of the roaring-boy professor. He was not without credentials. Rutgers University supported his work with a grant. His major work on post-colonial development of the Arab world did not, perhaps, make much progress, but the chapters that had been seen powerfully refuted any Zionist claims of Israeli preeminence in the Middle East. His principal output was profiles of Arab "leaders," most of them expatriate. More than a dozen obscure and violence-haunted mendicants, owners of evanescent but venomous "movements" and "parties," had rejoiced in seeing their tantrums and threats discussed as policies, their henchmen and hangers-on totaled up as popular support, and the whole published under the aegis of a Western Ph.D. in "authoritative journals" of Arab affairs.

He took what he could get. He was there. Every evening he walked down from his apartment halfway up the summit of Montmartre, on the Rue Burq, down through the sober, thrifty streets of an almost vanished Paris, through the Greek restaurants and vivid vegetables of the Rue des Abbesses, braced himself for the sex strip – Brazilian transvestites eyeing German tourists, each reduced to unwholesome ghosts by the cruel neon around the Moulin Rouge – and then sank further into the limp gray, sad streets of the Arab quarter of Barbès. Nothing vivid here, nothing wild. The Arabian nights were crowded but not gay. He felt too big, too strong, the power he served too awesome, for these streets where middle-aged laborers stood with sad eyes in the little dignity of a secondhand suit, where shawled women shopped anxiously for oil and meal in shops made over from garages, where displays of used luggage, incredibly cheap, mocked the immigrant with no ticket money and no chance at home, where blonde French prostitutes, like aging scrubwomen, stood sagging under the nightly weight of thirty Arabs. He had to remind himself that barracudas swam among these gray, cowed fish.

So he was there. He rarely stalked his prey. He watched and moved about. He would go into a café – four tables with greasy oilcloth – and drink a coffee, strong and sweet, move on. Then into a "restaurant" advertised by the greasy gray smoke drifting from its door. A brochette of raw meat would be moved from its window clientele of flies and set on the fire for him, served with couscous and rough red wine. Sooner or later he would find a table of four or five sadly animated men; perhaps the leader of a squatters' colony eating with a courier from the PLO and a Communist exile from Morocco. He, who was tolerated, whose sympathies were well known, would sit down, ingratiate himself. And then would begin another evening among the jealousies, the internecine splits, the plans and fantasies of Arab expatriates as they plotted against their own governments, each others' governments, the French government, the Israeli government, and each other. He sat like a bleary guru, egging on each vicious dream, genially excusing each betrayal, and providing the assurance, like a warm, dirty blanket, that everything wrong with the Middle East was the fault of the Americans or the Jews. Michael McNaughton detested Jamie Donnelly

113

and loathed inhabiting him. He liked to go home, throw Donnelly in the closet, make coffee, and read Anthony Trollope or, if the evening had been particularly poisonous, play the violin partita of J. S. Bach on the record player. But the things that Donnelly heard, the confidences that Donnelly wormed out, the betrayals that seemed to take place spontaneously around him, had put the CIA possibly even on top of the French in its access to the febrile world of expatriate political Arabs. These thoughts, once in a long while and by an evil chance, resulted in actual change in the Arab world that made McNaughton's distasteful evenings worthwhile.

This afternoon, McNaughton was uneasy. He felt the unanswerable and partly superstitious unease of the deep-cover officer forced to change his territory and method. Wop Stear's men were not his usual prey. His approach had not been his usual approach. The Wop had pushed him. McNaughton had returned his call from the telephone booth of a cheap restaurant. He had, for no particular reason, the conviction that Wop was calling from the lobby of an extremely expensive hotel. The cultivated, mellifluous voice that reached him through the crash of dishes and shouts from the kitchen emerged, he was sure, from Wop's richly suited figure standing on an ankle-deep carpet, making restrained gestures with a manicured hand. He had gone through a range of emotions by now familiar when dealing with Wop Stears: irritation, amusement, but also respect for information ably picked up and intelligently assembled, and, come to that, for more balls than he would have thought, too. It was true, he thought, even now that glossy Wop was all but a pro. But not pro enough to put himself in McNaughton's shoes and give him time for a proper contact.

So he had initiated contact himself (which was not his method) with people he had never himself observed; distinguished American academic needs interview, anti-Zionist views expressed, profiles done quick, meet you anywhere. Crap. Fuck Stears.

So here they were, not in his usual locale of smoky evening dive but in a couscous palace of the French upper middle class, just off the dove-gray Avenue George V and across from Rochas's striking façade of a spaghetti tangle of tubular steel. The bar was all mirrored minarets behind which bottles glowed like the Prophet's nightmare or Aladdin's cave. Perfume blended with steam of peppered sauce. The meat came on skewers with rapier hilts and the couscous and chickpeas in copper bowls. The adventurous French drank Royal Kebir, a simple, rough Algerian red that costs a laborer's day wages. The room was full of silk ties and laughter. The food was good. His company was less so.

Wop had them about right, he thought. Khannafi was a jerk, sure enough. Yamadi could have been a loanshark or a croupier, but he searched for a memory more exact. There had been a man in Saigon, of mixed blood and undefined influence, who had for a time been able to sell, at a standard tariff, the release of suspects from the "tiger cages," the torture dungeons. It was rumored that he also published the suspicions that brought the arrests. Yamadi had eyes like that man. As for Khamal, McNaughton had not quite believed him. Stears was not used to the violent world, did not know its animal strength. He had expected to find in Khamal an ordinary terrorist, which was bad enough and would have seemed worse to Wop. Well, he wasn't. He was pure, refined death. Handsome, casual, insolent, and fit, he had the dark, electric angelism of the pure-hearted killer. He fitted into an investment group like a whore in church.

The lawyer, Hussein Yamadi, said in a voice of polite question with dismissal close behind, "Really, Dr. Donnelly, I do not see what a scholar of your eminence can hope to learn from mere private businessmen. Indeed, I was not aware that our project was yet well known outside of a small group of North African investors."

The contact was not even going well. It could not.

There had been no time for satisfactory common ground to be prepared.

McNaughton answered, making Donnelly positively Ivy League, austere, "Your project is no doubt known only to a small and distinguished circle, but that is a circle to which a wise man must listen with care. And you are wrong, gentlemen. The scholar must deal with those who think, who reflect, not with those who merely react. The politician is often the froth. The investor is the current beneath him. I am interested in all Arab investors of position. They are my most valued instructors. That is why I was grateful when Mr. Iruni agreed to introduce me to you."

He paused to let this sink in. Friendship, confidence, and finally understanding with Khalid Iruni, the aging and conservative doyen of North African finance in France, had been one of his most valuable cultivations. He had made an appointment with him the day after Wop had called and the day after that had gone to the small private bank in the gray town house on the Avenue Franklin Roosevelt. Iruni had taken his hand gently in his alabaster fingers, murmured a welcome, and caused a servant with a tray – sherry for McNaughton, coffee for himself – to materialize briefly and then shimmer away. Iruni was perhaps seventy-five years old and as delicate as an ivory figurine. He sat, in a dark and perfect suit, by a small coal fire. "In the autumn here," he said, "an old Moroccan already feels the cold. When are you going to make an old man happy again and join me for another evening of Bach?"

They had talked of concerts and performers. The room was mainly French, but the firelight glittered on a breakfront full of Moroccan silver, rosewater ewers delicate as cranes, and graceful high-necked coffee-pots. Then Iruni gently said, "Dr. Donnelly, I am keeping you, I think, from your real mission. Too much politeness may become rudeness. What did you wish to ask me?"

McNaughton had never been sure exactly what Iruni knew of him. He doubted very much that he knew his name. But he also knew that Iruni accepted without comment that Dr. Donnelly represented the interests of the American government and was thus, in many respects, the opposite of the Dr. Donnelly that other Arabs knew. Iruni must, therefore, have thought it at least possible that Donnelly was CIA, and might even have ascertained this for a fact. He would intuitively have trusted Iruni with his life.

"I would like your opinion of three men," McNaughton said. "And I will tell you something about them first."

Quickly he named the group, described them, gave the history of their dealings with Stears. He ended, "My friend in Geneva is an entirely honorable man. He was obliged to play a role, you understand."

Iruni nodded quickly and looked serenely into the fire before he spoke.

"Amal Khannafi is an undistinguished young man but of a known family. I will return to that in a moment. Of the other two, I know nothing. If they are North African, they are either men of no history or of assumed name. The former is, of course, just the kind of associate that young Khannafi would find. But this is most interesting, for young Khannafi does not have three and one half million dollars. Nor does his father. The shipping house of Khannafi rose quickly during the sixties and seventies, but it is now bankrupt. This is not well known, for it suits neither me nor certain others that this should become public knowledge, and the Khannafi family does not as yet live in the manner of bankrupts. But it is true. Young Khannafi has no money. Therefore he cannot possibly be the leader of this group. He can only rent out his name as camouflage. Therefore it is indeed unlikely, as you must think yourself, that this is a legitimate import-export venture. Especially since the firm they have bought has had a bad reputation. Have I helped you, Dr. Donnelly?"

McNaughton said, "Inestimably."

And to his great surprise, the little formal doll got up from his chair and placed his translucent fingers on McNaughton's shoulder. Iruni said, "Please be careful, Dr. Donnelly. I believe that we Arabs are the most dangerous of men, and these, I believe, may be dangerous Arabs. At my age one is conscious principally of waste. I should hate to know that a brain that loves Bach had been crushed in an alley."

And so, through tortuous and encumbered channels, to Witham, to whom Stears had sent an edited report, sufficient for action. McNaughton had set up a meeting at his safe house – the apartment, ostensibly, of the editor of a "little magazine" of Middle Eastern proclivities – to bargan for chips to play in Yamadi's game. Two came to mind. It would be child's play for the Company to assemble a sample of arms, enough to point to the existence of a third party who wished to use the academic Walter Winchell of Arab revolutionary circles to make a conditional offer of supply to Yamadi. The conditions could be such as would not, in the end, be attractive. It would still suffice for a contact. Easier yet, the Agency could quickly buy the services of any of a dozen underground smuggling operations in Marseilles or the southern ports. Again it would be easy to quote a price that would force Yamadi to take notice and, again, there would be, at a controlled point, conditions that would make the deal fall through.

Easy. But every way he looked at this operation gave him a sense of dreary, generalized, pointless, alarm. This was the way to approach it, the obvious way. But he was an intelligence man, pure in his craft, and he hated these setups, these scenarios, these charades. He felt as though he were going into action not cannily following his nose but carrying about a stockroom of flimsy scenery. Then, in the safe house, he knew he wasn't going to get it anyway.

He was to put his plan to an "operations analyst" – a brand-new species in the Agency – who would report to

Witham. McNaughton did not know him. One Wesley Reads. One look at him and McNaughton knew that Reads and Witham would think exactly alike and that he was in the presence of the CIA subspecies he respected least. Reads was under thirty, with the careful candor, the casual pin-stripe, and the wryly, funnily hipster speech of a liberal gone straight. He was a post-Watergate puritan, a Carter choirboy, a ball-less Henry Peckham, a Civil Service spook.

They sat in the living room, furnished out of advertisements in *Paris-Match* – blond oak bookshelves, white plastic flowerpots, light fixtures pointlessly imitating construction cranes, all insubstantially surrounding the huge, possibly pregnant armchairs in which they incongruously faced each other like a *Paris-Match* couple enjoying Sunday afternoon. McNaughton sagged forward like a bag of laundry and rumbled out his alternative projected plans, with details and comparisons of risk and cost. Not many people could meet McNaughton's eye, but Reads could; every time McNaughton looked up in challenge, Reads would hold his cold blue eyes in his own limpid guilelessness and murmur, "Fantastic" and "Beautiful" alternately.

McNaughton closed. "The hard data is we know they do have warehousing but we don't know that they have guns. So I say we accept the higher risk factor and go with the guns. Over to you."

Reads smiled and sighed and said, "Beautiful" one more time. He continued. "Of course, it's crude pre-Watergate stuff and we don't do it anymore."

McNaughton nodded slightly and very slowly. "You are now going," he said, "to try to explain to me about the Congressional committees."

"I could do that. We would have to get approval, seeing that this would be, in effect, an arms sale. But I want you to leave here, McNaughton, on the same wavelength as me. That was a wonderful piece of tradecraft you presented there, and of course that's all we used to think about. But you'll find that the Company's raising its consciousness now. Entrapment's not the American way, is it? We try and operate within our charter now and we find that with a little more ingenuity we always can. When I analyze an operation I try to think, *If I had to defend this in front of a Congressional committee and* Sixty Minutes, *would my palms sweat?* That's pretty existential, but that's how I think about it. Do you get what I'm communicating?"

McNaughton said, "Yeah. I get it. You're running scared. You don't like my plan because it means Agency cooperation. You don't like Agency cooperation because it looks like conspiracy on Capitol Hill. You're more scared of the *Washington Post* than of the KGB. You hope I've got some grubby little agent somewhere I can sic on to this so everybody can keep their hands clean. As it happens, it's what I expected. Do you get what I'm communicating?"

Reads looked at him sorrowfully. "It's your operation," he said.

So he used Ali Massoun instead.

Meanwhile, Khannafi, Khamal, and Yamadi reacted in their various ways to Iruni's name. Khannafi looked merely rudely bored. A callow lout, McNaughton thought, while Donnelly obsequiously smiled at him. Yamadi registered, perhaps sincerely, a proper cautious deference to a distinguished name. Khamal shook his sculptured head and smiled gently as a girl and with a radiance of death.

He said, "Mr. Iruni. Such a pillar of our old Mahgreb. Do you know him well, Dr. Donnelly?"

He didn't answer. The venomous little bastard wasn't asking a question any more than a gun barrel would. He merely wondered whom the gun was aimed at. *Not yet,* he thought, *at himself. Iruni? Or just anyone without a hand grenade for a soul?*

The lawyer spoke. "What precisely is your interest in us, Dr. Donnelly?"

McNaughton said, "You have been kind enough to call me a scholar, gentlemen. It is so in that I use the tools of scholarship, and it is so in that" – and here he gave his words a sudden puzzling emphasis – "I guard my reputation as a truthful man, an honorable man, a serious man, as jealously as a scholar must. But I am not an academic shut up in a tower. I am in the world, gentlemen. I regard myself as an ambassador from the much misunderstood Arab world to my own America. But, as the proberb says, 'At the tables of the wise, a scholar is always welcome,' and as a disinterested scholar I am welcomed at the tables of many Arabs, some of whom would be uneasy with each other. Therefore from time to time I am an ambassador from Arab to Arab."

He stopped abruptly. Khannafi, now, was gazing at the barmaid like a spaniel at sugar, but Yamadi and Khamal had settled into poses of courteous but vast indifference while tiny worms of interest stirred in their eyes.

Yamadi, the lawyer, said, "Your life must be a rich one."

McNaughton allowed himself an ironic smile and turned his voice a little from the Harvard Club to the Garment District. He said, "Of the mind, yes. Money, not so much. Foundation grants aren't what they used to be. As I say, gentlemen, I live in the world. Most often I am the ambassador of ideas. From time to time I am the ambassador of accommodation. Every now and again I have the opportunity to be the ambassador of interests, and when this occurs, I am not so proud that I reject what honor would accept."

Khamal spoke before Yamadi. He smiled luxuriously into his lap and looked at McNaughton intently, pleased, like a Doberman looking at a steak. McNaughton involuntarily, invisibly, shivered. Khamal said, "And which now, Dr. Donnelly? Which now?"

They all but jumped as Khannafi slipped a Gucci memo pad from his suit. Still looking at the barmaid, with his tongue running over his lips, he hesitantly wrote a message, folded it up, and signaled for a waiter.

Into all this McNaughton quietly said, "I have a friend who ships discreetly, in small boats. He specializes in powdered cargo. His regular clients are for the time being obliged to be unusually discreet. He needs work. He has never been arrested. He is good."

And in the second that Yamadi's eyes and Khamal's conferred, McNaughton saw through half-lowered lids that both were startled, took a moment, in fact, to work out what he had said, that they were both relieved but in Khamal's case behind the reasoned relief was an animal disappointment. *That is useful to know,* McNaughton thought. *If I had spoken just now of guns he might have killed me.*

Yamadi visibly shook his thoughts to order. His surprise, even his indignation, were not entirely false. "What in heaven's name, Dr. Donnelly, makes you think we are interested in such things as that?"

McNaughton relentlessly went on. "If you are asking why my friend is not here himself, merely think. You have bought a firm whose name is not unblemished. He, as I say, has never been arrested – but what man can know that his name has never been suspected? He does not want to be seen with you. You do not want him here. I am seen with every Arab of note in Paris. It does not matter."

And now one surmise seemed to come to Yamadi and Khamal simultaneously, and they both looked quickly at Khannafi. *Well, that's great,* thought McNaughton. *I hadn't even thought of that. If they think that's where the loose talk came from it ought to take them a day or two to sweat him hard enough to decide it didn't.* He did not envy Khannafi the next two days.

Khannafi, for the time being, saw nothing wrong with them. The barmaid was blond, pouty, poured into jiggling black, and wore her little soubrette apron like the presentable equivalent of a porno garter. She read the billet doux with indifference, holding its corner between two fingers, and without moving her elbows from the counter, asked the waiter where it came from. Then she looked at Amal Khannafi, who was now leaning back in the booth with an oily smirk, anxious around the edges. She looked levelly and long. She counted the watch, the suit, the diamond cuff links, and she registered "Arab." In a personal way, she registered Khamal, and her eye played longingly over his cold, angelic face and hyacinthine locks, but that did not seem to be where the chance was coming from and Khannafi was quickly rewarded with a merry, mischievous smile. She tapped her watch and mouthed, *"Trois heures,"* ending it with a tiny kiss. Cheap delights rose off her skin like the scent from a candy counter. Khannafi grinned more widely and fluttered his hand. Khamal looked at him sideways with anticipation, mockery, and contempt, and licked his lips slightly. Yamadi looked stone-faced at McNaughton. *It's great to have lunch out with the boys,* McNaughton thought.

Yamadi said, "You have come to us under false pretenses. That is not a basis for trust. You have perhaps insulted us, your hosts."

McNaughton answered, "I came to you as I could. One does not ask Khalid Iruni to introduce one as an arranger of this type. And I came to you as I am. This is not my livelihood. I am helping a friend who has helped me. If his offer is of no interest, my business is at an end and I will thank you for your hospitality and leave."

He tensed his arms and haunches as if to rise.

Yamadi, not looking at him, irritably waved him back. "Who is your friend?"

"He will tell you when you meet him."

"Where is his boat?"

"Primarily in Marseilles." McNaughton allowed himself sarcasm. "It is also capable of movement."

"We would meet at a place of my choosing. At least two of us. He, alone."

"You are the customer. Why not?"

Yamadi looked first at Khamal and then hard at McNaughton. "What I am, Dr. Donnelly, is no concern of yours and you would be a fool to make it so. You may be a fool already. You have already become my concern. I hope that you do not live to regret it. How will I contact your friend, should I wish to?"

"You would call this number tomorrow evening at six o'clock or at that time the next evening. Not before and not later. If not by then, the business is finished. The number is 226 72 63. Speak to whoever answers. Set a time and place."

He was too far from home to walk. He took a taxi. It left him unsatisfied, unsettled. From Barbès or Belleville he invariably trudged home. He liked his house, his street. Montmartre delighted this Chicago Irishman. It was as huddled and frowzy as the tenements of his youth. He felt quite at home. The gray houses supported the same obstinate human life as the Old Neighborhood. He liked the tiny stores; the permanent smell of soup around the grocery on the Rue Durantin; the overgrown garden, no bigger than a bathtub, opposite his house, the personal jungle of a white tomcat; windows full of plants and canaries and all the products of fierce, small, odd ambitions; even the scrape and bang of deliverymen in dungarees pleased his eye and ear. But this tenement kid had grown mellowed, and Montmarte also gave him grace: the grace of the Sacré Coeur on the summit of his hill, grace in the beveled glass on the door of the dark little hallway of the house next door, the grand seventeenth-century windows on the tiny Hôtel Corneloup, the pretty balconies on Number 5, and on this poor street, the Rue Burq, the amazing presence of a Tibetan jeweler with a window full of shinbones set in lapis lazuli and prayer wheels of silver and jade.

His apartment suited him, his cover, and his purse. But there was more. After every session of bile and treachery in the Arab streets he would walk home uphill, leaving the sad, gray bitterness below him. The Sexshops and Strip-non-Stops of the Place Pigalle, the huge bright sides and reek of German buses, were a positive astringent tonic, a slap in the face. Then, up more steeply on the Rue André Antoine and the Place des Abbesses into an enveloping decency of emerald-green, clean vegetable stores, a neat window full of scholarly books, the sky framed by intricate rooftops, and the lively, sensible face of Madame Taupin in the dry cleaner's near the corner of his street. His home was a refuge. He entered his street, his staircase, with daily pleasure. James Donnelly was on his doorplate, but it was Michael McNaughton, though they did not know it, to whom the shopkeepers nodded and whose ankle the concierge's cat rubbed with its marmalade side.

He scratched its ear. He walked heavily up the stairs. His eyes were half shut. His mind, with an image of riffling file cards, ran back and forth, seeking out any weakness in his treatment of the group at lunch. His eyes snapped open and fiercely quizzed the garbage chute. He paused on the second landing, which smelled of Madame Morrisot's old pug dog. He needed to see Ali Massoun again. Ali Massoun hung out, when he was in Paris, at the Café Safi in the Quartier du Sentier, the quarter of whores and drugs. The Café Safi was one of the more verminous and much the largest of the dives he visited) infested not only with pimps and cockroaches but with Libyans and hangers on of the KGB as well. Well, it would be different from lunch.

He opened James Donnelly's door and inhaled the comforting, sulfurous reek of two years' worth of Gauloises. He stood perfectly still in the hall – a habit he had picked up under another name, in another life, during five years in Saigon – like a big, clever bear with his senses at full pitch seeking any trace of alien visit or presence. There was none. He lit a cigarette and padded to the kitchen. He put on water for *tisane*, a French herbal country tea he had come to like. He was turning into a French old maid, he thought, though a French old maid might have had to renew the quart of rye less often. He went back to the living room.

The apartment was mainly his. Donnelly was allowed out of the closet only on the very rare occasions when he felt obliged to bring a source back home. Nonetheless, Donnelly's correspondence was strewn around, Donnelly's manuscript sat dog-eared on the writing table, and Donnelly's books and magazines, questionable productions tending to incandescent nationalism and anti-Jewishness, usurped the bookshelves. But the plants in the window were his, and he carefully checked them for dryness. He sat in the worn, fat armchair and reread a letter from his married daughter in Detroit. She was the only person on earth he could still be said to care for much more than he cared for the concierge's cat. The letter had been sent to a box number at American Express.

The kettle whistled. He made his brew and took it back to the chair. He had four hours before the Arab cafés filled up. They stayed full at night, so that it was his habit, if he could, to read and then nap in the afternoon. He relaxed carefully, limb by limb, the tension of lunch rising out of him. He picked up a small, old volume, dividing the pages with his nicotine-yellow thumb. It was Anthony Trollope's *Can You Forgive Her?* Glencora Palliser was on the terrace over the Rhine at Basle in the velvet, though flimsily staged, summer night. He read with pleasure.

The Rue du Caire led to the Rue St. Denis and beyond that was the Café Safi in the Rue d'Aboukir. The Rue St. Denis reeled under the neon of cheap boutiques, T shirts, hot pink pants exploding in the light of "Brigitte," "Oxford Street," and "Bijou Cash." A car could barely move. The street was clogged with customers. And whores. A sad-faced Negro with hands busy in his pockets gazed across the street at a teen-aged French girl leaning in a doorway in black boots that met a miniskirt at her crotch. She was the flagship of her establishment, the top of the line. Behind the doorway, in the corridor, would be the line of cheaper girls, all tastes and budgets catered for, down to thirty francs. And so on up the street. In comfort and close at hand, the pimps spent the evening at the Café Safi.

Neither the café nor its street were representative of Arab Paris. It was large. Forty tables, maybe, and a space in the middle. From time to time a dance of sorts was held here for pimps and their favored girls. Nor was it wholly Arab. Nine-tenths of Paris Arabs are decent people living arduous lives. One-tenth are hooligans. In the St. Denis quarter the proportions are reversed, and the Café Safi drew exclusively from the worst. The general, civilian population of pimps and their enforcers served as a cover for the rougher element.

In the Café Safi, Paris stretched out its hand to the ancient city of Marseilles: the drug shippers of Marseilles made their arrangements here for the Paris market, and their fellow citizens in the white slave trade, for whom it served as a commodity exchange, found homes for their meat in the hungrier cribs of the capital. A Corsican was nearly as common here as an Arab, and a Frenchman was not unknown. The rich compost of commerce served in turn as a cover for a third, smaller clientele of arms smugglers and gold smugglers, their political customers, and their rivals, watchers, enemies, and spies. Café Safi is not listed in Michelin, though its lamb is quite good.

Ali Massoun was there but McNaughton ignored him. He did not trust himself to know, all at once on entering, who was at the Safi, and Massoun must be allowed to make contact in his way and time. He stopped at the table of a spindly, bucktoothed Algerian who was thought to have murdered a French police informer the week before and talked to him gravely about Arab solidarity. This served two purposes: the more people he was seen

127

talking to, the less significance any one contact had; it was also a first step to finding out if the murder – a particularly revolting one with much carving of letters in flesh – was purely criminal, as he so far assumed, or in part political. The Arab grinned throughout in newly won notoriety. McNaughton picked a table in the same quarter of the room as Massoun's. The small waiter, with dirty apron and worse teeth, paused before him. McNaughton ordered coffee. The coffee at Café Safi was good. In the open kitchen, two thin-faced young Arabs in greasy shirts tended the saucepans and the spitted lamb.

From the corner of his eye he watched Ali Massoun. He was with two of his crew – McNaughton did not know them but he had seen them before. The three seemed to breathe a different air, perhaps one of wind and rain, from everybody else in the room. Massoun was a big man – at first sight he suggested not an Arab but a Turk – and he sat with the ramrod back and composed, commanding eye that befitted the Sandhurst-trained major of Libyan cavalry he once had been. His jacket was an ancient duffle coat and he wore it like a dress uniform. He worshiped his former royal master, hated Colonel Ghadaffi with a concealed but driven rage, was a skilled, principled, and daring agent of the CIA, hated communism above Ghadaffi; and was a successful, regular, and cynical smuggler of heroin, illegal labor, guns to non-Communists, and gold. As usual, he was drinking heavily, without visible effect.

The spits turned. McNaughton finished his coffee. Customers came and left. Massoun began to circulate among the tables, still not drunk but bestowing his conversation regally, like a minor medal. McNaughton ordered kibbouleh and wine. Massoun arrived soon after. He spoke with sudden politeness and sat down almost with deference.

He said, "There was a Libyan here who worries me. He is more intelligent than most of Ghaddafi's apes. But he is gone now. Did you meet with them?"

McNaughton nodded. "I think they took the bait." He smiled mirthlessly at Massoun. "That means you. And they're tougher bastards than I thought. Not Khannafi. He's a sucker and they're using his name. He probably doesn't know what's going on, and if he does know, I wouldn't want to sell him any life insurance. The other two are real bastards."

"Why should you be surprised, old chap? Were you expecting a couple of curates?" It was a never-failing shock to hear, out of the swarthy face above the seaman's clothes, the drawled, careless English of a Sandhurst officer.

"I mean they're higher-ranking bastards. I thought we had a couple of superior bagmen and runners. But I think I know these two. Not positive identification, and I can't get it, either. No photographs on file. But it seems right to me. Khamal is probably the man we know as Abdelatif Zebdi. Arms and murder specialist with a sideline in torture. He's a PLO special operator with KGB training. He got his big-time start when Sergei Kiktev was sent as Soviet ambassador to Morocco and wanted some Islamic thugs on the spot. George Habash sent him over, and Kiktev liked him. When they sent Kiktev to murder Monahajadim Gahiz in Kabul he may have used Zebdi on the job. Since then, Zebdi's shown up whenever the PLO wants to do something particularly dirty with KGB backing. We think he was in the embassy takeover in Teheran. In fact, the only photograph we have of him is a high-resolution satellite photograph in the embassy compound. No good for positive ID but he fits the type. As for Yamadi, we don't even have a firm name for him. He began in al-Fatah, but he seems to be mainly coordinated by the KGB now. He's by way of being a businessman – you might say an all-purpose manipulator. He turns up in deals that get violent or messy later but by then he's gone. We never get a fix on him early enough to get a photograph. That's one thing I can take care of now. If I'm wrong about one, I'm probably wrong about both. But I don't think I am."

Massoun finished his whiskey and refilled his glass with McNaughton's wine. "In other words, my dear fellow, you're bringing me big game instead of vermin. All the merrier."

"In other words," said McNaughton, "I am doing what I have no right to do. I am putting a makeshift operation up against senior talent with possible KGB support. You have every right to get out now."

Massoun said quietly, "That is almost insulting. How do you want me to proceed?"

"OK. So you're in. Your choice." McNaughton now spoke as by the book, without warmth and almost without inflection. "Your assignment is unchanged: to identify cargo, source, and destination. We assume guns. We need to know if we're talking about street terrorist weapons or weapons with significant military capability. We would like to know if they're NATO issue. We need the shipment date. That and the location of source may very well prove to be the limit of your capability. That's OK, but it's the minimum.

"They will reinitiate contact. The number they have is a special telephone at the safe house, and it will be answered by an operative. I guarantee they will get no lead on that telephone. They will set a time and place for meeting. I have to instruct you to operate under a false identity. These people may have access to the KGB data bank. The KGB will probably list you as a genuine criminal, but they will know your personal background and that might raise an alert. So we must accept the danger of false identity. If you are recognized in their presence from another source, you will claim police pressure as a last resort. Can you trust your crew?"

"Totally."

"I will have an identity sheet for you tomorrow. It will have to be minimal. Read it, instruct your crew, and destroy it. I will also have a carte d'identité for you. That is all they would expect you to have. I cannot give you comprehensive operating instructions. I cannot predict how close they will let you get, but I think they will play very close. If they deal with you at all, they will have to give you data on the size and location of the cargo and the port of shipment and the length of the voyage. That may be all. You may have to follow them. Do you have a competent tail?"

Massoun smiled. "Competent enough to photograph a French judge picking up a bribe from the American Mafia? I have one that good. The police stayed out of my hair for a year."

"You may need him. This is your number to call. It will be manned twenty-four hours a day. It is your number for reports and, in theory, it is your number for assistance. I say 'in theory' because, other than myself, I have no assistance to give. Do you understand that?"

"I understand it. And I do not like crowds."

"There is something else. I have not yet been given a budget for this operation. I have assumed in the past that any account I presented would be paid. I am no longer sure of that. If this becomes complicated, if you use extensive tailing, you may even be out of pocket. We can always promise to help you with the French police, but our capacity for that is frankly limited. I have no right to ask this."

Massoun shrugged and his face took on the uninterested look of an English gentleman preparing to say a serious thing. But the mask, before he spoke, broke up and he leaned forward and spoke with the whispered, staccato vehemence of an Arab on his mettle.

"Dr. Donnelly,' he said, "it is important that you understand. I am an officer of the King's Guard, as was my father. My grandfather was a leader among the Bedouin, and so for a thousand years. Honor, to us, has been more than bread. Now, because of Colonel Ghadaffi, I hide from the police and deal in drugs. This does not itself diminish me. It is no affair of mine that American Negroes and Paris Algerians and fools in the universities sell themselves for poison. Fools and weaklings are not of my people. I grow rich at the trade. It earns neither honor or dishonor. But a man must have honor, positively, and it is this that I earn when I fight by your side against the vermin that creep across Arabia. You are the enemy of my enemies and you give me the means to fight them significantly. My friend, when you give me such a chance, it is not I who give, but you. Do not concern yourself with accounting."

Massoun dramatically sat straight again and his eyes, grown suddenly younger, looked haughtily around the room. McNaughton thinking simultaneously, *Never trust an unpaid spy*, and, *He means it*, smiled without warmth and said, "You are most generous. I have no more instructions and we have been together long enough. Your identity sheet and carte will be in your drop tomorrow. Pick them up between two and three o'clock. The time, place, and conditions of meeting, if any, will be in the same place the next morning. Be sure to observe them strictly. Do not call your number unless you have a report. That is all."

He looked away. When Massoun had gone, he unhurriedly finished another glass of wine. On his way out, he stopped for some time at the table of the "editor" of a venomous and faltering newssheet that specialized in stirring up transient Arab workers against their French employers. The editor was eating cheaply. McNaughton spoke to him with pompous obsequiousness. The editor grandly half-promised to buy an article from Dr. Donnelly's pen.

He walked heavily home. In the Rue St. Denis, the teen-age French prostitute was leaning now in the doorway and her hair was dank. He guessed she had another four hours to go. She looked seventeen so was probably fifteen, and would no doubt celebrate her sixteenth birthday in the line of cheaper girls behind. More to the point, and with equal joy, he evaluated the operation. *Damn the Company*, he thought. *Makeshift operation. Guesswork. Premature contact. Covert action. And now a goddamn Arab hero. Crap!*

132

10

Fall had not yet come to Washington but it touched northern Virginia with a morning light as clear and delicate as the dew on a spider's web. At Franklin's Spring, the Drew estate, young Carroway, the three-quarter-bred roan hunter who had been sleeping in the field, raised his head heavily to the morning sun and then drew in through quivering nostrils a huge, noisy lungful of the newly minted air. Old Samuel, the Drew's head groom, paused at the door of his cottage, went back in, rooted around in the ancient steamer trunk on the bedroom floor, and pulled out a baggy wool sweater that smelled of pipe and horse. The crows were active this morning. They stepped back and forth along the oak limbs, cawed, and launched themselves in short, circling flights around their tree. The dogwoods had begun to blush.

Halfway between the main house and the farm, on a low ridge between two rich pastures, was a small Virginia farmhouse, simply built of stone and dating from before the time when Julia Drew's grandfather had bought up the surrounding land. It was shaded by an elm. It had a porch with a swing seat, steep, narrow stairs, low ceilings and small windows, and it still smelled faintly but sweetly of hearth fires and apples. It had been given to Julia when she finished college so that she could spend as much time at Franklin's Spring as she wanted to, even live there, and yet be with Mother and Daddy in the big house only when she chose. Daddy wanted, above everything in the world, for his big girl to be at home at home. From her bedroom window she could see her hunters out at grass – there were four there now – see the stables where Samuel was carrying a bucket of feed to her show jumper in the stalls, see Mother and Daddy's big brick house with its splendid white columns built in 1934, and see ridge after ridge of well-fenced rolling meadow with patches of blue-gray woodland stretching on toward Warrenton and the Blue Ridge far away. If it was a weekday, and she put her foot down in the Porsche, it took her only forty minutes to be on Massachusetts Avenue at work for the PLO.

She stirred in the four-poster bed under the quilt that Mother had brought back from Nova Scotia. She was a young girl, seven years old, warm by the fireside, in the sleepy gray of a winter afternoon. Something good had happened. It glowed like the fire. She remembered; yesterday she had won her first big show-jumping class on Candy, her first real horse. Only she and Candy had jumped the big five-bar gate. Only she and Candy had not been scared. Daddy was in the room too, in the big leather armchair. Mother had gone to Washington with friends. She left in a peach-colored dress. Then she was in Daddy's lap. "Did I ride Candy properly? Did I hold his head up like you said?" "Oh, yes. My little girl rode him wonderfully well. My little girl's as brave as a big girl now." She loved to smell her daddy, pipe tobacco and after-shave. It was nice being in the fire-warmth with her daddy and she put her arms around his neck and kissed him. Then the room was dark brown and the fire began to hiss like the snake they had found outside Candy's box on the Fourth of July the year before. Her daddy kissed her back and this time it frightened her but she didn't know why and because she was frightened she hugged him closer and he began to kiss her like he kissed her mommy when they didn't know she was there and he said, "My little girl, my beautiful little girl," like somebody who'd been running. He asked her if she loved him. She had always loved her daddy. She couldn't see because her face was in his jacket but she felt him playing with her clothes and then she felt her tummy and her legs were bare and the fire shone right on them. And then her dreaming memory remembered this dream and she mewed in fright because her daddy began to do things to her between her legs and he was cold and wet like a snake and then suddenly he was a snake and the snake was around her, cold and wet and strong and hissing. And the poker was in her hand and she began to hit with it and the snake began to be covered in blood and mush and it stopped and it was dead. And then she sobbed bottomlessly between waking and dream because she had turned her daddy into a snake and killed him and he was the only thing she had ever loved. And she woke terrified and ashamed and threw her body across the bed in the hope that there would be a loving alive male body there to receive her. She began in terror and in loss but, as her hands touched his chest, she got control of herself and stroked him sensuously, gently, and put her mouth up to be kissed. The Mullah Ibrahim, whose name in circumstances such as this was Hussein Shamak – Communist, Egyptian, and principal representative of the PLO in Berbia – had been awake and watching her struggling body with interest for some time. He held her still rigid flanks and kissed her in return and smiled.

"Bad dream?" he said.

She sat up in bed and laughed lightly, huskily. "No dream," she said. "Just affection, darling. But do you know," and now she looked at him with a small, quizzical challenge, "I bet there isn't a single American baronial estate that's had as many Arabs wake up on it as this one. I can even make Turkish coffee. Would you like some, darling?"

It had been part of his intention to find out about her. Even in the PLO, even in Palestinians for Peace, the American front where she worked, there were very few who knew that Julia Drew, the rich little American girl, the socialite, the fox-hunter, the show-jumper, the stylish and pretty receptionist, was also the principal PLO assassin in North America. No murderer had had to cross the Atlantic on the business of the PLO now for eighteen months. Julia Drew, never for an instant suspected by victim or police, had done it all. The West Bank Arab moderate in New York to testify at the UN had had no fear of the pretty redheaded girl walking behind him down the corridor of the Plaza. The Saudi prince, the admirer of Sadat, had been delighted to take to dinner the elegant young American he had met at the Palm Beach polo game. The anti-Communist editor of the Lebanese newspaper, who had come to Chicago on a journalistic junket, was pleasantly captivated by the aspiring girl interviewer from the *Washingtonian*. They were all neatly dead and the list went on. Her fame had reached George Habbash. But there were questions. American radicals were generally distrusted abroad as flighty and disturbed romantics. Her known and extreme promiscuity did not inspire complete confidence. The questions about Julia were these: was she reliable enough to be exported when a non-Arab face would be useful behind the trigger and, secondly, was she sane?

It had taken Hussein Shamak three days and two nights to decide that she was completely reliable and incurably mad.

She frightened even him. A man doomed enough to love her, would drown there – not sink without trace but be cast up, broken, on the rocks. A true Siren. Or, if not drowned, go mad – not with empty longing, God knew, but from being locked in a corridor where nothing could be seen except through distorting mirrors, improbable in themselves and inconceivable in combination. He was no stranger to women, but making love to Julia was an experience of an intensity he had never known, and one in which, even in its fullest flood, there was a base note of distemper, even of fear.

In wonder he looked at the demure room, the double

136

bed with its pleasant quilt, and felt as though he himself were recovering from a nightmare, unable to relate the room to what he had known in it. From her firm and clean-limbed body – barely even female if your hands were used to Arab girls – there rose a passion so desperate, so unreserved, and so wholly of self that a man would feel himself at one moment a giant, omnipotent, fertilizing the earth, and at the next, an insect swept up helplessly in a flood; coupled to her he had seemed to float in the night sky, to be carried by the gale of her lingering, exulting cry; and when, a scant two seconds after her convulsive finish, she had said to him, in exactly the same voice, though a little out of breath, that he had first heard her use at the Salfield woman's party, "Well, darling, that puts you pretty high on my list – maybe second or third," he had felt exactly as though he had been hurled, still flying, against a cliff.

Later, she had lain alongside him, her slight breast against his chest, and talked calmly and cozily of her craft of murder, her experiences with various victims, of special problems and personal pleasures, of various teachers, as though she were talking complacently of her children tucked up in bed. Her body had woken him into lust again. This time she made love calmly and considerately and exactly in the manner of a well-trained and somewhat absentminded prostitute. In the morning, her waking terror, her fleeting, utter need of comfort, as though her whole need of anything remotely resembling human love were compressed into one second between nightmare and day, was beyond anything he had ever seen in man or woman. God only knew, he thought, what lava boiled beneath her pleasant, ironic, capitalist charm by day. But he decided that it was most unlikely that night would ever break through day – except perhaps at the actual instant of pulling a trigger or guiding a knife past bone – and he regarded her with increasing excitement as one of the most perfectly crafted weapons he had ever seen.

137

All in all, as the scent of good coffee rose up the narrow stair, he felt pleased. The main, quite different purpose of his trip had turned out equally well. America had been good to him. He had been told by a PLO political expert, and had some difficulty in believing, that the easiest non-Moscow source to tap for funds to nourish a terrorist movement against an American ally was the established Protestant Christian churches in the form of the United Clergy Against American Militarism – an organization enjoying immense donations from the World Congregation of Churches.

For this particular operation – in which the fanatical and violently anti-Christian Brothers of Islam had already been selected and perverted to provide a front for the Moscow-dominated Baath Party – he would have merely to hold out his hand and present the bill.

It had indeed been true. America did things nicely. He had spent yesterday at the United Protestant Center. Somewhat to his surprise, he had been fawningly ushered in by the flower-faced young girl he had abused at the Salfield's party. Apparently she worked here. Proceedings had begun with an ecumenical service which he had insultingly refused to join. Then he had gone before the interdenominational panel. One look at the complacent, unformed faces before him in a half circle and he had known that the PLO expert was right. But there had been surprises. He had begun to lecture the Christian men of God about King Fahd's excesses, his fornications, his neglect of his spiritual role, but this had seemed to interest them very little, and he had had to turn the diatribe to the subject of American corporations' alleged contributions to the royal Swiss accounts. He had found, indeed, that although the Brothers' legendary fanaticism seemed to hold a sort of pornographic fascination for the assembled priests, it was better to stay away from topics such as God, religion, or faith. He had found, indeed, to his increasingly hilarious wonder, that he got on better if he addressed the Christians not as the bogus spiritual leader he had spent four years and much risk to become, but as a "Third World" Communist, daubed over with a narrow, primitive, Europe-hating xenophobia.

There had been one tricky moment. The Methodist on the panel, a moon-faced young man wearing a very small cross and a very large antinuclear pin, had firmly promised a donation in the form of medicine and food. Ibrahim had actually not known what to do. At a loss, he had simply stated that only he knew the needs, from moment to moment, of his flock and then, inspired, had taken the offensive and accused the fathers of racism, paternalism, and complicity in the plots of the CIA in refusing to give him unfettered funds for any purpose he chose to use them for. The Episcopal delegate, a youth who markedly possessed the transparent and exalted look of a medieval Christian ascetic, but who had principally asked odd questions about King Fahd's treatment of homosexuals, had been reduced almost to tears of remorse. It appeared that this man had attempted to go to Iran with Ramsey Clark to work with Khomeini on his exposure of American crimes and was regarded as the foreign policy doyen of the group.

All in all, three days' work had netted Ibrahim $2.5 million, which he would be able to transmit in a week to the PLO/Baath team now in Geneva for the purchase of stolen NATO weapons. The oddest part in all this was there was nothing odd in it at all. The priests, who were actually, apparently, what they seemed and not even on the payroll of the KGB, had furnished, from the pockets of American believers, funds for Communist terrorists in Zimbabwe operating against the biracial government of Bishop Muzorewa. The terrorists in question, with spectacular independence of mind, had murdered thirty-three missionaries. The group had also funded pro-Soviet guerrillas in Namibia and taken a paternal view of any cohort of homicidal savages with a sufficiently gory anti-Western bias. The Methodist delegate had been a guest of the Pol Pot regime in Cambodia – a fact of which he was loquaciously proud – and had defended that regime in publications of the church. It was, Ibrahim supposed, a species of painless martyrdom by proxy.

This was more than he had dared to hope for – as strange and shocking as his nights with Julia Drew. But America had yet more to offer. In al-Tabek, where his life was lived largely in view of his fervid faithful and in fear of the King's police, contacts with the PLO and the KGB were constrained and dangerous. Here, in America, the danger was very small. He had been able to have lengthy consultations with strategy experts attached both to Palestinians for Peace and various United Nations delegations. More important still, he was able to talk in detail to KGB specialists in North African policy and in CIA penetration. Paris was known as the site of a highly effective CIA operation surveilling Arab expatriates, and the PLO/Baath team now in place there had just reported a puzzling, though on balance probably not CIA, contact. Through an American KGB source, he would soon have details and names of the CIA operation there. That was truly invaluable. It had been promised by next Thursday, a mere three days. He had respect for the CIA. There were many in the PLO who laughed at it, especially since Iran. Its failures were indeed well known; its successes, he thought, much less so. He had seen the Russians and his fellow Communists expelled suddenly from Egypt and he had good reason to think that the Agency had done some very careful work, in very difficult circumstances, to accomplish that. It was largely by luck – the religious crisis of one native Berbian agent of the CIA – that he had even suspected that the CIA had infiltrated his own Brothers of Islam. It had been very difficult to identify the man, and he had done so, he thought, just in time. If his Muslim fanatics had learned that everything they had risked for three years had been in the service of foreign Communists, King Fahd could have sat easy on his American throne for another ten years. In short, he feared the CIA and doubted that anything less reliable than American treachery was enough to safely neutralize it.

He heard Julia's voice from below. She called up the stairs, "Coffee's ready, Hussein. I'm going to do you a Virginia breakfast, darling, so come on down." Her voice was composed, even merry; this surprised him, though he did not quite know why, and he responded to it with an unsettling hybrid of pity, affection, and lust.

She had pulled on a pair of blue jeans and a blouse she had not yet buttoned and she stood by the stove turning some kind of salt meat and stirring a saucepan of white mush. The kitchen had a stone floor and beams and a round oak table with pottery on it that seemed in the same cultural mode as the quilt upstairs. It was, he guessed, what they called "Early American." Outside, the unbelievable greenness, the misty indirectness of the light of this butter-rich land filled the kitchen with clear, gray light. He saw at once that she was a woman at home here – her movements were economical, satisfied, her manner full of generosity and grace – and it filled him with amazement and even shock that this sick, mad creature, this poisoned syringe, should on some level be protected, nourished, by what must be the simplest and most dignified of her people's ways. He felt a sense of actual desolation and then of panic. *This is absurd*, he thought. *It is unprofessional, dangerous.* He abruptly laughed. She looked up at him, puzzled.

"I know mullah's can't eat ham," she said. "But I don't see why commies shouldn't. That's grits. You'll hate it, I should think. Do have some coffee – it's good and getting cold."

At breakfast, she talked of business. She had made herself his secretary. She brought a little notebook to the table and read.

"We must get there by nine. At nine-thirty you've got a little secret news conference – the *Nation*, the religion

141

editor of the *Post* – he used to be a Maryknoll priest and
he's doing a very big article on spiritual rebirth being the
last best enemy of the profit motive, which is very
important because there's a man called George Gilder
who's persuading people of just the opposite – and the
National Catholic Reporter. You needn't worry – these are
all very reliable people. You'll recognize one of them from
the other night at Persephone's. Michael Glossop. He's
the *Nation*. It really is worth doing. These are big opinion
makers. You'll have to wear your mullah clothes all day. I
think they're under the bed. So you'd better start getting
religious, darling. Can you rave this morning?"

"Soon," he said. She had leaned sideways to read her
notes and he watched, through a faint steam of coffee,
the blouse fall away from her breast. He felt suddenly
very well. Orange juice was always good, even at this
odd time of day. She really could make coffee to his taste.
The ham had the tantalizing flavor of slightly poisonous
things, and the "grits," he supposed, were a kind of
couscous for invalids or for chickens. This trip, with its
relaxation of risk, the absence of his unprepossessing
faithful, and its extraordinary success, was putting him
in a holiday mood.

Julia went on. "That'll take all morning. Around
lunchtime, you're meeting with an imam from the
Washington mosque. That sounds tough, dear. Can you
handle it?" He nodded. She continued. "For the afternoon, we got a call from Sasha Pritkin – he's KGB over at
Aeroflot – he wants an hour with you about something.
That'll be in our secure room, of course. Tomorrow
morning you've got a meeting with Jonathan Snead. You
know about him. You've got another meeting with him
two days later, but I think he wants to check you out first.
Is this all very strange for you? Being in the midst of the
enemy and that sort of thing?"

"Oh, no. I was prepared. America's a little odd, but I
like it. I expected to. The KGB people seem to like
Washington even better than Paris. After all, the West is

nothing new. You know I did my postgraduate work in Geneva after Cairo." He paused and went on thoughtfully and very mildly. "In fact, if it had not been for Europe, I do not think that I would have remained a Communist. I think that I would have drifted out of it and become some kind of a good Egyptian nationalist. A good Nasserite engineer. Who knows, today I might be running the Aswan dam and going to symposiums with our new friends in Tel Aviv. It would have been an easier life. I would have forgotten the poverty of the villages, of the *bidonvilles* – which is something that you cannot imagine. Most of the Egyptians of the middle class forget. I was a very good engineer. I have to thank Europe for showing me a sickness, a historical corruption, beneath its pleasant face. I learned that the West was like a deadly, destroying fungus that cannot be fenced out and that will let nothing grow beside it. It can only be destroyed. And it will be destroyed, seductive though it is. Russia too, of course, in the end. But they must help us first. And after Russia, communism itself – that will be the last thing of Europe to go. Then healthy things will grow. But that part is after my time. For now, only communism can defeat the West." He looked at her, genuinely puzzled and even, in spite of himself, hopeful. "You must somehow have come to believe the same."

She shrugged, both surprised and bored. "That's what they all say. I never think about it myself. We'd better get dressed."

He thought, *I have just risen from the sluttish bed of an insane murdress and I am seduced into speaking from the heart.* He felt cold.

In the pretty bedroom, he pulled on the coarse black gown with a familiar sense of foreboding and elation. Back to work! He pushed the heavy gold ring past his finger joint. Deep inside him, the Mullah Ibrahim woke like a crow. He let his face settle experimentally into predatory zeal and felt a new fierceness and intemperance flow through his muscles. He enjoyed this grotesque profession. He had suspected for some time that he must be odder than he knew. But Ibrahim could wait a while. He watched Julia before the mirror, putting on a dress – simple, clinging, and, he guessed, expensive. Her short hair glowed. Her perfect skin gave back the milky freshness of the morning. When she bent to adjust her shoe, her body curved with easy tension of an athlete. For all its greater richness, he suddenly thought, the body of an Arab girl will seem oversweet and cloying now. She looked at him and said, "Ready?" He nodded. Fortunate, he thought, that when you looked at her with eyes of love, her own eyes warned you. There would be, at the beginning of a glance, a flash of green like faulty wiring. He had not thought "eyes of love."

The driveway to her house led between the pastures. He knew just enough of horses to know that these were good ones, though somehow less vivid than those of North Africa. She drove the Porsche slowly and they ambled closer. She called to them in her pleasant, angular, throaty voice. It occurred to him occasionally, with simple disbelief, that they were, in effect, in her father's house. He had mentioned that, one morning in bed, and her eyes had flashed and seemed to hang on the edge of a terrible and lasting change and her bright laugh afterward had held the remains of rage or terror. It had frightened him.

At the beginning of the public road, he braced himself. For she drove the Porsche not like a maniac at all, but like a cold, dispassionate scientist, inexorably and without cease extracting the last possible ounce of adhesion, the last degree of equilibrium, before the car exploded from the road, blew up. So the engine rose and fell in long, hysteric cries; the stone walls and hedges pushed themselves close up to the window in flickering blurs; each curve or hilltop brought a moment of sickening decision, of life rebought, and he, no timid man, began to sweat and cling and squirm. He looked at the

144

speedometer once and saw 120 on a country road. He battened down his voice and lightly asked, "Have you ever been in a wreck?"

She answered like someone nicely asked to lunch. "I've never been in a bad one. I'd like to be, though."

He said, "What? Why?"

"To see if I would whine."

So that was that. On the merciful expressway, where she had to slow down for the Virginia police, he got his voice back and began to talk of business. She interrupted him.

"I'd really like to do some work abroad. Especially in the Middle East. Europe, too, but especially the East."

He said, "Why? You serve the cause so well here. You've become a specialist. Too much travel might begin to raise alarms."

And she answered like a girl, not coy, just somewhat modest, telling her lover of a sexual fantasy.

"I think that to do it in a strange place would be purer, somehow. I think that it would mean more to me. I think that to just land in some strange Arab place where no one could help me and kill someone and just leave would be about the biggest thing there is. It makes me shiver. Can't you help me do it, Hussein?"

And he asked her, as he had sworn he never would, "Why do you do it at all?"

"Well, you'd know if you'd ever done it," she said. "I mean cold-bloodedly – any other way doesn't count. It's like sex, but you can't imagine how big it is. It makes me feel as though I'd just been made love to for a month. A whole month. It's wonderful."

She looked at him and he saw in her eyes that she was wondering whether he had believed her and suddenly, for a hundredth of a second, the wiring sparked completely beyond control. *She's not telling the truth*, he thought. *That's probably part of it, but it's much worse than that. She's not telling the truth at all.*

145

11

Ali Massoun turned up his collar. Chill, damp breezes off the river moved the sour breath of burning garbage over the island mud. Close and inaccessible, the Pont de Levallois, blazing with streetlights, thumped and hummed with traffic. His spine shook. That it shook for anything but the chill, he would not consider. He was on the Ile de la Jatte, the half-waste island in the loop of the Seine beyond Clichy. He stood, as ordered, in the very middle of a degraded field of stubble framed on two sides by the dark bulks of industrial garages. On the other sides, in the silences of traffic, the river sighed and gurgled against the black, encumbered coffin hulls of barges moored against the banks. On one, a guard dog suddenly, peremptorily, barked. The light from the bridge made it just possible to see any car or person in the field; the dimness made it unlikely that anyone not watching closely would do so. Yamadi and Khamal, Massoun thought, had picked the meeting place of a pro. There was only one wheeled access to the island, a bumpy road off a minor bridge. It was easily watched or closed. At this end, the Pont de Levallois touched the island, but only an iron ladder connected the island with the bridge. In the field, it would be impossible to place invisible confederates within easy reach. It would be as difficult as possible to place fixed recorders or cameras. It was impossible to be simply overheard. He had been told to come to the island alone, on foot. His potential clients would see his arrival and come by car. They would have the only means of quick departure. For a slower departure, the river would serve a corpse quite well.

A factory on the Asières bank let out a deep gasp of steam. Massoun started. He wriggled further into his woolen seacoat. He was going to have to sell his services extremely well. This, he was used to. He was also used to a livelier wish that they would be accepted. He reminded himself that he was not some kind of French alley-rat but a major of the Household Cavalry of the Kingdom of Libya on the military, if somewhat far-flung, business of his deposed King. He felt at once warmer and even stately. He tapped his cigarette in its ebony holder like a tiny swagger stick against his index finger. He waited for the car.

The glow of headlights swelled in the corner of his eye. The lights licked the side of the farthest garage, and then he saw the car. The lights bounced. There was a long splashing sound as it drove through a puddle of waste water. At the entrance to the field, the car slowed and corkscrewed and its lights searched back and forth over the briefly yellow stubble. He thought he saw the glint of a barrel within it. A gray Peugeot 505 – fast and completely unremarkable. A good choice. No chances. It stopped twenty meters away. Its headlights carefully blinded him.

Yamadi and Khamal, at least, as they separated from the glare, fitted Dr. Donnelly's description. "Playboy" was not the word he would have used for Khannafi. And, indeed, if a playboy, Khannafi now resembled one in the last of a series of moralistic Hogarth prints. He looked at nothing but the ground. He seemed in a stunned, hurt surprise. He walked bent over and slightly shuffling, as though his back or his kidneys hurt. The last two days, Massoun surmised, had not been spent entirely with his barmaid. *This*, he said to himself, *is what they do to their friends*.

He said to the approaching footsteps, courteously, that he was pleased to meet them. He spoke to the night.

Yamadi, for a moment, held the gun. Khamal frisked him efficiently, insolently, enjoying the insolence. So far, they had made Marseilles toughs look like gentlemen. *But perhaps that is how they think we act*, he thought.

Khamal said, "Clean."

And now Yamadi spoke. He said, "Who sent you?"

Massoun shrugged. "His name is profit."

"Why did you send the professor?"

"How else does he repay me for his drinks? He is a good messenger. The police do not care about him. He is trustworthy, within limits."

"How did you know of us?"

"That is not your business."

Yamadi said very quietly, "It is most of all our business."

Khamal minutely changed the angle of the gun. It now pointed at Massoun's kneecap. It carried a silencer. Khamal ran his tongue across his lips.

Massoun made himself take time. He answered in a voice instructive and even patient.

"You are foreigners, as I am. Perhaps you have not been in the *milieu*" – he meant the French underworld – "as long as I have. If you had been in it as long as I, you would know that two North Africans, whom nobody knows, cannot buy a transshipment warehouse in the Trade and keep it secret. Since I am a smuggler with a boat to feed, it is my business to know who has merchandise to ship. One of my men heard of your purchase in a Marseilles bar from one of the workmen of the former owner. You should have kept them on. They were good men and they would have been loyal to you. Then I went looking for the men you had to have inquired of when you were looking for a warehouse yourselves. They are necessarily friends of mine. Then I found out what you look like and where you are seen. Then I found out who you are. Then I sent my respectable professor. You are entirely safe, gentlemen. I am only a businessman whose business is complementary to yours. I hope both will be profitable."

148

Khannafi, whom everyone had forgotten, gave a sudden, bitter laugh and was ignored.

Yamadi said, "Who is your *caid?*"

And now Massoun knew beyond the shadow of a doubt that this man knew nothing of the drug trade, had not even taken time to learn it, for of all its branches, drug smuggling is the one that is never carried out by gang members under a *caid* but always by independents. *Now I know that it is guns*, he thought.

He said, "I am my own man. My boat is my own. She is fast. She carries fuel for eight hundred kilometers. She draws a meter and a half only. I can make landings. Especially, I transload at sea. I meet floating bags. When ships from Turkish ports approach French waters, the morphine base is thrown into the sea in packets tied to a buoyed line at night."

Yamadi and Khamal looked briefly at each other. Khamal minutely shrugged. He put the gun away.

Yamadi said, "How much can your boat carry?"

"If concealment is not important, she can carry a container on deck. She is a converted trawler. Belowdecks, perhaps half that much." He had rehearsed this part of the answer and he went on quickly. "I am used to carrying automobiles. Many people ship that way." *That ought to be big enough for them*, he thought. *They can hardly be shipping tanks.*

Yamadi said, "How we ship is our concern." But this time the toughness seemed to cover only indecision.

Massoun went on, the eager salesman. "She can do eighteen knots. Her engine is well silenced. I have had her at full speed at night within three hundred meters of a Spanish custom post and they did not hear."

Yamadi and Khamal now kept the sheepish silence of a family undecided in a television store. Yamadi took a step toward the car. Khamal leaped back into authority.

"Stay here," he said. "Don't move. You will be in range." He snapped his fingers at Khannafi. The three walked back to the Peugeot.

149

He could see the heads within it – Khannafi's slumped, unmoving and in misery in the corner, the other two close together, talking. The drone of a diesel pushed upon his ear. A heavy Seine barge with a bright yellow tractor like a flower perched incongruously on its deck crawled up the river. He would have liked very much to be on his boat, in the smell of the sea, earning honest money for one of his regular, trusted customers. But he was not, all in all, doing badly. He was almost certain that they believed him. He was even more sure that they had at least some need for services such as his. He thought it even probable that they would accept him. The heads drew apart. The doors opened. Khannafi did not move.

No gun this time. Yamadi and Khamal walked side by side and this time stopped at a normal distance, neither remote nor bullying. For a change, Khamal spoke.

"May one ask if you have a name?"

"Indeed. It is Mohamet Gibran."

"Is it worth inquiring whether that is real?"

Massoun shrugged. "It is the one I have used the longest. You would hardly believe that I have no others."

It was not a bad name. It's owner, a Moroccan who had a small reputation in the smuggling line, had not been seen for some months and was probably dead. If they were to ask about, they would hear faint echoes of his existence. It would take great ill luck for them to hear anything more, Gibran had had no political interests whatsoever and, Dr. Donnelly had said, would have interested the KGB too little for a thorough file.

Khamal said, "So we are dealing with a committee." He smiled in what Massoun took to be an effect of merry complicity. It was ghastly. It said, *You are only a poor hoodlum, then, and we can do whatever we like with you.*

Yamadi said, "We have a shipment."

Massoun, blandly courteous, encouraging, said, "There are only four things I have any need to know: the shape and weight of the cargo, the date of shipment, the length

150

of the voyage, whether it is to be a transshipment or a landing. If it is to be a landing, I must be told where, in detail, for that is the only way I can assess the risk. And, of course, the terms."

Yamadi answered, "There will be no landing. A small ship at sea, not more than eighty kilometers out from Marseilles. The cargo is crates, many crates. About a hundred and fifty kilos each. The ship has a crane. We are shipping," he said quickly, as though remembering, "in the cavities of machinery. Can you do this?"

"In a calm sea, easily. In a rough sea, it will be hard work. But I can do it. It will be at night?"

Yamadi nodded.

"Which night?"

"Within a week. You will have thirty-six hours' notice. Thirty-six, that is, to the rendezvous."

"That is not much."

Yamadi shrugged. "It is what you will get. If the boat is yours, it is enough."

"And the terms?"

"Twenty-five thousand francs. Paid on delivery."

Massoun laughed. "This is not the Christmas sale. Sixty thousand. And half in advance."

He was interested. Yamadi had named a figure two years out of date and two-thirds of the current going rate. It could be avarice or ignorance. His own figure was absurdly high and he waited for the reaction. Among real professionals, there was little haggling.

Yamadi said, "Fifty. Ten only in advance."

He offered too much. But, of course, he might not intend to pay it. And ten was cheap.

He nodded. "Accepted."

Yamadi said, "One more thing. No crew but you. We have our own."

"That is out of the question. My crew sails with me. Always. For all customers. I know them and they know the boat."

Yamadi answered quietly, "You do not understand.

151

That is how it will be. You have already accepted all conditions that I care to make."

"Not that condition."

Yamadi, looking disappointed, vexed, an overdriven man brought up against a foolish hindrance, said, "Then farewell," and nodded to Khamal. Khamal's arm slid, fluid, snakelike, into his jacket, under his arm, toward his gun. He looked Massoun full in the eye and smiled. Massoun felt ice in his belly.

He said, "I need one man. One man who knows my boat."

Yamadi motioned to Khamal. He paused in thought. "One man. All right. You are a lucky man. Be sure there are no more. We must be able to reach you at any time, at a place from which you can be in Marseilles within twelve hours. We will tell you where to go. You will receive the ten thousand then. What number will we call?"

Massoun gave it.

Yamadi, visibly relaxing, a man overdriven, overtired, with something accomplished for the day, said, "You are also a sensible man. Remain one."

They walked quickly to the car.

It drove off hard, its rear wheels almost digging into the soft stubble. On the road, its taillights at once bounced wildly in a rut and he had an idea he heard Khaddafi scream. Its headlights passed the garage, faded. He stood, coldly sweating, his stomach tight, his hearing at full pitch. After twenty seconds, he heard a motorcycle start. That was Stognacci, his Corsican, his bloodhound, concealed by a garage since the traffic of working hours. He was not without resources himself, and this thought soothed the chill within him. He walked to the shadow and waited several minutes, his eye on the Levallois bridge. As he expected, the gray Peugeot drove fast across it, out of town. He counted to ten, then fifteen. Then the motorcycle. Good. A long way behind. If he had to choose between losing them and their knowing of the tail, he would choose to lose them. He knew also that he feared them and, fearing them, could not allow himself to fail.

He constantly forgot that Dr. Donnelly was a soldier. That was his trouble in talking to him. On the telephone, he would hear the gravelly, peremptory, unyielding voice, or in person be fixed by the ungrateful cold blue eyes, and he would quiver with anger that such insolence could be visited upon him by a rumpled, scrounging, dishonorable civilian. Then he would remember that was all Dr. Donnelly's mask, a mask simply too convincing: that Dr. Donnelly was his superior officer – exposed, without doubt, to dangers he did not even know – in the nebulous hierarchy of the murky battle that he fought for his almost forgotten King and his own constantly re-membered honor. Then he would disconcertingly be flooded by admiration and respect for Dr. Donnelly – almost as much as, when a sixteen-year-old cadet, he had all but worshipped the horsemanship and authority of the venerable brigadier of the Household Cavalry. So, on the telephone, it went now.

McNaughton said, "So you lost them."

He answered, "Only after several miles. They were heading on the road toward Chartres, that we know – "

"They were heading on the road," said McNaughton, "toward two-thirds of France."

Massoun said, "Yes." And then, "I have discovered definitely that they are operating out of Marseilles. It is most certainly guns."

"Those, as it happens, are the facts that made me select you as the agent on the case a week ago. Where exactly did your tail, who you were telling me so much about in the Café Safi, succeed in losing them?"

"Outside Gometz. At the turn for Les Molières."

"The first or the second turn for Les Molières?"

Stognacci had not said nor had he asked him. "I do not know which."

"Is that so? Does anybody recollect the circumstances?"

"The traffic on D988 was heavy. The gray Peugeot – "

"The number?"

That, thank God, he had. "854 BFK 75."

"Good. Go on."

"The Peugeot was two hundred meters ahead of Stognacci. It would not have been a good idea, Dr. Donnelly, for him to have been closer."

"There I agree."

"There was a truck between them. That was good. Their positions had not altered for several miles. Suddenly the truck's brake lights went on for a few seconds. They were going around a bend at the time and Stognacci thought nothing of it. Still, a few seconds later, he pulled out to check on the Peugeot. It was not there. He remembered that there was a small side road near the bend. The Peugeot must have turned off onto it at high speed while he could not see it. It took him some time to turn in the traffic, and when he got back to it there was no trace of the Peugeot. Dr. Donnelly, if you are dealing with a professional, and you do not know where he is going, you can't be certain with a tail."

"You knew they were professionals. You should have sent two men."

And because he knew that Dr. Donnelly was right, he said indignantly, "Dr. Donnelly, I am not the police."

"At all events, we have lost them and we have no way of discovering, at least until you are on your boat, what the precise nature of the shipment is or where it has been obtained. You are therefore going to have to discover this in a situation of maximum danger. I am worried. Worried and disappointed."

"There is another possibility, Dr. Donnelly."

"What?"

Massoun said, impressively, "I could call on Colonel Deschaux."

McNaughton said, unimpressedly, "You know him, do you?"

Massoun, with simple dignity, said, "I know him as a fellow officer. He will receive me. I have once done business with him. If any man in France knows of illegal arms movements, it should be he. He may have heard echoes of these people's dealings, if no more than that. It might even be that we can find them again. I am willing to do this."

"You could give it a try. He'll probably try to pump you in return. Don't give him anything. We're not the broadcasting service."

Dr. Donnelly was not an easy man to work for.

Alexandre Petitsang was a top-ranking member of the UDR, the Gaullist party. From 1960 to 1962 he was a high official of the French national police. Jean Botto held a position equivalent to the American House Majority Whip. He was top police officer from 1962 to 1967. Both were close political and personal friends of Marcel Assisocho, gunman, gang boss, and principal heroin dealer of France. Assisocho was also, oddly enough, a policeman – a member of the Service d'Action Civique (SAC). His fellow officers included: Domenic Carburano, smuggler, gunrunner, dope dealer, and close associate of Gaston Dacier, former politician in Marseilles and now a cabinet minister in the French government; Joseph Ateo, hoodlum and hit man; Christian Saül, heroin smuggler, police-killer, gunrunner, and along with Ateo, sometime specialist in murdering foreign politicians; Marcel Batterio, jailed insurance agent, drug runner, and political campaign manager; and Mathieu Lucci, a chauffeur, whose mistress had the misfortune to be found with one hundred and ten pounds of heroin in her car. This singular law-enforcement agency acts as bodyguards during political rallies, is composed, to a great extent, of genuine heroes of the Resistance, is fervently anti-Communist, periodically murders more conventional policemen, and may in sober truth have saved both the life of General de Gaulle and the democratic institutions of the Fifth Republic in the late 1950s.

Under these circumstances, it is less surprising that when Ali Massoun, a Libyan refugee and minor criminal called on Colonel Alain Deschaux, a specialist in contraband and stolen guns, he should not only be calling on a policeman but should be a policeman himself. Massoun was a humble member of the SAC, recruited into it by a friendly *caid* of the Marseilles underworld, rather as a merchant might help his accountant into the Lions. Colonel Deschaux was one of its luminaries and founders, a former comrade-in-arms of General de Gaulle. The connection was gratifying. It mattered still more to Massoun that both he and the colonel were officers and gentlemen.

He stopped the car and breathed the smell of the woods. The colonel's château, some hundred kilometres from Paris, had a drive that wound through beech and chestnut to a small manor house of buttery stone, warm in the autumn sun and stained with weather and moss. No melodrama of Dobermans and guards. Just a soldier's manor, a gentleman's estate, in the mold, even, of de Gaulle's Colombey-les-deux-Églises. It made Massoun warm with pleasure that he was about to be received here, an accepted visitor, almost a guest. He calculated soberly that if he smuggled hard and successfully enough he could, in six or seven years, retire to a manor house just like this.

The colonel wore a sweater with leather shoulder pads. He clapped Massoun on the back of his best suit. The hallway smelled of the colonel's pipe. Madame Deschaux, comfortably middle-aged and trailing a wake of cocker spaniels, emerged from a paneled corridor and offered welcome and tea. The men retired to the study. The study looked through bow windows to the lawn. It had a fireplace; well used, disordered bookshelves; leather chairs; a rack of various hand grenades; a prayer

156

book and prayer stool; an enormous, littered desk; a display of submachine guns; an assault rifle in pieces on the windowsill; a decanter of Marsala with Baccarat glasses; and, in the corner, a mortar and a globe.

Formally, and with respect, holding his teacup stiffly in the easy chair, Massoun said, "I thank you for receiving me."

The colonel sat commanding and askew behind his desk, neatly balanced between hospitality and trade. "I had no reason not to. You were a sensible man at our last meeting. Did your friends receive those goods?"

"They received them. They did not live long to use them."

The colonel, sadly, easily resigned, spread his hands on the desk top. "What would you? Colonel Ghadaffi is not an easy man to kill. Theirs was the fifth attempt, I think. There have been others since. Is that the business you are here on?"

"No, Colonel. It is quite different. I am here for information. Even for advice."

Colonel Deschaux said, "That is often so much harder to obtain than this." He gestured good-humoredly around the domestic arsenal and looked Massoun directly in the eye. His eyes were disconcertingly like Dr. Donnelly's. A very old prayer went through Ali Massoun's head. *Oh, God protect us from the Christians!*

"I have some clients in the heroin trade."

The colonel delicately raised his hands. "That is not my business."

"I think it is not theirs, either."

The colonel considered. "An odd disguise for anything."

"I think that their business is ours. As you say, it is odd. There is one possible explanation. They must be people who have not only a normal desire to keep the details of their dealings secret, but people who cannot allow it to be thought that they have purchased arms at all. That is strange. To worry about interception, yes. To

make your enemy guess what you possess, yes again
But why go to such lengths to hide from your enemy tha
you are armed at all? And the French police will arres
nowadays for heroin but hardly ever for guns. It in
creases the risk. But suppose you are planning to d
something for which you wish some other party to b
blamed. Then you would at all cost disguise the fact tha
you yourselves had the means to do it. At all events, I an
being used as the dupe and I do not like this. It seems t
me that such purchases would be outside of the usua
patterns. It might be that you, or men of honor that yo
know, are supplying to Communists unawares. As
fellow officer of the SAC I felt I must warn you of this ac
as well as seek your advice."

The colonel turned full to face him. "And how, Major
do you, the duped, know that you are duped? Have yo
seen the cargo?"

Uneasily, Massoun said, "No."

"Then I think that you are asking for my help withou
telling me all that you know."

Massoun said nothing.

"You may have reasons, that is as it may be. But I, or
my side, have little reason to help you. You should no
invoke our SAC and then hold back from me, you
superior officer."

He drummed his fingers on the desk. The fire crackled
The old Bokhara rug lay richly on the floor. But there wa
now no warmth in them. The colonel knew how to brin
out an icy, honorable chill. Massoun felt desolate –
comradeship refused.

The colonel softened. "Perhaps you are unable to say
what you know now. But you can surely tell me what you
in future find out. It could benefit us both. If I tell you of
certain development, will you, as an officer of the SA
and as a gentleman, tell me if it passes through you
hands?"

Massoun, in deep gratitude, said, "Yes, my Colonel,
will."

The colonel rose and stood comfortably before the fire. "There is always a trade in weapons that are actually stolen. I am not talking about the criminal who buys a burgled pistol but of the serious arms trade. It is a special branch of it, for the risk is both increased and lessened. It is increased for obvious reasons; it is lessened because the line of supply becomes more hidden, almost impossible to prove. The greatest source of the stolen military weapons is the armies of the NATO powers. Especially the Americans. There is always a corporal who needs money, a sergeant who cannot pay his gambling debts, even an officer who is blackmailed. So there is a steady trickle of weapons for sale and there are merchants who specialize in buying them and collecting them into larger lots. It is not a major trade. But of late it has greatly increased and it has become more comprehensive. There are agents now actively persuading NATO soldiers to sell their weapons. Especially weapons that have signs of use. It is as though somebody is trying to arm artificial NATO units, or at least artificial NATO-supplied units. I do not understand this. I do not like developments in this trade that I do not understand. I would much like to know where these weapons are going. The customers you spoke of sound odd enough that it could just possibly be that they are a part of this. That is what I would need to know and I would need also, in such a case, to know who they are. I have your word, I think Major, that I shall."

12

On the Cours Belsunce, the great thoroughfare of Arab
Marseilles, the leaves of the plane trees fluttered and the
branches moved stiffly, uneasily, in the wind. They
moved over the crawling sidewalk; over the peddlers'
stalls heaped with crimson plastic tigers, boxes encrusted
with jewels of colored glass, thirty-franc chandeliers,
five-franc rings, and purple panties with a glass diamond
at the crotch; they moved over rusty charcoal stoves
giving out the strong smoke of grilling skewered
horsemeat; they moved over piles and heaps and racks of
secondhand clothing out of which there came a faint,
sharp smell of sweat. Ali Massoun, one of Marseilles'
hundred thousand Arabs, looked at the scene with
complete disfavor. The wind was rising strongly and he
was in the quarter where his people lived.

His rendezvous with Yamaki and Khamal was on the
Rue des Récolettes, off Belsunce, in the Café Rabat. The
grace of Belsunce did not extend to Récolettes. It was two
metres wide. His shoes crunched lightly in a crust of
garbage. He looked in the doorways, seeking the Rabat.
The corridor of a hamman, a public steambath, gave forth
a waft of aged urine. Next door, a balding prostitute,
looking surprisingly like a prison wardress in a miniskirt,
stood in concussed boredom, holding a yapping poodle
on a leash. The street was half black, half Arab. Red robes
and white robes outnumbered dirty shirts and ragged
pants. Thirty or forty radios played Arab music or
American Soul. The Café Rabat was in the poorest block.

He was offended. The Artistic and the Chez Toto,

where a great number of his smuggling contacts were made, were rackety places but not cesspools such as this. If Yamadi and Khamal wished to stay sunk within the Arab quarter, there were decent places on Belsunce – and if they wished to stay off Belsunce, where the police still went, there were better places by far than this. Then, as through the window he saw the knot of men, not much above tramps, milling around the staircase to the rooms upstairs, he realized that the Rabat was the waiting room of a "hotel," which on this street meant a brothel, which on this block meant a *maison d'abat*, or slaughterhouse, where the girls would entertain sixty or seventy customers each day or night. It was eleven in the morning and business was beginning to move. Since a thousand or so Arabs would pass through the room and back each day, it would be possible to move an army through it without exciting notice. Still, he thought, to use it suggested an instinct for degradation; he was disgusted and annoyed, and he entered tapping his cigarette holder against his finger with the expression of a major general.

And Khamal beckoned to him with his chin. He sat down faster than he intended at the greasy table, in the unmatched chair. Yamadi and Khamal were dressed, approximately, in truck drivers' clothes. Khamal looked like a racing driver. Yamadi looked like a lawyer, badly dressed.

Yamadi said, "This will not take long."

Massoun said firmly, "The wind is rising."

Yamadi, suddenly just a landsman, looked nonplussed and petulant and said, "What does that mean to us?"

"It is a southwester. By night, there will be breakers on all unprotected beaches. Offshore, the sea will be one and a half to two meters. Transloading crates will be a pig. It may also rain. Visibility would then be poor."

Khamal, leaning swiftly across the table so that his face was close, said quietly, "If you are trying to get out of this, it will be the most foolish thought you have ever had."

And Massoun made himself hold Khamal's eye and

say unhurriedly, "But I am not saying that. I am saying it will be unpleasant. I am saying that I will need a sheltered harbor to load. I am saying that you will have your ass in the air and your head over the side vomiting all night."

Khamal's face tightened, but Yamadi said, "Can you load at Niolon?"

Massoun thought. Niolon was a fishing village, ten kilometers from his berth at Estaque, the commercial fishing port of Marseilles. It had a breakwater.

He said, "Yes. It is not too public for you?"

"Not at night. There is no security guard. There is a good road there."

Massoun said, "What time? Where is the rendezvous? How will you load?"

"The rendezvous is sixty-eight kilometers from Niolon in the open sea. I will give you the position when we load. How long will it take you to get there? Can you find a ship without lights?"

"I can find a floating bottle if it is in the right place. What is the approximate course? I need to know how I will be meeting the sea."

"Roughly south."

"Then we will have the sea on the starboard bow. Three hours. We will return slightly faster."

"The rendezvous is at one-thirty A.M. Loading will take half an hour. So you should be there at ten. I would wish to be in port by dawn."

Massoun thought. He said, "In that sea, transloading will take an hour if the men on the ship are very good. We will be back at Niolon a very little before dawn if all goes well. There will be some activity there, perhaps, but not much. How will you load?"

"You bring your boat with the one man we have allowed you. We will have six men with us. We will load by hand. My men will sail with us. They are over there." He pointed to the knot of men around the stairway. "They are the ones who do not look sick."

And indeed, among the gray, sour-smelling customers who waited joylessly for their turn were six men who stood out like wolves among stray dogs. When a customer came in, he sat at a table and then, as his turn came near, stood by the stair. The stair was narrow, so that one customer had to fully descend before another could go up. This happened a little more than once in each minute, but these men had not moved to the stair. Under their stained shirts was clear skin, hard muscle. They were young and lean. It was clear that they had been told to appear abject, and they sat like six crack commandos from any army in the world, all with identical cricks in the neck. They gave Massoun a new and wholly frightening comparison of Yamadi's resources and his own.

I should not have told them of the seasickness, he thought. *It may be my only chance.* But he made himself say, "Are they planning to fuck here all day first? They will infect the whole boat if they do."

Yamadi acidly said, "No."

Khamal said, "You have your orders."

Massoun said, "But I do not have my ten thousand francs."

He thought Yamadi looked slightly guilty as he replied, "At the boat. At the boat. You do not need it this afternoon."

And Massoun, though the crude and brutal implication gave him a stab of fear, surprised himself by feeling mainly angry, or even disgusted, impatient, as at dangerous children. He hit his fist on the table and loudly said, "In five years in this trade I never met clients so stupid that they do not pay as agreed. You pay me the advance agreed on now or you can sit drinking coffee in this pesthole till you get syphilis of the teeth. I do not have to deal with such people as you."

Khamal and Yamadi looked at each other. Yamadi said, "We do not know you, either." He said it sulkily but he passed an envelope across. "Count it," he said. "It is there."

163

Massoun counted it with insulting care. He nodded.

Khamal said, "Get out. We see you at Niolon at ten. Walk straight to Belsunce. Do not hang around trying to watch us. You will be watched yourself."

Massoun walked swiftly down the Rue des Récolettes towards Belsunce. He walked in the middle of the street, looking to neither side, like a brave man running a gauntlet. The street stung his eyes, filled his stomach with bile. *This is Arab,* he said to himself. *This is what I am. Without courage, without honor, I would be this street.*

His own street was no wider, but he lived among the French. A steep street of high walls with washing hung between; but the walls were charcoal gray with age, not filth, the dark doorways led to family lives, and from the plumber's workshop and the carpenter's came the sound of decent work. The paint was peeling but the cobblestones were nearly clean. On a glossy poster, a plump young man in a good tweed suit, François Valdini, son, nephew, son-in-law, godson, cousin, and closest friend of Marseilles' higher mafiosi smiled in fatuous beneficence and offered himself as *Conseiller Général.* The street had voted for him. As a criminal of sorts, Massoun was nothing unusual here, but, like his neighbors, he brought no mayhem to this street. As an Arab he was unusual; but he was big and gracious, he wore decent clothes, he played no Arab music, his customers were French; he was neither ostracized nor befriended but simply left alone.

But his house and his bed were tokens, nothing more. In Libya, if Ghadaffi had not come, he would have basked in a placid, fecund wife, a sprawling house, daughters to hug, boys to teach to ride. In imagination, he saw himself rich, reserved, with a chestnut-shaded château and an auburn bride. In fact, he lived in a Marseilles slum with a slumming student, Marie-Claire, who got from him his handsome body, his melancholy eyes, a ring, every now and then, that she never wore, and the conviction that shacking up with an Arab smuggler was as authentic as you could get. And this Arab, after all, was clean. He had nothing against her. She was pleasant in the morning, comfortable to sleep beside. She took no advantage and brought nothing worse than an unfilled center in his hopes, an ache. She was in class by day.

He sat at the kitchen table, one elbow on it so it would not rock. The faucet dripped onto the worn enamel of the sink, a sound so constant it was comforting. Clearly, as Dr. Donnelly had feared, there would be no way to inspect the cargo before it arrived at the boat. So his task was simple and no doubt impossible: to inspect a crated, secret cargo during a three-hour voyage on a small vessel guarded by eight expert, suspicious men; to "find out" during transloading about an anonymous steamer so secretive that it would risk collision rather than carry lights; to excite no suspicion. That was all. If he caused no suspicion, he assumed that they would merely try to kill him and his crewman at the end of the voyage. Yamadi's attempt not to pay him could mean little else. They would obviously succeed; he would be able to pass nothing on, so the operation would be pointless. If he somehow killed them in self-defence, the operation would be equally pointless. Yamadi had everything to gain by killing him, while he, by killing Yamadi, would gain nothing but his life. Obviously, they should succeed, but he was resourceful and capable and he could think about that. As for the results of causing suspicion, his mind stopped cold.

One thing was clear. Of his three crewmen, he must use Stognacci. Stognacci was not the best sailor. For the most part, he was the courier, the tail, the man on land. On the other hand, he was good with the gun that he would not be able to use this time. And the other two had wives and children and them he could not take. So he must call Stognacci now.

And anything, anything at all that added difficulty,

confusion, danger, to the voyage could somehow be his
ally. The sea could be his ally. He blessed the rising wind.
It was a pity they would not be meeting it more on the
beam; his boat did not pitch that badly, but she rolled.
God bless her, like a sow. He wondered if his clients
knew navigation. One of them might easily know a little.
He whistled to himself. On the refrigerator door was a
little smiling fish, a magnet for holding messages. He
took it down. Marie-Claire was going to a movie, would
be late. Yamadi, no doubt, had six machine guns. He, on
the other hand, now had a fish. He willed his stomach to
unknot. He despised the bile of fear. He looked around
the gray apartment. He went to the telephone.

Under the floodlights of Estaque, his boat, *La Revanche*,
was gracious, white, serene. She lay at the far side of the
basin. He walked along the wharf. Stognacci would meet
him here. Work went on under the lights all night. He
walked by stacks of fresh wooden crates, ready for icing,
hand-packed with silver mackerel, head by tail. He
walked around spread nets. He nodded greeting to men
in yellow oilskins and blue jeans, Corsicans, Arabs,
French. Their boats had just come in. Their oilskins and
their hair were wet. He called to an Arab captain, "How
is it out?"

"Sweet as a pig's ass. The fish must be paying you well
tonight."

The captain smiled ironically. Massoun fished just
enough not to flaunt his occupation in authority's face.

His boat was his hope, his dignity, his ticket to life.
And so he loved her. He patted her gunwale, a daily
gesture, as he stepped on board. He felt her rock,
minutely. She was an eighteen-meter wooden trawler,
big for Provence and fine-hulled for a trawler, rigged for
sardine and mackerel, twenty years old. A fisherman
would note that her rigging was skimpy, her afterdeck
almost clear. A mechanic would have noted that her one
engine was not the standard Detroit Diesel 871 but a

fierce, turbocharged 1271 capable of throwing her forwards at a maximum speed, even for her narrow hull, of eighteen knots. Anyone would see that her wheelhouse bristled with antennae: loran C radar, VHF, SSB – all standard in the Atlantic fishery, unusual here. But, like a well-cleaned fishing boat, she smelled of iodine and salt.

In the wheelhouse, he felt his nerves relent, his manhood double. High and strong, the stubby bow rose up before him. His hands took the wheelspokes easily. Everything that he was going to do to his boat in the next half hour seemed to him a subtle, belitting insult like a snickering joke at a mistress.

He switched on the instrument lights. The compass card, heavy and lustrous in its bath of oil, glowed ruby in the binnacle. The boat lay at mooring near ESE, 120° – not so very far, as luck would have it, from his intended course. He took the silly little fish from his pocket and passed it in an arc around the compass, fifty centimeters distant. The card ponderously twitched. He halved the distance and the compass followed for 10° – a faithful, excellent instrument falling for a cheap pretense. For fifteen minutes, like a solemn child, Ali Massoun moved his magnetic fish back and forth on the console around the compass. He identified two points, twenty centimeters apart, and marked each with a tiny pencil cross. The first position would give a reading of approximately 180° on a true course of 160°. The second would show 190° on a true course of 200°. A course change of 40° would show as 10° on the compass. It was approximate, but in the sea tonight the compass would swing anyway.

The next was easier. He unscrewed the back of the low-oil-pressure alarm. He disconnected the leads from the sensor and wired the alarm behind the console directly to the instrument lights. The alarm immediately, loudly, screamed. He disconnected one lead. It stopped. He experimented with squeezing the stiff wires so he could make contact at will. The alarm sounded on and off. In a few minutes he had it so arranged that a quick motion of his fingers against the leads would set it off. It could no longer give a true signal but it could give a false one at will. He was satisfied. He had made his boat a liar.

He went below. In the engine room, the sharp reek of diesel pushed against his face. Squat and big, with six cylinders and six injectors on either side, the engine gleamed dully in the light. By reflex, his shoulder flinched away from the steel exhaust stack looming in the aft starboard corner – with the engine at speed, it became close to red-hot. In his main tanks he carried three thousand liters of fuel; in the auxiliary, three hundred. All were full. At close to full power, with the engine gulping fuel, the auxiliary tank would run dry in two and a quarter hours. Niolon was a half-hour run. He dumped twenty liters from the auxiliary tank, disobeying every pollution law in force. Perfect! He switched the fuel lines from the main tanks to the auxiliary. He was satisfied once more. He had made his boat a cripple.

Back in the wheelhouse, he woke the loran. Two lines of numbers leaped out of the dark, changed, fluttered, fell over each other, and finally settled down to the coordinates of his position, accurate to within twenty meters. His finger rested on the button. On the islands and headlands around Marseilles were numerous light-houses. Even in the rain he expected, even with a compass whose degree of untruth was not totally pre-dictable, most of the voyage could be made by pilotage. To find a blacked-out ship on a stormy night, loran was almost, but not absolutely, necessary. It could also betray him to anyone in the wheelhouse interested enough to study the chart, and it. He left it on. Landsmen in a heavy sea could be relied on for sullen, miserable immobility.

A motorcycle's engine died on the wharf. Footsteps and the slightest shifting of the boat announced Stognacci.

Stognacci called out, "Eheau, Capitaine!"

Like many Corsicans, he seemed made of rubber. He was short, broad-shouldered, bandy – lithe and wholly without grace. His eyes, intelligent, hard, cynical, and amused, looked out of a face plowed by sensuality, endurance, and – over the left jawbone, from throat to ear – a fellow convict's knife.

He said, "So we have favored customers tonight?"

Massoun took him gravely by the arm. "Tonight is not a joke."

Motionless as prisons, harshly lit, the tankers towered above them on either side. The *Revanche* sinuously acknowledged the port's slight, premonitory swell, a toy boat in a toy sea. The swell shortened as the harbor entrance neared. Massoun stood at the wheel, silent, serious. The comfortable rumbling of the engine, the vibration under his feet, shook the worst tension out of him. He was grateful for the presence of Stognacci, wedged into a corner, smoking a strong cigarette. They had made what plans they could. Beyond that, he would not pester fate.

But he was pleased to feel the sea. At the harbor entrance they met it broadside. The wind was strong and nervous, warm and smelling of rain. The sea was two meters now, sharp, black, and topped with foam. It would grow as the night went on. The boat's motion was heavy, laboring, confused. Even he himself found the bottom of his stomach stirring from time to time. His boat could take this and as much again without the smallest risk, but a landsman, he thought, would feel alarmed as well as miserable. He relaxed a little. He steered southwest along the coast for Niolon.

They were there. From beyond the breakwater, the few lights of the village silhouetted the truck. The small wharf was deserted. As he rounded the breakwater men flushed quickly from the truck. It carried the sign of a wholesale fish dealer. A flashlight signaled him to the farthest corner of the wharf. Stognacci threw the lines to two men who looked at him blankly before they picked them up. *They, at least*, thought Massoun, *are not seamen*.

Khamal was on the wharf. He said, "Are you ready to load?"

"Yes."

"The crates will go on the deck."

"Not in this sea. They will be soaked, and even if that does not matter, the boat would be unstable. They must go in the hold. Can four men carry them?"

"Yes."

"We need four men to carry them from the truck and four in the hold to receive them. I will put my man in the hold and I will help at the truck. You can split your men, all right?"

Khamal nodded. He called, still in Arabic, to the truck. Khamal's accent, while not North African, was also not easy to place. The voice that answered was pure Palestinian.

And the men were not workmen, not soldiers even, but commandos, al-Fatah's best. Their skins had the gloss, and their eyes the clarity of men in training. With four men to a crate, each man carried near forty kilos. The truck ramp was steep, the wharf was cobbled. They did not grunt, stagger, breathe hard, or rest. The truck quickly emptied. The hold quickly filled. Thirty minutes for sixteen crates. He guessed three thousand kilos. The nails holding down the lids of the crates were widely spaced. At least they would not be hard to open or nail back. The guards were the security. They might not be seamen but, damn, they looked good! The plan, the hope, of wearing them down on a sloppy boatride now seemed to him childish, feeble, doomed.

But they hadn't expected the sea. Just at the breakwater, as luck would have it, a bull wave, compressed by the bay, roared down out of the night, the boat reared like a mustang, hung suspended for a count of three, and fell. Unpracticed hands grabbed for handholds. Two men staggered, cursed. Khamal looked at Massoun sharply.

Stognacci idly said, "Think it will get much worse, Captain?"

And Massoun replied smoothly, "A little worse, I shouldn't wonder. Dirty night."

The first fine spots of rain misted the windshield. Clear of the little bay, he spun the wheel, opened the throttle. The engine began to slam the hull against the sea. The lying compass rocked around 180°. The boat headed at 200°, dead broadside to the sea. The narrow hull, better for speed than stability and now badly overpowered, gave her first hysterical lurch, then corkscrewed. Spray hit the wheelhouse like a shotgun blast. Massoun looked at Yamadi pleasantly.

"Your course," he said.

In a different world, beyond the churning water, the lights of Marseilles glowed to port. The light fragmented on drenched glass. The windshield wipers pounded. He kept the lighthouse of Château d'If 20° off the port bow. His false course took him close by the unlighted Cap Caveaux on Pomègues Island. The wind and sea could carry him onto it. He could not yet see the light of Ile Planier, much farther out. Just as well. On his proper course he would have passed it close to starboard. In fact, it would be distant. That was something elementary. But in fact it was difficult even to see the big light of Château d'If, and, on a night like this, landsmen were usually blind and witless.

Past Planier, an hour and thirty kilometers out, he began to study the men. The auxiliary would run dry in thirty minutes or less. One man was a shambles. He could hear moans and unremitting retching from the little bunk room just astern where the unshaded light swung wildly, and the wheelhouse air was full of vomit. Seasickness is a joke of course. It can also be a fatal joke; a man who retches long enough can rupture his throat and drown in his own blood. It is a very efficacious joke; a man close to death may be more clear thinking, more aware, than a man deeply seasick. It is not far from

171

torture. Sober businessmen in charter boats in a heavy sea have offered captains $5000 to call in a helicopter to take them off. Even at an early stage, it can degrade a fist-class man into an egoistical, slow-moving clod.

So he studied them. One more would soon be on the bunks. Two seemed immune. He had to expect that. They might at least be tiring. Incessant bracing, clinging, is exhausting to the inexperienced. Yamadi gazed at the corner in the still, silent immobility of wretchedness. He looked like a sodden drunk. Two men had a withdrawn, wary look. They were functional and might remain so, but they were half the men they had been. Khamal seemed in hell, and mastering it. He had grappled himself to the seat beside Massoun. At each lurch he would shudder and half fold up like a man hit in the solar plexus. He was white. But his eyes were fierce, angry, and totally aware. Khamal was a leader.

Massoun slapped him on the back. "Only two more hours," he said.

He felt on him eyes of hatred. But he had reduced the odds.

He felt, before he heard, the first falter of the engine. He held his breath, five seconds. Then it staggered, picked up, droned on. Khamal had heard it. He looked up at Massoun, hard, suspicious. Massoun let himself look puzzled. He counted three more. As the boat next lurched, his hand missed the wheel, brushed the oil-pressure lead. The alarm screamed. Then the engine stopped. He was pleased to see that only three men moved quickly – Khamal and the two unsuffering guards, and the guards, though quick, were uncertain. But Khamal burst out of his chair and, though he staggered, he gripped Massoun's shirt, pulling him closer and hanging on, and said, "What is this, you whore's bastard?"

And Massoun answered, in control, "It is possibly water in the fuel. It is possibly water in the oil. It is possibly the engine over-heating. It is possibly the whole engine fucked. The first three, I can fix. If you care to change your language, I will go below and look. Otherwise we can all drift to Italy."

They could hear the wind, now, and the rigging like a cello, and the hissing and tumbling of the sea, and the sudden crash of wave on hull. It was black. The last light was swallowed in the rain. Massoun risked a look at the loran and a quick study of the chart without putting his finger on it. They were about twenty-four kilometers on a bearing of 210° from the rendezvous. He was where he expected to be. The boat's motion had changed. It was ponderous, sudden, erratic, wide. The moans from the bunk room, he was happy to note, were slower but more shrill.

He said to Stognacci, "Take the wheel. Stand watch. Let no one near the starter. I will go below."

Khamal looked at his men. He picked the best one. He said, "Follow him. Watch him like a hawk." He said to Massoun, "You may think that we need you alive. Maybe we do. But it would give me pleasure to make you run this boat with your kneecaps nailed to the chair. Do you understand?"

Massoun nodded, with no pretense.

The engine hatch was on the foredeck. The wind grabbed their hair. The bow was too high for whole seas to break over it, but tongues of waves leaped up and wetted them. His guard was agile, strong, no doubt intelligent, but also unsure of his circumstances. Massoun went down the ladder first. He saw the guard's foot slip once. His shoes were street shoes, rubber only on the heel.

The engine room was stifling, reeking of hot oil. He watched his guard. The man looked around alertly, but not like a mechanic. He tried him. He said, "If you light a cigarette, we will go up like a bomb."

The man nodded emphatically. "I am not a fool," he said.

And you also do not know diesels.

He had to switch the fuel lines. But his repairs were not entirely to be faked, for air had entered the fuel lines from the empty tank and, on a diesel, such air must be bled out before the engine can be started. That would take ten minutes, working fast. Or he could stretch it out. Six feet away, the watertight door led to the fish hold and the crates. Three minutes was all he needed. Found in the fish hold, he would still have some excuse. Hydraulic lines led to the winches through the fish hold. A landsman would not realize what they were. He could claim to have inspected them. But he must be alone. He could send the guard on an errand, but the man would surely stand in the engine hatch, quite visible from the wheelhouse, and call for reinforcements. Not time enough. He stepped carefully around the engine, watchful for oil spots on the heavy metal floor. He had a thought.

He worked busily around the guard then stopped, exasperated.

"I cannot work through you," he said. "Please go over there." He point to the aft, starboard corner, clear of the engine, where the exhaust stack rose up from the floor. The man began to move. Massoun held his breath, gauging the sea. The boat began to settle steeply. She would rise up hard. He staggered backward. He felt the guard. He heard him curse. Their feet entangled. He pulled himself forward, burning his hand on a water pipe. He let himself fall. The guard fell heavily.

The guard fell the only way he could, his feet straight out, his head and his back on the exhaust stack. He seemed stunned. With the engine at full bore for ninety minutes, the exhaust stack was still much hotter than the hottest skillet.

For ten seconds the man lay there, still. Over the reek of diesel came the thicker smell of burning hair and cotton. Then the man screamed. His feet scrabbled on the metal floor. The boat rose sharply, pushing him more heavily against the stack. The smell now was of burning meat. He flung his arms up, finding only the stack to grip. He pulled himself up laboriously, screaming. *He is loud*, Massoun thought, *but they will not hear this above*. Pieces of his back pulled away, stayed stuck to the exhaust stack, smoking. His hands were stuck. He pulled them off, the palms gone. His face was twisted. He staggered backward, fell over Massoun, and landed on him, screaming in his ear. Massoun pulled him off, and up.

"Get up there," he said. "We have morphine. You are hurt. They can help you. Go."

He pushed him forward. The man blundered, sobbing. Massoun moved to the door of the fish hold. The screams receded. He wondered how his guard would deal with the engine hatch. It should slow him down.

He swung the door. The crates were there, the tops waist-level. With luck, he just had time. There would be confusion. Hammer and jimmy were in his tool pouch. He ripped the lid slats off three crates, opened them. Thirty seconds gone. Oiled metal gleamed within. Guns, of course. All disassembled, too. Damn! He hoped he could recognize the pieces. Forty seconds. His back crawled. Yes! That barrel – Belgian FN7.62mm. Standard NATO issue. Old weapons, used. The rest the same. Close that crate. One minute. The next, different. What the hell was that? He reached in, lifted it, looked. Parts of an M45B, a Swedish K, 9mm submachine gun. NATO also. Ninety seconds. Close the crate. Dull thuds of feet above him. Any fool could recognize the next – U.S. AR15s. About two hundred individual weapons in the hold, enough for a multipurpose NATO company. Move! That was a foot on the hatch ladder. He swung the door behind him.

The guard came in fast and angry. He was the other fit one. Massoun yelled at him first.

"Stay the fuck off the engine. Stay away from the stack. Hold on to something, then maybe you won't get hurt."

"I do not intend to."

175

Massoun worked calmly, neatly, wedged against the sea. He let himself take pleasure in the handling of the wrench. He passed the word up: fifteen minutes – the rendezvous could still be on time. His job was nearly done; he had seen the cargo and he had not been seen. Transloading would be a bitch, but an ordinary, seafaring bitch. For the guards, it would be sheer hell. He grinned. And it would take time. Time and confusion to study the steamer and find out, at least, the country of her crew. More important yet, time to get back to Niolon at full dawn with boats coming out of the harbor and the wharves crowded with men. There was not much to fear in a public place from sick, exhausted men. Then he could vanish. He was almost safe.

He pictured to himself Dr. Donnelly's approval, and Colonel Deschaux's. He would give them everything they could have hoped for. Dr. Donnelly's approval was largely a source of personal pride. Colonel Deschaux's was more concrete. There were grand possibilities in winning the trust of the man who stood at the top of the weapons trade. He felt his life move forward. He had taken every favorable circumstance and bent it to his use. And he had won. He tapped the wrench gently.

Above, the bunks were full. The two sickest commandos, long past vomiting, weakly retched. One, as men in extreme sickness often do, was sinking into sleep. The burned man was sinking into morphine. He lay on his stomach, moaning quietly. They had made Stognacci tend him. Stognacci, after a look around the black horizon and a final warning about the starter, had shrugged and obeyed. He nursed him gently. Activity had made the two remaining guards at least somewhat better. They moved slowly and sullenly, but they moved.

In the wheelhouse with Yamadi, Khamal thought. The boat pitched aimlessly. He was full of unformed suspicion, half-grounded fear. He had some experience of boats. He had once in a while been on fast petrol boats off

Libya, or, in the old days, off Lebanon, and once in a Russian "trawler." That had been in calm seas with large crews. He regarded vessels as machines, the sea as a medium, danger as aircraft. Of real seafaring, he knew nothing. He had given the weather scarcely a thought. The possibility that it could reduce a third of his men to invalids and himself to misery had never occurred to him. Yamadi was also useless, but this phase of the operation was not Yamadi's game. He need not have come. Khamal was anxious about the transloading, but he knew it would be done. He assumed three men and the captain's man could do it. And if the men on the bunks were needed, they would work. While a man lived, he could make him do anything. He had learned to know this. It was his strength and pride.

He had been suspicious of the breakdown, doubly so of the burning. And yet, he knew the captain feared him; he could see it in his eyes. He had bravado, but he had also fear. Machines had breakdowns – tanks broke down all the time. This one seemed to be brief. There would be little point in staging it. Little point in injuring one guard out of six. That could be argued, but the man's fear could not. He would want to do his job, get home, get paid, get safe. That might even happen. Khamal toyed with the idea of letting him live, using him again. To make a strong man fear, you went beyond crude threats; your soul had to envelop his, crush it, poison it; a strong man who feared you was an investment; such a man should sometimes be let live.

He looked idly at the loran. The numbers glowed within it. He knew quite well what it was, how it worked – though he had only seen them used, not used them. He was curious as to where they exactly were in relation to the rendezvous. The thought of poring over a chart made him almost vomit. He got up at once to do it. He would not let sickness master him.

He found the rendezvous marked. Found Niolon. Found no course line drawn between them. That, he

177

thought odd. He found the parabolic lines, minutely numbered, of the loran coordinates on the chart. He began laboriously checking them against the numbers on the machine. He fought back bile. And he had got it wrong. He began again. The same. His eyes began to harden, his fist to clench. He checked again the tiny charted numbers. No mistake. And the machine. The same. They were kilometers off course on a totally false bearing. He did not understand. He had trusted no one. The rendezvous had been set due south so that the course could easily be checked. He had seen the compass. It had rocked, but it had rocked around due south. He looked at the console, thinking fast. A smiling little fish – he had seen them in cheap shops – seemed suddenly grotesquely out of place among the serious wood and brass, the dials and meters. He touched it. It moved beneath his finger. Magnetic, he supposed. Magnetic? He snatched it up. Released, the compass swung. Khamal stood rigid, kneading the fish in his hand. And then he gently put it back. And then he smiled.

He went to the bunk room. Like a good officer, he spoke gently to his burned commando. He told Stognacci and the two guards to go forward to the wheelhouse – he would tend the man. He leaned over the commando.

"Tell me," he said, "exactly how it happened."

Deep in morphine, the man murmured, "It burned."

Khamal took the man's mouth and softly cupped it with his hand. Then his palm hovered over the man's back, seeking the deepest burns. He brought it down with all his force, three times. The man bit, convulsed, screamed into his hand. His eyes started from his head. Slowly, Khamal released his mouth. He softly said, "If I have your attention now, please tell me more."

When they closed with the steamer – she looked like a small black spider stuck to the edge of the black sea – it was 1:42, twelve minutes past rendezvous. *Not bad,*

Massoun thought. All had gone well. When he had climbed out of the engine room with his guard and gone to the wheelhouse, there had been anxious minutes while he looked for a chance to shift the fish to its new position by the compass. Khamal had been too attentive. But at length he looked away. Massoun had made the switch, his heart in his throat that every eye in the wheelhouse would spot it. Of course nobody had. So he had turned by 40°, the compass showing 10°. Khamal had asked at once why the sea seemed easier.

"We drifted during the repair," Massoun had said. "This course is changed a little. It makes a difference."

And Khamal had nodded thoughtfully and almost courteously said, "Of course. How foolish of me."

When they left the steamer, it was 3:45 – two hours both heart-stopping and endless. It was much too rough for this. Even in the lee of the steamer, the seas were rising to two meters and more. Her rusted plates, her jagged rivets, rushed appallingly up and down beside them, like a freight elevator driven by a madman. It had been a dreary, endless, wet succession of lurches, sudden tearing impacts, falling, cursing men, cables dangerously slack then suddenly string-taut and flying off the deck. He admired these Palestinians. Four of them had worked, including the one he would have thought too sick to stand. It would have been rough for seamen – even Stognacci had panted and cursed. He had even forgotten they were enemies. For a while, as his boat reared and staggered like a frightened horse beside an elephant, he had been as solicitous of them as of his boat. They had become his crew. He had yelled a warning when a cable had looped around a guard and threatened to tighten and tear him apart.

He has also done his job. The steamer was old and small. She was typical of the ships of family Arab shipping lines – a tramp steamer, certainly pre-war, most likely British built. Such ships were being squeezed off the seas by fast, efficient competition. Even with Arab wages, it was hard to run them for a profit. Her name had been blacked out. He could not see her colors.

But she was Arab. And her crew. The yelling back and forth had left no doubt of that. North African. There might be Palestinians on board, but the working crew, he was sure of it, was Berbian or Moroccan.

But there was one other thing. As they closed and were recognized, he had heard a cry from the bridge and an answer blown in the wind, in a language he did not know at all. Later he decided, Russian. It never came again. Dr. Donnelly would be most interested.

It was behind them now. Empty, his boat rode even worse, insanely, like a cork. But the sea was on their quarter, so the effect, in sum, was equal. He had pocketed the fish in the confusion of transloading and the compass now read true. In an hour they would see land – see land, not lights, for the dawn was on its way to save him, dawn and the morning fishing traffic heading out. Khamal had questioned the passing time, had even fretted. But he had not been suspicious. He was not a fool.

The hillsides of Provence looked sweet, though their scent was blown before him. He was in the bay, the breakwater two hundred meters ahead. There were boats and men. In the bay, as in all inlets, the seas were tricky, steep. He steered with attention.

He rounded the mole. The boat gave a final pitch. Then steadied. He picked a course through the crowded harbor. The wharf was twenty meters. The boat coasted, crept. He spoke, without turning to Stognacci, telling him to go on deck. In reply, Stognacci gurgled.

He turned, surprised. In the back of the wheelhouse, in the shadow, Stognacci was supported by a guard. His shirt was crimson. Then Massoun saw the arterial blood pumping from Stognacci's throat, saw the knife glimmer, saw Stognacci drop and die. He jumped from the wheel toward the deck. The back of his head exploded. The world went dark.

He was awake, It was dark. He was bound. It stank of fish. His head was split. He was sick. He was in the moving truck. He thought, and he was terrified.

Something was wrong. If they had decided simply to dispose of him, it would have been done as to Stognacci, quickly, at the end. They would not cart him around alive. They must suspect. Or know. And they must mean to find out more. He had a sense of physical compression. His flesh crawled. He was an officer of the King, a Sandhurst gentleman. These were the vermin who sought to poison his Arabia, to tear down every fair and decent thing, Ghadaffi's friends. If his poor body stood between them and what they needed to know, his poor body would stand. He began to drive, as with a hammer, all knowledge of Dr. Donnelly, of his mission, from his head. He was a wharf rat, a smuggler, a petty criminal only, a Moroccan named Mohamet Gibran. Perhaps he could fool them. Perhaps it would not be so bad. Though he was not his good servant, surely God would look with grace upon him. They were on the same side. He found tears in his eyes.

He felt traffic, a city. They were going to Marseilles. The streets became steep and slow. They stopped, reversed, stopped again. He heard the scrape and bang of a freight door opening. They reversed again. Then stopped. The door slammed shut. Footsteps. The truck was opened. He was pulled to his feet.

He was gagged but not blindfolded. They seemed to be in the service quarters of a filthy hotel. Then he realized. They were back at the Rabat, the brothel. It was their safe house.

Two guards pushed him up the stairs. It was early morning, of course, no customers. Khamal selected a door at random, opened it. On top of a ruinous bed, a woman lay naked, sleeping, Khamal said, "Out!" In stupefied sleep, she did not wake. One of the guards went across and kicked her. She opened her eyes, numbed, resentful, incurious. The guard repeated,

"Out!" She crawled off the bed and sat collecting herself on its edge, then stood up and blindly shuffled from the room. Khamal shut the door. The room stank like an animal's cage.

Khamal said, "Undress him." They pulled the clothes off him, cutting them where he was bound. He wanted either to cry or to be sick. Besides the bed, the room had a wooden bench. Khamal said something else. They tied him to it, his legs apart.

Yamadi, who had come in last, said in a bored way, a formality, "We know that you are not what you say you are. We discovered your trick with the compass. We want to know who you work for, what they know, what you were told, and what you had found out. We want to know why you wanted to follow us, how you heard of us, and what you think we are."

He took an object from his pocket. "This is a cyanide capsule. If you tell us what you know, honestly, you will be given this capsule and you will die painlessly, at once. If you do not tell us, in a few minutes this capsule will seem to you the most precious thing on earth. It will be kept where you can see it."

One of the guards went behind him. They changed the gag so it could be loosened or tightened at will. It was loosened. Massoun took a breath and said, "I know nothing. I am just a smuggler. I did nothing to the compass. You are clients like any others."

Khamal shrugged. He tightly bound Massoun's hands together in at attitude of prayer. He forced thin triangular blades of metal between his fingers. Then he threw his weight on them and began to grind them to and fro. Massoun leaped up, screaming, dragging the bench. The gag tightened. Khamal said, laughing, "Come, come now. That was hardly serious."

Yamadi said, "Now you have saved your honor and you can talk to us. Sooner or later you will certainly talk to us."

He heard his voice say, "I have nothing to say."

182

They were doing something between his legs. There was a wire. A guard, the one he had called to about the table, began to crank a handle. A knife began in his testicles and rushed up his spine. They released the gag for him to vomit and tightened it before he could scream. He no longer knew whether he was screaming or not. His brain thudded, "I am Mohamet Gibran. I am Mohamet Gibran." He thought he sometimes said it.

The wire went away. His legs were tied apart still wide. He could not breathe very well, so he gasped and panted. He saw Khamal come back with a small household hammer. He understood and began to scream before it happened. When it did happen, he found his lungs were not big enough for his screams. The world was crimson. Sometimes he had to draw in breath and cry, "Gibran. Gibran." Later, Khamal took a blowtorch, but by then he could not see.

By the time the house opened, the room was needed, he was dead.

13

Ibrahim came alone, black-robed, a mullah. In the lobby
of the Institute of American-Islamic Relations – it was a
high, softly echoing, octagonal room, floored with blue
Moroccan marble, and bearing on each of its cool white
walls, like a jewel lit from deep inside, an antique
Bokhara, Ghiordes, or Saruk – he passed, cadaverous yet
stately, a pious and proper figure. He inquired for the
whereabouts of the meeting on tourism to holy places.
The Institute had been set up in 1974, primarily with the
funds of American foundations, to foster American-
Islamic understanding. Though its funds were from Ford
and Du Pont, though it was registered with the IRS as a
tax-exempt charity, though it was listed by the State
Department as a suitable recipient of voluntary foreign
aid, its management was impeccably Third World.
Americans, it was felt from the first, had no business
setting the context for Arab-American "understanding."
Palestinians for Peace often used its conference room
when their own facilities seemed inappropriate. Especially since 1978, when the *Washington Post*, striking one
of its most vigorous blows for liberty, had revealed – the
result of a carpenter's felicitious clumsiness – that the FBI
had even reached into this haven of understanding and
respect with its bugs and probes. Heads had rolled. It
was very certain, now, that the bugs were gone.

If the lobby could have served as the Great Hall of a
modern palace (today only the Arabs understand royalty)
then the conference room was the *cabinet* of an urbane
and feline minister. An Iranian influence prevailed

The floor was wholly a mosaic of a Persian hunting scene. Over the head of a whimsical prince was set, in proletarian justice, the chair of Sasha Pritkin, of Aeroflot and KGB. He looked up at Ibrahim with soft goat eyes and the mouth of a youthful loanshark. He wore the blazer of an airline eager to please, eager to convey to holy places. Jonathan Snead had his back to the window, to the fountain, to the river, to the grand tranquillity of Washington Cathedral. At their first meeting, Ibrahim had brought away a sense of cold, metallic conviction, of unquestioned strength – the only potentially frightening American male he had met. Today – he saw it as soon as he, the latecomer, came into the room – Snead looked strained and shabby. Across from him, perched at a table with a secretarial pad, was Julia Drew. The pad, the office-girl prop, was purely provocative. She looked like a young leopard. He had watched bemused four hours earlier as the tailored silk blouse, satirically prim, falling over her perfect torso, had not veiled her energy or allure but simply carried it, mockingly, into the civilized, sane world. It was she, the luminousness of her skin, the glory of her hair, the sweetness of her breath, that made Snead look worn and cheap. That was sexual, but there was more; in the light of her awful innocence Snead was sourly, and, alone in the room, a traitor.

But it was Khalid Merak, executive director of Palestinians for Peace, who began this meeting. He was the spirit of the room. He had been one of the earliest resources of urbanity within the old dusty ranks of the PLO. He could have passed for a Gulf States minister shaped by Oxford out of oil.

He raised a Mont Blanc fountain pen from a tiny leather notebook and he said, "Mr. Shamak comes alone by our instruction. It is not convincing for a religious enthusiast, however revolutionary, to spend very much time with the PLO, and even the American press knows this. He will not be seen with us for the remaining two days of his stay. I think that we have all met and that it is unnecessary for me to emphasize that although Mr. Shamak was not born a Palestinian, he occupies a position requiring more daring and skill than any PLO member – outside, perhaps, or our armed teams operating within Israel itself. Nor that he is the prime mover in our attempt to make of Berbia the secure base, safe from the Israeli army, that we so imperatively need. Nor," and here he nodded to Sasha Pritkin, "that he is your prime hope in your struggle to prevent the growth of an American armed presence in western North Africa and of your efforts to add Berbia to the socialist camp. I sincerely consider it an honor to have been Mr. Shamak's host. What shall we call you, sir? That, or Imam?"

Ibrahim said, "Imam is better. I shall be going back to my people soon. It has been confusing to listen to Americans calling me 'Mullah,' as though I were a Persian. I thank you for your welcome. The trip has gone well. Even excellently so far. I hope that today will crown it."

Khalid Merak opened his hands toward him, a small, gracious offering of air. "And so do we all," he said. And then, in a voice with the soft authority of a cello, "And now to *Lyusi*. As with everything about this project, we have little time and much to do. Mr. Pritkin, you may be at a disadvantage here, for you have worked with this project a shorter time than the rest of us – though that is short enough. Is there anything you immediately wish to be told?"

Sasha Pritkin, in his aged twenties, did his best to be a resigned uncle among rash young things. "Moscow Center would particularly like to know," he said, "why the central project in the destabilization of a pivotal nation has been evolved at such frantic speed that security has suffered in places. But I will let that pass. At least I would like to understand the code name. It does not seem random. Why is a project to undermine the loyalty of the Berbian army through a misaccredited action named *Lyusi*?"

Twice as avuncular, Merak chided him gently. "You should know more of your Berbian history. Lyusi was a marabout, a saint. In the sixteenth century he successfully opposed the Sultan Mulay Ismail, who had sold his country's loyalties to the Western Emperor. Many of Ismail's soldiers followed Lyusi. Most did when the Sultan set out to persecute the saint. And Lyusi's *sayyid*, his tomb, on the day of the yearly pilgrimage to it, is where the event will take place. It reveals not too little but too much, which is why we use it only among ourselves. And I will answer your first question, too. It is being done quickly because it was not thought of sooner. And it can only be done on one day in the year. And to wait another year is to wait for the Americans to become established too firmly. There is an honest answer for Moscow Center."

Ibrahim took it up. "And the loyalty of the army must be destroyed. The Brothers of Islam can raise mobs forever, can frighten the merchants into dealing with the Baath, but with the army firmly behind King Fahd it is all meaningless. Remember Iran. The Shah survived twenty years of hatred without a bead of sweat on his brow until the day the army wavered. We make other efforts with the army. We sow converts here and there. The Brothers have some influence already in the barracks. But that is all too slow. By the time that it succeeds the Americans will be there with a base to protect and they will send an army to protect it. It is not as though Carter were still the President. *Lyusi* will fill the common soldier with such revulsion for the King he serves that the whole edifice will come down at once. With the army gone, the PLO and the Baath can control Berbia as well as anyone else – but the army must go."

Sasha Pritkin irritably nodded. "Of course that is fundamental. We had a revolution in Russia once. Have you succeeded in obtaining the supplies you need?"

Ibrahim said, "With difficulty. In haste. At some risk. With less ease that if you had furnished them. We know that you have a stock of these weapons."

And Pritkin, who had already learned very well the Soviet bureaucrat's heavy-mouthed, walled face, tapped his notepad with his pen top. "There will be no connection with your project that could by any possibility whatsoever become known. Experience has taught us that the PLO will be forgiven anything by its apologists and that it has no reputation to lose among its enemies. You could recover from this if it became known. For us to be connected with it would be unthinkable. The Soviet security organs wish your project well, but the decision to supply no matériel was taken at the highest level. Most of our Western weapons are of Vietnamese provenance and are not always identical to NATO issue. We do not know to what extent the CIA is able to trace the NATO weapons we do in fact possess. The KGB will supply security information and will participate in disinformation and publicity, but that is all. All. All. I repeat my question, Imam. Have you obtained the supplies you need?"

Ibrahim, now toneless, official, replied, "A first shipment has been sent. It comprises about sixty percent of the light arms required, including mortars. It has not been without incident, but I will return to that later. It does not include the armored car. There were not sufficient funds or shipping space for that. Since you are not guaranteeing us, we have been required to pay in full and at once. The funds that I have received from the American churches will be available for transmission to the Bank of Valletta in two days, then to our financial man in Geneva, and will be available for the second purchase in a week. That will be shipped immediately. The first shipment has already been received in the Khannafi family warehouses. Since you are taking it upon yourself to ask these questions, may I in turn ask if you have produced the security data we required? It is already late."

Jonathan Snead moved as though to speak, but Pritkin silenced him and said, "By all means we will talk about security – but we will talk about yours first. You spoke grandly of your financial man in Geneva. I have no knowledge of this. Is this man trustworthy? Who is he?"

Khalid Merak answered, "I can perhaps answer that better than the Imam. He is not trustworthy. It is simply that he knows nothing and cares less. He is a private investment consultant specializing in Arab clients. His name is Giovanni Stears. He handles all kinds of Middle Eastern accounts, and in that business one does not ask questions. He is too successful to be stupidly inquisitive. Our business will be no odder than much that he handles. Besides, he is more or less a stateless person – a sort of Italian-French-American – a luxurious bourgeois with no loyalties."

Pritkin said, "Nonetheless, we will take a look at him. Have you any reason to suspect attempted penetration during the buying or shipping operation?"

Ibrahim, now with the dogged confidence of the remotely uneasy, replied, "In the end, no. But that is what I must return to. Our team in France, who are, as you know, Hussein Kebbaj and Abdelatif Zebdi, Dr. Habbash's people working as Hussein Yamadi and Hussein Khamal, were operating under the cover of Berbian heroin entrepreneurs seeking a smuggler. One was eventually recommended to them. They had expected this to happen, but the contact was an unusual one and came rather quickly. They thought at first that Amal Khannafi had talked without their knowledge, but Zebdi attended to him for a day and decided that that was not so. There were limits, of course, as to how far he could go with young Khannafi. The smuggler, however, appeared legitimate and satisfactory. His name was Mohamet Girban, a Moroccan. The KGB in Paris knew a little of him, but nothing that was bad. He clearly knew the work. But during the passage out to the ship, Zebdi discovered that he had taken intricate pains to examine the cargo. There is no doubt that he discovered its nature. I am assured that it is at least unusual for a professional smuggler to take such an interest, though I am also told that some may have contracts with major gangsters to discover all they can. He could not, of course, be allowed to live, but Zebdi, very wisely, did not reveal that he had discovered him and let him transload the cargo as planned. Afterwards, he examined him. I have seen Zebdi at work on a spy for the Israelis once at our training camp, and, to be honest with you, in thirty minutes I began to vomit. The smuggler did not give up any information that suggested he was anything beyond a criminal with the hope of collecting a payoff for his inquisitiveness. The conclusion is almost inescapable that he had no other information to give. It is hardly improbable that the underworld would want to know about a new operation in the heroin trade. Zebdi does think that his name was not Gibran and that he was not a Moroccan. But that came at the end when the man was more or less insane, and it does not mean much – all these gangsters have various names and identities. I would say, then, that penetration has neither been attempted nor effected, for that was the only dubious contact. But we would feel much safer if we had the details of the CIA expatriate surveillance operation in Paris. We know this to be formidable and we are carrying out a difficult and dangerous operation in its immediate vicinity. I had been told that I would receive this today. Am I to be disappointed?"

Pritkin said, "No."

Jonathan Snead turned in his chair toward Ibrahim and then winced as the sun, which had climbed above the cathedral, struck him in the eye. Under his feet, in mosaic, a stag stood beside a forest full of golden birds. His shoes were blunt and scratched, but his head, with the light behind it, was dark and the features indistinguishable. His voice, however, suggested complacency.

"Exposing a CIA network is not always quite as easy as opening a newspaper, though it may be one day. I want you to understand that we have made your business the main assignment of a source that took luck to find and a great deal of skill to cultivate, and that we have exposed him on this business to an unprecedented and dangerous degree. This is not all we have done. We have an agent of sympathy, a Mason Salfield, on the House Armed Services Committee, whom I have coerced into a position far more exposed than he realizes, providing very delicate data on the covert Berbian aid programme. He would have lasted forever as an agent of sympathy, but he will not last like this and I have in effect sacrificed him to *Lyusi*. We have your answer. We have it at some sacrifice. The PLO should remember that it is again in the debt of the Soviet Union." He possibily smiled. "The fraternal debt."

"Our initial information was that the CIA's Arab expatriate surveillance in France was the work of one officer and one only. We did not immediately believe this, and there was some delay, and some further risk exposure while we had this confirmed for you. It appears to be the truth. The operation consists of a deep-cover career officer. It is an unusual operation in that the officer both pursues intelligence himself and controls agents. The agent network appears to be fairly extensive but not highly paid. This officer's expense claims vary between $1000 and $3000 a month, so his agents must either be of conviction or not highly placed. The officer appears to be given considerable latitude in running his operation. That suggests a high degree of success in past operations as well as this one. We do not know the officer's past assignments. Indeed, we do not know his real name – even with high-level penetration it is difficult to match a CIA officer's real name with his cover name and it will take us a few more days to do this. The cover name is James Donnelly, Ph.D. His cover legend is a left-wing American academic, resident in Paris, specializing in Arab subjects. He has a reputation as an anti-Zionist. He receives a genuine study-grant but he is on the borderline between academic and journalist. He has obliged a

191

number of expatriate activists by publishing sympathetic profiles in the Western press. He is well know in Arab circles and enjoys if not respect, at least a high degree of tolerance. He frequents cafés in the Arab quarter and is often ready to do small errands for money, of which he seems in need. Many Arabs seem to enjoy using an American as a lackey. He lives on the Rue Burq. There are more details, but those are the main ones. He has held this assignment for five years. The KGB is in the process of reconstructing what this man has discovered. There is too much already. It is fortunate that it is now over."

Ibrahim, at the name of Donnelly, had felt disaster lurch, but as long as Snead was talking he had held the thought with effort that the names could be merely similar, that he could have remembered wrong, that it could not have happened. But as the voice ended in this self-satisfaction, the thought clattered to the ground. He looked at Merak, blandly interested, and at Pritkin, primly in control, and he forced himself to say, "There is one more detail. It is Dr. Donnelly who made contact with Kebbaj and Zebdi and furnished them with their smuggler. Our shipping firm has been the CIA."

He turned to Sasha Prikin, speaking to the small, unforgiving mouth. "You will be interested to hear that KGB Paris was asked about Dr. Donnelly. We have done nothing without the advice of our Soviet brothers. Vyacheslav Frolov had investigated him in 1980. As a matter of fact, I have the exact phrase Frolov used, for it happened to catch Kebbaj's fancy. He called him 'a typical left-wing American clown.' "

But Pritkin, who would perhaps go far, managed without a second's pause, "Moscow will not be impressed by an operation with so total an absence of safeguards." He contrived even a self-satisfied sucking motion of his lips. "Perhaps you can get away with this kind of thing in the Lebanon. Have you any plans to get out of the trap you have dug for yourselves, or will that be KGB's role?"

Which was fielded gracefully by Merak, who pleasantly said, "Let us at least be sure we are in a trap. What does the CIA know? Did this smuggler avail himself of a break in Zebdi's ministrations to telephone his control? I doubt it very much. Let us be sure that we know where we stand. The CIA has suspicions, but that is its job. It does not immediately seem likely that it has knowledge. We do not know yet how these suspicions arose or what their nature is, but perhaps with calm thought we can reach some conclusion. Let me ask you this, Comrade Pritkin. The American government does not like drugs. If the CIA accepted the story of drugs, would they investigate on that basis?"

"No."

"So they suspected something else. But the beauty of *Lyusi* is that it is so improbable that nobody would quickly imagine it unless they knew of it. And until the very moment of the event, the truth of *Lyusi* will be known to hardly a dozen people outside this room. I am willing to say to you categorically that the CIA does not know of *Lyusi*. I believe that the most they could know is that allies of the Baath are smuggling weapons into Berbia. That can hardly be news to them, though it is naturally a matter of interest. I doubt, in fact, that they know that much about this particular shipment. They most likely only know that somebody is shipping weapons, perhaps to Berbia. That is a thousand miles from *Lyusi*."

Ibrahim, who had not achieved urbanity, said, "But what if they know that they are NATO weapons? This could lead the CIA to *Lyusi*. After the event, it is true, but that could be even worse."

Julia, not really with conviction, simply like someone saying the nearest thing to a witticism at an awful moment, said, "Not that anyone ever believes them."

And was smiled at beatifically by Merak, as at the brightest pupil.

He said, "That is half of what I was going to say. If the CIA did suspect the fact of *Lyusi*, there is little they could do – short of a signed confession from each of its participants. *Lyusi* is primarily an exercise in disinformation. The CIA would hardly be believed in Berbia, even if anyone was listening. In America, an allegation by the CIA as strange as *Lyusi* would be laughed at automatically by every serious medium. If the CIA cannot get attention by a quite adequate proof that its adversary is applying neurotoxin to much of Southeast Asia, it is unlikely that it will get far with our little *Lyusi*. And King Fahd is the kind of American ally who is blamed in advance by Americans of conscience for anything that anybody chooses to allege of him. Mr. Snead can publish whatever we decide in his magazine and it will eventually come to be believed by every American who can write a coherent letter. Secrecy is indeed vital with *Lyusi*, but let us not be too alarmist. But this is jumping ahead, for I do not suppose that the CIA does not know that these are NATO weapons. I think this: that they are possibly beginning to become aware that more NATO weapons than usual are missing and that they would like very much to know where they are going. Our shipment was one possibility among many. They would have known if their man had survived. Now they do not know. We have had a brush with danger. But we are not caught."

He let it hang there. The sense of disaster gathered itself slowly up and floated from the room.

Sasha Pritkin said to Ibrahim, "At least you can now understand why there could be no direct involvement with the KGB."

But it lacked force, it slipped off the side of Merak's unctuousness, and Ibrahim wasted no time on it, answering instead, "Who should eliminate Donnelly? Your people or ours? Zebdi is talented, I assure you."

He saw Julia lean forward and her face come beautifully to life. But Jonathan Snead abruptly said, "You can't touch him. Not in Paris. Absolutely not."

And Sasha Pritkin said, "I agree."

Snead went on precisely and urgently, "This man's

cover has survived for five years. Our source had to take extraordinary action to obtain it. That is to say, he had to act outside of his normal role to do so. This is dangerous in itself. We are not dealing with an expendable source. The KGB cannot allow this officer's execution to be associated with our source's acts."

Pritkin, listening carefully, nodded, satisfied, and flatly added, "*Lyusi*, in fact, is of lower priority than the integrity of this source."

Merak attended graciously and gently said, "But he must, after all, be stopped. We can hardly expect him to let Zebdi and Kebbaj alone now that his agent has vanished, and Kebbaj and Zebdi must make another shipment. He is much too likely to find them again. Let us all think. We must be creative now. Pritkin, have you nothing positive to suggest today? It is, after all, your trade." He looked pleasantly around.

Pritkin primly said, "My trade is also to find out how this Donnelly found your people. He seems to have been waiting for them in Paris. That is either remarkably unlucky or slipshod even by your standards. This is the first I have heard of your 'financial man' in Geneva, this Stears, who was certainly not cleared by us. I shall need full details of this later." *A nice job for Yuri Chestnoy*, he thought – *KGB in Geneva and he even looks a little like a rich investor.* "As to Donnelly, yes, if he could be induced to step outside of his cover, to expose himself, he could be eliminated safely. That is theory. I do not know how it would be accomplished."

But this idea, for the first time, found no one to take it up. Merak, managing the benign expression of one who has walked into a restaurant nicer than he expected, drew neat, small patterns with his fountain pen. Snead looked sulky and determined, as though he had with difficulty saved a dear possession and expected it to be grasped at again. *Americans*, a KGB officer had once told Ibrahim, *are formidable but they conspire like dogs walking upright: it is not done well and one is surprised to see it done at*

195

all. It fell terrifically on Ibrahim that, concerning *Lyusi*, he was the leader, the man most at risk in a plan whose daring and enormity made him sometimes cold and that his closest and safest collaborators, in this close, safe room, were concerned with jealousies and poses and protecting other squares of turf. His eyes were taken by the floor, by the crimson saddle of a prancing steed, and he made himself search for its full pattern. Two parties of princes, trailing bannerettes like comets, had driven a lion, a stag, an onager, and a unicorn against the walls of a pleasance in a wood and were commencing a gay and witty massacre. Beyond the forest lay the royal arms of Iran. He played with that omen, whether it was good or bad, gave it up, and idly said, "He could easily be killed in Berbia."

To which Sasha Pritkin, loving his own obviousness, replied, "But he is not there."

Khalid Merak said softly to his pen. "But he might be."

He let it float in silence and then with growing emphasis went on, "We do not know very much about this man, but we can guess that he is dedicated, self-reliant, and unconventional. We do not know much about his operation except that it seems, like much of the CIA, somewhat underfunded and undermanned. There is one thing we do not know at all. We do not know how seriously he or his superiors take the business of the pair they know as Yamadi and Khamal. Berbia must be worrying them a great deal. Even if the importance they attach to this arms shipment is relatively small – and it may well be – it is possible that they would risk much for the chance of being led to the heart of things in Berbia. An intelligence service that has lost its eyes in a sensitive place may grasp at desperate expedients. I think that if Zebdi and Kebbaj were to make themselves easy to follow now, our Dr. Donnelly might perhaps follow them, even to Berbia, so long as they were careful to appear to know nothing of him that he has not told them himself. He might have misgivings – he is certainly no fool – but I suspect that in certain circumstances this man might follow even with considerable misgivings."

Sasha Pritkin said, "He would never do so. That is outside his station. He would go to his superiors and put the matter in their hands. They would perhaps assign an agent."

Merak looked at him with caressing affection. "That is what you would do, Sasha, I am perfectly sure. But, Sasha, this man may not be like you. He may not be like you at all."

Pritkin now looked sulky.

Ibrahim said, most of all to Jonathan Snead, "Believe me, I understand what you have said. But in al-Tabek a dozen reasons can be found to kill this man. If nothing else, a street robbery – they are common enough by now. And suppose that his superiors do think that he was killed for what he really is, would they not surmise that he was discovered precisely *outside* of his covered role? Surely that is more likely than that his colleagues betrayed him? Merak is right. Let us try this. He may not follow. But if he does, it will be our privilege to destroy a man who is dangerous to us both. Let us try."

He had pitched it so, for he had expected Snead to doggedly resist. But the features that he could not quite see had changed during Merak's description to something that resembled a contemptuous distaste, a jealous anger. Ibrahim suddenly thought, *I would not trust this man in danger.* And when he answered, Snead's voice held greed.

"If you make him break his cover you can do what you want. Maybe your Zebdi could work him over first. He's got a lot we'd like to know."

Merak said carefully, "That would be ideal. But this man is not gullible. He is no fool. He would treat Zebdi with great care. We must think of this at leisure. And Sasha, yes, we must indeed also try to reconstruct how it was that Donnelly became concerned with Zebdi and Kebbaj at all. But just to kill a man like Donnelly will of

197

itself not be easy. We will need someone in Berbia who is above suspicion."

Julia stirred. Ibrahim, across the room, felt her light astringent scent at the edge of his senses. She spoke to him. Her voice was soft and shy.

"I could go to Berbia."

Her small teeth glistened through her parted lips and her eyes glowed.

"The highest likelihood is that he was terminated by the opposition within his cover. That is to say, they accepted him as a criminal for hire and preferred not to take the residual risk that he would talk about them. I always assumed that that might occur. In that case, my exposure is nil. Even if he was found examining the shipment, that is not outside the parameters of a criminal, apolitical, role. His extermination, of course, would then be assured. Even then, my exposure is minor. I put those aggregate probabilities at seventy percent. In my opinion there is a ten-percent aggregate probability of accident, unforeseen circumstance, or agent-turning – the last, in this case, very improbable. The residual possibility is that his criminal identity was never accepted or that he was efficiently interrogated. In that case, the Donnelly cover is largely exposed."

Reads nodded thoughtfully. He said, "That's objective."

But the little prick's not quite listening, McNaughton thought. *He doesn't entirely care. That's interesting.*

Reads went on. "Of course I can't speak for Jason, but my own feeling is, this operation's got to go on."

He could have spoken for Jason very easily.

Jason Witham said – the scrambler telephone giving his voice an additional level of artificiality – "One thing I can promise you, Michael, and you know me well enough for this. I'm not going to sit here and tell you how to run an operation in France. Wesley's a tiger and he'll give you all the help you need, but basically we're going to keep our hands off. You get the results, we leave you alone. Just one word I'm going to whisper in your ear: Tempo, Michael, keep the tempo going. Keep it going a little better than it's been. A lot of people are starting to notice Berbia now, and there's been a little disappointment that we aren't hearing more from you. So over to you, Michael. Over to you all the way."

This was after he had heard, with a silence much like Wesley Reads', that contact with Yamadi and Khamal was broken and that cover would have to be pushed as out of shape as a broken umbrella to reestablish it.

Before he left, McNaughton said to Reads, "Thanks for the gift. I want them tailed. Starting today. Found and tailed. Can we still do that?"

Wesley smiled charmingly. He smiled like Jason Witham. *Jesus*, McNaughton thought, *Do they teach it now?*

"Of course," said Wesley. "They'll be tailed. Good luck."

On the stairs of the St. Denis Métro station, at eleven o'clock at night, between a trampled McDonald's wrapper and an Arab addict crumpled against the wall, Khamal touched Dr. Donnelly on the arm. McNaughton blinked. He was required to believe one of two impossible things: that he had been tailed without knowing it; that the coincidence was real.

He said, as though searching his memory, "Ah, Monsieur Khamal. I remember our lunch. I hope your business was satisfactory."

Khamal said, "It is fortunate to meet you. We have more business for your friend. Perhaps you can help us again. We have failed to find him."

He had to raise his voice. Outside, a bus from Hamburg and a bus from Manchester ground forward in the direction of the Folies-Bergère.

"I regret that I have not seen him," McNaughton said. "You have had contact with him long since I have. He calls me when he will. He is rarely in Paris and I do not know his home in Marseilles. I am sorry that I cannot help you. In his business one must be discreet. I trust your arrangements with him were satisfactory?"

Khamal smiled. "They were highly satisfactory. But perhaps you will be able to help us after all. Perhaps you have other friends. We are often to be found at the restaurant Timgad, Rue Brunel. We are established in Clichy. This time our gratitude would be shown to you directly. The matter is somewhat urgent. Goodnight to you, Dr. Donnelly."

He smiled, hard and handsome as a stone Apollo. He was smoothly at the top of the stairs before McNaughton, bemused, heavy, had covered three steps. In the light of the Métro entrance, two fair-skinned shopgirls looked at him with pleasure. Khamal preened for an instant, for himself, then vanished into the crowd. At the top of the stairs, McNaughton stopped to cough. He looked to see if there were any of the Company tails he knew, or any tail, behind Khamal. There were not.

What was most strange, Khamal might have told one truth.

Wop Stears called from Geneva. The urbane voice was uneasy at the edge.

"They're back," he said. "Yamadi at least. He called me out to the airport."

"He came himself?"

"I'll get to that." Urbanity, with an effort, pushed out tension. "Business is booming. They got another $1.3 million last week, and my instructions were to switch it into bearer bonds and stir it around, the usual farce. And then where do you think they want it?"

"Marseilles."

"Metz."

McNaughton said, "North of France. Near the German border. Near NATO. But still in France and not so obvious as Strasbourg. Get around, don't they?"

Stears said, "Yamadi grilled me. He started off thanking me for the valuable introduction to the distinguished doctor. I looked perfectly blank, of course, and said, 'What doctor?' Then he went into his oily threat routine and said that I had spoken of contacts in Paris, I said, yes I had but there hadn't been any, it was just a chance and all that, didn't know they needed a doctor. Acutally, I think he believed me. He just looked surly. Then he gave me a present, nicely wrapped."

"Yes?"

"A photograph. Pompini drowning."

"Christ. They took a picture when they threw him in the river?"

"Oh, no. He didn't drown in any river. He drowned in a handbasin. There was an arm holding his head. With a towel. No bruises. They took him out to take the photograph. He wasn't dead yet."

"Did you recognize the room?"

"No, McNaughton, I didn't. Not even the basin. He had left by the time I had it open. I still think he believed me. This was just employee relations, I would say. On balance, I think it's good. He knows I'll be a good boy now."

He stopped and then he said, "I knew things like that happened. I did. But you wouldn't notice Yamadi, you see. He'll sit by someone in the airplane who'll never know. I never thought of that."

McNaughton had again the image of Stears standing in English shoes in a lobby brushed with the exhalation of Havanas, but this time he saw it with respect: for fear held in, for a sniper holding on in what was suddenly bad ground. There were pros and pros.

McNaughton said, but not dismissively, "That's the way it is. Khamal contacted me. He wants another contact in the ports. The best assumption is that he accepts my cover and Yamadi was checking you to be sure. So I'm agreeing with you, Stears. There are other possibilities, but that's the one I'll go with. I'm going to let it simmer as long as I can. We've got them under surveillance here. Might find something useful. God knows. Trouble is, Witham's breathing down my neck and I've got some sort of new control here whom I would professionally judge to be a little prick. We will do what we can."

He heard Stears say hesitantly, as though fearful of offending an etiquette he didn't know, "I'm sorry about your man."

"So am I. He was better than most."

"There's something else, McNaughton. This money's not Libyan and it's not KGB. This money's American. It

204

originated at the Chase. Now I have a friend at the Chase Manhattan and I called him and got a little digging done."

McNaughton said, "So whose is it? Teddy Kennedy's?"

"No," Stears said. "Before it was laundered it was the United Clergy Against American Militarism. A.k.a. lefties in the American Protestant churches."

"The KGB," said McNaughton, "can use anybody's lies."

Reads did not entirely fail him. Reports came in. Yamadi and Khamal really were seen in Clichy, the most decent of the Paris Arab quarters – a suburb, really, a small provincial town with three-story buildings, bakers' shops, and squares mysteriously, as for a surrealist movie, full of caftans. They operated their export-import business, still called Michelet et Cie., with its dusty office, a new secretary with bracelets and a downy lip, and even occasional clients. Its operations appeared to make no particular sense now – but small Arab businesses, in McNaughton's experience, usually did not. Most of the clients were unknown to the CIA; none had profiles beyond that of small-time left-wing nationalist hangers-on – and that was a category that included a fifth of Paris Arabs. So the business might, as far as it went, still be real; it might equally be the meeting place for new terrorists of an untraced crop.

Yamadi and Khamal went to and fro. They were seen at the offices of *Al-Watan al-Arabi*, the left-wing Paris Arab weekly – the only paper to which "Carlos" ever talked. They went to dingy political clubs with known KGB connections. They had the habit of making telephone calls from restaurants – rarely from the same restaurant. It was highly nonspecific. What was noticeable was this: they were easy to follow, but when it actually came to eavesdropping, to effectively tracing a call, then quietly and impenetrably they developed every trick in the

agent's book. He was being played with. They could
vanish at will. The days were passing. The shipment
must be close.

And then again, he might not be being played with at
all, for the veil was at least double. Their skill under
surveillance, their equivocality, could simply be the
constant mode of highly practiced clandestine agents –
and that, for sure, they were. The near certainty that they
had killed Massoun did not of itself negate the possibility, the probability, that they accepted Dr. Donnelly as
the character he was meant to be and thought that a
contact made through an American left-winger of unsav-
ory acquaintance and scrounging habits had certain
specific advantages in security over the available channels of the PLO. And Dr. Donnelly, those who knew him
well would know, would not be stopped by the suspicion
that they had killed one friend from offering up a second
one if the price were right.

In short, to believe in the trap he scented, he had to
disbelieve in his own cover, his own skill.

He went to the Timgad. The poor Arabs of Paris might
dine on grease among flies, but true terrorists ate well.
The Timgad was a richly Moorish fantasy and, predict-
ably, the only Arab restaurant in Paris to boast a Michelin
star. It was twelve o'clock. The Islamic bar had an
acceptable rye. He ordered it straight up. He waited.

This was not the trap. He had not the slightest doubt
that Khamal himself, or any faceless hit-man (and there
would be twenty or thirty of these available to the PLO in
Paris at any time), could have picked him off at will.
Whatever they wanted him for it was not, here and now,
a corpse. He sipped his rye. Above the sagging
shoulders, his mind, poised and elegant, sought in vain
the sweetness of lucidity. He was in the midst of a
quadratic equation. The available data yielded two
answers, one positive, one negative. The deciding
datum, given the skill of his opponents, would be
difficult or, soberly, without luck, impossible to get.

They were expected. They were Yamadi and Khamal. McNaughton was interested to learn that those names were in use in Arab Clichy. It suggested the imprecise possibility that those names were the only ones they used in Paris and that their role was perhaps of a greater secrecy than the PLO usually bothered, nowadays, to maintain.

They came straight to him, to the bar. They ordered nothing. His breath, he knew, smelled strongly of whiskey at a little after noon. He made his eyes vague.

Yamadi said, "You have found your friend? Or a new one?"

Dr. Donnelly gestured loosely, ending it at Khamal. He said, "Your friend spoke of a reward. Times are not the best. What would it be?"

Yamadi said, "What do you owe?"

"Three thousand francs would help." It sounded seedy and greedy, both.

Yamadi said, "Good enough. If you find us a good man, it is yours."

"I would not have to share it with him?"

"No."

"Then I will seek my friend Gibran."

Khamal said, "Look also elsewhere. It may be that you are right and that Gibran is very hard to find."

Dr. Donnelly listened with understanding and gave a crafty look. "It might have to be four thousand. I do not have an unlimited supply of friends."

Yamadi said, "Three."

Dr. Donnelly shrugged. "You will remain here in Clichy?"

Yamadi said, "No. We leave shortly for Marseilles. The business is there. It is much the same as the last time. You can find us there through this number: 33 19 84."

Dr. Donnelly said, "If I cannot find Gibran, I may have to go there myself. I have friends that I can find there. The ticket costs money. I do not have a car."

Yamadi said, "It costs three hundred francs. So you can well afford it, a rich man like you."

Dr. Donnelly said morosely, "I will try."

He left, abruptly. As an actor and a Catholic, it gave him pleasure to stick al-Fatah for two shots of rye.

Marseilles drew him in with dirty fingers. First, the gracious blue-gray hillsides set with cypress and tiled homesteads; then tangled industrial slum threading through the valleys like rising, dirty water; then a sour yellow haze on the right from the refineries around the Etang de Berre; then the shantytowns and stagnant ditches; then a ring of soiled white apartment buildings stuck harshly to the dry rock; then he was off the autoroute and in the clogged, hot, tawdry center of Marseilles. And yet McNaughton almost liked Marseilles. The Chicago in him responded to it. It was a city of shoulder and belly, greedy and crude, without pity, embarrassment, or grace. And it crawled with life. It was a city of whores, hoods, peddlers, even tramps, but not of beggars. Marseilles bellowed, snarled, cursed, and sneered, but hardly ever did it whine. He would take Marseilles over Georgetown any day. Stuck in traffic, he shifted behind the wheel. It had been a long drive from Paris. His neck was stiff.

He was here as a flatfoot. He had one agent, no other means, no plan. His aims were crude and broad: to get close enough to Yamadi and Khamal to discover, in descending order of importance, the nature, date, and destination of their shipment, their associates – if any – and why and how they had disposed of Massoun. Success was far from certain. They were not hiding from him. The fiction that he was finding them a captain – he had none – could be good for one more contact. In Marseilles, he had a few well-placed French friends. But he felt like a chessmaster shooting craps in the dark. Against killers.

Killers, he had no doubt at all. But a part of him had

208

begun to find them farcical as well – and that, he knew, was dangerous. He could not help it. The idea had grown in him of late that the inexorable and endless replication of "liberators," "armies," "gangs," "brigades," of shootings, kidnappings, kneecappings, blowings-up, of half-witted slogans, posturings, transparent lies, of brutalities and braveries crazy and grotesque, was in the end nothing but a ghastly joke and that he, and the world, would die at the hands of a Satanic children's party.

His contact number was a restaurant. Of course. The Piment Rouge. In the Arab quarter. Of course. The best. Of course. Yamadi and Khamal, he thought, were terrifying and tiresome, both at once.

Two prongs, elementary enough. He would go to the restaurant himself, direct contact. He would have the Company's general-purpose agent in Marseilles stake out the place and tail them after the contact. The Company's man, an ex-detective, Gaston Lacrampe, was competent, and a merely competent man, behind Yamadi and Khamal, would find out precisely what they wished him to. But if they accepted his cover, they would not expect a tail, and in Marseilles they might not expect surveillance at all.

So he sat at another bar. No rye at the Piment Rouge; he ordered Pastis. The barman poured, added water. The Pastis neatly performed its trick of turning from clear amber to cloudy milk. The barman crossed the room to telephone. So they had a photograph. Outside, across the street, Lacrampe sat in a neat blue Renault, a briefcase on his knee, a salesman busy with his forms. No Moorish efforts at the Piment Rouge. It was a tiled, cool, white, high-ceilinged place with solid tables under old white cloths. Four Marseilles businessmen, lunching early, sat at one table – munching jowls over good blue suits. The rest were empty. No place to hide.

For the first time, he felt at risk. He did not know why. Nothing had overtly changed. It was, he suspected, superstition. Paris, Paris itself, Paris physically, had

209

come to seem a part of his cover, a gray labyrinthine shell. He felt it dissolving under an alien sun. That was not intelligent.

Twenty minutes after the phone call, they came. Not far, then. Again no Khannafi. Yamadi sat on his left; Khamal, on his right. Both sat close. He felt the presence of Khamal like that of a German shepherd. He allowed himself to squirm.

Yamadi said, "What is his name?"

McNaughton said, "I do not have a captain yet. There are several I could see. I need money."

Khamal leaned closer. He said, "You came for nothing?"

It frightened him that he was pleased that he could whine. He said, "I have forty francs in my pocket after the train. I do not see why I should do your work for nothing."

Yamadi opened his wallet and flipped onto the bar two hundred-franc bills. "Now you have money. This will come out of the three thousand."

McNaughton let himself whine on.

"I need to know when and where you will be loading. The captain will need to know that."

With gratitude he heard Yamadi give the expected, the normal answer. "We will tell him that ourselves."

But then Khamal leaned closer and quietly said, "Why should not Dr. Donnelly know what he needs? I am sure that he would not betray us – we could so easily find him. Niolon. Tomorrow. At ten P.M."

McNaughton said, "That is a help."

Three possibilities. He decoded them as he raised the Pastis nervously to his lips. One: Khamal was indiscreet. Two: Khamal, secure in Dr. Donnelly's character, meant precisely what he said. Three: He was already halfway down a trap. He looked as though regretfully at the empty glass. He called the barman – another Pastis. The small ploy worked.

Yamadi said, "We have better things to do than watch

you drink. I expect success. I have already paid you money."

They left. He watched them through the window. Their car was parked fifty meters ahead of Lacrampe's on the other side of a one-way street – good placing, as luck would have it. Khamal drove. McNaughton drifted from the bar to the window, seeking a table. He could see the street for two hundred meters. Khamal placed the car in gear and scanned the mirror minutely. So he was on his guard for a tail. It could be habit. Lacrampe moved at the same instant – too soon. A man like Khamal would see that. The cars moved off, sixty meters apart. Lacrampe was out of luck. A traffic light changed to amber just before Khamal. He would go through it and Lacrampe could not.

But Khamal braked instantly, reflexes like a trigger, as no normal driver would. The car behind him hooted. Lacrampe caught up. The light changed. The cars drove off.

He expected a tail. He fed the tail. McNaughton, by a sudden light, saw the glint of the teeth of the trap. His priorities changed in an instant. It was now imperative, at whatever cost of compromise, to find out what had been done with Massoun. He would go knowingly into danger, but he was damned if he was going blind.

He heard later from Lacrampe. Yamadi and Khamal had gone to one of the lowest brothels of the Arab quarter. They had not come out. It was inconceivable that they had gone for recreation – they must be established there. The brothel would not be easy to open up. Expensive arrangements were in force. He knew that for a fact.

He went to the *Préfecture* – the seat and power of the Paris government. Two policemen in capes, sweating in the midday autumn sun, flanked a gracious gate of scrolled wrought-iron. In the courtyard was a ready phalanx of the slab-sided vans with barred windows and bristling

211

antennae that the French police use as flying fortresses. The scene was military. In Marseilles, the gloves are off. He was not stopped. Tweed coat, big shoulders, undeviating, unhurried stride, creased face and cool blue eyes subliminally murmured "cop." He picked an entrance. He was in a long, dim gallery of seventeenth-century stone, smelling of tobacco and lined every thirty meters with red fire buckets full of sand. He walked past a reception room with secretary to a door marked "private." He went in. François Peyrejac, assistant to the *préfet*, formerly of the SDECE and now effective representative of Paris in Marseilles, looked up from his desk without pleasure. His pleasure diminished. He said, "An American in need of assistance. You have lost your passport, perhaps? You cannot find your hotel? A taxi driver cheated you? Go away, Michael. The *Préfecture* does not deal with the CIA. You know that."

McNaughton said, "Disappearance. Ostensibly drug related. Pretend I am with the Bureau of Narcotics. An Arab you must know well. Massoun, Ali. But your narcotics people will not know the people who did this. This is armed destabilization of a French ally. Berbia. And it bears upon Morocco. The SDECE would love to know about it."

"And will it?"

"Not for two weeks or so. I need space. But it will. That will be the deal. You'll find out about it, François. All by yourself. That will be agreeable."

McNaughton had taken a seat. François Peyrejac looked at him down a sharp, thin nose. His Adam's apple rolled as he lightly sucked his pipe. They sat composedly at the desk, two senior professors at an excellent private school, entertaining a disagreement over the curriculum. Peyrejac's ashtray was several millimeters out of alignment with the blotter. He corrected it.

He said, "Circumstances?"

McNaughton said, "On the eighth, he was to have made contact with two men working as Hussein Khamal

212

nd Yamadi. I will give you Khamal's real name later. You
will know it. We do not know Yamadi's. He was to have
furnished his boat to take them and a cargo to a waiting
ship. The cargo was ostensibly drugs. We are assuming it
was guns. He was to investigate the cargo and report
back to me. I do not know the time or position of
rendezvous. I do not know the harbor where they
loaded. If you have a corpse that might be my man's, I
would like to know its condition. There is a small chance
he was interrogated."

Peyrejac said, sadly, sincerely, "You should not be
doing this on French soil. You should be working with the
Sûreté. We are not Latin America, you know."

McNaughton said, "I do know."

"Yes, you do. And our government is too fond of oil.
Offhand, I know nothing. We can look at the reports."

From the table by his desk, he took a stack of onionskin
copies of double-spaced paper typed in blue. He read
them from his lap, quickly, completely, the professor
justly judging papers. At one he made a bitter-face,
involuntarily clenched his hand. He laid it aside. He read
on. He finished.

He said, "There is only one. In all probability it has
nothing to do with you, but the possibility exists. You
can go and see. In fact, it will be your punishment for
disturbing my morning. Our deal is on?"

"Yes."

"Go to the *Charité*. Tell the police that you are author-
ized to question the woman Anna Merin. A nun will have
to be with you. In less than three weeks I will call for your
end of the bargain. But do not come back here. Now you
may read this. It is not pretty. On the other hand, much
of may be fantasy or spite. The police think so."

"The *Charité*?"

"The *Charité*."

Beside Michael McNaughton, the sister's shoes whispered
on the floor. The floor was bare. The walls were white.

213

The nun wore black. Michael McNaughton's stomac
clenched. He was being taken to the principal, Fathe
O'Shea. His hands flinched beneath the stick. He laughe
sourly to himself. He looked at the nun. Her face wa
kind – worn and solid as a well-scrubbed floor. Like Siste
Theresa, Math.

He said, "How was she found?"

"By the garbagemen, Monsieur. There are big garbag
cans behind one of the hotels on Belsunce. She wa
thrown behind them. They expected her to die befor
morning, you understand. She was bleeding very badly
That is quite commonly done when the girls are very sick
They do not like them to die in the houses. It make
trouble."

They passed a door open to the chapel. The huge, dim
space under Puget's dome waited, tremendous, like
silent bell. It had the terrible serenity of sufferin
accepted and resolved. Its parish had been of dyin
galley-slaves, syphilitics, beggars, prostitutes, and thieves

Double-spaced, in blue, the police report stampe
through McNaughton's memory. All at once h
perceived, like a boot in the stomach, that the real horror
began behind it. His own presence nauseated him an
he said, "She has recovered enough to be safely ques
tioned?"

And the kind face gently, appallingly, replied, "No
Monsieur, but I think she will die whether you question
her or not. The important thing is that she will die among
us, with God. If her talking to you will serve God's work
then she must do it. If it will not, then the sin is on you
soul. It is not one that I would wish to carry. Put the mask
on, please. There is severe anemia and no resistance t
infection."

Which was why, no doubt, she was alone. The nun'
chair, still warm, was beside her bed. He would have
guessed the woman was about forty-five. The medica
records estimated twenty-three.

Her face was dead. Chalk-white, except for a mask o

214

muddy blue around the eyes, fading toward each ear, and fallen-cheeked, it pointed to the ceiling, fragile and misplaced like a piece of broken figurine. The lips did not move when she breathed. On one exposed shoulder, flaccid skin appeared to be draped loosely over bone. He had the idea that if he took hold of it, it would come away like cheese. Her eyes were conscious and dead as lard.

The sister said, "This man must speak to you, my child. It is important. You must try to answer."

Quietly, nursing energy, she spoke. "Shit, they haven't finished?"

Quickly, McNaughton said, "The man who beat you, the second one who beat you badly, what did he look like?"

He thought at first that she spoke to the nun who stood by the bed, erect and gracious as a cypress. But it was only that her eyes did not move and she looked straight upward. She spoke as though from a laundry list.

"Oh, he was a handsome turd, that one. An Arab, like the Boss. Curly hair. He had beautiful teeth. Like a film star. He was tall. When he'd finished with me, he changed his shirt."

"Do you know what they call him?"

"One of those names they have. Ali . . . Abdul."

"Abdelatif?"

"Yeah. That's it."

"Did they ever call him Zebdi?"

"Yeah. Maybe. I don't know. Something like that, once."

"And the voice next door. The screaming. You are sure it was a man?"

"Oh, yeah. They had a guy in there. I thought it was the new man teaching one of the girls, at first, like he taught me, but they must have left the gag off once and I knew it was a guy. That's why I noticed. It was a guy in the van, too, the body. It had short hair. I noticed that, too."

215

"Can you tell me all of it. From the beginning. Like you told the other man?"

"Fuck, don't you ever get tired? You don't believe me, anyway. Not about the stiff. That's what the others said. They said I was trying to make trouble. They said we're all like that."

But somebody, he thought, *believed her. It got into the report.*

He said, "Anna, some of us believe you. We want to get that man. That Zebdi. If you help us, maybe we can. Wouldn't you like that?"

And for a minute he thought she wouldn't. Wouldn't bother. That she would just stop. That there was nothing left. That she would die, still breathing.

But for the first time she moved – shrugged – and said, even thoughtfully, "I'd like to get that guy. He didn't have to do it, see. Not like the Boss. He didn't have to. Well, it was like this. I was sick, see. I was bleeding and it hurt, and I said I wouldn't fuck. And the Boss said I was lazy and he beat me and I still said I wouldn't and he'd have let me off. But that new guy was there, he laughed and said the Boss was soft and he could make me do anything. That's what he said. And he said he'd show him how. So he beat me a new way. He had a sort of whippy stick with a steel ball at the end and he beat me over the kidneys till he was sweaty and I thought I'd die. Then he said he was going off that night but if I didn't work he'd beat me when he got back in the morning. And I said I would and he laughed and said, see, it was easy and went to change his shirt. So I worked that night but then I started bleeding really bad and fainting. And they locked me up that day and that's when I heard the noise next door and the guy screaming. But I didn't think about it much, you know, because I was in and out, sometimes I wasn't conscious. Then I came to and they had me downstairs at the van. I knew I was going to croak because that's what they do when girls aren't going to make it. It was dark in the van and I put my hand out and

216

there was a face and it was cold, you know, a stiff. A guy.
I guess it was the screaming guy. Then they dumped me,
you know. Then I was still alive and I was here. I don't
know where they put the guy."

His ears were ringing and his bowels were cold. He
saw that the sister was stroking the girl's hair, slowly,
with one hand. It was blond and thin. The exposed
shoulder shuddered. He gritted his teeth and said,
"Where was this house?"

"I don't know. On a narrow street, I think. I never
went outside. It must have been the Arab part. All we
fucked was Arabs."

There was nothing more. He needed to retreat into the
cool, clean rooms of calculation, to plot a path through
the wreckage of his operation, undisturbed by such of its
realities as the one on the bed. He allowed himself a
measured, seeing look. Death had become as unsurpris-
ing to him as the body of an aging mistress, but
decomposition could still shock. This, he said to himself,
had been made out of a living woman by craftsmanship
slower and more careful than that used upon Massoun.
And over both floated the face of Khamal/Zebdi, handsome, perfect, sure, and brave – the revolutionary, the
liberator, the new warrior.

He said to the nun, "That is all I need." He said to the
woman, "Mademoiselle, I thank you. We will do what
we can."

And, the last he saw of her, she shrugged.

He walked with the nun down the high white corridor.
An electrocardiograph, on a trolley, sat beneath a crucifix
of ancient, ebonized wood.

His escort said, "Pray for her, Monsieur. Pray even
if you are Protestant. God will be merciful, for she has
seen hell already. But hell is still upon her. It seeks its
own."

He said, "I am not a Protestant. I will pray."

Outside, he found a telephone. He called Peyrejac. He
said, "No good, but thanks for trying. Not my man. And

I'd say she's mostly lying. Maybe psychosis. Maybe spite. Not worth investigating, I'd say myself. But the deal's still on. Don't worry."

François Peyrejac said, "I understand. How kind of you. That is also of the deal? That she is lying? At least that she is lying for two weeks?"

"Right," McNaughton said. "You got it."

And that's all I need, he thought. *To have to keep the bastard safe from the French police.*

McNaughton was alone. Dr. Donnelly was a tattered rag blowing in the wind. The alien sun shone full upon him. He sat in the armchair of the second-class hotel room, rejecting the bed. It was very fortunate that he had gone to no hotel before the *Préfecture*, before the *Charité*. James Donnelly had been nowhere in Marseilles. Here, he was Michael McNaughton. He would be hard to find. The ceiling fan reminded him of Saigon. He switched it off. He analyzed the damage.

Anything that Massoun knew was known. To imagine otherwise was childish. Furthermore, what Massoun had said must now be assumed to be in the KGB computers. Not only did the KGB exact such tribute from the PLO, but the PLO's ability to analyze intelligence on its own was modest. Dr. Donnelly's brief life, then, was being combed with electronic speed.

But only Dr. Donnelly. The essential fact was that his cover was penetrated only through the very bottom, through Massoun. The lines that led upward from Dr. Donnelly to Washington were secure. McNaughton was secure. As McNaughton or as anybody else he had only to fear facial recognition. Dr. Donnelly's apartment, the tisane and the plants, even Glencora Palliser, unfinished on the shelf, his last five years, were gone like smoke. Dr. Donnelly could be examined with great profit for five years back. But at five years, he vanished. The Company knew its craft.

He still had regard for the Company but not for his

chief. Jason Witham was the new CIA, and between him and Witham was Wesley Reads. In the final stage of this operation, if he reported its present status to Reads, he feared a response in which craftsmanship would be swamped by appearances and greed. In particular, he feared an immediate and ill-crafted second identity. McNaughton was safer than that. The penetration of Dr. Donnelly had, absolutely, to be reported. But he could discover it next week.

As before in his career, he thought of his one high contact. He had one, higher than even the summits of the CIA, on the National Intelligence Advisory Board itself. Nelson Aldrytch had been his major in the OSS, had gotten this son of a Chicago Irish barman his commission, had given him his start in the earliest, formative days of the CIA. He respected Nelson Aldrytch as he respected few other men. At moments of crisis, of catastrophe, of doubt, the long equine face, known now from news photographs with Presidents, with secretaries of state, would float before him, remote and accessible. He had had no contact with him now for thirty years. He had thought of him in Saigon when his own intelligence conflicted with the entire framework of belief of the U.S. Command. He had thought of him a few years ago in Paris when the sudden activity around the obscure exile Ruhallah Khomeini attracted no interest, for the Shah was known to be secure. Nelson Aldrytch was not of the Company, but above it. McNaughton had resolved before, and he thought it even now, that when the day came on which he had to go outside the Company to do the Company's work, then his work was over. He let the old distinguished face drift further, out of sight.

On a certain level, he could still function. Visual surveillance. Back to the earliest beginning of his craft, the tail. He could find what Massoun was to have found. Had found. It was very possible that he would go no further. Khamal and Yamadi did not know what he knew. That was his strength. The Dr. Donnelly they

219

expected in their trap would vanish. McNaughton, unseen, would watch. He would go to Niolon.

He went shopping. He bought black shirt, black jeans, black sneakers. At a lingerie shop, he bought sheer black stockings, a rumpled old man with a sleek new mistress. He tried it on. He was a fat old punk. He put a stocking over his head. He was Black September.

He went to his suitcase. He took out a king-size can of Barbasol. He had not used it since Saigon. He unscrewed it from the middle. Inside it were miniaturized tools, the equivalent of stethoscope, thermometer, rubber mallet. He rejected a recorder with directional microphone. He rejected a voice-transmitting bug – nice but he lacked the backup to use it. He rejected a cyanide capsule, firmly. He took an optic probe and an 8mm camera with infrared film. He took the smallest signal transmitter with magnetic base. It could be quickly placed on a vehicle and allow it to be tracked, at least for a short distance. The little instruments were expensive, solid, good. They recalled his youth. He felt his craft quicken at its roots. He had never carried a gun.

He wrapped his new clothes around the instruments. As the sun set, he drove to Niolon.

It was a village still, under the Estaque hills, and it smelled of hillside herbs, not petroleum. From the television in the waterfront café came the tinny voice of the evening news. The hillside fell into the sea. The harbor – wharves and breakfront bulging into the sea – was below the main street, down stone steps for pedestrians, a ramp for trucks. He parked in a dim place a little way from the ramp, his Paris license plate against the wall, and changed into his seaside clothes, his black. He walked quietly toward the ramp. Three men lingered around one fishing boat, but the harbor was otherwise deserted and not well lit. Most of the boats had been in for two hours and a few would go out until dawn. There was a boat tied to the nearest wharf. He crept on board and lay on deck, right under the gunwale, safe from a sweeping light. He settled himself. It smelled sweetly of cleaned fish.

It was now 9:00 o'clock. He had long ago trained himself to wait. An hour was short. He lay still – movement could minutely rock the boat and a careful eye might see it. He kept his watch in sight. What happened or did not happen now would equally answer questions. If they did not come at all, that would at least suggest that their reliance on him for a captain was still real.

They came. At 9:53, the murmur of a throttled-down diesel came in from the sea. It was in the harbor. The deck under him shifted to its rippling wake. Its dark shape passed in front of him, no lights. It tied to the bollards at the farthest corner of the wharf. So they had a boat. Their need of him was pretense, an excuse for contact. And they knew his cover. And they waited for his tail. He gently raised his head. He had the impression that the captain was alone. He did not expect to recognize him. Boats were not McNaughton's subject, but this one seemed to be a Mediterranean fishing boat, fairly big, but designed for voyages of two hundred kilometers or less. Then there must be a steamer somewhere.

And then the truck. Headlights at the top of the ramp swept over the harbor at mast height, then plunged. A fish wholesaler's truck – FRANCOIS RIGAULT ET FILS, POISSONS ET FRUITS DE MER EN GROS – perhaps it was not even them. But it stopped close to the wall, within fifty meters of the boat. It was them. The truck could not be hidden; neither was it easy to see.

Four men in the cab. Khamal, Yamadi, and two tough young men. They opened the freight door. Three more jumped out. They stood in a circle, listening to instructions, dimly lit by one of the streetlights scattered thinly on the wharves. They had the general look not of urban guerrillas, but of troops – fit, uncomplicated, young. One of them shone a flashlight around the wharves. It was perfunctory, he thought, and that surprised him.

Khamal spoke to the captain on the boat. He could see

their arms gesturing like semaphores around the afterdeck. They were going to load on deck. No reason not to. The night was calm. But it suggested that they would unload again before first light.

The loading began, four men to a crate. The crates were wood, rectangular, about a meter and a half in length, and heavy even for strong men. The work went slowly. The fifth man worked with the captain, on the deck. The weight of the crates varied, that was clear. They were of the size to contain rifles, ammunition clips, even machine guns and light mortars. Or oranges. Or potatoes. The light was bad.

He was in luck. The captain was loading from the port side, the outer side, so that a solid wall of crates grew up toward starboard across the deck. He was loading carefully, Khamal was watching. He called out, "Wait." Four men with a crate stopped, spoke, set down the crate. They set it down in the light. He could see it plain.

DRAGUNOV. The name stared at him in heavy, stenciled letters. Dragunov: sniper rifle, 7.6mm, Soviet army issue. Smaller writing in numbers and Cyrillic – Red Army codes. So that was it. The provenance was East Germany, not West. A weapon better than those used by any but the one elite royal regiment of the Berbian army, much of which was still armed with American M-1s and even venerable British Lee-Enfields. Only that regiment was equipped with the current NATO weapons equal to weapons such as that.

It happened four times more: the cry of "Wait!"; the soldiers gratefully laying down their burden in the light. As he had suspected, the crates were not the same. The next one, heavy indeed, was SKODA – the Czech munitions factory. Skoda made weapons of many different kinds. The next was 120mm shells, correctly marked. The Skoda, then, was probably a mortar. The last was KALASHNIKOV. A useful general weapon. His luck amazed him. He was seeing a guerilla's shopping list beneath the light.

222

He laughed at the crudeness of the trick.

But not entirely crude. It would have worked if he had not discovered how Massoun had died. It would have worked if he had not seen them accommodate his tail. Most men saw what they expected to see. One could, after all, ignore the fact that no sane man would simply choose to drive weapons stenciled by the Warsaw Pact through France. Most men hiding on a deck, in a shadow, under a wall, would be pleased, not puzzled, by the perfunctory flashlight, the unattempted search. And most agents, seeing the crates pass through the light, would believe in their own brave, clever luck.

So let's stay here and be smart, he thought, *because the next part's not going to be such fun.* The advertisement was "Warsaw Pact." Now for the reality.

He knew how to do it and he pushed it from his mind. He thought of Intelligence: find the provenance; kick it back to Stears; intercept at sea; use the Berbian network. There was no Berbian network; you do not intercept neutral vessels at sea; this was not Stears's job; the provenance was buried. It was here and now. He looked at the water.

The boat was loaded port to starboard. The crates were stacked high as a man's eye. A man on deck could not see a man coming over the side from port. He could not feel him, either. Under the loading, the boat shifted constantly. Its freeboard and its cleats were low. They made good handholds.

He rejected the idea completely. He was no gonzo. This was not his job. He rolled across the deck.

He slipped over quietly. This early in the fall, the water was only cool. His shiver came from the thought of the manner of Massoun's death. The water was black. In black, the stocking over his head, he was in truth invisible unless he splashed.

He paddled slowly. Fifty meters.

He grasped the cleat, arms outstretched. His sneakers found some purchase on the uncleaned hull. But his body was strange. He knew it as a sack he carried, a sack that coughed and ached in winter. It told him nothing of how to raise it up. He loosened his grip. *Stupid old man. But I can paddle safely back.*

The boat lurched under loading. This was the moment. He convulsed himself. He was at the level of the deck. He almost fell backward, like a sack. *Jesus, that would do it.* He steadied himself. *Christ almighty, he was there!*

And he was calm. There was, in truth, a wall between them. He could breathe. Very carefully he removed the stocking. In it was the optic probe, still dry. He put the stocking back. From his pocket, he took a small hand drill. He set to work.

The wood drilled easily with a whisper like a mouse. It was not thick. The drill burst through. He took it out and, in its place, worked in the probe. On its tiny proboscis was both a lens and a light. He looked. He could see. He could see metal. It had no meaning.

He expected that. The lens was wide-angled but, so close to the subject, what it showed was nine times out of ten unidentifiable. He had to drill and probe, drill and probe, until he found a detail he could recognize. It was like doing a jigsaw puzzle in the dark. And it was not quite silent. And they would not load all night.

It took four tries. His hands began to hurry. Soon, they would shake. But his reward was there: curved by the wide-angle lens, shading off into darkness, but unmistakable, clear, was the trigger and breach assembly of a Belgian Fabrique Nationale FAL40. The bread and butter weapon of NATO infantry. He looked at the marking of its crate: SKODA.

He made himself do it once again. This time, only two tries were needed. This time an M-14 in a crate marked KALASHNIKOV. That was enough. He needed to live, survive, reflect. The sense of physical danger now hit him like a blow. Slipping off the side, he almost lost his grip. He paddled imperceptibly, wincing at each voice. He paddled beyond the boat he had first hidden in to the dark shadow under the quay. Here, almost for certain, he was safe. He was cold. He shivered.

Chill was in his bones. He changed clothes in the car, throwing the black garments in a sodden heap on the floor. But even at the outskirts of Marseilles, his skin was still clammy and his back shook. On the highway he saw the lights of a small restaurant, catering to truck drivers, still open. He stopped. He ordered *bourride* and a bottle of Gigondas, a lusty red wine. He drank half of the wine from a tumbler before the soup arrived. It poured straight into his veins. His body unlocked.

Their plan was by no means illogical. "Yamadi" and Khamal/Zebedi knew by now that he had information linking them to Berbia and guns – but where that information came from they could not know. Stears was safe so far. Instead of hiding from him, they had chosen to mislead him – that had the smell more of the KGB than of the PLO. He grunted approval. It was aggressive, but the risk was well contained. That arms were reaching the Baath in Berbia was hardly a secret; one modest arms shipment hardly counted among the floating arsenals of the Arab world. Even if the CIA could have stopped the shipment without blowing Dr. Donnelly's valuable cover, it would be far more interested in surveying it. And the French, though they valued stable governments in North Africa, rarely found the courage to obstruct the PLO – for the PLO, Paris was all but friendly territory. Supposing even that the CIA had informed the French, the French would move slowly, if at all.

The plan was sound. The question was its point. The PLO, operating through the Baath (or, just conceivably, through the Brothers of Islam), either positively wished to advertise that they were receiving weapons from the Warsaw Pact or were willing so to advertise to conceal what the weapons really were. The only possible motive for the first would be to draw the KGB further into an operation of the PLO. That sounded cumbersome and odd. The second would suggest either a wish to safe-guard a source of supply or to confuse any possible tracking of weapons inside Berbia.

And at that point, McNaughton passed from firm ground to swamp. He had no idea. Stears had no clue, who "Yamadi" and Khamal/Zebdi were operationally or what, precisely, they intended to do. They were opera-tives of some hard-line, probably Habbash, splinter of the PLO with KGB connections on loan to destabilizing forces inside Berbia, and currently acting as purchasing agents or transfer experts. So far so good and there it stopped. Who their Berbian connections were, what their operation was, were deeply buried. He and Stears had combed every piece of knowledge they shared for an indication. There was none. Without one, Yamadi's motive for disinforming the CIA, through McNaughton, as to weapons source could not be guessed. That was an intricate and urgent job for the Berbian network. And the Berbian network was dead.

He spat out a fish bone. The *bourride* was good, and trilled with warming garlic. The weapons were now at sea, on their way to a waiting ship. Marseilles to al-Tabek would be three days on a slow vessel. This might well not be the last of the shipment – by successful guerrilla standards it was small. Unless the rest of the shipment were due within a day or two, it was improbable that the steamer would be kept loitering off the coast. The French flew routine coastal reconnaissance missions. After about a week, an unexplained vessel would begin to draw suspicion – toward the drug traffic, at least, the French were becoming aggressive. Thus it was probable that the weapons would soon arrive in Berbia. They would be passed through the docks effectively, in secret. Both the Baath and the Brothers of Islam were strong enough on the al-Tabek docks to manage that with ease. They would disappear. They would reappear some-where at a moment of crisis. Too late.

Change the subject. The opposition knew Dr. Donnelly

as CIA. They did not know that he knew this. They knew nothing of McNaughton. They quite certainly knew enough of CIA practice, if not by themselves then through the KGB, to know that a deep-cover established agent like Donnelly/McNaughton would not all at once change his sector. Therefore, they would not expect Dr. Donnelly in al-Tabek. They would not be surprised to see him travel – he would take the intelligence that they would assume he had gathered in Niolon back to Paris, no doubt with photographs. He could travel from Paris to al-Tabek in reasonable safety either as McNaughton or under his emergency passport as Albert Weston. As McNaughton he could with luck establish a minimal and ad hoc surveillance capacity in al-Tabek – it should not be for nothing that his information on Berbia all but over-whelmed his memory. He could collaborate with Stears as easily there as anywhere else – Stears could perhaps introduce a confusion in Geneva that would distract Yamadi and Khamal.

What was more, the port of al-Tabek was small enough that he would have a reasonable chance of knowing when the weapons ship arrived. It would almost certainly be a small Arab steamer arriving in three days to a week. If he then appeared as Dr. Donnelly, maximally exposed, something would surely happen. His presence would be enough of a surprise that something would be changed at the last moment or something would be done to stop him. That something, no doubt, would only be a thread. Threads unravel.

That something could also be his death. He did not have to do this.

He mopped up the *bourride* with his bread. He ordered coffee. He ordered marc. He had an honest choice. His own. He thought about it, content, warm at last, at leisure.

He was fifty-eight. His cover of five years was blown. His next and last assignment would be a desk at Langley. That, and then retirement. The business in the harbor

227

had not been bad. Bad? Hell! It had been first-class active surveillance under exposure. There was a lot in him yet.

He thought about Khamal. He thought about Massoun. He thought about the woman at the *Charité*. He thought of his own sudden fear at the Piment Rouge. Khamal, he decided, could be personally disliked.

He would go to Berbia. He would go at once.

At Marseilles airport, a man stood two behind him in the ticket line. He was an Arab. At Marseilles airport, an Arab is nothing odd. But he did not board the plane.

At Charles de Gaulle, a French left-wing student in a denim coat watched the Air France counter for North Africa. Then he watched the Berbair counter. He was well drilled and he reached the Royal Air Maroc counter two hours before the flight to Casablanca by al-Tabek. He found his man. Donnelly/McNaughton was traveling as Albert Weston. That, Yamadi thought, was clever; he expected him to appear in Berbia as McNaughton.

The green and orange coast, the almond trees, the birthday cake city, and the sapphire sea unrolled beneath him. He felt disengaged, in orbit, free. He was on his own, his own choosing, his own danger, his own way. His danger, by his own timing, would be very great in three or four days. For the present he rested in the sense of his own reflexes, his proved skill. His performance in the harbor now seemed to him literally like an icy shower, washing away old staleness, old doubt. This was his last assignment. He was at his peak. He felt younger. He was lightheaded from fatigue.

He had never been here. He knew almost every block by photograph, the name of every street. He knew the photograph, name, and dossier of over two hundred of al-Tabek's citizens. He knew intimately people who did not know he existed. The airport was air conditioned, European. He took the shortcut to the baggage counter. His memory meshed with the ground. He did not stand in line for taxis. Nobody who lived here did. He told is driver, "The Hotel Sultan." And "The old way, not the new. There is no traffic at this time of day." Only the heat surprised him. He had forgotten about the heat.

There was no air conditioning at the Sultan, but the lobby was shaded, dim, and cool. It was the old hotel, less sybaritic than the French Reine de Carthage and fustier than the al-Tabek Hilton. But it was clean and quiet, and the streets around it were crowded and obscure. He could work from it with ease. Room 28 was known to be unbugged. He asked for it. It was free.

The taps worked. The toilet flushed. Bulbs were in the lights. The lock was good. He dismissed the bellboy. Through the window lattice, shafts of sun were scattered on the tiled floor as opals. The street noises drifted through at the same volume as the fly that bumped against the lattice. The bed was high and white and soft. If he slept now he would lose his edge. He unpacked. He sat at the feminine and spindly desk, deep in concentration, riffling through the dossiers in his head. He wrote down abbreviations in a hand like an electrocardiogram. He went downstairs.

So he was not to be the only American. A girl was checking in. He stood close beside her as he gave the clerk his key. He was suddenly aware of her. She was in her early twenties. Her hair was auburn and shining and short. She had sapphire eyes. But he saw that through a surrounding radiance of perfect vitality and perfect grace – a glowing animal, an athlete, a floating and glorious girl. Her scent was light and clean. His senses swung toward her like a compass needle. He had the same sense of overpowering life as when he had stood beside Khamal. But Khamal's presence was like an arrow in the spleen, and beside this girl, in his orbiting and exalted state, he felt an explosion within him of regret and joy; he longed to touch her, to hold her, to know her, to be her, to drink from her, to be lost in the glorious music of her self. And he nodded, but she was locked in battle with the clerk. She didn't even see him and she said, "But I had another suitcase. I had three. Just like the other ones. It was in the taxi. I know it was. It was stolen. Stolen here. Right in the lobby. In your hotel."

Her hand tapped the dark wood counter: a girl's and a woman's both – light but with authority and jewels. No little hippie, this. Even McNaughton knew that the haircut and the dress were good. He knew her accent from his Washington days: Virginia.

The clerk was soft and dark. His eyes turned muddy and opaque. He said, "Madame, madame, on my honor, when you arrived there were only two. Maybe the taxi driver, madame. The porter say that taxi driver is bad, very dishonest man."

But she hardly listened – nor did she see McNaughton, to whom she turned. She ran her hands up through her hair and carried on, "I mean, my God. Really. My God, what a place. I mean damn, really, with these fucking people, what am I supposed to do?"

She still hadn't looked at him and she turned to the clerk.

McNaughton said, "It isn't stolen."

She registered and turned and said, "I beg your pardon."

He said, "It'll turn up. It isn't stolen. The police don't let them steal from tourists at good hotels. It will turn up. You'll be grateful and you'll give somebody another tip. That's the idea. Don't worry."

Her eyes opened full upon him and he felt it in his chest. She said, "Do you really know that?"

He smiled. He said, "Yes, I do. Relax. Go up to your room. And don't tip too much."

And she smiled, elegant and happy, and said, "Well, how very nice of you. I will. They'd have taken me for a real dumb American, wouldn't they? Thanks so much. Maybe I'll see you later." Impulsively, she gave him her hand. It was light and cool and strong. "I'm Julia Longleat," she said.

"Michael McNaughton."

He left. She watched him through the door. The porter appeared and looked at her with question. She beckoned and nodded. He came back with a small suitcase like the other two.

"Good," she said. She gave him five dollars. The clerk stared and shrugged. She gave him five dollars, too. He smiled.

Life was what it was. He sat at the bar that evening. Simply life. A woman like that would wash off fear, would wash off doubt, would wash off compromise, would wash off the sight of living death he still carried with him from the *Charité*. Well, anyway. He brought his mind back to business. He had seen a coffee merchant in the bazaar, a sleeping agent of the Company. He would not be active. A low-level surveillance of the bazaar would be assembled within two days. It was a beginning. It was not enough. It had taken time. She was in the door.

He loved her hesitation. Should she be there alone? How difficult for a woman traveling! She sized it up and thought it was not proper. She turned to go. He caught her eye. She smiled and shrugged. She came to join him.

She said, "I hate American women who make exhibitions of themselves. I shouldn't be here, should I? But the room's so dreary. Thanks again. I got my luggage back. Just like you said. I only tipped five dollars."

He said, "Why are you here?"

"Buying horses. Daddy has a stud farm. They have wonderful Arabs here. What are you?"

Just an Arabist. A scholar. How terribly interesting. So he knew all about this place? All she knew was the horses. He must tell her everything.

He had been handsome once. He had not lacked for women. And even now, the worldly, hard-lived face lit by the cool and piercing eyes could still find conquests. But not like this. He felt, as they talked, as they dined, as they talked, the happy reassessment of himself, the grand, self-altering gift, the growth like a tree, of a truly beautiful woman's liking.

For she did. He was telling acerbic stories of visits with the Saudi royal family. (He had never made such visits or met the family. He knew its blood pressures, sexual predilections, and private bank accounts.) He caught in her eyes a look of delight, like a grown-up child, not so much in the story as in his telling of it, in himself, and when he leaned closer she colored slightly and lowered her eyes. But, at the point of the story, her laugh was strong and rich. He had the feeling, and it made him shiver with lust, that he was in the presence both of a modest lady and a mountain lion. They walked on the terrace after dinner. The old hotel was surrounded on three sides by a tangle of small streets, degenerating into slum. A single radio played music. There were isolated, incomprehensible shouts. It was high enough to see the lights of the port below them. He thought for a moment of the secrets and savageries of the streets and wharves that he must penetrate tomorrow.

But Julia put her arm on his and said, "Isn't it beautiful? Just like the Arabian Nights."

And he had to struggle not to paw her like a teenager.

Then she said, "Well. Stables wake up early." She said it softly and with regret.

She took his hand in hers and held it gravely, gently, as if considering, then dropped it and kissed him warmly on the cheek. "Thanks," she said.

He took her hand again and looked straight into her sapphire eyes and said quietly, "I want you."

Her eyes didn't drop and she looked at him seriously and slowly and then slightly smiled and said, "Can you spare tomorrow night?" And squeezed his hand to seal it. She turned and walked quickly away from him to the hotel door. She was not the kind of girl to look back and linger.

She hung over the next day like a springtime sun – nothing to do with what he was doing, but improving its aspect. He worked with extreme care. His task, essentially, was to activate the sleepers in a network – agents recruited and even paid, but never used, never contacted, never compromised. None had ever seen him or heard of him. There was a roster of a score of them. He needed only four or five. He considered only those whom he could contact without any initial guess on their part as to his role. Even the sleeper network might be penetrated at points unknown. It had to be handled with the utmost delicacy. He chose a taxi driver, a customs clerk at the port, a baggage boy at the al-Tabek Hilton, and a desk sergeant of the police. The customs clerk had camera skills. He arranged for detailed, multiangled photographs of every vessel entering the port, beginning tomorrow. The taxi driver, who could quietly assemble two friends, would monitor the movements of certain drivers with known connections to the Baath and to the Brothers. It took time to make and test these contacts. He would do more tomorrow. It would still be quite inadequate – but the Berbian network was creeping back to an embryonic life. He made no contact with the embassy.

He called Stears. His travels had been so precipitate that he had not done so yet. He had also been uncertain what to say. This was in a sense Stears's operation – Yamadi and Khamal had been found by Stears and passed to McNaughton as a package fairly neatly tied. If the risk and effort had lately been mainly his, it was because of a collaboration that had been his idea. And as for risk, Stears would be anything but safe if Yamadi in any way connected them. He no longer doubted Stears. Anything that could be done in Geneva, Stears would do well.

But do what? He found himself uncharacteristically tentative as he spoke. He told Stears of the shipment and the double bluff. He told him in terms that would not be understood by an unbriefed listener. Of a briefed listener, he had as yet no fear. He set up a time of second contact.

233

Stears said, "This had gone far enough. You're unsupported. You need reinforcements. We have to go to Witham in the end. Why not now?"

It even crossed McNaughton's mind to agree. But he said, "No. This is my kind of game. I understand it. I don't want some bastard tripping me up. Give me five days. If I can't do anything by then, we go to Witham. Same if I don't make my next contact."

And Stears had been silent and then said slowly, "Difficult clients, those. Don't take chances."

It was as much anxiety, McNaughton knew, as he could allow himself to show.

He played with fantasies. He accepted, flatly, that that was what they were, but he allowed himself to see one small bright corner where they might be real. The iron, sharp duties of his life were cracking open, breaking up. In a week they would be finished. When he had looked toward his future, he had dimly seen a desk job at Langley, a small house in McLean, then a cranky old man spending Christmas with his daughter. He did not complain. But now, today, beginning with the rebaptism of youth at Niolon, he saw just the chance – it was like finding a gorgeous present locked within his own chest – that he might be given love, life, succulence, a second chance. He could not take seriously a life with Julia Longleat – she was simply above him. But she might be the gate through which he walked into a richer life. He was almost nervous.

This evening she seemed to him more delicate. This was a date. He waited for her in the lobby. She came out of the elevator in a soft silk dress, younger, less sophisticated than before. As they sat in the bar, it suited the acerbic, gruffly cyncial protection he couldn't seem to lose, to say, "If this was a respectable country I'd have to say you were my daughter."

And it seemed to him, oddly, even in the dim light that her eyes crackled like faulty wiring and her arm went rigid. But the moment passed and she laid her hand gently on his thigh and said, "You couldn't begin to imagine how boring most young men are."

And as she spoke, her breast within the soft silk dress drew his eyes as to joy, life, music, and she saw it and didn't move and lightly stroked his knee.

He let her talk this evening. They dined on lamb cooked with orange blossom. He could not forbear champagne. She talked of parties, horses, friends, but seriously, with judgment and concern. She handled her own rich girl's life with a funny, modest irony, but not with guilt. She was beautiful and her life was filled with pleasure and she neither wasted it nor hated it but watered it, pruned it, loved it, and hoped that others would love it too. It occurred to him that there were lives in which deception, cruelty, conquest, the use of others as disposable tools, existed in a small, squalid corner, if at all. He felt suddenly unworthy of her, like a poisonous old crab pulled from a narrow, dirty shell.

But he loved and, yes, respected her, most of all, for she seemed to have slipped like an arrow straight between coyness and immodesty. She had simply annihilated the guessing, the fumbling, the asking of an affair's first night. The fact that she found him wonderful stood beside them, assured, complete, and giving no explanation of itself. She was his mistress already, receptive and loving.

She said, "You're real. Do you understand that? You're not a promise. You're not a possibility. You're not an idea. You're a man. You've lived."

They were on the terrace again, walking slowly around it. They did not touch and the space between them sweetly ached.

She went on, "I don't quite know how to say this, but it's not as though you're older, it's as though you're what's right. You're whole. The others were little fractions. And for once I'm scared, I really am, that it's me that's not enough. That I'm not ready for you. I think I

235

would be one day – but perhaps not now. So," she smiled at what she said, "as they say, be kind to me."

And his arms went out to her as though from an electric shock. He held her to him and said, "Now. Let's not wait any longer. Now."

She kissed him strongly and firmly and said, "Yes."

She preferred her room. Her dress flowed down her like water to the ground. He was seeing perfection, and, urgent as he was, he touched her at first as though she was actually fragile, with respect. She surprised him. He had not expected a virgin, but he had not guessed that on the billowing, old-fashioned bed, all hesitation, her serenity, her gentleness, would so utterly drop away. He felt the body he had touched with loving fingertips goading him, covering him, driving him, giving up its secret prodigally, too fast. He even felt, as he caressed her, loved her, entered her at last, that she was falling father and farther from him and that now, this moment, he would be left in her, obsessed with her, alone.

But still her glorious hair hung over him, and her breasts moved across his face as she stretched her arms above him, and she leaned back so he could see her whole. She said, "Kiss me." And he raised his head toward her.

And saw, like a blow in the head, the glint of the steel wire between her hands. He stopped frozen, not so much held beneath her thighs as simply from the brain's convulsive wrench between one world and another. And the wire was around his neck. He roared then, and bucked and threw her from him. She held on with her ankles as his breath choked. He rose up under her, carrying her weight with him and heard her, the last thing he ever heard, exclaim, "Oh Jesus Christ! Goddamn! Goddamn!"

Then he was standing, flailing, by the bed, and she hung from him, white-knuckled, by the wire. Then the thin wire bit had vanished and in its place on his throat were lines of blood, then streamlets. She felt the wire cutting her own hands and cursed again. He staggered once, a second time, then fell on her. She had to push him off, wipe blood from her face, before she went to get the finishing ice pick from the bureau drawer. He was heavy to turn over. She stabbed once, economically. She stood a moment, panting. She considered. She would leave searching the clothes to Ibrahim. He would be here very soon. She knew that McNaughton had his room key. That was good. She could hardly have done better. She went to the bathroom. She turned on the tap.

Part Three

15

Madame Oubad was Moroccan. One would have said she was from Nice. She divided her time between the golf course, the swimming pool, and Elizabeth Arden, and looked, in consequence, like a lacquered lizard. She was Lady Champion of North Africa. She said to Wop, "Next time you must go to the Atlas Mountains. St. Moritz is riffraff now. Nobody believes me, but Morocco has the most charming skiing in the world. You can look down from the snow and see the almond trees below and, more importantly, only the best people know about it. You must tell me when you go and I will see that the hotel looks after you." She leaned closer and poked him in the knee – no coyness between friends. "Marie-Sophie would love it."

Sidi Oubad, talking to Marie-Sophie, overheard and said, "Don't listen to her. The Atlas is for beginners. You two ski like guides. It is just that she owns the hotel, you know, and nobody goes there." He had put his English tweeds on, for October, but his collar was open, for Sunday and sun. He was director general of the World Council on Arid Lands of the United Nations.

Marie-Sophie said, "Sidi, you are terrible. People *do* go there. It was in *Vogue* last month. I saw it. The Vicomtesse de Noailles was there and so were the von Thyssens. It's a beautiful place. I should love to go there."

They were her friends. Artificially close friends but friends from before she knew him. Sunday lunches with acquaintances plucked haphazardly from the past were an intermittent imperative of their lives. "Do you realize," she would say, "how long it is since we've seen the Rienzis?" He would try to remember who the Rienzis were. Visual memory was of little help. All of Marie-Sophie's Geneva friends were interchangable – tanned men in gold Rolexes and creamy suits and reptilian women in jewels. He knew for a fact that they without exception scared her and cared nothing about her at all. She would be hilarious, sophisticated, warm. She would even name-drop. She would pay for lunch. Then, having proved that she knew everybody there was to know, knew smarter people than he did himself, had her own place and life, didn't, in fact, depend on him in the slightest bit, she would be absolutely, trustingly, and exclusively his all month. And that made his heart ache. And lunch was good. Today, lobster by the lake under the turning chestnut trees in the autumn sun. And McNaughton was out of sector, at risk, alone.

He said, "There are metaphors I will not mix. I refuse to contemplate a ski teacher in a burnoose."

Madame Oubad poked him in the knee again. Golf had developed her fingers. "You're terrible," she said. She turned to Marie-Sophie. "He's terrible," she said.

He felt doom and he did not know why. He recognized McNaughton's skill in his craft, recognized its certainty, recognized it as superior to his own as easily as he would have recognized, for that matter, a ski teacher's. In continuing an operation under compromised cover, McNaughton was going against the book, the whole book preface to index, no doubt about that. It was true that Witham, in Bern, had told McNaughton to infiltrate expatriate groups returning to Berbia – something like that – but the instruction was vague, and, in case of failure, would certainly be interpreted to McNaughton's disadvantage. Nonetheless, it was not, on its own merits, indefensible. There was no possible compromise of the McNaughton identity. Visual recognition was an undeniable risk, but skill could reduce it – and Donnelly had never been in Berbia. In activating a sleeper network

of doubtful status, he was taking an unquantifiable risk –
but it was arguably a necessary one and would be managed
as far as possible by expertise bordering on intuition.
Seen as a continuing operation, it had impossible holes,
but as a quick in-and-out job the rewards might well repay
the risks. And Berbia was in principle friendly ground.

When McNaughton called, he had had the image of a
man locked in the last dry compartment of a sinking ship.

Madame Oubad said, "Yes, but still it is a long way
away. Once the firing got so close that we could hear it at
the hotel, but still it was many miles away. The guests
left, but most came back again. I do not fear the Polisario
yet. Not for four or five years. Then, perhaps, it is
finished. But Berbia will have to go before Morocco, and
that will not be this year."

And it should have been remarkable, but it wasn't –
Madame Oubad, of Palm Beach, Cannes, and golf,
speaking of the end of her investment, her country, her
world, as an end that by great good fortune was a few
years off. It was becoming not only usual but the rich
Arab's inescapable mode of thought.

It hadn't been said to him, but he replied, "Yes, but the
equation's been changed and you forget that. America
will play its proper part now. The area of stability will
expand, not contract."

Sidi Oubad absorbed a paupiette of sole and said
equably, "The Americans cannot even control the Nazis
in Israel, and they will destroy us all. Khomeini is the
future. Ghadaffi is the future. Hassad is the future. We
shall all be boat people." He smiled. "That is why I keep a
yacht." He gestured to the sapphire lake.

And even Marie-Sophie sadly shrugged. "I think so
too," she said.

The Arab world leaked like a sieve. There, indeed,
Stears agreed. Hard to remember, here in Switzerland,
where life rolled as smoothly as a trolley of desserts, that
in the lands he watched over the trick was not to discover
that arms were being shipped; the trick was not even to

243

find them – that being only marginally more difficult than finding sand there; the trick was to deduce which of forty-seven different factions had brought them in. NATO posing as Warsaw Pact. Warsaw Pact positively advertised. But why? You couldn't pretend when you used them, anyway. Anybody with two days of training could tell you what weapons had been used on a battlefield. Two days before McNaughton's next contact. He felt Marie-Sophie's toes against his shin. He was to offer liqueurs? He supposed so. He played host. And her warm hand, with credit card, beneath the table. He squeezed it. He endured these lunches better because they led to languorous long Sunday afternoons.

He said to Sidi, "I almost forgot. A very pleasant young man came to my office the other day – Amal Khannafi, from al-Tabek. He's become a client of mine, he and his associates. He said he knew you a little and that his father knew you better. I thought we might get together for lunch the next time he comes through." He added, throwing it away, "He might have room for more investors." And closely watched.

Sidi smiled. His eyes turned still. Below the smile, bolts and shutters slid quietly into place. He gestured expansively. He said, "Sure thing. Give me a call. You know, I do not know him very well. But give me a call. Maybe I can break away. No promises."

Which was as close to a refusal as an Arab would give. And to an invitation baited with one of the richer names of North Africa. Sidi Oubad was a meeter of professional caliber. That was confirmation. There was something wrong with the house of Khannafi that the Western bankers did not yet know. McNaughton's Moroccan was right. He turned to Madame Oubad.

"And when is your next tournament? I can't keep up with you."

"Marrakech," she said. "Next week. It is only a small tournament. Really very dull. On the other hand, I shall win it."

244

The back of the Oubad's Bentley withdrew under the chestnuts down the drive. They waited for Sear's Jaguar on the restaurant steps. Marie-Sophie stood beside him with a warm, requited smile.

"That was so nice," she said. "Was that not nice, Giovanni? I so enjoy having Sunday lunch with interesting old friends. The Oubads are some of the best people in Morocco, you know. And maybe you have made a business friend. We do not have enough social life. If I left it to you we should live like hermits. Do you know what I should like to do now? I should like to go and see the new Alain Resnais movie. It is on at the Elysée at eight."

"That," he said, "is five hours from now."

"Yes," she said. "I do suppose that we shall have to wait. But I am tired of my house, Giovanni."

He touched her neck and gently smoothed a small tangle of necklace and collar.

"There is always, I suppose, mine."

In the car, she said, "Cannes will be so nice. It is so long since I've been away."

He nodded. Two or three times a year, he saw clients in the South of France. This time, for the first time, she was to go with him. They were to drive down the next Sunday.

"I hope we can trust the Jaguar," he said. "It's three weeks since it was in the shop."

"I think my Alfa is not running very well," she said.

He thought. "Well, put it in the shop this week and I'll drive you and if the Jaguar breaks down next week, we'll take the Alfa instead."

From time to time he wondered if he had, unbeknownst to himself, already married her. He said, "You know, we can never leave each other. Not with an Alfa and a Jag between us."

She smiled.

His apartment was up a steep street in the old city, Voltaire's Geneva, Rousseau not welcome, reason in stone. He had the long third floor of the left-hand wing of a gravely grand façade meditating upon a courtyard. For the same rent, he could have enjoyed a pink malachite lobby looking on the lake and a Saudi on every floor. His rooms were high and strict. There, reserve ended. His taste in furniture was frankly grand, luxurious, even Neapolitan. His entrance hall had an inlaid cabinet with Triton and Naiads on the lower half and Olympus on the upper. His dining table was green marble. His bed had claws and wings and painted shepherdesses. And Marie-Sophie. She lay replete and soft as down, gazing at the ceiling through half-closed eyes. He looked down her gently breathing length and felt a reflected warmth both of spirit and of body. Champagne had been generously poured at lunch. He briefly closed his eyes.

She must have noticed. She murmured, "Let's really not forget the movie. Shall I set a clock?"

"No, no," he said. "Don't bother."

He had been asleep. His head was on her shoulder, which was moving also to the telephone's sudden ring. She sat up quickly.

"I'll get it," he said.

"Have we missed the movie?"

He looked at the clock. "No. There's time. It's lucky that the telephone rang, though. You'd better get dressed." He padded to the next room, to the telephone, in the last late-evening light. It was on a small gilded corner table. He picked it up. He answered in French, as always. The voice was American, unknown, friendly.

"Stears," it said. "This is Jonathan Winters. How're you doing, boy?"

"Fine," he said. "Jonathan Winters" was this week's code name for an emergency contact from the Agency. Warmth and sleep and Marie-Sophie vanished.

"Got some news for you on that prospectus you're interested in. It's finished. Wrapped up sometime last

246

night. Don't know how they did it. We'll be getting back to you tomorrow."

"Thanks," he said. "So long." So McNaughton was dead. Was murdered.

By lunch the next day, he had had no contact. He considered initiating it himself and thought better of it at once. No idle chatter. Cairo would need time to think.

Lunch with Hajji Melouf. Wop arrived first. The headwaiter smiled and murmured greeting. Wop sat at the mahogany bar. At once, unbidden, a chilled dry sherry appeared before him. A silver dish of salted almonds was placed by his hand. They brought him the Paris paper. The weather, the barman thought, was nice. A fine October is the finest month of all. He agreed. Shot, drowned, butchered in an alley, pray God not treated like that Arab smuggler, McNaughton passed before him. The half-formed thought, *I set this up, this was my operation,* knocked at his head. For the third time that morning, he pushed it violently away.

Hajji was worried. Hajji did not look well. Hajji failed to smile dreamily at the copperplate menu.

"I could easily have seen you next week in Nice," said Wop. "I hope you didn't come here just for me."

"No, no, Mr. Stears. Other things." Hajji vaguely waved his cigar. "But I will not say that I am not anxious to hear what you have done since our last meeting."

Wop nodded. He reached to the window ledge for his briefcase. The plane trees, deep green at their last meeting, were tinged with copper now, and summer shirts were gone. But the lake was still its summer sapphire. In a month it would be winter black.

"Here are the details. In essence, I did exactly as you said. I liquidated $3.2 million of assorted Kingdom of Berbia issues. I very much regret to say that I did so at a discount. Your issues carried coupons of 9.25 percent, 9.5 percent, and 10 percent, averaging about 9.5 percent, tax free. They had good ratings. On that, they should have

247

gone for about 90 percent of par in the present market.
All I could get was 83 percent, averaged. Too much
Berbian paper is being sold. It's not a panic, and Western
investors are picking up the bargains, but more is coming
onto the market than the market wants to pick up. I'm
sorry. But then, Mr. Melouf, this is not my strategy."

And it isn't even now, he thought. *There's nothing going
on in Berbia that a boatload of guns is going to change. Not this
year. Madame Oubad's right.*

But Hajji nodded and even seemed to taste his cigar.

"Do not worry, Mr. Stears. You have done well. Many
have done worse. I should like to know about the mineral
rights."

"Essentially, it is the same story. The rights are good.
There seems little doubt that the tungsten is there or that
it's extractable. The world market is down, but not
forever. That's Polisario country, of course, and they're a
nuisance – so we have to expect a discount for that. I
should have said that your Erg Iguidi acreage was worth
$1.5 million and your Erg Ahram a bit less because it's
more remote. Say $1.25 million. Berbia is in general an
excellent climate for Western business. But I'm not
getting it. I have heard that 12,000 acres of Berbian
ore-bearing acreage hit the market this month. The
market can't absorb it. My best offer is this: I can sell a
ninety-day option at $2.2 million to Kerr McGee for
$250,000. My guess is that in ninety days this spate of
selling will be over and that Kerr McGee will take it up. So
you'll get $2,450,000. Otherwise I shall have to let it go for
about $1.5 million. That's a pittance. Even if it is twice
what you paid for it."

Poor Hajji was upset again.

"No option, Mr. Stears." He swallowed his smoked
salmon like porridge. "No ninety days. Take what you
can get. Even," and this caused pain, "$1.5 million."

Formally, Wop nodded. Reflexively, he scratched his
pad with his pen.

He said, "Now there is something I want to take up

248

with you. Your ships – " and stopped. Hajji's eyes were pure mud. Hajji reached for his cigar like a stealthy poker player.

"My ships are fine, Mr. Stears. No reason to worry about my ships."

"Your ships are terrible. Revenue has almost dried up, and your ships are too old. They cost more in maintenance than they can earn. You've had one in and out of the yards in Marseilles for a month and apparently it's not right yet. I'm not a shipping man, Mr. Melouf, but I know these are ten-knot British tramp steamers of the 1930s and they can't compete. The game's not worth the candle. Even when the freight market picks up again it will not go to your vessels. It will go to thirty-knot container ships. You've lost $75,000 on three ships in six months. And it's going to get worse. Let me get rid of them."

Hajji said, looking only at his empty plate, "I have confidence in my ships, Mr. Stears. The refit in Marseilles is nearly over – I have the yard's word on that. There is an Arab coastal market that you do not know much about, I think. My ships will be profitable again."

But he looks absolutely miserable, thought Wop. He tried again.

"It's not logical."

But Hajji, suddenly straightening up, brightening, said, "Another time, Mr. Stears. For now, this discussion is closed. Tell me what investments you are buying with the funds from Berbia."

Below his office, the Levantine Commercial Credit murmured with Arabs. A ranking Kuwaiti – he knew the face – flowed in white robes from an inner office and gathered in his wake two stone-faced bodyguards camped by the door. The robes were never as impressive close up. One had the impression of pajamas worn too long. Three intense Lebanese surrounded an Empire desk in tripartite attack on an unperturbed and chilly Swiss. On a

boudoir sofa was a solitary, awry figure like two Hajji
Meloufs stuffed into a single suit peering anxiously into a
bulging briefcase. He had the sudden feeling of dropping
into a room of sordid mysteries, of utter, hostile foreign-
ness, of an incomprehensible charade. He flinched in
sudden, unprepared distaste and then, as quickly,
thought of Marie-Sophie. He waited for the sedan chair
to descend. He thought, surprised, *If her body wasn't the
sweetest place in the world, I don't think I could do this
anymore. It's she that makes them human. They matter because
of her.*

He cancelled his appointments for the afternoon. He
closed his office door. He stood by his desk, one hand
toward the telephone, and looked upon the lake. The
crowds were gone from the lakefront. Half the ice cream
stalls were boarded up. Among the first falling leaves,
one last old man offered his stock of windmills and
balloons. The steamers still swam to and fro, but they
were nearly empty and would stop next month. Empty
steamers. The thought caught at him for a moment and
was gone.

There was now no doubt in his mind at all that Berbia
was collapsing, crumbling from within even while its
outer walls stood solid in plain daylight, without a crack.
He did not know when the fall would come. Probably not
for a year or two. It would be as astonishing as Iran's, as
Libya's, as Iraq's. There would be a heap of rubble –
Marie-Sophies mangled underneath it and Khamals
building blockhouses on top. King Fahd, of course, was
corrupt. He wondered how often he would have to hear
it. There was poverty. How new! The society was threatened by Western ways. Well, lucky old Afghanistan!
There was invariably a mechanism of subversion, an
actual, identifiable method, that reduced a structure
merely a little shabby, a little used, a little weak, to a
wreck. Things were not always more complex than they
seemed. It was easy to confuse the complexity of the
structure destroyed with the cheapness of the crowbar

that destroyed it. The crowbar could in principle be grabbed away before it struck. And then another crowbar and another. But it could be done. It could be done if the crowbar could be found. It was a thing worth doing.

Witham called. The telephone, waited for, made him jump. It was a direct line to his desk, secure.

Witham sounded like a patient man pushed far by the folly of others.

He said, "I will give you the details because to some extent they affect you. The body was found in an alley near one of the bazaars. It may or may not have been moved there – there is evidence that it was dragged a short distance. Manner of death was garroting with a stab to finish it off. And that fits in with a bazaar-type murder. It's the local method. There is no evidence of interrogation. We are assuming that he was engaged in some kind of direct surveillance in the bazaar quarter, was discovered, and was terminated by a low-level operative on the spot. Perhaps a guard. Frankly, we hope that's what happened. There's another dimension you have to know about. He was working under exposed cover. The Donnelly cover was broken and he was there as McNaughton."

Wop said, and instantly regretted it, "I know."

"You *what?* How do you know?"

"He told me."

"When?"

Drearily, he said, "Three days ago."

There was silence and then – the first emotion he had known in Witham – genuine anger, just controlled.

"Well, you have had the advantage of me, Stears, because I received this remarkable information in a handwriten letter this morning. It had apparently been written by McNaughton and taken to the embassy in al-Tabek by another hand. It is coded and it is genuine. It was not part of your fireside chat. I had thought that you were trustworthy, for a noncareer man – and that McNaughton was a professional. I find I am wrong on

251

both points. Is there any other information you could trust me with?"

Stears said, "The agent, the smuggler, was interrogated. McNaughton discovered this. I do not know how. He nonetheless ran surveillance on the loading of the second cargo and discovered NATO weapons labelled as Warsaw Pact. He deduced that surveillance was expected and desired as regards the Warsaw Pact cover. He went immediately to Berbia to activate the sleeper network in order to effect surveillance of the weapons on arrival. It was a risk but he did not have much time. That's all I know."

"Very well. If I thought that this collaboration was your idea I would sever you from the Agency. I assume, however, that it was McNaughton's. He seems to have paid the price. We have to take into account the possibility that he was followed from Marseilles and killed as Donnelly, in which case the sleeper network, if we still have one, will have been damaged incalculably. We so far reject this on the grounds of the manner of death, which suggests a low-level event, and the lack of interrogation. It's all very crude. I find it astonishing that an operation in a benign environment should have been totally hamstrung by amateurishness and back-alley murders. It does not help the image of the Agency."

Into the brief silence, Wop said, "I am beginning a written advisory on the Berbian situation. It will be extremely pessimistic. My contacts with Berbian financial sources are revealing a total and stunning ebb of confidence. I have never seen confidence in an economy decline so fast, and the decline is most complete precisely among those whom I consider to have the best insights. Something is going on in Berbia that we have not penetrated, and I have the impression that everybody is too scared to tell us. The collapse may even be imminent. It would be coincidence, I suppose, if this were a major part of it."

Witham said, "You will send such a report to me only.

But write it, Stears. Write it. That's what we hired you for. I expect you will decide that you are seeing a financial panic, which is hardly the imminent collapse of a government. Even if the situation in Berbia were a great deal worse, the army would buy time for several years. Berbia has unstable elements and we know about them. As a whole, the place is pretty solid. Now, to get back to present issues. We need to plug this leak of NATO weapons. This particular arms shipment is of only medium importance, but we cannot tolerate having our weapons floating around dressed up as Warsaw Pact for any reason at all. McNaughton's last data were valuable. The conclusion is that these people wished us to think that the increasing theft of weapons has nothing to do with them and that we should look elsewhere. Military intelligence will be working on it on the spot, in Germany. You are our only remaining link between Yamadi and Khamal. Can you reinitiate contact with them?"

"It would be difficult. I have instructions from them not to. I have really no way of doing it. I could make a mistake, I suppose. I could fumble a payment. That might bring them up. I don't like it, but I suppose I could."

Witham was thinking. Then he said, "Maybe you could do a little better. Maybe you could do something that looked a little – sleazy. That would make them think that you had light fingers. After all, you're a Latin, up to a point, aren't you? It would be in character. That should bring them up."

Bastard!

Stears said, "No. I make my living at this. By reputation. I shall make a mistake. It will be adequate." He finished sweetly, "Sacrifice is not in our character."

Witham agreed. "No. I suppose not. But we need them back in contact, Stears. That's up to you. When you get them, it will be your responsibility to keep them for an hour or two until we can put in priority-one long-term surveillance. Do you think that contact might be established outside of Geneva?"

"Paris is a possibility, I think. So is the South of France. Anywhere else seems unlikely."

"We will be prepared." Witham hesitated. "This will be the most significant thing you have done." And finished with a Witham flourish, "I am, of course, quite confident that you will do it very well."

He dined at home, alone. One corner of his drawing room window looked over steeply descending roofs to the lake. He sat in an armchair, coffee beside him, a motet of Thomas Tallis cleansing the air of McNaughton's murder. He watched the lights around the lake. An old moored steamer served as a restaurant. He had once taken Marie-Sophie there. Maybe Hajji could use his ships for that in al-Tabek. He smiled. Or in Marseilles, since one seemed to be stuck there. He stopped smiling. His hand, reaching for his demitasse, stayed still in space. He shook his head and drank his coffee. He got up and walked around the room. He stopped at the telephone. It was the telephone that had rung for McNaughton's death. He dialed Marie-Sophie's number.

She answered, "Hello, my dear. Is that you? I thought it was you."

He said, "Could you spend an extra two days in France?"

He liked it that she never answered lightly. She thought.

"I believe I could," she said. "We are not very busy at the Commission. I think that Wageman would let me." Wageman was her Belgian boss. "You know I'd like to."

"Good," he said. "After the Riviera, we'll drive over to Les Baux. It's the nicest place in the world and you've never been there. We'll stay there two days."

"That sounds all right," she said.

"I'll be in Marseilles during the day. There are some clients I have to see there."

"How nasty for you," said Marie-Sophie. "Are they gangsters?"

He laughed. "What a question."

16

After dinner, Stears and Marie-Sophie sat on the terrace outside the hotel above St.-Paul-de-Vence. Marie-Sophie wore a silk shawl over her bare shoulders. Even on the Riviera, the nights were now cool in the hills. The village lights were close below them. Far below, between the hills and the sea, floated the constellation of Nice and the distant nebulae of Juan-les-Pins and Cannes. The waiter came with coffee. Marie-Sophie drew the shawl more closely round her.

"Are you chilly?" he said. "Maybe we should have stayed in Cannes after all."

"Oh, no," she said. "You wouldn't believe how nice the air smells in the day up here. Why should I want to stay by the sea when I live by the lake? And Cannes is so noisy. And the Carlton is so stiff. I should have brought something wool. Tell me some more about that Egyptian woman."

He smiled. "Remarkable," he said. "She was an aging beauty of the Farouk court and she's lived at the Carlton ever since. Half of one wing of the third floor. Never leaves it. And she will never use the telephone and she will not see anybody except her servant and her chamberlain. Yes, chamberlain. So twice a year I go there and I sit with my briefcase in a drawing room like a set from *Aïda* and a citizen in a court uniform comes in and takes my proposals – without a word, mind you – and vanishes. And I sit there drinking sweet coffee for a couple of hours. Then he comes back and my proposals are covered with objections in pencil. So I rework it and send it down to be typed by the hotel. Then I wait some more and a woman with a flute wanders in and plays to me for half an hour and disappears – I'm not making this up. Then we send the papers back in and a mound of caviar appears to keep me company. They come back with more objections. Down to the typist. Finally, about four o'clock, the chamberlain comes back and at the bottom of my papers is a little penciled word, 'Proceed.' That's it. I've never laid eyes on her. I think I manage about one-fifth of her business and there's millions of it. It's very profitable. She's quite sharp as a matter of fact. Never say Cannes is dull."

Indeed, he loved the Riviera. Loved money and women and sun. It gave him considerable satisfaction, on these trips, to perfect the financial arrangements that brought forth jewel-like villas among cliffs and pines, crisp yachts, and gatherings of lobster and flowers and champagne. He also liked to stay above it and fly the Jaguar – which was behaving very well – up the hill each night to a small and expensive aerie. He hoped, with a twinge of guilt, that Marie-Sophie was not bored.

She laughed. "Oh, those Egyptians," she said. "They are not like other people. What else did you do?"

"There wasn't much time left by then. I saw Maroudi. He's fatter than ever. He's thinking of selling his place in Montreux and staying down here all year."

She leaned back. "So this is a day you can tell me about?" she said.

"What?" he said. "Yes, of course."

"Not a day like yesterday when you half drop your eyes and say, 'No big problems, but those clients are difficult'?"

In her flawless French she was a sly imitation of his trace of Boston. He heard it with apprehension. She had never done that.

"I don't know what you mean," he said. He knew very well. Much of yesterday had been spent in the tangled affairs of a development company which provided the

257

front for a group of rich and militant Libyan refugees. The less said about it the better.

"Is it because," she said, "there are things one does not bother to tell a little Arab girl?"

He looked for at least a trace of a smile. There was none. Her back was rigid.

"It's perfectly all right. It's perfectly all right. I was very well used to it with my husband. I would ask him something about our vineyards, because that was our life, and he would wave his hand and say, 'We just do it the usual way.' So I can quite understand that there are things that don't have to do with the drawing room or the bed that a clever European would not bother to tell a little *Arabe* about. Why should you be better than him? Or is it because I am too stupid to understand very much? I went to school in Paris, but I shouldn't think I could have understood it all, should you?"

It was too sudden, too much without cause, and besides, this did not happen to them. He said, with small aplomb, "I've just finished telling you what I did all day."

"And the other days? Are you doing something dishonest? Are you a crook? Or are you seeing someone else? Did you bring me down here to sit on a mountain while you go and see some woman in Nice?"

"Do you believe that? Either one?"

"No. Not really," she said drearily.

"You could have come yesterday, or today. You could have shopped in Cannes. You said you didn't want to."

"You didn't seem to want me. Why should I want to shop all day alone? Do you know how much it hurts to ask you all this? It's just I don't know what I'm for. I have this stupid job at home and I spend my time waiting for you and I don't know what you intend for us and when you take me on vacation you leave me alone all day, and then you're evasive and vague."

He had a sudden odd vision of Witham laughing at him and thought, *This wouldn't happen to the real CIA*, but

258

he put it aside at once because what mattered was in front of him. Marie-Sophie's face, in the vagrant light of the terrace candles, was damply dismal, and the change from the glorious, dark luster of her eyes by night to the watery and blinking ones before him now made him grasp her hand, much too hard, and be rewarded by a tremendous and uneven sniff. He thought, *I am still going to have to lie.*

He said, "Let's walk down the path. Will you walk with me?"

She shook her head, then nodded it, both silently. He thought as fast as he could. The path wandered through the hotel garden. Floodlit beds of roses and begonias glowed through groves of pine.

He said, "Do you know what it's like to have a hundred secret Arab accounts?"

She minutely smiled. "That would be a lot of secrets."

"I'm buried in secrets. Half my clients know each other and half of them are trying to cheat each other. If they even knew who else I advised they'd get frightened and run away. I keep secrets from Arab governments. I keep secrets from the Swiss. I keep my appointments secret. My office has a secret door, you've seen it. I don't even have names on my files – just numbers. I think in secrets. I have to. Do you understand that?"

She nodded doubtfully.

"I escape from them to you. You'd never be jealous of them if you know how they made me feel. Sometimes I am even afraid of them. The secrets could change me into something I do not want to be. It is you that heals me. I would begin to die without you. I don't have secrets from you. Just a habit. Maybe I want to look a little better to you than I am."

She stopped in front of him. "Is that really true?" she said.

Her face was in shadow. Beyond her, lighted roses glowed like blood in the night.

"Yes."

"Oh," she said. She took his hand and held it close and silent.

Oh, God, he thought. *That was easy*. He thought it with self-disgust.

He thought she was asleep. Through the open window came the faintest smell of pine, the hoot of an owl higher up the hill, and the lingering cicadas. His arm was around her. Her back was warm against his chest. The crown of her hair moved just perceptibly against his nose.

She said thoughtfully and quite awake, "Is it the Americans you work for?"

He almost put his foot through the bottom of the bed.

"What do you mean? What Americans?"

"Why, the government. The CIA, of course." She spoke as though to a slightly backward child.

"That's the most ridiculous thing I ever heard!"

She spoke still with sweet reason. "I wouldn't mind if it was true. I've been thinking about it. It's just a question of what it means for us."

"Go to sleep," he said.

"Yes, but we must talk about it soon. Good night."

He woke late but with unease. Marie-Sophie was rested, warm, serene. She ate a croissant for breakfast instead of unsugared fruit. She dressed in a silk skirt and vest which played at being tweed. This was the day they were to leave St.-Paul-de-Vence. Les Baux, in the limestone crags at the far north of the Marseilles plain, was halfway across southern France. The Jaguar would do it in three hours.

She rode almost in silence. That was no cause for alarm. On long drives, she nearly always did so. Her scent prevailed discreetly over leather. It occurred to him that she wore the scent she knew to be his favorite. He was grateful for her silence. When he drove fast, his thinking, relaxed and concentrated, was unusually clear.

It might have all but knocked him out of bed, but in the light of day her guess seemed neither disastrous nor odd. She was observant and clever and he knew the intermittent clarity of eyes of love. He could deny it. Completely and with force. She would believe him and be left with a sour broth of doubt. He rejected that out of hand. He thanked God she was not a fool. He would deny it *pro forma*, letting her know that she was right, and she would comprehend instantly and accept that compromise. He guessed she had already. His trust in her was never in doubt.

So there was no problem. How fortunate for him. How untrue. Her guess had put Witham beside them in the car and, next to Marie-Sophie, Witham did not look nice. For Witham had failed him.

Stears was a private soldier in the war against communism. Well and good. To that he was committed. Wop did not so much hate communism abstractly as resent it concretely. Its theology, at once fantastic and banal, its armies of morose thugs with bad teeth, its crude and noisy lies placed the totalitarian world, for him, fair and square in the dilapidated outskirts of hell – watched over by varicose concierges and smelling of cabbage. In the most concrete terms, the only ones that mattered, the victory of communism would be the replacement of Marie-Sophie by a prison wardress. In grander terms, it seemed to him that Berbia, Kuwait, Saudi Arabia, were places where the human spirit could more or less decently live while South Yemen physically and morally stank. To know that creatures like Yamadi and Khamal had been illuminated in their dirty basement by his foxiness, his guess, his brain, was a warm and personal pleasure.

So what was wrong with Witham, his commanding officer in this pleasant war? Witham cheated. Witham made duplicity dishonest. It was stupid to say "Witham." Witham was the Company. The Company cheated. It was all very well – it was a captivating game – to lie to

261

your clients, to lie to the country you lived in, to lie to your love if your lies produced the precious ammunition for a noble war. It was something else if the war were an office brawl. This had been, as Witham said, his most significant operation to date. He had seen the Company's long fingers move. It had also opened his eyes. He had seen the Company lie to itself – feebly repeating an official doctrine that its own data contradicted. He had seen McNaughton hide data from the Company. He had seen the dribble of information that he himself sent to his chief – hiding even this from McNaughton – used to push McNaughton into an unsupported operation for the sake of Witham's institutional prestige. He had revered McNaughton. He had seen McNaughton blamed for his own failure and his own death. He guessed now that he was seeing McNaughton's death misinterpreted.

He was not shocked. The Company had turned out merely to be on a level with the rest of his life. He had no right to shock. He looked at his sleeve of English wool, his Gübelin cuff links, the gold bracelet of his Vacheron watch, his Jaguar. If one changed Wop Stears for Sidi Oubad, would the difference be so great? He was a half-stateless, luxurious *grand bourgeois* living by his wits in a neutral city. His work was secrets, tax avoidance, smart deals, stealth. He was very good at it. He had taken a heritage of Massachusetts puritan and Tuscan count and lived as the new European aristocracy – an aristocracy not of fragile châteaux but of deluxe, replaceable restaurants and hotels, an aristocracy smooth and resilient as grease. What was more, he liked it. If he thought that a stainless, warrior CIA would turn his eyes at least morally blue, his jaw square, would even make him an American, was that the fault of the Company?

It had not even entirely failed him. Not altogether. His life since school in England – before that, since the first understood stories of other boys' fathers in the war – had been corrupted by his own father's half-committed, half-thought, not quite intended, and ill-defined treason.

262

A waste – so little gained, so little escaped from, so much thrown away. He could weep at times for his clever father, his pretty mother – friend of Dos Passos, daughter of a count, published, photographed, and even liked – in their frivolous and fatal cowardice. If it was really even that. He suspected that his father had run in 1940 to Vichy France with the same cool shrug with which he would have refused to worry about an unpaid bill. The food was good there and it wasn't his war. He had not been a traitor. Some snobbish satires of democracy do not make a traitor, even written in the wrong time and place, even translated into German, even reviewed in Berlin. It had been just enough to ensure that his son grew up with ostracized and exiled parents, snickers from the village boys, a fear of opening his mouth at school, and a growing knot of love and anger. All that, the Company had in part redeemed. He had worked for it first with love.

But not if it led toward treacheries of its own. So drop it? He couldn't now. If he was at the beginning of the chain that had brought about McNaughton's death, he would at least, if he could, complete that chain. But then? Quit the pretense? The idea gave him a sudden pleasure. It would be one layer of duplicity gone. It came to him that he had known since waking that he would have to be more guarded with Marie-Sophie now, not less. She would never know, she would always guess, where Giovanni stopped and the CIA began. She would assume that he spied upon her friends. And so he did. Well, he could be free of it. Two years of Choate and four of Yale, a Boston surname, quite certainly did not impose upon a wandering Italian Genevese loyalties that Americans themselves, so far as he could see, almost universally rejected. Give it up!

And from now on the extent of his life would be intricate lunches, subtle advice, acquaintance sought for profit, unquestioning loyalty to the wealth of clients. He would get richer and richer. The game was absorbing. He enjoyed success. The compensations were innumerable. He sighed.

Marie-Sophie laid her hand on his knee. A red-tiled farmhouse, closeted with cypresses on a terraced hill, swept past them, the vine-rows flickering. He had opened the roof, and through it, even on the autoroute, came the smell of herbal hillsides under the midday sun.

"Such a sigh!" she said. She patted his knee and let her hand rest on it comfortably. It carried both affection and confidence and he heard her, as clearly as if she had actually said it, convey, *I am not going to be difficult. There is nothing to dread.* He smiled and shrugged and flashed his lights at a truck with ambitions to the fast lane, far ahead.

He could have her, he knew, forever. She would marry him with joy. Was that it? The note of grace? Was anything more really needed? He, an ordinary rich man, living in no particular place, doing well a job of no great mystery or merit, with no loyalties or adventure or cause, had beside him as a free offering her body as adventure, her moods as mystery, her needs, her happiness for loyalty and cause. He was given to quick certainties, which he immediately distrusted. He knew all at once that this was where joy lay waiting only to be noticed. He thought that it might even be true.

The surroundings, that evening, did their best to persuade him so. The Bergerie at Les Baux, all fourteen rooms of it, a Provençal *mas* surrounded by improbable limestone crags furnished by the Siennese masters, was his favorite resort in Europe, and its dining room, he maintained dogmatically, unchallenged in the world. He enjoyed her discovery of it. He walked her up to a mountain in the afternoon, through groves of olive. Butterflies flew above the maquis. Thyme and rosemary, bruised by their feet, hung in the air like resin. On the ridge, the air was suddenly sharp. The tight group of hills was set down on the plain like an arbitary and eccentric decoration. Far away was the smudge of Marseilles. The ruins of the Château des Baux looked like the skull of the adjoining hill. Marie-Sophie looked at it with growing approval.

She said, "Look, Giovanni, it faces the sea. It was against us. Against my Moroccans. We weren't always so feeble, you know. You Europeans forget that. You had to build castles to keep us out."

"I wouldn't really bother," he said.

"Now seriously," she said, "you should remember that. I think we should go down. I want to wash my hair."

Bathed and dressed, sitting by an autumnal fire of olive wood in the vaulted lounge, she glowed. She was the most beautiful woman in the room; she always was and was so by a kind of law of nature. Those more remarkable than Marie-Sophie, for they did exist, invariably used their bodies as a bludgeon or a monument or a shield, while hers was tentatively offered, gratefully known, but not absolutely believed by her.

On the night he had first taken her to bed, they had drunk Roederer Cristal Brut in the transparent bottle. It had become the wine not of their routine extravagance but of events. He studied, in the firelight, the list of colossal Burgundies, antique Bordeaux, and then, surprising himself, ordered Cristal Brut.

It came while they ate translucent, fenneled sheets of sea bass and salmon, rose and pearl. She looked at the clear bottle with a small surprise and unhidden pleasure, following it with her eyes until it went back into the bucket and the waiter bowed and left. She sipped it and sighed and said, "That's so nice." And then seriously, "But I don't want a prize for being a bitch."

Tonight her eyes had reverted from puddles to grottoes, and he looked into them with the familiar sense of vertigo and smiled and shook his head. But she went on.

"Or a prying bitch."

He said hurriedly, "That's all right," but she swept him aside and said, "But you have no idea how much happier I feel. I was getting so resentful and confused.

265

Now I know what you're doing it's all right, even if it's terrible. I mean, what you're *not* doing, don't I? I'm going to have to learn to talk backwards now, aren't I?" She laughed. It was close to a giggle.

Genuinely horrified, he said, "No! That's enough!"

She nodded dutifully and said, "Of course. I'll stop. Right there. Never again. You'll see."

Wop said seriously and quietly, "So may I."

But she looked at him then straightly and firmly and shook her head and said, "No. Not just like that. Not because of this. Because it must have been serious if you were doing it at all. I know from my father that these things are not toys. You pretend to be so fashionable and careless. Giovanni. But you are the only serious man I know. And I am a grown woman, not a child."

Much later, sinking into sleep in the Marie-Sophie-scented bed, he thought vaguely. *Serious, serious. It's too damn serious for them.* He thought drowsily of Marseilles tomorrow. It seemed incongruous. His bright idea of a week ago, about the ship, improbable and even childish. He considered reaching up and unsetting the alarm clock, spending the day with her. *No,* he thought, *it's a stone to be turned. Methodically. Perhaps the last.* He left the clock.

17

Stears did not go directly to the port. He had no precise plan. He rejected the idea of presenting himself with credentials, with authority. It would work but it would be remembered. Pretense of some sort would be necessary. Instinct told him that to pretend at all he would need to rub off some outer layers not only of the Riviera but of himself. He parked the Jaguar and walked.

He loathed Marseilles. It seemed to him a concatenation of Naples and Detroit. Naples as to moral order and Detroit as to air. He parked near La Canebière, Marseilles's great and fabled street, and walked down toward the center, the old harbor. La Canebière was given over to five-and-dime stores, shady foreign-exchange establishments, and pornographic films. He stopped to buy a cheap watch in a department store smelling of mothballs and sweat. He rubbed shoulders with sailors, Marseilles housewives with tight blouses squeezing flaccid flesh, and Arab laborers. It struck him as promising, though not agreeable, that he was perceived as one of them. Before the alarm clock had rung, while Marie-Sophie slept with her chin tucked into her neck, he had pulled from the corner of a suitcase a coarse black sweater and a pair of jeans. The permanent space around him, the space bought by a Savile Row suit, was gone. The Arabs, this year, were wearing wollen ski caps. He would tell Madame Oubad. It should encourage her.

He wandered toward the shopping district. He sought a clean café for breakfast. Opposite the Stock Exchange, a mountebank, in circus fetters and stripped to the waist, harangued the crowd before rolling on the sidewalk in broken glass. Wop looked at the shop windows. He crossed to Hermès' shop, the idea of a blouse for Marie-Sophie piercing the circumstances like a ray of light. There was a bundle on the sidewalk. He began to step around it, then stopped, transfixed. Below him was a tramp, the face almost hidden in stained white hair, the body heaped with rags, and in its lap a half-plucked, half-singed, half-bloody, half-eaten, strangled city pigeon. Wop abandoned simultaneously the project of the blouse and his own breakfast. He had been in Marseilles forty minutes and he felt seedy and depressed. The sweater scratched his skin and was already damp in the armpits. He thought he could manage to be a wop sailor at the port.

He took the bus. He stood. The port stretched five kilometers, north to south. He knew it just enough to think that the repair yards were somewhere in the center of it. Access worried him – how undocumented working stiffs were handled, he simply did not know. He got off at the passenger terminal for North Africa and Corsica at the southern extremity of the port. There at least there would be crowds. He decided he would speak French only if necessary. It was a pity his Italian was the noblest Tuscan, but few would notice.

He was not used to physical subterfuge. The terminal parking lot was surrounded by a chain-link fence. Beyond it, open, were the ranks of yellowed hangars, wharves, rails, and concealing traffic. There was an unwatched gap in the fence. He knew that he hesitated. He was used to open doors. *Remember that!* he thought. He sidled through, the fence wire catching his sweater. Well, he had begun.

He must not look lost. He walked fast, preoccupied, with the traffic, tending north. He tried to classify. He was at first in an area of general freight and then, it seemed, of cereals. The ships were for the most part aggressively modern, high, square-lined, and clean.

Here and there, at long intervals, he saw with gratitude, were dirty, rounded tramp steamers like disheveled ghosts from Conrad and Kipling. Forklift trucks scooted in arbitrary directions. Switching locomotives lurched into sudden motion. It worried him that there were few men on foot. Thereafter he kept close to loading bays. He felt as insignificant and ignorant as a bug on a desk. As yet, he had not had to speak to anybody.

Before him, the nature of the cranes had changed. They were huge, squat, rectangular. The repair yards must be close. He feared another barrier. He rounded the side of a hangar, keeping on the outskirts of the men around a line of loading trucks, and saw the yards. Impossible sight! A vast black hull, on dry land, blocking out the sky, was sawed neatly through the middle, like a fire log, and the two halves were being drawn inexorably apart. The air changed – no longer heavy with corn and diesel, it had the high, sharp smell of metal welded, riveted, and drilled. A forklift glided past his shoulder. He had never heard it among the shrieks of steel.

He studied the immediate prospect. Security seemed to be more general to the port than peculiar to sections. The north-south internal artery of the docks crossed the back of the repair yards. There was a checkpoint, but traffic was heavy and it was lightly manned. Most traffic was waved through. When a truck was stopped, it was the cargo, not the driver, that was checked. A theft control, he decided – pilferage in repair yards was rampant worldwide. A man on foot could not be suspected of toting very much. He waited until a mighty diesel was stopped and roaring at the gate. He walked angrily past the cab, shouting to the guard, "Now they tell me the bugger's over here!" He wondered what he meant. The guard shrugged, preoccupied. He was through. Wop very nearly grinned. The abstract, misty thought of taking a canny look at Hajji's ship was turning step by step into a concrete and exhilarating game.

But he was as lost as ever. He vaguely knew that 70

percent of the marine repair of France was taking place around him. Out of the huge sheer sides of a dry dock, the stern of a tanker projected like a topographical feature. Closer by, a freighter had had its entire superstructure lifted off and stacked neatly on dry land beside it. A block the size of several locomotives hung by a thread over another ship. He supposed it was an engine. Here, where the grandest vessels were treated as casually as Tinkertoys, the work on Hajji's little ship – something to do with leaking steam-lines and boilers – would be the equivalent of fooling with an outboard. He looked hopefully for some humbler section, some mechanical slum. He thought, and guessed that Hajji's ship would be berthed where the cranes were smallest. He studied the skyline and turned right.

He had it! He could not see the name, but four berths away a small, foul steamer, sprouting irregular winches like an untidy bug, lay grappled to the wharf. It seemed to be in one piece. A haze, in fact, rose from its smokestack. He slowed to as near a saunter as he dared and studied it. Now he could see the name – it was, rather touchingly, the only fresh paint on the ship. The *Leah*. Named after Hajji's oldest daughter. That was it, then. A gangplank was in place.

And, after all, he thought, *nothing of interest has occurred today*. Hajji's worn-out ship was in the yards, where it was supposed to be. It had not, by any evidence in sight, undergone any grand or startling metamorphosis. This part of the yards showed general signs – a crank-shaft here, a generator on a forklift over there – of being concerned with things like engines. The haze over the smokestack – steam must be up or getting there – surprised him vaguely. But Hajji had stressed that the repairs were finally close to finished and they would naturally run some kinds of tests. It occurred to him with irritation that he could just as well have driven up as Hajji's representative, strolled aboard, found out as much or more, and been back for lunch with

Marie-Sophie and a truffled quail. At least he could have walked openly on board.

As he could have done now, and didn't. There was no one immediately around the ship, and he had no doubt that if his purposeful, preoccupied walk had taken him through a checkpoint and two kilometers of dock it could take him down a gangplank too. He even looked. The gangplank led directly to a hatch and the companionway vanished into gloom, rust, and the bilious light of a distant bulb. It repelled. He felt a need for knowledge as for a flashlight.

He looked around the wharf. Activity – lathing noises, the sudden, violet glow of welding – seemed confined to the recesses of the hangar behind. There was no one on this wharf. But the forklift with the generator throbbed unattended in the center of the yard and it must have a driver somewhere. He crossed to it and waited in its oil-scented shade – a man belonging, but not rushed.

He saw at once that the driver was Italian. A big man, older than himself, in denim from neck to ankle, with gray hair and spectacles delicately set over a stonemason's, a centurion's, a foreman's face. He would be more than just a driver. He came from the hangar with papers in his hand, quickly but not scurrying, a man of authority interrupted in a task. Wop thought, *It is Italians like this who keep Europe running*, and, just as quickly, *He'll be hard to fool*. The man swung up on the other side of the forklift. He had not yet seen Stears. Stears loudly said,

"Buon giorno!"

The man looked down and covered surprise with irony. *"Buon giorno, Signore."*

Genoese, thought Stears. He saw the man look at him with polite and undisguised reserve as though doubtfully matching clothes to face.

"What do you want?" he said.

"I am engaged on the *Leah*," Stears said, "when she sails. But the company does not say when that will be. If it is still a day or two, there is some business here that I

271

can do. I came to see for myself. It seems all screwed up to me." *And if that's nonsense*, he thought, *the most they can do is arrest me*.

But it seemed that it wasn't, after all. The foreman shifted his eyes from Wop to look in grand contempt at the *Leah* from the height of the forklift.

"You should not have very long to wait," he said. "My colleague tells me that she is holding pressure now. He also tells me that if she comes back again he will personally scuttle her. Some crew has been arriving this morning to clean her up" – he quickly laughed – "as a matter of fact. You are working for cretins of course." He looked at Wop, puzzled but with suspicion in reserve. "What are you doing on an Arab scow like that? You're not an officer."

"Electrical fitter," said Wop. He wondered how many investment counselors it took to change a light bulb. "There is work to be done at sea. She is not my kind of ship but there is a slump in shipping. You may have heard of it."

Less convinced than uninterested, the foreman said, "You know best. Of course she is not worth repairing."

Wop nodded judiciously. "She is a little old."

The foreman laughed again, once, like a fox's bark. "Her boilers are rotten. I was worried for our men down there. Her steam pipes have more patch than metal. Her condenser is about to go. And she belongs to the worst kind of owner in the world – the kind that will not stick to a repair he begins. My countryman, you have a fine berth."

And now Wop's ears were pricked. The Hajji he knew was not a vacillator. "Doesn't stick to it, eh?" he said. "That's bad."

The foreman slapped the side of the forklift and settled back in it as on a judgment seat. "Brought her in a month ago. Major overhaul of the steam system. But stretch it out – don't run up the bills too fast. Stupid bastards ended up paying as much in wharf charges as in shopwork. Ten days later they tell us to stop work, patch her up for sea. She's got a valuable cargo. Valuable cargo! So the old wreck farts off in a storm, no less, spends two days out, and comes back leaking steam like a sauna. We start work again. Ten days later, if you can believe this, the same thing happens – the steam pipes are patched by then and they say the boilers can wait. Thirty-six hours out. They even contrive to break a winch, God knows how. When they come limping back that time I try to refuse the job – a ship like that has no business in a yard like this – but I am overruled. I tell you this because I do not like to see an Italian in such a crew, whoever you are. And now, after all this fucking about, we are told to get her ready to sail any time in the next forty-eight hours. Do you see why I am not impressed?"

Wop shrugged. Ten days had been the approximate period between shipments. But then again, she could not have gone very far in thirty-six hours. It occurred to him, the wildest guess seeming improbably, grotesquely true, that she could very well indeed have sailed to a rendez-vous and back.

He said, "Most of these small owners are a pest. There is no room at sea for ships like that."

The foreman briefly frowned as one slightly contra-dicted. "There are limits," he said. "And I am not the cicerone here. I have work to do. You will make your choices." He put the forklift in gear. It rocked away on bulbous tires toward a dapper, small container ship with a sky-blue hull – the *Anna Beiner*, *Bremen*.

He looked again at the *Leah*. She was still unwatched. Whatever crew she had aboard was still below. If, fantastically, he was right; if the clever thought of a Geneva evening that Hajji had behaved too oddly about a ship too conveniently placed had somehow struck the mark, then the poor despised *Leah*, this patched and stained and broken toy, carried in her holds, like a bomb, a vicious charge of mayhem. He looked again at the gangplank. For one already here, disguised, covert, for an investment counselor of his own free will converted into a ferret, an "agent," a spook, there was only one possible next step that did not imply that he had turned tail and run. There was nothing more he could find out up here. It was greatly in his favor that the ship was still under the repair yard's influence, if only tenuously, and that the crew, therefore, whoever they were and whatever their orders, could not be very greatly surprised to see a stranger on board. If he could help it, they would see nothing.

His first impression was her smell. The hatchway breathed out an air that seemed compounded of heavy oil, a filthy seafood house, and the public lavatory of an ill-kept racetrack. His second was that she was wet – condensation gleamed on the companionway, streaks of damp rust ran down the bulkheads. His third was that she was built for dwarfs. Moving quickly down a passageway, he struck his head against a steel insert put there, apparently, for spite. Below deck, she was alive. He could hear the sound of hammering, conducted through metal from God knew where, and intermittent, distant, footsteps. Ventilators moved warm, four air. He had no clue as to her layout. He passed an open door that seemed to open into a sluttish dormitory. He smelled the stink of a latrine. Naked bulbs glowed at long intervals over narrow stairways pointing downward. Downward he went. He had the impression that he was approaching engine rooms. There would be people there and, besides, that was not his objective. He should find the holds. He realized that he did not know what one looked like.

He stopped. As soon as he touched the bottom of the steps, the noises of activity, vague and distant until now, leaped into his presence as though he had opened a door. They came from the passageway, left and right. Doors were open, lights on behind them, in one a shadow moved to and fro. He felt cheated, deceived. He had formed the idea of a ship barely peopled by furtive presences. It occurred to him that he had simply wandered through the crew quarters, which were temporarily vacated, and was now on a working deck, which was occupied. He stood still. From one of the doors a voice, in Arabic, loudened, a footstep sounded more purposefully, a shadow rose in the door. He backed into the stair. A man came out, a small Arab seaman in dirty dungarees, with ruined teeth, and walked away from him down the passageway. He sighed in relief. Then froze. There was a footstep above him, near the head of the stair. Anyone who started down the stair would see him almost at once. The passageway, again, was empty. He flushed into it. To the left, he thought toward the bow, there was a door open, no light behind. He dodged into it. It appeared to be a small bare office, not much used. He looked through the crack of the door. A man came down the stair, two men. Quite different from the little seaman. These were young, Arab also, hard and fit, in pressed pants and khaki shirts. They moved with authority. They crossed before his door. One said, as though ending a discussion, "The moon cannot be helped." The other shrugged. Officers, Wop guessed. But damned if they didn't look more like the junior officers of a warship than of a dissolute tramp.

He noticed all at once that a huge, cold object had come into his belly, as though he had swallowed a rock. It was, he realized, fear; it was Yamadi and Khamal. He had changed worlds. His gallant, merry enterprise had to do with Hajji's little ship, and with Hajji there was no risk at all. He might have to explain himself over a meal. Just conceivably, he might lose an account. But dark, smelling corridors, hard young men, had nothing to do with Hajji. They had to do with Yamadi and Khamal.

He withdrew into the dark and forced himself to think. He was not sure, the acoustics were confusing, but it seemed that there was movement above him that had not been there before. Possibly, more men had come aboard. Possibly, men were moving around the ship. Possibly he was wrong. In any case, it was obvious that the ship was being gradually crewed, made ready, woken up. He had to recognize that his way out, unseen, had become doubtful. The rock inside him grew. He reminded himself that his situation was more embarrassing than grave. He could always, at the end, play his role of a yard workman with late business on board. If the ship were innocent, there would be no problem. If his wild guess were right, then her officers would want a contretemps at the Marseilles docks less than anything in the world. Of course that was true. He could leave getting off until later. The question was, should he look further now?

For the moment the passageway was clear. It occurred to him that if there was one place on a ship where a visiting mechanic had no business being found, it was in a ship's office. There was no security in staying there. He looked, listened, and slipped out.

He knew his way around a yacht, but not a freighter. He had not thought of that when he had conceived of looking over the ship. He had no clear idea of how the living and working quarters would relate to the cargo holds. He seemed to have blundered into the most populated part of the ship. No doubt that was why the passageways and stairs had led there. He was obviously above both engine room and hold. The engine room would be astern or amidships. The cargo must be down and forward. There were three lighted doorways ahead of him. Beyond that, the passageway seemed dim, empty, and ended at an unlighted stairhead. He moved quickly. He passed an antediluvian radio room and a room with a long, stained table – presumably a mess. These were empty. An Arab in a tattered undershirt stood vacantly and scratched his armpits in the galley. So far he had seen four men and heard, he guessed, two more. That was not a crew. Whether the rest were absent or elsewhere on the ship, he could not know. He reached the stairhead.

At the bottom, it was almost dark. The light came from

aft. The air smelled of hot oil. One door immediately faced him. Forward, the passage ran two meters and stopped at a massive vault. Astern, a bare passageway ran toward a lighted door and noises of metal. Perhaps the engine room. He opened the door in front. He shut it quickly. It opened on a fuseboard of antique design in which small blue sparks crept ominously. He quickly resigned his post as electrician. He turned to the vault. He suspected he was at his goal. This was a waterproof door of the heaviest kind. Its fastening was at its center, a capstan screw wide enough for both arms extended. If there was light behind it, it would certainly not show through. There was a risk in opening it. He thrust it from his mind. He threw his weight on the capstan.

It did not budge. He tried again. The third time he breathed deeply, positioned his feet for the greatest leverage, and pulled in short, shuddering spasms. He heard his joints crack. The capstan was solid as a stanchion. He looked more closely, his eyes now accustomed to dim light. What he had taken for paint was rust. The capstan was frozen solid. He looked further. The flange and sill of the waterproof door were fused with rust. He leaned against it, thinking, and knowing he was right. This was indeed the door connecting to the hold. It was never used. The invariable access was through the cargo hatch. The cargo hatch would be in full view of bridge and deck and, no doubt, required a winch to raise it.

So the Secret Agent, having tracked down a rusty door, could now go home. On the way out, he could go over the mannifest with the captain, perhaps, and sell him a bond or two. This game was over. He could alert Witham to his frail deduction and, if Witham listened, the ship could perhaps be tracked and examined upon landing. By whom and how, he did not know. He did not know this: the chance of his chain of command working fast enough to bring the French on board the *Leah* before she sailed was nil.

He slowly climbed the stair. The acoustics were such that he could hear little from the upper passageway until he was halfway to it. The crown of his head would rise above the stair before he could see farther.

There was more activity. Feet walked the passage. More than one man's. He could hear two or three voices in quick succession. They were not extremely close; he had the impression that movement was still confined to the same areas as before. The stairhead, he remembered, was in shadow. He crept on up.

His eyes reached the passageway as three men came down into it. They wore cheap trousers and dirty shirts – seamen. He flinched as one walked towards him but saw him turn into the galley and heard his voice; the other man must still be in there. Then another. This one wore a white shirt with mangled epaulets, one hanging loosely by its threads. An officer, then. The officer walked quickly down the passageway, looking into each door in turn, speaking briefly – a tour of quick inspection. He turned and headed back up the stair. There could be no doubt that the ship was being progressively crewed. It seemed that the men were arriving in twos and threes. What proportion of the crew was now aboard, how near she was to being able to sail, he did not know. She had been in the yards ten days. A ship, even an old small ship, was clearly not a motorboat to be started up all at once. And when she would in fact sail was another matter yet. If she were a virtuous tramp, then presumably as soon as possible – and to a cargo wharf. If she were what he increasingly found himself assuming her to be, then she was no doubt headed for another rendezvous, the last, off the coast. That would be at night. The rendezvous would be outside the shipping lanes, outside lights, beyond routine patrols; it would be pointless for it to be much farther. Say, seventy-five to one hundred kilometers at most. She could surely do ten knots. Eight hours at most to rendezvous. That would hardly be before ten at night. Most likely, it would be later. It was now eleven A.M. Innocent or guilty, it seemed likely that she might move in a few hours, but not quite yet. That was grand. He could lounge about. He discovered that his spine was now continuously crawling, that to be discovered had somehow changed from an embarrassment into a fright, and that his way out unseen would by now be a matter of the purest chance. The situation seemed unlikely to improve. It was time to take the bull by the horns, get up, walk out, and trust to luck, surprise, and wit.

So he tensed in preparation. He began to rise. Then hung back as more footsteps, swift, authoritative, came down from above: the three officers – the two in khaki and the one with the torn epaulet. He realized all at once that the three made no possible group. Epaulets was clerically thin, a man in his mid-thirties, a discontented mouth, a face marked by worried, dutiful authority and the promise of dyspeptic breath. It bore now a look of small and weary protest. He carried a notebook. His colleagues had a look that Stears had seen twice in photographs and once in life: on an Israeli paratrooper, on a French commando, and on the German shepherd of a Cuban client with Batista loyalties and a walled villa by the lake. It was a look in which fear, doubt, mercy, or wavering were not so much not present as simply laughed to scorn. They carried machine pistols. They treated Epaulets with a swift, passionless bullying. They separated. One stood sentry in the passageway. The other, accompanied by Epaulets, went to the far end of it and entered a cabin there. They came out. They entered the next one. There were curt voices there. The seaman with the itching armpits wandered out of the galley, speaking back over his shoulder to his friend inside. He had a monkey's crazy, kindly face. He set off up the corridor. He had not yet seen the sentry. The sentry barked at him, "Stop!"

The man's back showed sudden fear and also, lesser, dignity. He said reasonably, "I am going to my bunk. I

need to get my medicine." It was clear that he knew th
sentry.

The sentry said, "Get back in there. Wait for inspec
tion. Have your papers ready."

"I will be back before they get here. And why do yo
need my papers? You have known me for two months."
He said it weakly and bravely and he started toward th
stair.

The sentry walked toward him with a smile. "Yes," h
said. "I know you." He was within a foot of the other an
he brought up the butt of the machine pistol like a ma
pitching up a shovel and struck its corner into the man'
breastbone. The seaman gasped and staggered. Stear
winced. The sentry took the man by his shoulders
turned him, and pushed him back toward the galley.

"And you know me," he said. He turned, still quit
relaxed, and walked back to the stair. The seaman wa
probably not injured, and the incident was not impor
tant. Epaulets and his colleague inspected another
closer cabin – quickly, silently, perhaps an empty one
Soon they would be at the office he had first run into. H
was no longer frightened. He was terrified.

He thought again, shuffling the cards, looking at fact
discarding personal panic. First, the case was proved
These men, their arms, their actions, had no possibl
function on a lawful freighter. The thought arose tha
they were merely private security guards on the lookou
for stowaways and petty theft. The thought fade
without trace. And his own situation? Escape unsee
was for the moment impossible, and for the future
doubtful. Bluff was still not quite impossible. Thes
people could not risk association with the mysteriou
vanishing of a French shipyard worker. If they doubte
him they would still, surely, have to take him ashore t
check his story and, once ashore, he had nothing wors
to fear than the French. The danger was that they woul
not doubt him but simply disbelieve him altogether. H
had no papers. He had, he realized suddenly, no tools

He could never pass an interrogation on things mechanical. He had a vivid vision of the doubt in those hard, able faces flickering out, replaced by a sneering certitude of pitiable fraud. It made him cold. That moment might be close. It was possible that they might end their search before the stairhead; it also seemed improbable. So his needs were these: a place to hide, where he could wait until there was at least no posted guard and he could perhaps rush off the ship by surprise and speed; a place that would at least add to the likelihood, if he were found, that his disguise was genuine. The area of the engine room seemed his best, bad hope.

So he started down the stair. As his eye sank below it he saw the face of the sentry swing toward him as though attracted by the movement. He was halfway down before he heard the footsteps. They were not urgent. They were deliberate, even quiet. But they were unpausing. The man was coming to look.

He turned toward the engine room. Even if he ran, tearing pretense to tatters, the guard would be at the stairway before he was there. The passage had other doorways, but they were not close, looked securely shut, and might well be locked. The cargo door was sealed as a tomb. The footsteps, muffled now, were nearer. The door in front of him, he remembered, had opened easily. The fuseboard. It was the size of a broom closet. He opened it. Small, random worms of violet sparks awoke and died in front of him. He got in as if it were a den of snakes. He turned his back and shut the door. a connection behind him hissed briefly. He did not know whether to touch a point would be to be shocked, burned, or simply turned to ashes. He heard the guard's steps descend the stairway slowly, then stop, wait, then more swiftly reascend, recede. None of this, absolutely none of it, was happening to Giovanni Stears.

In the darkness, he leaned against the door, his forehead to the metal, his back sucked in from the wires behind. The darkness was strangely comforting. It suggested surrender, permanence, peace. He had to force his hand to open the door a crack, then further. He looked onto dim iron bulkheads. There were intricate footfalls somewhat to stern above his head. The inspection of the corridor was proceeding and must be coming to its end. Whether the guard, having then found nothing, would search there with extra care or not at all seemed equally likely. He shut the door again. If in ten minutes he heard no footstep on the stair, he would assume the search would go no further.

He waited, bathing his forehead with the cool metal door. His hearing grew better. Ten minutes passed. There was no footfall on the stair, but those above his head continued. He waited. There was a flaw, he realized, in his plan: he had no means of knowing whether these sounds were the search minutely progressing or merely some activity in, perhaps, the galley. The commandos might be gone to the hold, the bridge, the devil. They might be standing in the corridor. He sought some clue, some indication, any. He was becoming paralyzed. He noted it with disgust and dread. He waited. In five minutes, no matter what, he'd move.

He thought at first that the pulse in the metal was his blood. It knocked faintly at his temple. Then it strengthened and he felt it in his feet. It quickened and the iron around him shivered. His heart beat with it then and he convinced himself that the pulse was his. It slowed and became regular and strong. He knew it then. Steam pistons moving. The throttle had been opened. The shaft was slowly turning. His ship had sailed.

His first sensation was of black, hopeless, formless panic. The second was of weak relief. Now there was nothing that he had immediately to do. Escape was obviously impossible. Unless it was a mariners' custom to repair to the fuses upon sailing, he could stay there, he and his fear, for thirty minutes, an hour or two, a day. Liberty Hall! His third sensation was of self-contempt. He, a successful, a clever, a significant man had followed a bumbling and puerile trail into danger both farcical and deadly. He was conscious of a number of layers of squalid terror. He saw himself lingering in hunger and thirst. He saw himself fried by voltage should the ship suddenly roll. He saw himself hunted, beaten, tortured, shot, flung over the side, drowned. He reached final truth: he needed to urinate and feared electrocution if he did so. He suddenly, silently, began to laugh. Having laughed, he thought.

He slowly opened the door. There was no reason he could think of why anyone should be there. With the ship at sea, the obsession with security would lessen. A routine would grow. The ship did not seem heavily manned and the crew would soon be divided into shifts. He could not contemplate survival for days or a week – it could hardly be more – but each half hour in turn could conceivably be managed. He had survived the most critical time already. Once he had lived for six months with a slipped disc. Six months of pain is unimaginable. A day could be faced. He guessed it was the same with terror.

He noted that which he should have seen before. Under the stairway was a dim, tall space. Within it, he could be almost comfortable, could monitor the corridor above. For the long term it was near the galley. Considering the general sanitariness of the ship, attention to his immediate need would leave no sensible trace. These considerations were a thin membrane stretched above paralysis. They gave him an unexpected satisfaction and pride. He began to wait as he had never waited before. He waited, perhaps, for night.

The motion of his ship, first tentative, then real. The forced attempt, in his iron dungeon, to visualize the harbor of Marseilles: the Railroad Byzantine cathedrals, La Major and Notre-Dame-de-Garde on its opposing hill; the small scrolled lighthouses at the harbor mouth where big ships pass between old men's cane poles; the painted fishing boats; Fort St. Jean with fig trees growing out of its sheer, soft stone; the Château d'If. Enough. Waves of fear, then unease, and finally forced attention as feet approached and receded from his stair. The beginning of smells from the galley. Hunger. The thought of Marseilles prawns, their saltiness and taste relating to Atlantic ones as violins to a double bass. A sexual reverie of Marie-Sophie awakening into the cold of fear. The thought that she would not yet expect him back – and what if she did? She had no clue where he was gone. The pain in his legs. The immobility of his watch. Time, the jailer. And the fear of change.

But patterns developed. No one came seriously near his stair. He became confident enough to creep halfway up it. He could duck down again before it could be reached. The commandos were nowhere to be seen. No doubt they were on the bridge or resting. Epaulets came once to his own former office, briefly. The galley worked. Random transmissions, most in French, emanated from the radio room. At six o'clock the clanging from the galley loudened. A slovenly steward appeared, went in, spoke irritably, and finally staggered out with a tray piled high with dented covers. A bell rang. There was a rush of footsteps. He dared to raise his head to count the men entering the mess. Twelve, he thought. They ate and chattered. He tantalized himself with the far-fetched, magnificent idea that in four or five hours he might creep up for an Arab seaman's leavings.

The ship did not visibly go to bed. Men, not particularly employed, loafed as though waiting. The engines pulsed on. Out of endless, thirsty, dismal time the probability congealed that this would be the night of rendezvous. A second, separate landscape of fear attached to it. When the rendezvous took place, it would surely be his task to formulate some unimaginable strategy, to leave his safe, appalling niche, to find a vantage point, to spy. He tried to plan, but realized that knowing nothing of the general layout of the ship or the crew's future actions, such planning would not far from mysticism. At half past nine, the expected, unimaginable surprise – the engine stopped.

And nothing happened. The roaring and gurgling in the ship's belly stopped. She lay slightly wallowing. A man in pressed pants and a cheap aviator's shirt came out of the radio cabin, stretched, wandered into the galley, and came out again with a cup of coffee. Stears hugged the wall of his stair. When he was nine years old he had been sent alone, by train, from his parents' house in what had recently been Vichy France to his new English boarding school. His father, grandly and with a little speech he had later found in *Tom Brown's School Days*, had given him almost half the pocket money he needed for the trip. He had missed his train in Paris. He had sat up all night in the Gare du Nord in his strange, brand-new school uniform, his suitcase on his lap and Algerian soldiers all around. After the taxi he had had money to buy one roll. Then as now he had been ashamed to cry.

The ship's horn sounded – once, quickly, like a melodious hiccup. A bell rang harshly. Now it had begun. The ship murmured with footsteps. On his corridor, men roused from waiting or dozing came out of the cabin and disappeared up the stair. He had by now a tolerable estimate of how many men there were in each cabin. Except for the radio operator, the corridor was deserted. The cooks left the galley empty. His stomach churned them a farewell.

The stewed mutton was disgusting – scorched, greasy, and by now congealed. The fava beans were slimy with overcooking and lay in a thin gray gruel. There were roaches suspiciously close to each, receding. He assumed they had been in it. He ate with a cooking spoon in gulps, scarcely chewing, alternating with wads of pita bread. Dimly he remembered the dining room at the Bergerie. He dined in ninety seconds. Fearing unboiled water – dysentry would not improve his situation – he gulped cold bitter coffee. He looked for some wine. Damn all Muslims! So much for dinnertime.

Food and reflection propelled him on. He recognized that in his heart he had thought that having swallowed scraps, he would scuttle to his hole. But there were no footsteps above him – as Eskimos are said to have names of forty-seven different kinds of snow, so he was developing an acute perception of feet. He remembered that above him were the crew quarters, surely of all places in the ship the least occupied during a demanding task. Above that was the open deck. Hurry was the order of the hour. A man moving fast, preoccupied, would be nothing odd. On deck it was full night. He dimly knew that to burrow back when action at least was possible was to squeeze himself another notch into cramp and fear. To seize a chance would be a rush of blood, a breath of air, a meal for the heart.

So he padded down the passage. The radio operator sat with his back to the door. He gained the bottom of the stair. He listened, scurried up. The door of the latrine was open now and the metal floor was filmed with dirty water. The dormitory was littered with dunnage and smelled of cheap tobacco. The companionway was unguarded. Beyond that, sweet-smelling night!

But not quite dark. A half-moon was up. Still, he saw at once, the crew was gathered around the winches and the cargo hatch, this area was lighted, and it would be difficult to see into the dimness beyond. His clothes were dark. The men were clearly set off by the light, grouped in a rough circle around the path of the winch, talking, gesturing, somehow weirdly suggestive of a Cape Cod clambake. The winch whined. A shout came from the sea below – he could not see the boat. A dark bulk rose up, caught the light, and blossomed into a crate with stenciled markings. The winch arthritically turned toward the cargo hatch. Outstretched arms steadied the crate. Voices called into the hold, were answered. The crate jerked down into its mouth.

He was too visible. He was gawping like a yokel. He saw the two commandos and an officer he did not know pacing around the men or looking urgently over the side. One looked in his direction and his chest froze. He crept behind a ventilator cowl. He considered crossing the deck to see the boat below and rejected it. There would be a risk and he would see an anonymous vessle with an unknown crew. What mattered was the cargo. Here, behind his cowl, he was a few meters closer. The stencils were on the tantalizing edge of visibility. The crates moved slowly through the light, but they also swung; just as a marking registered on the brain, the crate would rotate dreamily and brush it from view. Besides, he knew nothing of military abbreviations or weapons codes. But there were no Cyrillic letters here – no doubt of that. And the stars were American, not red. The eye quickly caught "U.S." So disguises were over. He was seeing, or nearly seeing, the real thing.

And suddenly the sharp edge of fear inside him shifted a little and turned into fierce triumph. He ruled the game. He, the amateur, the humble "noncareer," had reached up and caught Yamadi and Khamal in their secret progress. He, from all the ocean, had set his finger upon this vessel. He, a man of business and rich hotels, had crept through this stinking steamer, beaten the search, fed from his enemies' table, and now seen more than McNaughton himself had ever seen. He could survive the voyage – al–Tabek, even at a bicycle's speed, was less than three days' sailing. He would ride the ship like a secret nemesis. It would be almost a routine – unpleasant, even desperate, but possible. Once off the ship, he was the master. A call to the embassy, even a shout to the police, and all was finished. He had seen enough now. Best to get back while the work was in full progress.

He turned. The entry, some five meters away, glowed dully from within. He moved toward it slowly. Something behind him caught his eye. He stopped. Where he had stood, the cowl, was washed in a small pool of light.

He looked at it, startled. At once, the light moved, rushed past him, and played around the door. It trembled, swung, and rushed again – this time, he knew, straight for him. He jumped, half stumbled, and heard his own feet thud. The light veered toward him. He twisted. He heard a voice speak sharp above him. *The bridge – of course, the bridge!* He had forgotten that not only the deck had eyes. The light was behind him. He was between it and the door. He scuttled, stopped. From the corner of his eye he saw it circle, stop, and then swoop horribly up behind him. He felt more than he saw it bathe his face. A whistle blew. The voice, this time, shouted. He looked up. He was almost blinded, but the lights wavered for a moment and he could see a man in a peaked cap leaning over the open, outer railing of the bridge, a flashlight in his hand. He moved again. A huge, invisible hammer struck the metal by his feet. A shock struck his ear. A bullet, he realized. Another voice above him said almost conversationally, "Stay still, or you are dead."

He was bound so as to frighten, to blind, to hurt. One of the commandos, the one who had been sentry, did it with quiet, professional satisfaction. He smelled like an athlete, not a workman. Stears was tied with his knees bent and his head forced between them. The commando said caustically, "See you later." He said it in Arabic. He said it again in French.

This was done in the wardroom. He heard the winch continue to whine and thump a long time. Then a little silence. Then a heavier thud that slightly shook the ship. Then footsteps and engines. He could not move a muscle. His position caused at first acute discomfort and then pain building from hints, to waves, to torrents, perhaps towards infinity. He could not lessen it for a second. This was a new experience, even after the slipped disc.

He was kicked onto his side. It was easier, thus, to cut

him loose. He was told to get up. He failed. The other commando massaged his knees and back with a genial and hard amusement. "Stiff, are you?" he said. He pulled him to his feet. He could stand. The commando pointed to the stairs toward the bridge. "Up," he said. "Don't try anything." He didn't.

The captain said, "What do you speak?" He had a plump, sad, disillusioned, sweat-dewed face. He had spoken in French.

Stears said, "Italian. A little French."

There were four others on the bridge: the two commandos; a man in a baggy sportscoat, with a northern face, gray eyes, and short gray hair; and Epaulets, who stood near the binnacle, looked forward, never looked at them, and who appeared to have the watch. There were also two seamen.

The captain went on in French. "Who are you?"

Stears said, "I am with the dockyard. I was left on board." he said it without conviction.

Into the silence the captain slowly and regretfully shrugged. "That is not possible," he said. "That is not even intelligent."

The first commando, who was leaning in the door, walked thoughtfully across and stood in front of Stears's chair. He patted each of Stears's cheeks gently with the back of his hand while Stears looked straight in front of him in rigid fascination and then slapped him full from the shoulder, left and right. Stears had not been struck since he was fourteen years old. He did not feel slapped; he felt as if the earth had shaken. The commando looked at him. He saw him through watery eyes. Even so, he decided that the commando was not intelligent; as in a totalitarian poster of idealized youth, his energies had run down from his eyes into his chin, bypassing his mouth, which was self-satisfied.

The commando said, "Now . . . who are you?"

Stears, at the end of his strength, confessed. His mouth tasted of blood. "I was running from the police. I have no passport. I wanted a ship to Naples or Genoa, but there wasn't time. I won't make any trouble for you. I can work. First port you come to, just dump me, you know. I'll be all right. I don't want trouble. I don't care what your business is." He went on, inspired, "Don't dump me in France though. I can't take prison there, again."

The captain looked at him, pursing heavy lips. Epaulets turned and looked curiously, briefly. The Northerner lit a cigarette and studied its burning tip. The captain said, "What have you done in France?"

Stears shrugged. He said, "Smuggling," unashamed.

There was silence again. The captain nodded slowly. The Northerner looked Stears quickly in the eye, a beam of gray. He got out of his chair, as though annoyed by the effort, and walked over to him. He took Stears's wrist firmly and impersonally, and held his hand to the light. Traces of grime set off the precision of the manicure, and one broken nail pointed the regularity of the rest. He turned it slowly before each face in the room. He shrugged. He said, "He was in a prison for hairdressers, perhaps." He spoke in Arabic, heavily accented. He held the cigarette in the other hand. He went on, "It is a soft hand. My cigarette will burn it badly. Watch." Stears flinched and, as quickly, cursed himself. The Northerner said, "And its owner speaks Arabic." He dropped the hand. He sat down and looked at nothing.

The captain dropped his eyes and slightly shook his head. *He's not part of this*, thought Stears. *He's just an ordinary captain. Note that. Note everything. Note that the ape who hit your face thinks slowly. Note that the accent in that Arabic sounded Russian. If you note fast enough nothing else may happen and you may not scream.*

The commando beside him said, "He must be killed."

The other said, "He must first be made to talk." But he sounded uncertain.

The Russian said, "No." He said it almost as to himself and looked at no one. All looked at him. Stears found that

290

his eyes were pleading and he looked away. The Russian went on, "You are not interrogators. I am, but I doubt that I have all the facts. I am inclined to think that this may be important. This man should be saved for Khamal. Khamal will know what to ask, and, of course, he will be answered." He looked reflectively beyond the bridge to the black and moon-sown sea. "That at least would be my advice," he said, and then, as if kindly clarifying, "You could break him down a little, but do not dull him, you see."

18

He had choices: three, three pains. If he leaned forward, the pain was in his arms. His arms were behind him, around a cold metal pipe. If he sat straight, the pain was in his legs. The floor was metal and studded with rivets. If he leaned against the pipe, the pain was in his back. The change of pain was an important decision, not to be lightly made. Freedom remained in the choice of pain, and to fritter it away into thrashing and flailing would be to slide toward despair. Outside the door, the footsteps of those for whom reality was not an iron pipe passed up and down. An unidentified absurdity hung over all. In time, he recognized it: his situation was undesired, displeasing; therefore somebody should be summoned to change it. It would not be changed.

Why Hajji? Money did not make sense. Hajji's interest in a stable, pro-capital North Africa hugely exceeded whatever sum the Left might pay for the use of his ships. Ideology? The mind boggled at fat Hajji as a Communist of secret conscience. A deal? If Hajji had made a deal in the destabilization of Berbia, then the deal had cost him well upward of a million dollars in investments in a month. Entrapment, force? But why and how? The Russians, the PLO, the Baath between them could easily find a ship. Why Hajji?

Thought helped. It filled the space with shapes of his own choosing. He was in an unused, bare cabin. The pipe was in the corner, floor to ceiling. No, deck to deck. Facing him, supported by chains from the wall – no bulkhead – was an unfolded folding bunk. There was a porthole. It was black, still night. The light was on, and harsh. The floor rose and sank between him, monotonously but not quite in rhythm. Nausea slowly swelled in him. The thought of lying in vomit made him shudder, sickened him more.

But he slept, after a fashion: it was like going through a subway tunnel, dark, but full of lurching and noise. He woke with his back on fire and almost immovable. The porthole above him was no longer black. He could not see out of it.

Footsteps stopped at the door. The lock turned. Obviously, they had to feed him and they would do so now. He had a moment of new fear. If they did not untie him, they would have to feed him with a spoon and he would then throw up. Most likely they would untie him. Easier for all.

The two commandos came in. There was a difference in caliber between them. The one who had slapped him would have been oafish had he not been self-confident and fit. The other had the face of a good young sergeant, hard but with responsibility, with thought. Neither spoke. They moved on either side of him, toward his head, toward the pipe, no doubt to untie him. Conversation with the second one would be impossible, he thought. It would be good to lay a foundation. His muscles knew in advance the bliss of stretching free.

The first kick was to his elbow. He had not seen the shoe move and he drew in his breath in utter astonishment as a cone of dark-blue pain entered and surged up his arm. He saw the second. It was to his kneecap and he moved in time. The next was to the pit of his stomach so that he could no longer move and the kneecap became a stable target. The commandos breathed hard. He had the impression that he, and their kicks, were far away from them, somewhere at the bottom of a pit. He vaguely noted that they concentrated on his back, his joints, his ribs. He quickly ceased to feel the separate blows; his body was a pool of pain into which tributary rivers, from all parts of him, carried dark surges and floods. Pain turned to exhaustion. He heard himself whining, *"Non, non, non!"* He wondered why he said it in French and dimly remembered that he should be glad that he had. Then it stopped.

The commandos left, slightly disheveled, as by brisk and useful work. He lay wholly absorbed in his body and himself, floating on pain as on the surface of the sea, time stationary overhead. There was one intrusive individual pain like a flame rising and falling on his side. He supposed that they had broken a rib. After a long time, pain began to recede, to break up into separate parts, and the walls of the cabin became visible through it.

The lock turned again and he flinched. There was also the smell of coffee. He saw that the Russian stood in the door, a mug in his hand, looking down at him with mild approval as at a piece of useful furniture.

The Russian said, "I imagine that you are having a disagreeable trip." He said it in English. Stears did not answer, only because he had nothing to say. Then he remembered that he did not speak English.

The Russian put the coffee on the bunk. He walked toward Stears, towards his head. Stears shut his eyes. He felt his arms being tugged and moved and then knew that they were free.

The Russian said, "We can dispense with these for the present."

He got the coffee and brought it to Stears. Stears sat up with great difficulty, gasped at his rib, took the coffee and looked down into it. The Russian sat on the bunk, in silence. He let Stears drink half the coffee before he spoke.

He said, "I have decided that you are inevitably CIA, though I must say that you seem a little unusual for them. There was the theoretical possibility that you were Bureau of Narcotics only. But no, you are not that." He shook his head. "I tried to place you with the British service or even with Mossad, but it did not work. I am quite certain that you are not French. No. CIA."

He had the expression of a sympathetic but unpersuaded banker, and his voice was mild. Stears looked at him, remembering to look blank.

"It would be possible, indeed, to do this in French but I find it foolish of you to conceal your English when you could not even conceal your Arabic. Let us make this facile. Unless, of course, we speak Russian. I would be interested as to whether you speak Russian."

His English was that either of a melodrama villain or of a textbook, presumably the latter. And the collar of his jacket was ill cut and the tweed not English. Among his teeth were crude fillings. His skin suggested strong soap. Stears noticed this and thought. *Not one of their Westernized smoothies, then. Not a senior talent. First thing they do is run to a New York dentist. A midlevel KGB working stiff keeping an eye on the Arabs. But they train them well.* He tried to shrug but thought better of it. The coffee helped, but not enough.

He said, *"Je ne parle pas l'anglais. Suis italien."*

The Russian more successfully shrugged. *"Bon, alors, parlons français."* He went on, "But I do not believe a word of it and I shall assume that you understand what I said before. I could certainly make you speak English but I am not going to do that sort of thing." He looked Stears over with appreciative interest. "That is not your customary wristwatch," he said, "for it does not fit your suntan. And your inexpensive pants are almost new. If the CIA had trained you for this nature of work you would not have made such errors. You are interesting. Maybe you are not CIA. If you are not, I should tell you that you will die a most unpleasant death in North Africa, for you will have been able to tell me nothing and I shall have been unable to help you. But I am sure that you are."

The trouble is, he thought, *sometimes these are smarter than the smoothies. Like with us.* It occurred to him, *He's a McNaughton. McNaughtonski.* He babbled on to himself, *No. "Mac" means "son of." So does "ski." So Naughtonski. That's it — Naughtonski.*

The Russian said, "Dr. Donnelly. Does that mean anything to you? I wonder where you fit in."

Stears shook his head. "You are mad. I am an Italian. I have worked in the French *milieu*. I speak Arabic because I have Arab customers. You are mad." It was strangely believable, enough so that he could whine in frustration that this man did not believe him. He felt irrecoverably far from him who had dressed amid Marie-Sophie's makeup and then walked past flowerbeds to a Jaguar. He moved and his side stabbed him. That was reliable. That was quite real.

The Russian smiled sourly but then said, "Of course. I understand that you cannot commit yourself in advance. I will state my business and you may consider it in solitude – unless our hosts come back to visit you. I will not encourage them to do so, but they may do so nonetheless. You present me with an unparalleled opportunity for coercion. As you well know, my department does not normally employ extreme methods of persuasion upon American officers of the CIA. No more than you do with us. It is in the end unproductive. There is almost a rule against it. But in this case, unless I very strongly intervene, you will be taken off this ship and turned over to the attentions of a man named Zebdi, of whom I may soon learn that you know a great deal. If you happen not to know about him, I can tell you that he is one of two things: a very skillful interrogator or a sadistic lunatic. Probably he is both. So in him I can use a threat that is not of my making. The CIA knows that he is not part of us. I will have broken no rule and he is outside rules.

"You will naturally pay me in information. First, about yourself. It is not inconceivable that the CIA has surveillance operatives on a large number of ships sailing between France and North Africa. But you are not such an operative. You do not have the training and you are not the type. You are some species of desk officer or specialized agent. We know, of course, about your Dr.

Donnelly, whose cover has been terminated, and we thought he was your only significant contact with us. Your presence suggests some parallel lines, not dependent upon him. It also suggests that it has developed very quickly, too quickly for normal CIA surveillance methods to be used. That would be the case if you did not intend more than a brief inspection of this ship – as is possible. I wish to know about that. I wish to know where you are placed, what your area of surveillance is, what led you here. I wish to know what, if any, connection you had with Dr. Donnelly's operation.

"The rest is more problematical, for one never knows what, precisely, beyond his own instructions, an opposition agent knows. But I wish to be told, as far as possible, what this operation represents to the CIA, how it is evaluated, and how it is surveilled. I will be the judge of whether you are telling me all you know.

"It is a professional relationship, you see. You have become accessible to me. It is to my advantage that your information be developed professionally by us, and not messily by our clients. After all, we are in a profession, not the movies. We shall cover your tracks as far as possible with the CIA. Perhaps we can discuss a long-term relationship. I should like it if you would now speak English. It is reasonable of you to maintain an element of doubt, but I really do not have any doubt and it would make no difference to you if I did. Let me give you a name. You can call me Boris. You can easily remember Boris, can you not?"

Drearily, with the feeling of playing a failed farce to the bitter end, Stears beat his hand on the floor, feebly, and said with beseeching petulance, and in French, "You are mad. Mad. Mad. I know nothing of these things." And then looked up and was rewarded by the slightest trace of alarm in "Boris's" eyes, as at the first shadow of doubt surrounding a childishly easy prize. He went on, "Do I look like a Yank to you, eh? Do I look like a Yank spy?"

But the alarm quickly changed, and with it the mild

and patient face, into a twitch of truculent arrogance – the professional challenged by the mainly pitiable. He said, this time in English, "You are obstinate. You are stupid. I should tie you up again. But why bother? Maybe I will send the Arabs in again. You have until tomorrow to decide. Don't think you can make your own deal. I do not need you." He opened the door and paused. "You are a stupid son of a bitch," he said.

Stears looked at the departing heels and the closing door. *Yes*, he thought, *you're right. But you do need me. You need me a lot.*

That was why, as he pulled himself through a pool of pain across the floor, ribs blazing, joints aching or giving way, toward the bunk, he had the first distant sense that there was opportunity to be grasped as well – not as blissfully simple as a urine-stained and verminous bunk, but in the longer run, his ticket.

For "Boris" needed him, knew it, and knew that he knew it, too. That had been the alarm – the alarm of a pretty good larcenous poker player with his money on the table making his first guess that his sucker might be anything but.

Boris needed him, first, for himself. Stears was a beautiful big fish. Boris was in his late forties. From the evidence of his English and French – excellently taught but not much used – this was his first assignment in the West, or very nearly so – and, in truth, playing nanny to a boatload of Arabs between Marseilles and al-Tabek, whatever the importance of the mission, was not, in KGB terms a real, wonderful, succulent "Western Assignment" at all. Boris must have had bad luck. He seemed pretty good, but his career so far could have been no great shakes. Even for a KGB man with a brilliant past, the opportunity to debrief, perhaps even to turn, an officer of the CIA did not come often. For a man like Boris it was a miracle that it had come at all. Skillfully handled, it could change his whole career, and that, in as class-ridden

298

a society as the Comrades ran, meant living in a bright, entirely new world. He would be terrified of letting it slip through his fingers. So Stears was like the magic flounder, hooked but too valuable to kill.

And there was more. For him to be interrogated by Khamal/Zebdi – his skin turned wet and his bowels melted at the thought – would not be a matter of indifference to the KGB at all. The KGB, desperately and with only partial success striving to impose Russian will upon the Middle East, had a daily battle to control its Arab clients. From the PLO – now threatening to dissolve into anarchy itself – to the smallest scattered bands of urban guerrillas and private assassins, the pro-Left forces of the Arab world had wayward wills of their own. They frequently also had money, from frightened merchants or frightened kings, and with money they could buy what weapons they chose. The KGB had far too little control. What it could control was information. It was by doling out intelligence, by being the eyes and ears of its murderous pets, that it achieved a good part of the inadequate influence that it possessed. The minor gangs and militias posed no particular threat to this partial monopoly. But the larger groups, the Baath, perhaps, and above all, the PLO had an intelligence potential of their own. To the extent that they developed it, the influence of the KGB would be diminished. The KGB must have considered it a most regrettable accident that McNaughton's Arab smuggler had fallen into Khamal's hands – for the KGB to penetrate Donnelly through the PLO was not the way the traffic was supposed to move. For a CIA officer with unknowable areas of information to spill all to Khamal would be a virtual small disaster for the KGB. If Boris allowed that to happen, and it was judged that it had not been necessary, then Boris would be heading East. Calm thought revealed Boris as his choiceless savior. It was to prevent calm thought that his savior had had him kicked to a pulp. Calm thought also foretold that to prevent calm thought in future he would almost certainly be kicked to a pulp again. He groaned. He beat his healing fist against the mattress. Thus agitated, it gave off a smell of unrine.

That was the theory, the big picture; he'd back a client's investment in it. There was always the doubt, the fear of the little special fact you could not know that pulled the big picture inside out. The investor's successful courage was to go with what you knew, to accept the inevitable rare failures. The penalty for failure, this time, was Khamal. His handling of Boris must be perfect. He settled down to think.

But he couldn't think. The simplest methods worked. This time the kicks came later; they began with fists. He had been brought down instantly to the bottom of the world of a police dog. The lock had turned. He knew he cowered when he saw their feet. The first, the oaf, held him from behind, elbows locked under his armpits; he was held close, he could feel and smell him. The sergeant hit him regularly, in cadence, unbelievably, slowly up one side, in the stomach, in the side, in the chest, in the ribs; he screamed, was hit again. A thick brown flood of pain, humiliation, terror, disgust, and fear rolled indistinguishably over him. He was hit again in the stomach. He vomited. It touched the sergeant. The sergeant cursed, backed off. The sergeant balanced himself and kicked him terrifically in the groin.

They tied him as he lay, doubled up and keening. What was there was not a superior man insulted by baboons. What was there, was: stupid, terrified, foul smelling, and confused. He was nonetheless not significantly injured. Men such as his commandos are widely and quite casually employed. Nothing remarkable had happened.

In time, he tried to crawl back to himself. He recognized it as a race: between Boris's timing and his own. Boris would not come while he could only babble and groan. Boris would certainly not wait for him to heal. Boris would come when he could talk and slightly think but would be too weak to take the initiative, too hurt to take risk. Such a time would come. He knew it now. He knew what he would have never guessed; that between his subtlety and a hooligan's boot there was no competition. None at all. He must simply progress faster than Boris would predict. His head split.

Boris did not untie him. Stears could only see his feet. Boris said, "This does not happen to officers of the CIA. It happens to Italian gangsters." He said it in English.

"And to Russian poets," said Stears.

"Ah," said Boris. "Progress." There was again a smell of coffee. This time it was for Boris. He drank it in silence. His feet were just in the air, where the bunk was. "Overrated ones," he said. "And the Tsar imprisoned Dostoievsky. You are not really stupid, I hope? I have respect for your service."

Stears weakly said, "Untie me."

"Why should I help an Italian hooligan who reads the anti-Soviet press?"

Stears said, "Melouf."

"Better." One foot rose up and came down across the other.

"They nearly killed me."

"No. No danger of that. How did you get to Melouf?"

"Cut me loose. I want some food. And a glass of wine. I need a doctor."

"There is no doctor. There is no wine. How did you get to Melouf?"

"There are such things as shipping registers."

There was a rustle of the mattress. Boris warmly said, "Yes. There are. But Melouf is not listed as the owner of the *Leah*."

"*Leah* is registered to the Compagnie de Navigation Littoral du Mahgreb. Melouf is its principal shareholder. The company is registered in Tunisia. The ships are registered in Berbia." Stears said it in a dull monotone, and then, with the petulance of a fish flapping on the earth, "This is elementary. Do you think we can't read?" This was also getting much too close to Giovanni Stears. He said, seizing one favor from surrender, "I can't go on talking like this. You'll have to cut me loose."

"One thing first. A name."

"Harry Winston."

He sensed, although he could not see, a perfect stillness on the bunk. He had chosen an emergency, unused identity of McNaughton's – an identity that McNaughton's smuggler could not conceivably have known – simply to increase, for himself alone, his own consistency. The stillness on the bunk surprised the corner of his mind that noticed it. Boris must either be searching his memory in vain or have some preconceived notion.

Boris said, "I see."

His feet dropped to the floor. He walked toward him. Stears piteously flinched. It was not difficult. His wrists were tied to his ankles.

Boris cut the cord. Stears tried to straighten. A spark jumped from his ribs to his back. He groaned, spontaneously. Boris looked down at him and shook his head with the pleasure of an unfavorable professional judgment.

"You would not last long with Khamal," he said.

But that was an aside. Boris was preoccupied. He sat back on the bunk, while Stears made the tentative movements of a crippled bug, and began twice to speak and twice stopped.

Boris said, "Harry Winston. Cover, code, or real?"

"You know it is not code." Code names are single and in capitals. MCSWEENEY.

Boris looked at him in silence. He said mildly, "I could bring the Arabs back again."

Stears thought, *Not while there are questions on the table.* He humbly said, "You could get me some coffee."

"Yes. I wonder which it will be." Silence. "And what was Harry Winston's sector?"

It was a not unreasonable guess that Harry Winston was cover.

"Politics. Report to Paris but geographically non-specific."

Boris paused, considering. "Were you associated with Dr. Donnelly?" The accent was on "associated."

"I was desk. He was field."

The game was risky enough to make each bruise and joint ache in dread each time he lied; yet it was not, for the present, excessively so. Nothing the smuggler could have said would have indicated how McNaughton was "controlled." His own false version was more probable than the solitary truth. And Boris had picked him as a deskman. But Boris, he had found, could not simultaneously operate in English and completely control his voice; behind the next question he heard a mixture of excitement and doubt. It puzzled him.

"Donnelly was field, then? Field only?"

Stears said irritably, "Yes. Of course." But a network was trying to join up, catch the light, within his mind. He felt its threads straining to come together. He had to give it attention and to cover himself. He said, "You should know. You penetrated his cover."

Which was not what Boris had said. Boris had said, "Whose cover has been terminated." Nobody said that. Cover was "penetrated." An agent, in that event, was "burned." An agent was also "terminated" – killed. Donnelly had not been killed. McNaughton had been killed, out of cover and in a "low-level" event. The KGB should not know that McNaughton had been killed. The KGB should not know that Donnelly was McNaughton. Then why the slip of the tongue?

"What was the objective of this surveillance effort?"

"Expatriate Arabs." They would have worked that out already.

And to "Harry Winston," now that he thought of it,

Boris's ears had jumped off his head. Why? It should have been a name like any other. Why . . .

"Be more specific."

Stears, as one buttressed by cowardice and growing treason, now firmly said, "Coffee. And soon food."

And Boris nodded. He moved toward the door.

"You would not run away and hide, I hope."

Stears shook his head. Why the doubt that Donnelly was a field man with a desk control? It was what he should have been, except he wasn't. Why the effort to conceal the doubt?

Because the source was not the smuggler. Not alone.

Because the exposure was from above. Not from below.

Because McNaughton had died, not by accident, not by scraps torn from some poor bastard in hell, but by comprehensive treason.

Boris came back. He gave Stears a cup scorching to the touch, the steam from which held a rich, high smell of grape.

"The brandy is my own," said Boris. "There will be food in due course. Go on."

The priorities were changed. Nothing takes precedence over the integrity of the Agency itself. He had three duties now: to survive; to uncover any perceptible clue to the nature, the source, the extent of McNaughton's penetration; to escape with a brain intact. Information that would have been sacrosanct when only he was at stake could be spent, if needed, now. But before he came to that, there was a whole worthless account to be paid out first. He could reveal what they already knew, with minor, misleading variations.

He said, "In the beginning Donnelly was a solo operation. It grew beyond expectation. It was getting disorganized. I was put in as desk control. Donnelly didn't like that, if you want to know."

"What was Donnelly's real name?"

He breathed the coffee's vapor. Just at the outermost

edges, pain and degradation lifted from his flesh. On the ship's deck he had had a stupid confidence in skills he did not own. The skills needed now, he had. He had two cards to play. Boris would never guess, would not be humble enough to conceive, that his prey had seen through him to the truth. And in due time Boris would have to keep him from Khamal.

He began to play.

"McNaughton," he said.

19

It was not a mosque but a back room, a warehouse, of the bazaar. So much the better! How bitter to be barred from speaking to God within his holy house! Now, at Friday's noon, the most divine of hours, all men went to mosque: the weak of faith, the lax of prayer, the covetous, the lustful, the wine-bibbers, the rich, all stood in the infinite mercy of God and spoke the sweet words of prayer toward Mecca, to the *mirhab*. All but his faithful. For in the mosques also were concealed the King's police and the Brothers of Islam – whose poverty, whose ignorance, whose low estate were only a tattered cloak over souls that blazed with God – they, the God-famished, must hide to pray. Good and very good, thought Ibrahim. For they had learned to hate their King and would tear at his throat with the teeth of God. He praised to himself the love of God that turned in an eyeblink to the hatred of men. It was, in its own way, wonderful; even a ghost could work for Marx.

He led the prayers. Prayer in a mosque, Mohammed said, exceeded by twenty-seven times the worth of other prayer, yet was not imperative. The Brothers took what crumbs of God they could here in their hiding place, in the smell of sesame and oil. He liked to lead the prayers. They were part of his boyhood, part of his tongue's flesh. He prayed. "God is great. I extol the holiness of my Lord, the Great." His body, unbidden, took the position prescribed, standing, waist inclined, head humble, hands decorous against the knees. A hundred bodies followed him. It thrilled him to fill these sober, courtly motions with the fire of passion. He straightened, cried aloud, "God hears him who praises Him!"

He was softly answered, "O Lord, thou art praised."

He threw himself onto his knees, his forehead to the gound, as though the earth embraced him.

"God is great! I extol the holiness of my God, the most high!"

He had no quarrel with Islam. It was an admirable lie. If a Big Man Up in the Sky were needed to teach self-sacrifice, if one were needed to teach that all men are equal at least in the eyes of God, to tell the Arabs that they were greater than the mighty West, to overthrow the King, then let him stay up there for a while at least. His people's children would come to Marx, perhaps, not they themselves. But they would serve purposes that they would not understand.

He raised himself upon his knees, spine taut with fervor, and prayed as though the sentences could not wait upon their own slow stateliness. "The adorations of the tongue are for God and also the adorations of the body, and alms-giving. Peace be upon us and upon God's righteous servants."

He turned his head slowly to left and right in the binding *salaam* of brotherhood.

"The peace and mercy of God be with you. The peace and mercy of God be with you."

He lifted his eyes to his people. All were men. Pinched faces, lantern jaws, flat eyes that had looked on little but the crudest labor, clothes patched and soft as silk with age, breath of the pepper and garlic of poverty. He looked, however, into a collective, requited smile; the week's great bestowal had been received and tasted, life was lit by heaven. He was stabbed by a sense of waste and thought, *They could be braver, better, than the Old Bolsheviks if only they believed.*

He would do his best. It was time for the *khutbah*, the weekly sermon, the last before the pilgrimage. He raised himself, as though tearing himself from God's sweet ground, and walked, emaciated, weary, to the pulpit improvised from packing crates, the *mimbar*.

He began slowly and gently, as though hating to lay a burden upon them, and in the unstilted language of the mosque. "Brothers, who never had anything and who gave the little that you had to God, do you still have the strength to give?"

He looked into their eyes and accepted the answer given not only by the muttered "Yes" but by the setting of their shoulders; in their lives questions were not rhetorical and actions were not symbolic.

"It is good," he said. "God loves you."

But he spoke first of their poverty; the docks that employed a fifth of them that needed work; the pitiable wages; the price of bread, from grain sold by the American devils who held children's hunger hostage; the filth of the shanty towns where a Muslim could not make himself clean for his God; the arrogance of the bosses, the foreigners, the shopkeepers, the police; the vile, mocking offer of wages if they worked in the nest of vermin, the American base. He looked closely as he talked. Yussuf's eye infection, it was clear, was worse. He could see the discharge from where he stood. Yussuf would be blind before long and would be supported from the fund – would have been. Hussein, a young man of spectacular holiness in a red striped gown actually in tatters, now wore upon his face a look both vacant and intense that Ibrahim suspected to be hunger. He would be fed. No other visible emergencies. He would ask about the children later.

His voice rose a level and turned wild at the edges as he talked of the King, the generals, and the foreigners: the whoring on soft beds; the swilling of wines that cost a year's wages; the gambling at heathen tables; the mocking of God. Old stuff. He said it once a week, but with time, like a cancer, it hurt not less, but more.

And now they were ready. Now to *Lyusi!* His chest tightened. Now was the real beginning. He saw before him the first of the blood-torrent that would drown the King.

"Do you think that you are the first to know these filthy things? You are not. Do you think that you are the first that a king has mocked in their faith? You are not. Why do we praise the saint, Lyusi? Why do we travel to his tomb to pray? Why does his virtue flow among us like the scent of roses? Four hundred years ago, brothers, in our own al-Tabek, the wicked Sultan Mulay Ismail crept on his belly to the Christian Kings. Wine was guzzled in his palace. His people wept and starved. Who rose up against him? The Imam Lyusi, the marabout. He did not have to, brothers. Lyusi had a good life. He was a court imam, a favorite of the King. But God rose in him and he took the path of persecution and of truth. He preached to the people the filth of Mulay Ismail. He brought back to men's minds that God was stronger than their King. The people no longer wept. Now they shouted and shook their fists. The King unleashed the regiments of his anger against Lyusi. Lyusi stood fast in virtue. Therefore we praise him.

"But we praise him also because in him God showed his strength. The King sent men to take the saint and his disciples like wild beasts in the desert. They came upon the holy band: twenty men, twenty-three women, their children, and their camels. The soldiers came in tens of scores. But God moved in the hearts of the soldiers and they could make no move against Lyusi. No! The soldiers stood in their ranks and Lyusi, whom they had come to slay, moved and preached among them and his women brought them water. And when the sun set, Lyusi led the soldiers' prayers. And those soldiers turned on Mulay Ismail, and other soldiers with them, and Mulay Ismail was driven from his filthy palace and his life thereafter was a dog's, and Lyusi led Berbia back into the arms of God. Therefore we praise him.

"In four days, when Lyusi's holy birthday comes, let our pilgrimage be great! Go into the streets! Tell all men who love God, who do not fatten on the palace foulness, to join us in our march of holiness. Can a man not walk a day for God? Tell them to bring their women and little children, for children are most pleasing to the Lord.

"And do not fear so very much. God was with Lyusi and he who bends before Lyusi's tomb is himself, in some degree, Lyusi. Think of our brothers in Iran! The Imam Khomeini told the holy people to bare their breasts against the soldiers' bullets. They did so, trembling. And what happened, brothers? The soldiers turned and fled. Some of the holy died, it is true, and they rejoice in heaven. But the armies melted and the Shah ran shrieking to America on his way to hell and Iran now rejoices and is free. Would not you rather live proud and happy, as in Iran, than in shame and grief, as we do in Berbia? Then if the King sends men against us on our pilgrimage, do not fear too much. Bare your breasts. Show your children to them. Trust in God. All will be as God desires."

He stopped. His arm, which had been outstretched, the gold ring shining on the index finger, slowly dropped. He leaned forward, all passion spent. When he spoke again, it was in the softest of conversational tones.

"There is nothing more. We meet on Thursday, by the fountain of the bazaar, at dawn. Go in peace."

His arms dismissed them. They left, by cautious custom, in threes and fours, melting into the bazaar outside. He walked among them as they waited, talking— leader, help, and friend. He talked gently to Yussuf and to Hussein.

He was the last to leave. He looked around the bare, dim room, its white walls smudged here and there with smoke. He had been at his best, here. He sniffed the air, smelling grain and oil and older smells of leather. He shrugged. He would not be coming back.

His rooms were dim, but the noises of the street were unmuffled in them. The clip of a donkey's feet could have

310

come from his writing desk and the cry of the dateseller from beside his bed. He lived in the slums. His rooms were small and smelled of his neighbors' charcoal and food, but they were clean. He kept them so. Any pious woman on the street would gladly have swept the Imam's lodging, but he made it known that the intensity of his devotions, his unceasing studies, made it imperative that his rooms be left alone. Outside, al-Tabek lived in the streets, like an opened ants' nest. Looking through his shutters, he could see, mating excepted, any conceivable aspect of his people's lives, and, sooner or later, any of his people themselves. He could perhaps also see police. He must be watched. But he knew that the decision had been taken long ago that the benefits of arresting a revered imam were not worth the inevitable explosion, however subversive and obnoxious the imam. So the surveillance would be occasional and remote – though the CIA's penetration of the Brothers' inner circle still sometimes made him cold – and his rooms were in a warren. It would be impossible to tell who came to him. Thus she could come. She would come any minute. Thank God she would come.

He moved constantly around the room. He was now entirely Hussein Shamak. Ibrahim's black robe almost surprised him. He straightened a book, a carpet, things that did not need straightening, not out of nervousness but because to move, to manipulate, the simplest of an engineer's acts, relieved his body's urgency. He was infatuated. He knew it. He knew it as he knew that he would someday die. He could analyze his condition as easily as he could write a will. He knew that the culmination of the work, *Lyusi*, the imminence of gigantic change, the risk, the urgency, the certain stunning violence, had raised him almost to an exalted state and that those great energies, by an almost random chance, had focused erotically upon Julia. No doubt of it. But why should he be torn to fragments? Crude, copulative images of her breasts, her tawny loins, her throaty cry, rolled thunderously over him and were replaced by the most poignant need to pity, to protect; the memory of her in McNaughton's room, naked, blood-spattered, out of breath, and suddenly sweet with lust appeared to him one moment as an exhilarating drug and at the next, as horror. To make love to the bravest of comrades, did that not fill his heart with life? And from its cool room, an engineer's voice said, *You are infatuated with a madwoman, certainly a murderess, and quite possibly a monster, and such an experience cannot but disturb.*

There was no street door to listen for. He heard feet on the stone flags below and thought that they were hers and knew that they were as she climbed the stair. He opened the door to the sharp smoke of charcoal. She was dressed as a modern Arab student might be, going back to see her family: jeans, a plain blouse, and a scarf so cleverly worn that it hid her flaming hair and shadowed her northern skin. A surreptitious American young woman would be in danger in this quarter, and Julia would not have passed an instant's close inspection. Her radiant smile, her lighted eye, were not for him but for the enjoyment of danger controlled by skill. Her vitality, her courage, were as strong to him as the raw scent of a lion. He was overwhelmed by love and by her safety with him and he threw his arms around her and said, "I'm so glad you came."

She let herself be briefly kissed, then pulled away and said, her voice unchangingly composed, ironic, "Hello, darling. You wouldn't believe what a bore that hotel is getting to be. Being the Peck and Peck girl for a week is not my thing."

She kicked the door closed with her heel and walked toward the bed, trailing her scarf in one hand. She unbuckled her belt and ran her fingers up the buttons of her blouse, then looked at him, who had not moved, and said, surprised or slightly irritated, "Is something the matter?"

"No," he said. She shrugged and slipped off jeans,

312

blouse, all, standing now in the dim room like a pale wax candle tipped with fire. He looked at her again in wonder and again in surprise. He should know by now to expect not the shadow, not the memory, not the pretense, of shyness, modesty, flirtatiousness, or romance. It excited him, no doubt of it; her matchless body needed no fluttering, no frills. Nor, he thought, would that of a lioness. The thought hung in a corner, and was pushed away, that he had known more womanliness in a dockside whore.

He started toward her, pulling his robe up by its hem, and heard her say, "One thing I like about mullahs is they don't have to fiddle with flies." He pulled it over his head. "Or underwear," she said.

He ran his lips upon her nipples, hearing himself groan with pleasure and smelling the sweetness of her sweat. He felt her stiffen and grasp his thighs. She sank beneath him, guiding him to the bed. He was lost in her, and she, in herself. He knew that too, by now. Her lovemaking was wholly unreserved, wholly passionate, ingenious, and wholly private. He was not received; he was taken, tantalized, driven on. His sense of her climax was both dark and lurid, lava in the night. And of late, by night, in dreams, he both ached for her and feared her. But he felt all his body now yearn to flow within her, his skin dissolved on hers, her breath was warm and sweet inside his mouth, his body surged, and in his ears was the roaring of his heart, his voice, or hers.

She had made his breakfast in Virginia, but that was not because she was woman but because she was host. Her lack of domesticity startled him still, not because it was great but because it was absolute; her domesticity was as absent as a missing tooth. Never, in his house, had he seen her hand so much as stray to straighten a pillow or touch a plate. So, as the sun set, and she lay on the bed, he found himself gathering together a loaf of bread, olives, cold lamb, dates, the plates and glasses – he, an

Arab, doing for a woman a woman's work and hoping that she might be pleased.

And she was pleased. She would be. Every time, in the corners of his mind, that his picture of her became monstrous, perverted, strange, she banished it by her presence. He brought the plates back to the room. The table was low. They sat on cushions. It would not have done for Ibrahim to have Western chairs. She sat gracefully, unlike most Europeans. He remembered Virginia again; the same half-buttoned blouse and jeans, the same ease of company, the same angular and candid voice, a gracious comradeship.

She said, "You know, it's not half bad. Wouldn't an Arab slum be slummier than this?"

"Oh, yes," he said.

In his room were a worn carpet on the wall, a table to eat from, a table to write at, a bed, some cushions. The walls were white. It had the serenity of a successful abstract painting. Beyond was a kitchen. It had a charcoal grate. There was no running water.

He went on, "This is a slum to you and perhaps to me but not to the people who live here. The real slums are *bidonvilles*, shantytowns. The people here have some kind of work, some hope. Of course the other rooms have eight people living there, sometimes more, and they have beans, not lamb and dates. But no, it is not a slum."

She said sociably, "It's all less filthy than I would have thought."

"The Arabs are not a dirty people. I saw more filth in Washington than you would find on this street. Of course, the *bidonvilles* are different, and the poorer villages. What would you expect? A thousand people camped with no latrine. There the children go blind for the flies upon their faces. But they are retarded already from malnutrition, so perhaps they do not care." He heard his own voice and said, "I am sorry. I am lecturing." And then, in spite of himself, "One must be kind to the conscience of an American."

She sopped up the liquid of the olives with her bread and said, "You really do hate us, don't you? That's not an act."

He said, "I hate what you do. Perhaps it is that I hate what happens because of you. It would be unreasonable to think that you could help it. It is simply the logic of your historical position. That is why the West must be destroyed, not changed. I hate the British, of course, but that is different and not very important."

"Why the British? Of course, you're Egyptian. They were there, weren't they?"

"Yes," he said. "They were there. It's odd how little we know of each other. You do not know, for example, that my father was shot."

He waited for her reaction. She said, interested, with no pretended shock, "By the Brits?"

"Yes. I told you that my father was the chief man in his village. He was not a peasant. In European terms he was a farmer, or even the poorest kind of squire. He was a very gentle man and very pious. That is why I can so easily seem to be a pious Muslim. I have seen it and loved it, you see. Like many Egyptians during the war, he supported the Germans. Not because he was a Fascist but because Rommel might have ridden us of the English. I have never known exactly what my father did. I was a little boy then. It cannot have been very much. Perhaps he passed messages, perhaps he reported the movements of troops. One day, four British soldiers came – a great red-faced sergeant and three men." He stopped. He felt weary and depressed. He went on in a voice deliberately flat. "You will think that I hate the British because they arrested, perhaps tried, and shot my father. That is not so at all. They were fighting a war and I can forgive them that. I cannot forgive the expression on the soldiers' faces, an expression so plain that a little boy could know it. They had no doubt at all that they were picking up a dirty little Arab traitor. That this educated, gentle, frightened man might be braver and better than

315

they never crossed their minds. It couldn't have. That is why I hate them. But it doesn't matter. I do what I do because it is right. Not because it satisfies me."

She thought about it and said with the same calm interest, "But you hate your own people too."

He looked at her, astonished, searching her face for some complexity of meaning. But it was said and meant flatly.

"How can you say that? I risk my life for them. I give my life for them."

"Oh, come on," she said. "With what you're about to do? Maybe you like power." She looked at him irritably. "I'm not blaming you. It doesn't matter to me. Just don't talk crap."

He felt a sense of futility, which he understood, and desolation, which he did not. He said quietly, "You do not understand. You have never seen hopelessness. You do not know what it is. You have never seen, *seen*, poverty and ignorance and disease reproducing itself to the end of time, like rats in a pit. How can I make it plain to you? You who are twenty-four years old, Julia, do you know what you would be in the villages? You would be an old woman with fallen breasts and rotten teeth. You would be sick with parasites because your water is foul. When you picked up your children there would be a cloud of flies. Can you understand that this is so, that this is true? Can you understand that this has been so since the Pyramids, that it is truer than anything you know? There is nothing, nothing that could happen to one generation of these people that would not be worth it if it changed the future. What do you think could happen to the poor of Berbia that is worse than another day of life? *That is Lyusi.* It must be done in that manner, for that is their level of development. Lenin taught us that. Have you never understood?"

"Oh, yes," she said. "I keep forgetting you're a commie. And most of the ones I meet are Trots and they're a little different." She ate the last of her dates and

316

looked at him with thoughtful interest. "Has it taken a lot out of you, doing this mullah thing? It seems a hell of a thing to keep up, to me. But it seems to rev you up." She smiled sociably. "Even in bed."

He took his time, for he hardly knew himself. "First," he said, "I believe in it passionately. It was a daring, almost maniacal strategy but I was sure that I could make it work. As for the act itself, I think that any deep enactment of any strong emotion opens up the psyche as strong exercise opens up the lungs. I knew a soprano, once . . ."

He stopped, for the air of desolation had risen to a gale and he understood it now. *She doesn't care. She's interested. This is entirely for her. She's screwed, she's eaten, and now she'd like to find something out. She's her own appetites and nothing else.* The thought approached him. *She has no soul. Can't you see it? She is dead.* But he refused to encompass it.

"Tell me about her," she said. Her violet eyes were on him and her breasts moved silently within the shadow of the blouse. He longed for her to understand.

But at his silence she shrugged and said, "Anyway, we'd better talk about Thursday. I've been hanging around with the Dutch television people and they don't have any doubt that I'm a nice American journalist. When I come running to them with a horror story they'll listen. It's a stroke of luck they're here. But I need to know when you'll have your tableau all set up, dear. I don't know when to bring them."

Detail soothed him. He felt a purpose again. He said, "Late morning. About midday. Yes, we must talk now."

20

Boris said, "I would give you a change of clothes if I could, but we are different sizes." And added with facetious malice, "Besides, I have heard that a gentleman does not dress on the last day out."

"The last night," said Wop. "The last night."

Boris had become to him like an uncle, of the most objectionable sort. He was full of heavy humor, easy disparagement, and funny menace to which he added a Soviet contribution of class wit. Wop was delighted. He had made him smug.

Boris looked through the porthole. He said, "You can see Berbia now. It should be of interest to you since it has caused you so much trouble."

Wop nodded. Since it hurt to move, he did not. His circumstances had been advanced by the addition of a chair. He was also made free of the bunk when Boris was not sitting on it. He had not been let out of the cabin. The Arabs had not come back.

"As you know," said Boris, "we have no embassy here – your government has seen to that – and thus no legal network. I fear that makes it more difficult to safeguard you. The PLO has more power here than I do. But I think I shall succeed. As you know yourself, the dock area is almost entirely under the joint influence of the Baath Party and the Brothers of Islam. It would be a great mistake for you to try and escape from me there. If you were to succeed, you would be found, but perhaps not by me. I am your hope. We know that, I think."

Wop nodded. This was the first spoken acknowledgment that Boris would keep him from Khamal. Unspoken, it had been long established. He had managed the disinformation of Boris well. He knew it. Intelligence is trade. He had given Boris information. The value of intelligence, either accurate or new, that Boris had received was negligible in comparison with the intelligence that McNaughton had been penetrated from above – and, if McNaughton, who else? Boris, unaware that he had gotten a quarter for five bucks, was pleased with his quarter and figured he might have fifty cents to go.

But Boris's money was in the bank and his own was a long way from one. Now was the hiatus of calm, the pleasures of the cruise behind one, life ashore not begun. He should be terrified. The unspeakable, the all too dreamable – interrogation by Khamal – was not now a serious danger, but that it could be figured in at all was bad enough, was worse, in fact, than anything he had ever had to fear. The probable was less frightful, but still exceedingly grave. He was presumably a captive of the KGB. That was bad enough. If he remained so very long, the dubiousness of the information he had given to Boris would begin to come to light. He still might not face torture or death, but nothing else was sure. He had no idea of what would take place on land, of Boris's arrangements. He had no plan. Yet in fact he was not terrified. He had a sense, almost lightheaded, of tautness and of chance. It surprised him. He was sure it was not courage.

"I must leave you now," said Boris. "There is much to do."

"Of course," said Wop. "You are excused."

They came with no warning. He was made to rush. Of course. He must be kept confused. He had in fact gone to the porthole, seen the distant white city and azure sky, seen the painted fishing dhows, seen floating garbage

319

begin to spot the sea, seen the thick layer of shanties, like tidal sludge, rise up between the dockyards and the Moorish walls, seen the wharves as the ship crept by them – crowded with labor, not much mechanized – seen the steel hangar opposite move slower and slower and finally stop. He felt the ship bump gently. Then nothing. Feet in the corridor. Hollow thuds of hatches. It was interesting, at least, that this pirate ship felt at ease in the very center of al-Tabek harbor. Doubtless bluff and ingenuity were being used, but it still suggested both confidence and haste. He must tell Witham. The thought of Witham was distant, distasteful, secure, like the memory of a childhood schoolmaster. Time passed. They had taken his watch.

Boris came with the commandos. Since all were now in suits, Boris's the worst-cut, they had the air of partners in a dubious carpet business. They did not carry guns. That was not accurate. The sergeant took an automatic from his jacket pocket and showed it to Wop. He put it back. He stood behind him. The other took him by the elbow, hard. "Move," he said.

They rushed him through the ship. The sun hit like a hammer. It was hot. The wharf was crowded with laborers. At the end of the gangplank was a dusty Buick, a European driver standing by its door. The driver, Boris, and Wop were the only Europeans. The commmando did not relax his grip. Wop was half dragged down the gangway. The driver walked around and opened the curbside rear door. Wop was pushed in. Boris greeted the driver in Russian, then sat down beside Wop.

The two commandos walked to the front, with the driver. Both smiled and spoke to him. The second extended his hand in greeting. The driver, puzzled, took it. He was a very young man, fair-haired, with a rabbit face and the eager, uncertain air of a first assignment. The sergeant took the automatic from his pocket and hit the driver on the face with it, three times. The second pulled the man down so that his face was pressed against

320

the hood. The sergeant hit him twice more on the back of the head, then pushed the man away. Blood trickled down the hot metal of the car, turning quickly to paste. Boris had opened his door and was halfway out of it. The sergeant turned. His automatic pointed at Boris from across the car. "Get back in," he said.

From the crowd of dockworkers, a dozen quietly approached the car. They surrounded the body of the driver. Those inside stooped and raised the burden. It was moved unhurriedly, unseen in the bodies around it, toward the water.

Boris muttered to himself in Russian. The sergeant opened Boris's door. "Get in front," he said. It was now the sergeant who sat next to Wop. His colleague took the wheel.

The sergeant said to Boris, "Yamadi gives orders here, not you. And you do not steal prisoners you have been questioning for three days. The PLO are not your servants."

Boris shrugged, a gesture both impotent and Olympian, a professor played a trick by a little boy. He said, "The death of an employee of the KGB will not be excused. This was unnecessary." He said to Wop, in French, "I regret this, genuinely. For me this is an annoyance. For you, I fear that it is worse."

Fear was in his heart, his bowels, his blood. It made him cold. It made him sick. But in his head was a frantic, whining anger at Boris, the avuncular, the professional, the disparaging, the duped. He was driven toward his doom silently beating his fist and shouting, *You stupid Ivan bastard, you muzhik dolt, don't you know you're meant to be in charge?* He couldn't think why he didn't shout aloud. It seemed to him incredible, an insult of fate, a vulgar excess, that he should be destroyed by the incompetence of the KGB.

They stayed clear of the city. He had a moment of hope at the security gate, but the Arabs showed no trace of

321

doubt; the guard looked at them, looked even at the slaughterhouse car, clearly recognized them, and nervously waved them through. So much for the forces of order. They drove fast through shantytown. They came to a modern, four-lane highway built through blue-gray hillsides of parched, aromatic scrub blessed here and there with almond trees and cypress. So far from desert, they appeared to be in suburb – the city, from here formal, biblical, remained in sight. Concrete villas, each in a small explosion of flowers and young trees, dotted the hills. The earth, where it was unflowered, was rawly graded. All seemed new and, in the manner of the homes of the Arab newly rich, were built perhaps by the bastard grandchild of Le Corbusier and decorated by his cook.

Boris was not alarmed. The back of his neck was thoughtful. Boris was not lost. He braced before they braked. They turned onto a road into the hillside, unpaved but smooth. They passed two villas separated by two or three hundred meters of untouched scrub. Before each house, at the center of each contrived oasis, behind the gated low stone walls, a Cadillac glinted in the sun. They went a mile farther, to an encircling wall that was high enough to block the view. The driver blew the horn. The gate was opened, and not by a dingy Arab gardener but by a hard young man in a khaki shirt. Behind the wall, unseen outside, he had a colleague. The colleague had an M-14. The grounds were larger than at the other villas and less well kept. He should, he dimly knew, observe everything, catalogue each chance, take his bearings, size up the guards. He couldn't do it. His brain slipped and stumbled. He studied his one defeated protector. He found some hope in Boris's neck.

They kept him in the car. This villa, too, was new, a sharp-edged, deep rectangle, white enough to hurt his eyes and bordered with formal beds of flowers dying in the sun. Its lower windows were shuttered and barred with sturdy arabesques. A flight of twelve wide steps led up to the entrance. The entrance was flanked by massive marble pots full of the skeletons of geraniums in cracked earth; by each pot stood an armed guard. The sergeant walked up eagerly. Boris walked heavily up behind. Both were known, admitted. The driver stood by Stears's door easily, holding a gun with insolent carelessness. The car windows were closed. Sweat ran down Stears's face through dirty stubble. His own clothes sickened him.

The house door opened. There was about this place a curious mixture of the violent and the sluttish. The sergeant merely stood in the door and beckoned for him like a rude receptionist. His guard threw open the car door and pulled him by the elbow, unbalancing him completely so that he landed in the gravel, on his knees, kicked him to his feet, and pulled him up the steps – but all mechanically, as though obeying the arbitary etiquette of the house.

It was cool inside. It was dim. While his eyes darkened he foresaw Yamadi and Khamal ranged somehow in judgment, astonished and triumphant. His sight returned. He was in a drawing room, half Arab, half gaudy European, turned into the semblance of an office or campaign room by dragging filing cabinets and a trestle table – now covered with papers, maps, and a solitary, dismantled gun – in among the stuffed sofas and by hanging a bulletin board half over a dubious Venetian oil. His eyes, compelled, sought Khamal. He saw no Khamal. Boris was there, by the trestle table, looking exasperated and placatory at once; the sergeant was there, looking self-righteous, pleased; a red-haired girl, in a pink armchair, looked interested, in fact amused; and there, in the dark suit, anxious, sharp-faced, secret, and quiet, was Khamal's other half. Yamadi, his customer, his client, his penultimate doom. He waited numbly to be named.

Yamadi said, "So this is the man?"

The sergeant nodded, secure in a job well done. "Yes.

323

We found him on deck when we were loading. Verkhelsky talked to him for two days. We even helped him, but Verkhelsky kept the answers to himself. Then he tried to take him off to his people when we landed. We did what was necessary."

Boris said quietly, "In short, your orderly took it upon himself to murder an employee of the KGB, to cause an incident, however minor, on the dock, to invade the intelligence function of the KGB, and to risk an incident with the French secret service. You are fortunate in your men."

Across the room, Yamadi looked incuriously at Stears. Stears, filthy, bearded, bruised, cowed of shoulder, wild of eye, looked back dumbly. Yamadi shrugged. "Very fortunate, since they obey orders," he said. "This is a joint operation. As usual, you were taking the benefits and leaving the risk to us. They have contingency instructions for just this. You needed a lesson. Who is this man?"

With patient authority, Boris explained. "He is a French surveillance operative. He is not important. He tried to pass himself off as an Italian criminal, and there is even a degree of truth in that. A small degree. He comes out of the SAC. The French have an army of such people. He is part of the Marseilles drug world. He claims that he has never been convicted and this is probably true – the French keep such people on a leash for just such purposes as this. He claims that he was watching the ship for the French government and the Mafia at once. I can believe him. It would be unreasonable for you to expect the ship to have caused no interest at all. It does not matter. The French are fond of information but they do not act upon it. If he had succeeded in his task they would have filed the information and taken no action whatsoever. If they had been seriously concerned they would have sent a more skillful man. This one is entirely expendable. You will find out all this for yourself when Zebdi questions him. I am frankly sorry that

that cannot be until tomorrow. I would like to get this over with."

Stears heard it through a frozen brain, as though from a radio in another room, but he was filled with a choking gratitude. His protector was at his side. Boris was playing high cards. Boris – Verkhelsky? – must have a plan. Numb as he was, he knew it might be a frail one. Boris himself was untouchable – he did not have to fear being found in a lie. But to try it at all he must have something – if nothing but time. He was stunned with fortune at Yamadi's blindness. He remembered the suit, the tie, he himself had worn at their last meeting. He remembered Marie-Sophie's hand in his as she happily left the gallery, deciding where her new Fragonard would hang. On the way to the office, he had eaten oysters at the Cintra, standing up. No. All that was the time before. The last time, Yamadi had given him Pompini's picture. He shivered suddenly, first at the squalid memory and then with yearning for his life. What surrounded him now – he saw it even above his fear – was most of all disgusting, twisted, mad. He felt contempt like a sudden gift. For Boris even. Whatever happened now, he had lived as they had not, in sunlight.

Yamadi said, "And on this expendable man, you spent two days of work?"

He walked slowly across the room toward Stears, circumambulating a fat, brocaded pouf of rosy silk near the trestle table.

Boris prosed on. "I would have spent two weeks. There is always something of value to find out. But it is of value to a comprehensive intelligence organization – not to a guerrilla operation. You do not understand that. If you insist that Zebdi examine this man, he had better do so now. Then we can get this interruption out of the way."

Yamadi now stood by Stears, his head level with Stears's chin. He spoke to Boris and pointed at Stears in conventional, contemptuous demonstration.

"It is two days before *Lyusi*. Zebdi is supervising the distribution of weapons. Then he has to go over the ground with the men. It is their first and last chance to see it, as you know. If I was sure that I believed you, I would save time and have this man simply shot. But I am not sure."

He turned and looked at Stears, his eyes unseeing, for dramatic effect. Stears felt Yamadi's face, near his, play over him, and almost leave him. And at the last second Yamadi's pupils froze.

He felt the shock himself. He was as close to Yamadi's eyes, almost, as in a kiss. It was like seeing a stuffed rodent come to life; the small black eyes became liquid, furtive, shocked. Yamadi breathed out, and an odor of Sen-Sen reached him. Yamadi opened his mouth, but into Yamadi's eyes, still intimately on his, came thought, and close behind that something inexplicably like terror. Yamadi turned away. He assumed, from so close, an air of ghastly nonchalance. He turned to the sergeant commando. He asked judiciously, tying up a small detail, "Has this fellow had any chance, any chance at all, of contacting his superiors? At any time?"

And, confident again of merit, the sergeant said, "No. We thought of that. He had no kind of radio when captured and there was none on the deck or elsewhere. We searched. I do not think that he could have thrown one overboard. As for the ship's radio, it was manned at all times."

"Could he have seen the cargo that was already on board and have reported earlier? Could he have examined it before you sailed?"

"I do not see how. It is not possible to go from the forecastle to the hold. The cargo hatches were closed and locked and he could not possibly have broken into them unobserved. Anyway, the hatches were not disturbed. He could only have witnessed the transloading and he could not have reported that."

Yamadi nodded. He said to Boris lightly, "Are you sure of this man's identity?"

"Yes."

Yamadi thought, judged, decided. "Zebdi has much on his hands now. I would not wish his concentration disturbed by something that may be of no importance. There is no need to involve him. Put this man away. We will deal with him when we can."

He felt, then saw, the girl's eyes upon him. She was looking at him with pleasure, lips slightly parted, with affection, even with lust. It was intense enough to startle him. When he looked back, she sought his eye. And then it chilled him. What she sought in his eye was terror. It had not been there, but at her eye he flinched. She quietly smiled. It would be their secret.

He sat in the corner of the room, on his haunches, clasping his knees, feeling the solid wall against each shoulder. The room was bare. The corner seemed right. He was far beyond panic, his mind was clear. This immobility seemed precious, seemed like peace. Strong bars of sunlight flowed through the chinked shutters and made patterns on the walls and floor. There were vaguely heard steps and voices, from time to time a voice that must have been the girl's. Cars drew up, crunching the gravel, a curiously unhurried rhythm of arrival and departure. A bee droned and knocked against the shutter. A house party at St. Tropez in summer. He had retired to his room.

It made some sense. The surveillance network of the CIA had almost worked. Yamadi did not look very good. His operation had been penetrated by McNaughton in Paris – who had even succeeded in getting an operative on board. Yamadi's people knew that. McNaughton had been blown by treachery, which was almost certainly a gift to Yamadi, not his own doing. What McNaughton's smuggler had screamed out was almost irrelevant – what they had needed had come from on top. Now Yamadi found, and only Yamadi knew, that his operation had been snared at its very base, its financing. Giovanni

Stears, if not precisely Yamadi's choice, had certainly been his responsibility. Yamadi, except for luck, had been beaten by the CIA. In his world, mistakes were dangerous. This one, by luck, could be swept under the rug. It could be swept quietly. Wop would not protest. There was always Khamal. Khamal was so useful.

So he would be killed.

And surely soon. He wondered when and how. Not here, he thought. He would pass through this room, leave it to its sunbeams and its bee. It was no doubt the last room he would know. Odd that it should be this particular one.

They came for him. They tied his hands. He looked at them with surprise. He had assumed it would be the commandos, or others like them. But the two who came were Berbian – North African for sure; young men with the driven, defiant look of radical students, not the satisfied brutality of the terrorist camps. Perhaps. But they were sure of themselves, these two, no doubt of that. And one of them easily carried an Uzi, deadly and small. They would make a success of this. No doubt the commandos were Khamal's boys, and these, Yamadi's. They wore jeans and shirts, not khaki and not cheap. The one who tied his hands wore a Rolex watch. He tied them quickly and well, scrupulously avoiding contact with his skin. Stears asked them mildly. *"Qui êtes vous?"* The one with the Uzi replied, *"Tais-toi. Allons, depèche-toi."* It was not gutter French. he did not hit him.

So, a Jeep. A drive into the country, then. The driver was an ordinary Arab, a servant, he guessed, a gardener or chauffeur with a face unquestioning and satisfied. The driver sat alone in front. Stears sat in the middle of the back seat, wedged between his escorts. The seat burned. The Jeep was started. The house door opened and Yamadi stood there, small, dark, neat, alone. He watched with no expression.

The city dropped behind them. Life was stripped away. The houses ended. The highway, empty for a mile, stopped abruptly with a ragged edge of concrete and became a track. The track climbed. The hot wind fanned their faces without freshness. There were no more herbs. Then the shrubs thinned. He found himself looking at the few that they still passed, victories of dusty green over rock, for comfort or a message. He knew with certainty when they saw the last. They were in a stony, barren valley crawling into low hills. The sun breathed upon the rock. The Jeep bucked and rattled; its metal was too hot to touch. His escorts looked straight ahead in silence.

His mind was at once stunned and clear, knowing but not feeling. If he protested, talked, told them what he was, it was highly likely that they would turn around. He would of course be taken to Khamal. At that he could not even look. If he cooperated utterly, told all – more than that, let Boris turn him, he would perhaps escape Khamal. He rejected that with weariness, distaste, and the dreary foreknowledge of what his life would be. Neither courage nor cowardice governed either one. Neither treason nor torture was a possible choice.

They would stop, he assumed, at any moment. One rock here did not seem better suited for murder than the next. He felt tears on his face. At a particularly violent motion of the Jeep, the face of the gun-carrying escort was thrown towards his. He saw on the face a slight, unyielding sympathy. But the tears were for the sweetness of his former life, and as it gathered itself up and floated away – snow beneath his skis, Marie-Sophie's voice and breasts, chestnut trees turning by the lake, the welcome of old friends in weekend houses, the smell of a suit freshly valeted, intelligence, success – he didn't know if they were for gratitude or loss. His death, he supposed, would be a little confusion, and a blow.

He saw the place at once. It was a narrow ravine leading back into the rock, pretty well concealed from all directions. Worth a little extra trip. His spine, of a sudden, froze. The Jeep stopped a few meters past it. His escorts jumped out. The driver moved, was told to stay. The younger escort without the gun beckoned to him. He did his best, but to get from the high Jeep with his hands tied was difficult. He said so. The boy looked oddly surprised and held up a helping hand. They walked on either side of him toward the ravine's mouth. He stumbled on shifting stones. He was supported. He saw the solitary boulder, the place he would be put against to die. He said, "Give me a moment." He said it again because the first time he had not made any sound. "Give me a moment. I won't make trouble, but give me a moment." He faced the wall of the ravine.

He turned again. The boy with the Uzi said, "American."

He nodded numbly. Of course. He had spoken English. One boy looked at the other. He felt a moment of fear, even of horror. He had accepted this. His life was ended. Now he had blundered into a resurrection of knives, of screams, of crimson. But the boy with the Uzi shrugged. he said, "Go over there. By the rock. Sit." And then, remembering the proper form, "Do you want a blindfold?"

He didn't answer. He sat by the rock. It scorched his back while his belly froze. The other boy went to the mouth of the ravine. The one with the Uzi backed up. He raised the little gun, like a Christmas toy. Wop saw the edge of the muzzle.

The noise was overwhelming, vast. He felt a hundred cuts and blows like stinging bees. The noise ended. He looked at a smashed hand, beginning to ooze blood. He saw it. He saw chips of broken rock on his leg. His ear rang. One eye was blind. He blinked. He saw through blood. He saw his executioner turn to his colleagues behind and nod. He saw him turn back to him and give a sign, thumb up. The executioner walked toward him. He feebly raised his hand. The boy gently pushed his hand away, said, "Later." The boy took the Uzi by its barrel, wincing at the heat, and swung it at his head.

When the young men were aboard, the driver turned the Jeep. As he started back, he looked curiously into the ravine. The foreign spy was lying pitched forward on the dry rock and his blood was around him. It was appropriate that infidels and traitors should so die.

21

His pillow was too hard. It cut his forehead. His head was full of a boiling, sour fluid. He wanted to vomit. He tried to move his right hand to wipe his face. His hand was stuck. He closed his eyes and groaned.

He opened them and turned his head. Saw rock. The stone bit his cheek. The other side of his head ached, on fire. With neither effort nor welcome, memory reported back for duty. He lost interest in moving. He groaned again, this time with meaning.

His body needed to move. His brain, without any urging from himself, seemed to pull itself out of glue and turn faster. Perhaps there was somebody about. It seemed foolish to ignore the fact that he was alive. He pulled himself into a fetal ball. Rib, aches, cuts, and lacerations all protested, but feebly and from a distance. He got his legs under him and sat up, squatting. His hands were tied. His left hand, smashed by ricocheting bullet or flying rock, was welded to the right hand by dried blood. He looked around him.

It was now evening. The sun had left the ravine. Through the mouth of the ravine he looked across the dry valley to stone hills yellow in the sinking light. He could have stretched out his hand and touched them, put his finger in a dimple of the rock. The air was of the utter clarity that is paradoxically palpable, ether, a Zeiss lens. The stillness was perfect, the stillness of bones, of the moon, of space. It shocked him; such stillness as he had known before, of pine forest, of hay meadow, of evening river were by comparison a chaos, a riot in the street. At an infinite distance, invisible, a circling bird whistled in comment. He drew in his breath and yelled. He stopped at once, terrified.

The sun was switched off. The rock glowed silver under darkness. A furlong or so above his head, the stars came out. There was barely room for them. They covered the sky, single intense fires and silver blotches against jet black. They weighed upon him. He sank onto the boulder. His thirst was moderate but worrying. His body's pains and smell were almost comforting. They kept him company. He began to count the individual pains but gave up.

He was not alone. Behind him in the ravine he heard a small, dry rattling. His scalp froze. Then the merest whisper, as of skin on rock. Then a tiny, angry stirring of small stones. He grew terrified of the boulder behind him, expecting around its edge a sly, sudden, deadly snout. He levered himself to his feet and stood in the open, turning. On every side the rock stared back at him. He never heard the sound again. In due course, the still space around him seemed more terrible and he crept back against his rock.

It was extremely cold. His teeth began to chatter. He could not control them and he lay like a mechanical toy gone mad, chattering and shaking. He felt an utter desolation, a loneliness on the edge of tears. For a second, he had the sensation of Marie-Sophie's body warm beside him, and longing flowed through him like wine. He wondered where she was. He had the impression that he cried, but through clattering teeth it was difficult to tell.

Sanity and prosaic torment returned with light. So did thought. The rock turned a gray, hard yellow. His thirst was much worse. The slender chain of fact and effect suggested that at the last moment he had not been shot because he had revealed himself as an American. Nor had he been taken back to Yamadi and Khamal. A divergence of interest between his executioners and his captors seemed indicated, but beyond that he could not go further. Other possibilities: this whole performance was a charade to break his nerve. Khamal could have broken it in twenty seconds – and it had been broken all to pieces anyway since the hijacking on the dock. This could be no more than a particularly sadistic execution. He doubted that; he assumed that somebody would come back. It gave him some but little comfort. The thread of chance seemed as frail as gossamer, and he did not have much time left.

For already around him there was the dry breath of an oven. The ravine took the morning sun. It scalded his eyes. He shuffled around to face the rock, sat hunched. Thirst began to constrict his throat like a tightening gag. The sun climbed upon his head. He and the sun were the only things that moved. The hours were counted by the movement of the sun and the minutes by the contractions of his throat.

The thought of liquid drove out all else. He imagined basins, waterfalls, bottles of white wine, the dew on the bottles. It occurred to him to shuffle off up the ravine in search of springs amid the rock. After twenty meters he grew too tired, and he was frightened without his boulder. A thought returned to him from training sessions in far-off Virginia. It was possible – ribald comment from the class – to drink one's urine. The thought seemed slighly less wonderful than an ice bucket, but very slightly. There was a problem. His hands were tied, could not form cups. He thought for several minutes. A concave rock would do. He shuffled eagerly about. At length he found one. It was not convenient, but if he braced his feet and leaned his head against the rock wall and stretched, it could, anatomically, be done. With thumbs alone, he struggled with his fly.

He realized later that he had heard the drone, but he was too busy; it was only the change of gear that registered. He scuttled to the mouth of the ravine. There, in perfect clarity and very far away, was a Jeep, every rivet of its metal visible. On rock, it stirred little dust. It came up the valley fast. There were two indistinguishable figures in it, Arabs in burnooses.

He supposed he should hide until he could see them better. It seemed, however, pointless, friend or enemy knew where to find him; any stranger would be better than death. He stood at the mouth, his eyes fixed on the Jeep, watching it turn from toy into reality. He was ready to jump out and wave if it gave signs of going past, but when it was still a hundred meters away it turned slightly from the center of the valley and he could see its wheels pointed straight toward him. For better or worse, it came for him.

It stopped where it had stopped before. The Arabs got out, cowled, anonymous. His heart leaped; one carried a water flask. They paced toward him. A voice came from within the cowl. "We are truly sorry. You were not to have been here so long." It was spoken in good French. The cowl was lifted. His executioners had returned. They had returned with water.

He knelt naked by the spring and poured water from a wooden bucket over his shoulders and his head, gasping and shaking with delight as it ran down his belly and his thighs. It was cold Atlas water. The stiff grass was springy under his knees. He reached into the spring for a palmful of sand gleaming with mica and rubbed his body with it. His hand, free from its crust of blood, was stiff and painful but not much damaged. He heard sheep bleat in the higher pasture. He looked up and saw them on the slope, like soft, moving rocks. Aziz, the older of his escorts, came out of the cabin. He heard his voice speak back to Hassan, his brother, inside. He dried himself with a bit of old blanket, though the sun would have done it in minutes. His body, washed, felt frail and tender, but its leaden aches were gone. The clothes he had pulled from the suitcase at the Bergerie lay stiff and filthy where he had thrown them across the spring. He did not care to touch them. He picked up from the grass the long, unfamiliar burnoose, wondering how the devil one put it on. He fought his way into it – it smelled faintly but sweetly of raw wool – and emerged beneath the cowl. He moved, and felt it strangely flow around his limbs. He looked at himself and laughed; he was a shepherd in a Christian play.

The cabin was plaster, white and low, blackened inside by tallow candles. It smelled of smoke and sheep. The Jeep sat outside its door, blocking some of the only light; the cabin was dim but he could see on the rough table a pie of sorts and bread and wine. Hassan indicated a blanket on the floor. He spoke in French.

"Sit here," he said. "There are no chairs in a place like this. That is a pigeon pie. Very Berbian. Quite folklore. Eat and drink first. You need it. Then we will talk."

He did, and looked at them. They were a type he knew well. Their burnooses, he imagined, were as unfamiliar to them as to him. He guessed Aziz was twenty-four, Hassan two years younger. They had the sharp, mannered, preening air of young Arabs at the Sorbonne or in Nice – but not at all the spoiled and puzzled look of callow young Gulf sheikhlings. They were of good North African merchant family, educated and trained to work; they were probably intelligent, and neither French beaches nor French girls nor the thin gold chain around Azis's neck would have blunted a character both smart and tough. He had taken them for radicals. Now he was not quite sure. They had learned all that, he thought; they had the arrogance of the Left; good Third World French students. But they would go in the end with power and conceivably even with responsibility. He had liked men of their type before.

The wine was strong. As soon as he had sat down, he knew that he was lightheaded with exhaustion. He ate and drank little. Sleep pressed on him like bricks. His thoughts floated. He pulled them together with an actual contraction of his brow when Aziz spoke. "Now tell us who you are."

He lacked the strength for intricacy. He shoved his money on a bet that seemed reasonable on its face, shrugged, and said, "I am American. I work for the American government."

Hassan said, "That is not what Yamadi told us."

He said, "But it is true."

"Of course it is. When you spoke in English back there you were too frightened to think. There is no arguing about that. It saved you. If you had been what Yamadi and the Russian said, you could not have helped us. Of course you are CIA?"

Stears shrugged and said nothing.

Aziz took over. "Does the Russian know that?"

"Yes."

"And you did not tell Yamadi." Aziz thought. "Yes. That makes sense. Yamadi is cautious. If he thought the CIA even had his scent he might have changed his plans and maybe the Russians would not have liked that. It makes sense."

Stears choked back the words in his mouth and said instead, "What are you? Why did you do what you did?"

Aziz and Hassan looked at each other in silence. Aziz said seriously, "We will tell you what you need to know. Our family, like many others in Berbia, knows, as you Americans do not, that the days of King Fahd are over. Maybe not this year, but next year, or the next. There are two forces – one must take his place. You know them both; the Baath socialists and the Brothers of Islam. Our family ranged itself behind the Baath. We helped persuade them; they would have stayed committed to the King and they would have been destroyed. For us, the Baath was justice; for the family, it was better than the Brothers of Islam – everyone has seen Iran. But the Baath accepted help from the Russians. Of course it did – how else could it fight against the American King? Then,

337

when the PLO was dispersed from the Lebanon, the Russians and Ghaddafi in Libya gave us PLO 'volunteers' and 'experts' and 'trainers.' Yamadi and Zebdi were two of them. Before long, all the Russian and the Libyan money came to the Baath through the PLO, and before much longer the PLO was not *helping* the Baath, it *was* the Baath. And then we saw the truth. The PLO would run the Baath, and the Baath would topple the King, and Berbia would be ruled by the Baath, and the Baath by the PLO, and Berbia would be the new Lebanon. Libya and the PLO would rule in the Mahgreb. It is a grand plan. But we, you see, are only Berbians."

Aziz stopped. His eyes challenged any accusation that he had made a mistake. Fair enough, thought Wop; he hadn't – he had been tricked into one. Few things would be more reliable than a young Arab's enmity to the forces that had duped him. Stears had the absolute conviction that the time had come to invest everything he had. He said, "And I will tell you what you need to know of me. Yamadi also knows what I am. He did not until yesterday, but he knew then, and not because the Russian told him. Khamal – your Zebdi – does not know yet. I doubt he ever will. I have observed Yamadi for some little time. You need not ask how. He had no cause to suspect me. But Zebdi also would have known if he had seen me. That was what Yamadi did not want."

He stopped, grave and deliberately grand. The condemned man babbling English and the poor scarecrow at the ravine's mouth needed a counterweighing image. He leaned back.

It had an effect. Both looked at him in silence, not trying to disguise that they were prepared for him to be a liar. But Hassan slowly nodded and said with decision, "Yes. That is why we were used. We thought that it was to test our loyalty, or our nerve. Or even that the Palestinians were too busy. But the Palestinians are first and foremost Zebdi's men. If Yamadi wanted to destroy you quietly, it would have been a risk to use them. He did not trust us, either. I heard him questioning the driver. I believe you. What do you know of Zebdi and Yamadi?"

"That they had been buying weapons. Western weapons. Not enough for a serious guerrilla army, but a considerable number nonetheless. That they have shipped them here. That the weapons arrived yesterday. That they are financed in part by Libya. That the Russians wish to control them."

With a gesture purely of Paris. Aziz poured three dashes of purple wine into the leather cups on the peasant table. A gesture of partnership. He said, "We also know that, more or less. But we have a suspicion that this is more than a normal terrorist operation. We think that it is the mainspring of Yamadi's plan. We think that you, the CIA, can help us. This is why we took a risk at the last moment and did not kill you. But we must tell you more.

"It is also a fact that a large number of Palestinian guerrillas arrived three days ago on another ship. Two or three of their officers have been at the villa, but the rest have been seen only by Zebdi. We are almost certain of three things. They are not expected to stay here very long – we have no evidence that they are to be infiltrated into the guerrilla fighters in the city, and if they were to reinforce the Polisario they would have come in through the south. We are sure these weapons are for their use. There has been some anxiety about these weapons. We think that there was some doubt that they would be here on time."

Hassan broke in on his elder brother. "But on time for what? That is what we do not know. Fifty, seventy-five men cannot do much against the King's army. We do not think that any special disturbance has been planned for al-Tabek. Only one great thing is about to happen in Berbia. Tomorrow is the yearly pilgrimage to the tomb of Lyusi."

Stears said, "Lyusi? The old saint?"

"Yes. You know of that? The Brothers of Islam have made a cult of him. They always have, but there is a new holy man among them this year and he has turned it into a hysteria. Berbian Islam is very primitive, you know. This man has a great following among the al-Tabek rabble, and it seems that he is going to lead a huge crowd from the city out to the tomb. The government is nervous, but it tolerates it and will probably leave them strictly alone. An incident in a religious procession is the last thing they want – they saw Iran, too."

He paused and Aziz, judicious, elder, took it up. "We believe that this operation is connected with the pilgrimage. We do not know how. Probably Palestinian thugs will join the pilgrims and there will be an incident of some kind. It there were armed men among the pilgrims the government would be forced to take some action. Maybe that is what Yamadi wants. But it is important. Make no mistake of that. Everything Yamadi and Zebdi have done for the past two months seems to be directed at this. We believe that what is planned tomorrow may start a landslide that cannot be stopped."

Aziz paused. He waited impressively. Too long – Hassan beat him to the punch. Hassan said, "Except, perhaps, by the Americans."

Aziz frowned, went on. "Yes. Except, perhaps, by the Americans. We do not know what will happen, but some strange incident will take place, something about which no one will ever really know the truth. That is how things unravel in the Arab world. In Europe, this or that happens. Here *something* happens, God knows what. If Yamadi plays his cards right, by the time it is known what has happened, it will be too late. Berbia will be beyond control. We do not wish Fahd to rule forever. We do not want your American base. But Berbia must choose its own time. We will not see our country stampeded by a trick. And that, you see, is why we did not shoot you. Do you understand? You are to be our witness. The witness for the Americans."

340

It made, Stears thought, a general and schematic sense. He reserved doubt and simply said, "How?"

Aziz said, "Our first idea was that you should join in the procession. But that would not be safe. You cannot play that role. We doubt that anything will happen before the pilgrimage reaches the tomb. That is when emotion will be highest and somehow, surely, that emotion will be used. That is where you must watch. There are hills there – it is grazing country, not so unlike here – and you can be concealed. Besides, at a distance, dressed as you are, you pass for an Arab pretty well. We shall take you there. You must stay here alone tonight. It would cause some suspicion if we remained away. No one will come here. It is our uncle's land and the cabin is not used. We will fetch you before dawn. The village of Lyusi's tomb is perhaps an hour from here. Perhaps we will watch with you, perhaps not. It will be safest for us to do whatever Yamadi wants. But we shall also get you back. Tomorrow we will know how. Will you do this? You do not have much choice."

Stears answered the hint of threat with deliberate severity.

"Why did you wait for me to fall into your hands? Why did not patriots like you go to the American embassy before?"

He knew that answer. Hassan laughed.

"They would not have listened. They see what they want to see. They think King Fahd is here forever. Your eyes have been torn open. And besides, it would have been dangerous for us. Your embassy is close to the King's police."

Stears nodded. His eyes were lead, his body sodden with fatigue. He said, "I will do as you say. It is not so bad a plan. It is your responsibility to get me to the embassy. That is your undertaking."

Aziz said, "Of course."

He wondered if he would collapse in front of them, but they did not stay much longer. He watched the Jeep

341

snake down through the rocky pastures and finally, a mile away, rejoin a threadlike track. He was alone, for the time being at no great risk. It seemed to his ringing brain an unimaginable luxury. For a minute he watched the hills, the distant sheep. Peace settled on him like a brief shower in a drought. It was near dusk. He went into the cabin and picked up the blanket from the floor. He wrapped himself in it, lay down, and slept.

22

They drove in darkness, in the confederacy of those up before the light. Stears sat in the back alone. The air was cool. He had slept deeply; only the headlights of the Jeep in the cabin door had wakened him. He had had time only to grab a handful of pie and a cup of wine, but to be rested was a feeling bright and new as dew. Hassan drove fast and without hesitation. They went downhill at first, then across a broad valley, then began to climb. They were never on highways. The stony tracks were creamy gray in the headlights. Before each village, Hassan switched off the lights. The villages were white cubicles with black windows and disembodied dogs.

Hassan again switched off the lights and ran the Jeep off the track. It ran over grass toward a blot of greater darkness, a grove of trees. He switched off the engine.

Aziz said, "Now we walk. About twenty minutes. It should not be too bad. There will soon be some light."

It would have been fine in boots; it was a bitch in robe and sandals. He had a sudden sympathy for all biblical people, and for women. But the sky was the faintest gray and the stones and thorn bushes were at least visible. They were near the head of a valley in moderate hills. There was a village below them, surrounded on three sides by slopes at first gentle and then steepening. The road came up the valley to the village and went no farther. The lower slopes were rocky pasture – some of the rocks moved and bleated; the upper slopes were a stony maquis. They kept to the edge of the maquis, a kilometer or so from the village, circling it toward the slopes behind it. Aziz and Hassan, it seemed, knew the roads but not the slopes.

Aziz muttered, "Shouldn't we stay away from the sheep? Don't sheep have dogs?"

When the cock crowed, Hassan and Aziz jumped.

They were behind the village. It was now grayly visible, as in an engraving. The road, ending in the center of it, gave it the semblance of a public square. The houses were small, white, and almost identical. The village succeeded in being both crowded and straggling. At the back of it, where the road ended, was a small, domed mosque. The village did not quite end there. A broad footpath led slightly uphill, two hundred meters, toward a sparse grove of low trees. In the center of the grove was a square building, also domed, its roof a little higher than the trees and, alone in the village, built of stone. The earth around it was meticulously swept. Aziz nudged him and pointed. "Lyusi's tomb. This is a good place to watch from, but we must find some cover."

So they waited. It was even peaceful. A jagged boulder, three or four feet high, sat in a small concavity of the slope. The boulder's brown-gray color was not much different from their clothes – shoulder or headcloth could show without danger. They whispered, unnecessarily. Aziz and Hassan, far from being needed by Yamadi, had been strictly told to be in al-Tabek, to have no contact with the Baath, to be seen, if possible, with friends or family, to come nowhere near the villa. They had debated leaving Stears alone. They had decided that in making their way back there was more danger than in staying put.

So while the sun grew hot and the grass whined and ticked with grasshoppers, they watched the village, sharing Aziz's binoculars. The cry came from the mosque at dawn. Men with sleep in their steps hurried to it. Women moved in the streets toward the wall. Charcoal hearths were lit in courtyards. He imagined that he smelled coffee. He had the sense of a demonstration done for him.

So through the dawn. After that, this special day, the village scurried like an antheap. They put up canvas booths on the road. In a small, bloody pen, three men skinned slaughtered lambs. There was a smell of fire and meat. And all the time, the footpath to Lyusi's tomb was walked by families in small groups. They prostrated themselves on the earth outside and left some offering on the ground – bread, flowers, he saw even a picture frame and a copper pot. It looked disconcertingly like a garage sale.

Hassan looked at his watch. Stears remembered uncomfortably the same gold Rolex on the wrist that had bound his hands. Nine o'clock. Hassan counted to himself. "The pilgrims will have left the city at dawn. It should take them four hours to get here, I think. So an hour more, perhaps."

Stears said, "Will the village people not know more exactly?"

"How? There is no telephone here. This is not Algeria or Egypt. Nothing is more remote than a Berbian hill village."

At first it was like a trail of multicolored smoke blowing into the end of the valley. The reports would later say ten thousand. Stears doubted it. He never thought more than three. But on the narrow road, at a walking pace, it was like the emptying of a reservoir; when the leaders were plainly seen, the rear guard still crawled into the valley. That was cloudlike, tatterdermalion, but the leaders positively made him duck. They made a tight mob, perhaps a hundred, around one central figure, all men, not in step, in every kind of gown, but they seemed as indivisible as a boulder rolling down the road. He looked into the intense, vacant faces, the blind righteousness, and saw that he was witnessing something that he knew of but had never seen: anger and exultation,

345

violence and God. "Pilgrimage" had meant something quite other to him; he was as shocked as if he had seen the College of Cardinals rush out in leather jackets.

But if the leaders as a group were ominous, the leader of them all made him blink. The Imam moved in a small space in the pack. The black robe put him in the frame of a priest. The emaciated, staring face was from the mold of saintly wretchedness. He moved without ceasing, encouraging, glorifying, exultantly lifting his arms and capering like a dervish, a figure of antic holiness drawing the whole assembly on. So. A fanatic native. And then Stears stopped, uneasy. He played with the binoculars' focus. He felt a physical need to be closer, to see what he only apprehended from here. For the frolic turning was not entirely random – the Imam had the whole rout constantly in view; the urging, the prayer-shouts were directed at any loosening of the leaders. He did not know if he was right, but he had the sudden thought of a holy fool counting the take.

Aziz whispered, "That is the new Imam." The whisper was ridiculous in the hubbub now rising from below, and he went on in a normal voice. "His name is Ibrahim. If Berbia had a Khomeini, it would be he. But he is much worse. Khomeini is a scholar of sorts. This man deals in nothing but violence and ignorance and hate. You will see when he speaks. He is the reason why families like mine support the Baath."

He was drunk with the smell of the crowd, sweat and dust, sharp and dense. He danced with no pretense. *Dictatorship of the Proletariat* – not a formula but a living force strong and dense as sex. The poorest of the slums poured their small, sad energies into him, a thousand times, five thousand, until in him they compressed and caught fire. He felt more than human now: his "real" self, Shamak, the engineer, not even within reach, even Ibrahim transcended. His wit, his courage, his limbs, his loins blazed with strength, blazed back into the mob.

346

And through him these jobless laborers, fly-speckled children, worn-out mothers of the slums, became a piston of the Dialectic carrying History, King, and Fate before it. Dancing, turning, gesturing, he should have been at the limit of his lungs and legs, but the breath of the crowd and the tremor of the red earth beneath his feet renourished him like warm new blood.

This part, the march, was over. The villagers had put out booths: bread, lamb, sugar drinks, sweets. His people must be at the limit of their strength. Lethargy at the last could be fatal. He made a gesture of gracious, brief permission. He beckoned for lemon water for himself. The thought of its taste in the mouth of a child delighted him truly. He watched his people's careful modesty – a small pie among a family of four, a slice of lamb considered and forgone – with love and awe. For a moment he was struck with sadness.

But turned from it. The march was the smallest, the easiest of his work. He had allotted it an atmosphere of exalted merriment, more or less of holiday. Now for anger. Soon for rage. He made anger well up within him; he felt the change in his spine and face. He saw, with pleasure, two girls who had relaxed in his leniency, gratefully chattering and eating, look at him again and turn suddenly abashed.

He saw the consecrated bull. A white animal, its flanks still heaving, its eyes bleary and afraid. Its drivers were around it. Beyond them the six lean drummers who had carried their instruments from the city. His plan was formed from the materials at hand. It was time now to lead on to Lyusi's tomb. There, Lyusi's ancient anger would speak through him, would lead to the prayers and the celebration. The people's own ritual, the extreme of the debased Islam of the Mahgreb, would set fire to rage. He beckoned to the drummers.

Stears watched. The commandos, any of Khamal's Palestinians, would have stood out among this frazzled mob like prizefighters among tramps. A few special groups – the heavies around the Mullah, some drummers, a cow, for some reason – all seemed safely of the day. He said so to Hassan.

Hassan shrugged doubtfully. "There is time yet. They are not even at the tomb. I would not have expected anything yet."

"What are you looking for?" said Stears. Hassan shrugged again. The drummers gave a sudden, staccato burst. The cow was goaded to its feet. The crowd began to move.

"Now," said Hassan, "he will take them to the tomb. No doubt he will speak to them. You will understand what I said."

In the forecourt of the tomb a flat white rock cropped out, a natural and established pulpit. Ibrahim spoke there, his back to the tomb. He now began to watch the valley road. He could see it perfectly, beyond the flat white roofs of the village, five kilometers until the valley curved. All other eyes in the village looked the other way, to Lyusi and to him.

He, a Marxist leader of terrorists, waited for machines and preached the word of Allah in a scene of timeless and perfect pastorality before a house of sanctified old bones.

He perfectly grasped the unity: that only the martyr lives; that anger, passing through the People and purging them, is the only useful love; that the Marxist Dialectic alone can effect that love, breaking the stalemate of History and setting the martyred people free. He spoke terrifically and wholly without effort. He spoke of the anger of Lyusi. He brought before them their hunger, their poverty of spirit, the ancient meekness of their class, their thirst for righteousness.

He saw the trucks. Four, crawling into the valley. Precisely on time, under the most difficult circumstances. And behind them, the armored car. His heart jumped. His voice soared still higher. The hysteria of the crowd had now to be pushed to blindness. He beckoned to the drummers again.

Stears listened to the voice; less to the words. Ibrahim spoke of the life of Lyusi, whom Stears knew chiefly as a sanguinary and vindictive zealot. He spoke of the King, the Americans, the rich. Aside from the delivery, which was terrific, it was the same stuff, empty, rambling, and malevolent that Stears had seen on a hundred smudged newssheets or heard on the news from hirsute saboteurs, a sad and sour wind. He was, besides, distracted. A small flock of sheep had ambled toward their rock, and a lamb had seen, at first snoofing in alarm, then fascinated, the three men lying flat on the grass. So while the voice from below, wild but attenuated, shifted swiftly between politics and God, preached of the hatred and revenge of heaven, he felt on his face the sweet milky breath, felt the small mouth pluck at his sleeve, tried first to push it away, and ended by surreptitiously throwing handfuls of grass to it, which it first pretended to be frightened of and then ate. No doubt about the locals, though – Preacher had them buffaloed.

He had been watching the square, but a movement on the periphery of sight made him raise his eyes. At the farthest point of the valley he saw the vehicles like four black bugs coming up the road. Dust rose above them. He nudged Hassan and pointed. Hassan looked and stiffened. He put binoculars to his eyes, studied, and somewhat relaxed.

"Army trucks," he said. "And an armored car behind. I am surprised, but I suppose the government wants to take precautions. They will not come very close."

In the time the trucks and troops needed to deploy, the plan would stand or fall. If the crowd saw the deployment, then its action would be unpredictable and the tableau would fail. This was the timing that he had rehearsed again and again. For this he had accustomed

349

the Brothers to his rhetoric so that they moved to his emotion like a horse to his legs. The Brothers would sway the rest. He felt the drums around him like the charged air of a thunderstorm. He knew that his shouts were almost inaudible, but he shouted still. The trucks, now two kilometers into the valley, peeled off the road, two on either side, onto the flat pasture. The armored car took the lead.

The pilgrims were now dancing singly to the drums. In their exaltation they achieved an individuality he had never seen in them before, as though washed clean of resignation. Some he had known for a year and more. Yussuf, a boy with a cleft palate and downcast eyes – who could have guessed that he would tremble in the air with joy? Mohammed, a stiff and bitter elder, moved to the bass drum's slower beat in sensual and amazing grace. A few, here and there, were sinking into trance, their eyes and faces blank as meat above bodies jerking in spasms agonized and copulative at once. These were reverently guided toward the bull. The crowd was far too large for the courtyard of the tomb. That, also, he had foreseen. The stony path to the village pulsed with bodies and, below that, others were still pressed in the space around the mosque. He looked at the trucks again. Much closer now. Five minutes, at most, for all.

A hundred meters from the village the trucks stopped abruptly in a line across the valley. The armored car went fifty meters farther, right up to the beginning of the booths. The backs of the trucks were opened.

"This is insane," said Aziz. "I can understand them putting some troops into the area, but this is madness!"

The soldiers now began to jump out of the trucks. Stears saw them and blinked. He was looking at platoons which were, except for the Arab faces, American Marines.

Hassan saw it too and stiffened, but he said, "That is the palace regiment. They are called the King's Own

Light Infantry. They were trained by your Marines, and their uniforms are quite different from the rest of the army. Their weapons, too. They are King Fahd's own tribesmen. He never uses them for things like this. He's lost his mind. People who go on pilgrimages with the Brothers of Islam hate all the troops, but they hate these more."

For now, it hardly mattered. Theology had been abandoned for a dance. Even up here they had to speak loudly. The Imam was howling like a banshee, and, though he could certainly see the troops, was evidently not going to let them spoil the show. Some particularly ominous citizens, apparently in a moving trance, had surrounded the poor cow. The note of the drums slowed and deepened.

Perhaps it gained something if you were there. First he thought that two adepts were hitting the cow about the neck with sticks. Then the neck turned crimson – the sticks were swords. The cow sank to its knees, looking up at the Imam. Its head fell off, rolled a little way, and lay looking into the air. A lake of blood began to spread.

What happened then appalled him. Fresh blood is as forbidden to a Muslim as to a Jew. Yet he saw the entranced dancers, under their Imam's feet, rush forward to cup their hands at the bubbling throat, raise the blood to their mouths, and drink. Meanwhile the crowd pushed forward, and those close enough capered like mud larks in a clay of dust and blood and smeared their clothes and skin. Stears made a sound of disgust and saw that Hassan's face was rigid with embarrassment. He made himself say equably, "I did not know that Muslims did this."

And Hassan forced his upper lip into a Frenchman's curl and said, "A folkloric manifestation. I told you it would be improving."

He looked back now to the troops. The line had moved. He was looking, he thought, at about a hundred men. Two groups of about twenty-five each had advanced

351

on either flank of the village so that it was surrounded on three sides. Aziz and Hassan's Jeep, within its grove of trees, was a good thousand meters behind them. He looked at the men more closely now. Their weapons, he saw, were Armalites and M-14s.

The rest of the men were drawn up behind the armored car. An officer spoke to the troops behind the car and then into a radio. The engine ground coarsely. The car moved slowly up the village street. It appeared to be a French Panhard with gleaming paint and the royal arms emblazoned on the turret. The soldiers followed – not crouching, confident.

Aziz said, "There is only one possibility. The government has decided to arrest the leadership of the Brothers of Islam and thinks that it would be safer here than in al-Tabek. That may be why they are using the royal regiment – their discipline is good. But they are still mad. To arrest pilgrims at a shrine is bad enough. If there is an incident, it will set Berbia on fire."

Stears saw it intimately and safely as a scene on a jigsaw puzzle. He saw it with a morbid fascination. The troops, a tight, olive-dun line behind the camouflaged toy armored car. The patchwork mob now pressed into the last third of the space before the mosque and flowing from it, as from an hourglass. The bare, red earth. The street from a children's Bible, the armored car now almost to the end of it. He felt a sense of vicarious nakedness when the car was suddenly in the square, with the pilgrims, only the empty earth between them, the troops fanning out. The rear of the crowd had seen them now and were shouting in alarm. The troops and the car halted, and the only movement was the struggling and turning, first individual, then in a mass, inside the crowd. So, when the turret of the car opened and an officer's figure, like a Jack-in-the-box, rose out of it, the officer faced a crowd stunned, immobile, incredulous, but fixed on him.

Perhaps the officer counted on it; to shock the crowd

352

into movement before it thought. His cap shaded his face; Stears could see little of him, but he had the impression that the officer was lean, taut, and young. He soon had the certainty that he was a fool.

His voice, from a bullhorn, cut across the square, cold and remote.

"This is an illegal assembly. You are under arrest. Come forward. Come forward now."

And the troops raised their weapons.

It was inane. The crowd, not even mutinous, not even panicked yet, gaped at the line of muzzles it was invited to walk toward. And the voice, now even worse, with an edge of shrillness.

"Come forward at once. Come forward or it will be the worse for you."

And now the Imam moved. Stears saw him all at once, running down the footpath, which opened for him, like a black ferret, a pack of adepts behind. The mob, too, parted for him. He bored through it, sable and fierce. Then he was on the white steps of the mosque. Black against them, he seemed to pulse. And when he spoke. Stears groaned.

For he screamed, *"Sheitan!* Shit of the King!" And then to his own: "Will you turn from the worship of God for the fear of this filth? Will God himself not defend this holy place?"

The words went on. But out of the crowd now came a sight of nightmare, an eruption from its front of crimson, dripping figures, a dozen or more, reeling and spinning, bodies from a flaying pit in their last agony. Stears gaped, wondering what horror he had missed. He had forgotten the entranced dancers. Sodden with the bull's blood, conscious of nothing beyond their Imam's voice, they were moving out of the crowd, now, a weird vanguard descending upon the troops. Soldiers, horrified, shifted on their feet. The officer, either shocked himself or simply forgetting his last order, cried, "Halt! Stay where you are!" But the dancers were running now and the officer spoke inaudibly but urgently to his troops and Stears saw their hands move on their weapons and he raised his eyes and saw the Imam stretched forward like a mantis in a final howl of vituperation. And then he heard the shots.

They were ragged, thought Ibrahim. They were brief, short, like the chatter of fireworks, not the crash of Fate. Bodies fell to the hot earth, but casually, scattered. And they moved. Every step toward this movement had been imagined, timed; the moment itself, he had never thought to picture. This was wretched. Not the future storming in, but sudden silence and single bodies crawling vaguely in the dust. All at once, he feared. That it would somehow stick; that the Palestinians would blanch; that it would crumble from a seizing of History to a squalid accident. He drew in breath to lash his people on, but words and rhythm failed him. With the shots, the virtue had gone out of him.

Then Fate woke up. On the outer fringe of the crowd, terrified families struggled back, away from the guns. But now the crowd itself began to swell like a bladder. The larger mob around Lyusi's tomb had heard their Imam from the mosque, had turned and flowed back down the path. To them, the ragged, faraway firing had been not a terror but an outrage. The Imam's own congregation was at the farthest rear; it drove down like a piston. So the screaming families were flung outward toward the troops. The troops saw hurled toward them an avalanche of struggling flesh. The troops were the embodiment of a lie, their uniforms counterfeit, their weapons stolen. But their choice was real: stop the crowd or run.

They stood. Ibrahim saw the mob roll down on them, the space of earth between narrowing from field to ribbon; they seemed futile, debris to be blown away. But then he flinched. From the square came a long concussion, shaking his skull. He had heard before individual soldiers firing single shots. This was like a hat of noise forced down upon his ears.

And the crowd stopped. At first he thought so. And the noise went on. But the crowd had stopped moving forward only; its edge moved upward now, it climbed upon itself like a breaking wave. Its boundary was a line of falling bodies, but still the pressure from behind was such that more were carried over them and – with their faces toward the crowd, fighting back into it like swimmers against the current – were cut down themselves. Ibrahim looked at the faces of the troops. A few he even knew. All were veterans of the terrorist camps. Each he had insisted, had successfully carried out operations against civilians before. They seemed mesmerized by the tide flowing down upon them. The faces of some were dreamy, of others, set. The shell casings sprayed from the breaches, the magazines littered the ground, the barrels shimmered; the noise roared on; the crowd weltered at its deadly edge; time stuck. The panic in his head was gone. Fate had come to his calling. And his bowels were touched with cold.

The officer stopped it. A sudden, deeper pulse began, the heavy machine gun of the armored car, firing down upon the crowd – not at its edges but at its center. The center now recoiled. The surge on the path began again, but now uphill. The whimpering vanguard rocked once and then pushed back.

Ibrahim knew that he must leave the steps. He was safe there – alone, his identity obvious. No soldier would fire at him. But he must be seen to help his people. He was shocked, however, into stillness. He moved with difficulty down the steps.

He moved into a new sound, vague and distant. The crowd was nearly silent, but the wall of fallen bodies was not still. It trembled and shuddered. A hand, fingers splayed, rose out of it, fell back, and from its center came a rippling whimpering, babbling, a stifled scream. He had not thought that annihilation would leave sobs behind. From the bottom, blood seeped already, forming mud. In one place, the heap stirred and heaved. Like a bloody worm from a rotten fruit, a child crawled out and crept upon the ground.

A girl, talking silently to herself, looked at him blankly. He remembered her from the booths. He tried to speak, but he had forgotten what Ibrahim would say. He had the sudden fear that his treachery was already known. He pushed it from his mind. It could not be. *Lyusi* had already exceeded his wildest hopes. Horror had grown with the logic of Fate. He had never thought to use the dancers so. The finger of History had reached down. It was a pity that the cameras, not due yet, could not have seen them too.

He flinched. Another burst of fire. A few of the crowd had tried to break away by fleeing to the edge of the square, among the village houses. They had been stopped, correctly. The plan had to be followed, the tableau set up, the sacrifice made perfect, the effect assured. He could not bear to waste the People's blood. A woman blundered against him, her eyes on a wad of sticky crimson in her arms. From the wad, a child's foot protruded.

He found that he was running. The last shots had stampeded the crowd. They surged back toward the tomb, carrying him along. He smelled the bodies of his people. It frightened him to be within the mob, unrecognized. He fought his way to the edge of it. He tripped over a stumbled body and, looking down, saw a despairing face looking up at his. He saw a pall of smoke come from the armored car. Good. On cue. The car was to be damaged and left behind, a photogenic witness.

He must be Ibrahim. He ran beside the crowd toward the tomb. The chaos around him affected him. He had a sudden new fear that *Lyusi* would be wasted; that he would lose control, that Ibrahim would disintegrate, that the rage and horror would find no focus. He saw the rock before the tomb with dread and exultation. If he could not recapture them here he could do so never.

356

Exultation triumphed. He stood above them and spread his arms. They knew him. At the motion, a cloud of flies rose from the carcass of the bull. The phrases of a sermon flashed through his head, but he looked at the faces before him, a young man searching frantically, a woman with her fingers thrust into her mouth, and knew that his hold on them was short. He cried, "My children! It is I they seek. Save yourselves. God will not forget. Tell the city of the horror you have seen."

He pointed to the hills.

Hassan wept. Stears looked away. He took his hand from Aziz's. He had had to reach up and pull him to his knees when Aziz had leaped to his feet at the first volley. Stears felt as though the world had burned and left its ashes in his head. *So this is what they are behind the names, he thought. Guernica, Katyn Forest, Babi Yar.*

Hassan turned to him. The assured and handsome face was wet. Stears thought for a moment that he spoke to him in a fury, then knew he was holding back a sob. Hassan said, "This is the King I wanted to save from the Baath. This is the King." He looked at Stears as though suddenly seeing him and added, "Do you like the King you bought? Does this suit the CIA?"

Stears passed his hand before his face and drearily, pointlessly murmured, "I am sorry."

Hassan beat his forehead on the grass.

They saw the Imam point to the way of escape, the hills above the village, above the troops. The crowd streamed, leaderless and straggling. Beneath his horror, Stears was puzzled. The massacre had seemed to begin out of a grotesque concatenation: an inexperienced officer, the crazy dancers, a poor plan, nervous troops, the unspeakable Imam. An accident. And yet . . . The officer had first called for an arrest. His force could never have taken custody of such a mob. The third burst of fire, upon those fleeing, had seemed vindictive beyond measure.

The guns began again. He looked in disbelief. The

357

crowd was scattered over the slopes, well above the village, straggling away from it toward the city. Bodies in it began to fall randomly. Then, from the shadowed interior of a truck, he saw squirts of orange flame. The machine gun fired in bursts, as if idly swatting flies, as if to no end but to increase the panic. The ragged figures struggled on, and here and there were plucked up and flung upon the ground. The slope was dotted with bodies, or bundles of old clothes. He thought, *They are being driven past the guns, like grouse.*

In the shadow of the tomb, Ibrahim waited. He would be assumed to be in hiding. *Assumed by whom?* he wondered. His congregation was struggling to al-Tabek like the rats of a plague of nightmare. The Dutch television crew, drawn dutifully by Julia's shocked rumor, would meet them on the road. Julia would guide them. They would arrive at the village with morbid expectation. He wondered how strong their stomachs were.

The Palestinians were leaving. He could not see much from here, but he glimpsed a knot of men around a truck, smoking, not talking much. The trucks would vanish into the desert. A Libyan transport would land at night. The trucks would be burned. They would be found one day, but it hardly mattered. What counted was the next four days. The Palestinians would wait in Libya and return if needed.

The village burned in places. The armored car, the royal arms blackened, sat in totemic guilt. He knew that magazines cases, a jammed M-14, a general small litter of the first-line NATO weapons that only the King's Own Regiment used, had been left on the ground. All was in place, perfect. The unbelievable plan had worked. He cowered in the shadow.

He had the impulse to run to the troops. He dreaded being left here. Without cease, without accent, like random spirits wandering over the ground, came

358

whimpers, pleading, cries. He saw with horror, twenty meters away, a body come to motion, sit up, and look toward him before it slumped again. Out of sight, a child cried with mechanical hysteria. He became aware of a growing diapason note rising and falling at the limit of hearing. It puzzled him until he knew it as a swelling swarm of flies. It had been planned, at the last, that the arriving cameras should find him, accusation made more terrible by mercy, alone with the suffering. He had agreed. Suffering, no doubt, was a category of annihilation. But he could not do it now. He had a vision of shattered hands drawing him down to bloody faces, of strangled breathing confidential in his ear. He had not foreseen that the vanguard of the future would be groans and flies.

He watched the Dutch, two bearded young men, a girl – they the technicians, she the reporter. Clean, carefully untidy young people of the North. They were in the square. The air buzzed now as from a cello overhead. The cameraman took his hands from his eyes and raised his camera. It hid his face, but his tawny beard came out beneath it. He panned experimentally. He spoke in a small voice to the girl. The girl, blonde with the trim, complacent face of decent Western socialism, had been staring vacantly at a woman sprawled on two small children. She raised the microphone, put it down again, stood closer to a tangle of corpses, flinched, then screwed up her small shoulders and raised the microphone again.

His eyes sought Julia. Amid death and disgust she stood untainted, beautiful, removed. Her hands were in her jeans' hip pockets. She walked past death scattered or heaped, neither hurrying nor flinching but with the distant attentiveness of a viewer at a gallery. A young man's body stirred spasmodically. She watched it gravely. Help had been called, by radio. It ceased to move. She shrugged, walked on. She saw him look at her and smiled. She turned away again and walked, the unhurried tourist, up the path toward the tomb. He looked. The Dutch were preoccupied. He followed her. The glow of her skin banished his sickness. The slight, unemphasized movement of her hips seemed to him life itself. He caught up with her. They were before the tomb, before the sparse trees. The body of the bull and its severed head, like disused party favors, lay beside the rock. She looked around, quizzical and amused, and said, with the husk in her throat that made his heart now leap, "This place is a mess." He pulled her to him, folding his arms around her strength and youth. She met him gladly. He felt bathed in balm. He kissed her. His weakness drained away. Her thighs pressed his. He felt both peace and the wild energies of Ibrahim reborn. She pushed him away gently.

She said, "We'd better watch out for the Dutch." Then looked him over merrily and added, "You know, you look like hell, darling. You really do."

He walked back down the path alone, Ibrahim again alive within him, the future in his hand. He looked up the stony slopes, to the bundled dead. Three men in country dress walked high up on the slope. They hurried, almost ran, but the terror of the fleeing faithful was absent in them. He wondered who they were and how they came there. He shrugged. The more witnesses the better.

Part Four

23

It should have chilled him, to lie again on bare rock, the dead mountains sharp and close and gray in starlight. Was it only two nights ago, his night of death? But Stears heard the soldiers' quiet Arabic, an officer's hissed reprimand, the chink of a touched weapon, and felt in his spine support and safety. Nevertheless, he felt naked. Surely eyes from above could see them as he could see the mountains. He looked slowly around the rock-strewn valley. It had been well done. Half a mile away, three random large boulders lay cold in the unmoving desert. Hard to believe that they had fluttered from the sky, that under the gray camouflage were Chinooks of the Berbian army. He could see the soldiers scattered among the rocks, but only as in a puzzle, pulling them out with his eyes. The airstrip was clearly visible. The two-thousand-meter slash of earth, only roughly graded but cleared of rocks, seemed in the night desert to be not an adjunct of material transport but a sign, a rune. Off to one side, the abandoned bulldozer, its covers blown off by winds, looked like a browsing skeleton. It would not be the easiest of landings. The Libyan pilots, if it was to be they who came first, would need their eyes for the strip.

The radio spoke, high and querulous. It was quickly turned down. He heard the rhythms of English. CIA, al-Tabek, then. He heard a live, softer voice reply, "Sidewinder." Cy Bennett acknowledging. Then a low squawking at the limit of hearing, at least a minute's transmission. Cy Bennett murmured, "Affirmative.

Nothing here yet. Sidewinder out," and then, as to someone close by, "You copy that?" Then a voice suggestive of beer and Chevies, a Deep South sheriff, "Shit, then we gotta stomp those suckers." Stears still half smiled at it. That would be Major the Sheikh Irun al-Quatani, of the King's Own Light Infantry, three years' exchange with the U.S. Marines at Camp Lejeune. They were a few meters from Stears. He was not spoken to. He was alone.

But he heard a foot on pebbles and smelled coffee. Cy Bennett squatted beside him and pushed a mug into his hand in silence, a gesture inclusive and even companionable. Stears, author of the operation, was acknowledged. He felt grateful. His gratitude annoyed him.

Cy Bennett, in imitation of the soldier he was not, looked around the unmoving prospect. He said, "All hell's broken out in al-T."

Stears looked at him, expecting more. Bennett, gimlet-eyed, quizzed the rocks. He was career Covert Action CIA. His face was reminiscent of Henry Peckham's, smoothly aggressive, close-mouthed, shallowly arcane. A little more evolved, however. Bennett's face was also like a television screen, but one in which embryonic stirrings of a third dimension had begun.

In revenge for his gratitude, Stears said, "Bit rowdy, I suppose?"

Bennett looked at him sharply and grinned slightly. "OK," he said. "What gives is this. The pilgrims hit the city about four o'clock, but there were rumors earlier – you know how it is. You and I were en route between the embassy and the barracks then but nothing blew until six – evening prayers. The news was all over the city, but it seems like people were just kind of stunned – Fahd's not that popular, but he'd never pulled a stunt like that. Well, when good Muslims are stunned they go to the mosque, which they did. Preachers must have stirred 'em up real good. It seems they went in like lambs and came out like a lynch mob – wonderful thing, religion. The police tried to keep control. The citizens fragged a few and then the police began to waver themselves. The docks and the *bidonvilles* are just plain out of control – there are various mobs following various imams. The better sections are controlled by the army, but, what that transmission was mainly about, the army's beginning to desert. Shit, they're Muslims too. It's working. The palace regiment, what of it isn't here, is holding the palace and the airport. No problems yet, but they can't hold off the whole country. So we figure we've got about eight hours to get a bunch of confessions, because after that nobody's going to listen." He added, an afterthought, "Your Imam's doing great. Nobody's seen the girl."

Stears said softly, to the rocks, to Bennett, to himself, "Of course it's working. I saw it. I was there. I believed it all. It was only when the girl kissed him. The girl from the villa."

But Bennett spoke over him. "Item two. Dutch television got priority on a satellite. It was all over Western Europe on the evening news. It seems that the pictures would make a hyena gag." His voice became precise and pious. "Some might even suspect that human rights had been violated. So it will be on the evening news at home. About now, in fact. American ally and so forth. Ought to knock El Salvador right off the map."

He did not hear the major – not Marine training, he thought, but a Bedouin's almost feminine grace – but he felt him like a shadow by his side and smelled the rancid tobacco on the major's breath.

Al-Quatani said, "You guys oriented?"

Stears shook his head slightly. Al-Quatani pointed with a gesture slow and graceful, of a piece with the thin Bedouin face and the balanced body. "OK. Those pissants have to come over the hills about there." He pointed right, down and across the valley, to a shallow saddle in the barren hills. "There's a track up there. If they're driving with lights we'll see them real good. If they're not, we ought to catch the silhouette. Four trucks?"

"When they left the village," said Stears. "And I would say that they were full."

The major graciously inclined his head. "Yeah," he said. "No problem taking the suckers. Or the plane. The problem's not spooking whichever one comes first. Gotta hit 'em both. Ghadaffi's air force and the PLO." He looked at Bennett. "You guys ought to love it."

Bennett said, "We do." And added, "If they come."

Stears said, "What?"

Al-Quatani said quietly, still looking at the hills, "You don't know about the radio?"

And Stears replied in Arabic, with irony, "I know nothing but those things of which I tell my masters."

Al-Quatani smiled dryly. "When we hit the villa it was as sweet as it could be. They saw our trucks and uniforms and figured we were their own guys. They didn't think so for long, but it helped. We cleaned the place up in about three minutes. Of course they had a radio. You can bet the trucks have one too. The lawyer didn't know much about it, and the guys we sweated after him said that nobody had had time to send off a message. Could be that's the truth. Otherwise, no trucks, no bird, no nothing. We could find them. But not in time."

Stears nodded and said nothing. They lay in silence. He smelled a fresh cigarette with surprise; he had not seen the light. Al-Quatani smoked and then said, this time murmuring in Arabic, "You are a judge of men, Mr. Stears."

Stears said, "You are kind."

"Only one of them broke, and it was he of whom you told us. Yamadi, the lawyer. The others were men." He spat. "At Yamadi we had to look quite fiercely. They should not have told him so much. It is he to whom we owe this. It is his confession we will use on the terrorists."

Stears said, "I thought that it would be so."

Al-Quatani smoked in silence. Then he said, "And you were their prisoner? For many days?"

"For some."

The major looked delicately aside. "We are fortunate that you fight with us," he said.

Another shadow joined them. An officer murmured to al-Quatani, who nodded and turned to Bennett and to Stears. "Check you guys later," he said. "We don't have long."

Stears was alone again, the coffee cup turning chilly in his hand. It was of a piece with the disconnection of his life that it had not yet yielded a new watch. He knew little of stars. Without a moon, there was no time. He lay and watched the rocks and mountains all sharp at the edges and dark in their mass. He watched the mountain saddle, knowing quite well that a dozen eyes more skilled than his watched also. This operation was his child, his success, his doing, and he was the most unnecessary man there. He had the thought that nothing would ever come, that they would never move; that they had become part of the desert, a petrified army deployed until the end of time.

He had the conviction more than ever that he had been dealing, this last week, with the powers of darkness; that he had fallen from Marie-Sophie's bed into an infernal asylum. Everything permanent or committed in his own life seemed, from the perspective of this sewer, gracious and courageous; everything raffish or temporary, a cheap and dangerous joke. He had had some news of Marie-Sophie. Her intelligence and force filled him positively with desire. When he had not returned, she had called the embassy in Paris, refused to speak to anyone but the ambassador, laid seige to him, persuaded him at least to take cognizance of the fact that an American was missing on his government's service. She had even remembered that he had asked about Berbia. She had had the discipline, it seemed, not to call the Marseilles police but to talk only to the *préfet*. It had all even done some good – not to save him, but to make his appearance at the embassy in al-Tabek one small degree prepared for. He had not yet been able to talk to her. He felt the lack of it like air or water.

A shape moved toward him. The Anglo-Saxon face seemed soft and innocent among the lean Berbian troops. Cy Bennett said absently, "Pretty soon now. If they come."

Stears said, "Yes."

Salutation over, Bennett went on. "You're pretty solid about that penetration, aren't you? McNaughton's? From on top?"

Pulled abruptly from the desert, Stears answered, surprised and vehement, "Yes! Absolutely. There is no room for doubt, is there?"

Bennett replied, pleasant and condescending, "There's room. You didn't make many converts. Myself, I'd be willing to say there's a chance you're right. A small chance."

In the intimacy of night, of low voices, Stears heard himself plead, and hated it.

"Why? How? Didn't you all hear me? I am an agent of the CIA with a report of the highest importance. What doubt is there?" He even looked at Bennett, who looked at the mountains, then the mountains drew him back himself.

"We heard you. We heard a noncareer agent, a thousand miles from his field of expertise, give his impressions of a professional intelligence man's conversational slips and his own unqualified analysis of information sources. Yeah, we heard you. We hear a lot. The Company has more unqualified experts telling it the time of day than you can shake a stick at. We ran a check on it. There was a possibility someone could have missed a possible compromise that might have touched McNaughton. They can do that by computer now at Langley. Nothing. McNaughton's control chain was solid, right up to the top. There isn't even a third-hand association even with a suspect insecurity. You're asking us to take the judgment of a limited-assignment agent and turn the Company upside down. We know you're not a nut. You had hard evidence of this and we acted as fast as anybody could. We're not dumb, Stears. If this works, we owe you a lot. But don't expect too much to be made of the other. There are other explanations. Good ones."

Stears said, "Why are you even telling me this? I don't need to know. It doesn't matter what I think. I shouldn't give a damn. I'm not even in the club."

Very mildly, Bennett said, "I thought you'd like to know. It seemed like a good time." And even more mildly, looking at the saddle of the hills, "My, my, we got company."

It was orderly, it was peaceful; it was impossible, it couldn't be. His life had not healed. It couldn't have. Not yet. He was still in the world of searches, beatings, horrors, madness, fear. His body still ached. His rib still stabbed. And yet the troops were around him, armed, in order, and they had not been seen. And the trucks of the Palestinians, which had trundled across the desert without alarms or *brio*, were parked in line, five hundred meters away, silhouetted, peaceful as a truck stop. And far in the distance – he had not heard it until Bennett jogged his arm – was the drone of an unlighted transport letting down. A stroke of luck, even; the Palestinians were being kept in the trucks until the time to embark. Stears knew the plan – the moment of embarkation; the single rocket to immobilize the plane; the flares; the massed burst of fire; the blind helplessness of the enemy; the call to freeze and surrender. It was surgical. It could not fail. In the absence of a surrender, a second firestorm would be unleashed. There would be survivors – and the wounded would be, if anything, easier to force to witness and confess. If a few escaped into the desert, their bones would do no one any harm. It would be clockwork mayhem. It had been explained to him so dispassionately as military science by Bennett and the major that he had been a little shocked when he had asked, "But what if they don't surrender?" And the major had coldly smiled and said, "Then we will know that God is good."

So he lay there, stretched out on the ground, while the peaceful drone crept upon the night and the toy trucks sat in their sandlot, and rehearsed the infallibility of the plan. He could find no flaw. It was utterly unreal. He was terrified.

Reality came with the landing lights. The strip must have been easily visible from the air. The transport lowered straight toward it, unlit. It was a middle-aged Soviet Antonov An12, clearly seen but as though diaphanous in starlight; its high wings and extended undercarriage gave it the look of a child's plane, gawky and vulnerable. But a thousand meters from the strip its landing lights flared on; the circle of harsh illumination galloped over jagged rock; movement, threat, and metal suddenly were there.

The rough strip was no trouble for it – the Antonov was built for that. Its speed arrested, it rolled heavily down toward the trucks. The trucks were some two hundred meters from the airstrip, which ended in a loop just wide enough for a turn. The An12 loaded through the rear belly. The markings, Stears noticed, appeared to have been painted out. Well, Ghaddafi was not a fool.

And then, at last, the terrorists. They dropped from the backs of the trucks, dark shapes, multiplying. He heard around him a sudden collective exhalation, a breathed curse. It surprised him as much as the major's cold smile, and he realized that to the men around him these were foreign butchers come to smear a bloody crime on them. Small movements caught his eye, a hand tightening on a gun stock, a foot seeking purchase. The terrorists began to move from the trucks, not in order but walking fast. They carried their weapons casually.

Cy Bennett whispered in his ear, "Numbers look right? All there?"

Stears answered, "I think so. About a hundred. Yes."

The terrorists were halfway to the plane when one truck bloomed flame from its belly, then another, then the rest. The slight concussions struck them. Small timed charges. But the fuel tanks caught and the orange flame rushed up above the trucks. The fiery light reached the terrorists, flickering. They seemed now like black figures walking in flame. Stears heard al-Quatani curse – they could be seen themselves. Al-Quatani spoke orders quickly. The strike would have to be now. Two soldiers rose abruptly from the ground – one with the rocket launcher, one more with flares. The rest tensed like sprinters.

Later, he knew that he had heard an angry hissing, a bang, a short, shocked scream, and a bellowed curse from al-Quatani, but all that he registered was the light. It hurt. A white glare struck them from above. Not light, but a blow upon the eyes. He covered them, forced them open. He, Cy Bennett, the major, the rocks, the troops were there, washed in the glare as sharp and still as under a flashbulb. He saw the jagged edges of the flare launcher, and the soldier's blackened hand, and his shocked face. Straight above them, the misfired flare descended slowly. A black curtain had dropped around their cell of light. He heard al-Quatani shout, "Scatter! Return fire!"

And suddenly he saw chips begin to fly off the rocks around him. A soldier rose, grunted, and sat back down again. He saw the sergeant with the rocket launcher fire vaguely into the black and then pitch forward. Suddenly Stears's eyes stabbed him. The flare had come to rest on a rock some ten meters away, still burning. He stumbled in inky shadows as he ran. A man bumped him. A hammer struck a stone beside his foot and splintered it. Then the flare died.

At first it was like a black, wet cloth around his eyes. He could see nothing. The Berbians were firing wildly. It was only their rifles that told him he was still among the troops. His back crawled. He could easily be shot from behind. He thought that the incoming fire was less. He had no idea how far they had scattered.

Slowly, sight returned – first the burning trucks, then shapes around him, then the plane, then the enemy. The Palestinians made no move toward them. A rear guard kept up a fire in their direction – their vision could not be perfect either. But the rest were pressing through the wide loading bay of the transport – about half, he thought, were in already – and the plane was pointed down the runway and the engines ran. He heard al-Quatani's voice, registering that he was not dead. There were confused replies. Men scuttled around, attracting fire. Somewhere, beside some rock, under some body, lay the rocket launcher, like a misplaced toy. Beside the rear guard, only a short tail of Palestinians still stood behind the plane, whose flaps suddenly flexed up and down.

He heard al-Quatani shout, "Cease fire on the airplane. Cover the rear guard!" He wondered why. Even small arms might score a damaging hit on a plane. A slim chance at that range – but without the rockets, the only one they had. Then he saw the major leap up and run, not waving them on, but running, bounding across the stones, zigzagging, dodging, an antic, weird figure, a runner in a nightmare. He saw the terrorist rear guard turn their fire. He saw sprays of shattered stone around the major. But the rear guard were now the only men outside the plane, and as the Berbians turned their fire on them they ran for the loading bay themselves, still firing, but now wildly.

And for a moment the scene seemed almost motionless, the major bizarrely capering in place, the airplane still. Then the loading ramp began to rise, the slice of light between it and the belly narrowing, and the engines surged. When the plane first moved, the major was perhaps fifty meters from it. Almost at once, he was on the cleared airstrip, straining forward. It was heroic and absurd, a boy's pointless dare. The transport, on rough ground, gathered speed slowly. The major gained. He was under the wing now, but the plane was moving as fast as he. It was pulling away when al-Quatani, now a strange, windmilling figure under the landing lights, threw himself at the undercarriage, clasping the strut to his breast, hanging to it like a bag of laundry, flapping.

And suddenly there was a ball of orange where al-Quatani was and a momentary vision of jagged pieces separating, flying. The concussion reached them. The airplane lurched, staggered, and in a slow, despairing motion, fell on its unsupported wing.

They were all running now. A quarter of the Berbians, at the most, could have been hit. He wondered if any man there had known al-Quatani's purpose. He wondered how he had done it. Hand grenades? He had seemed to reach into his chest in the final dash. The airplane was not far now. It did not appear to be on fire. The loading bay was clearly jammed against the ground. He saw an auxiliary door four meters above the ground open and a man jump out. He saw men around him drop to their knees and fire in bursts. The man hit the ground and crumpled. Another, standing in the door, fell back. The thought went through Stear's head, *Fish in a barrel!* He laughed. He felt sick.

One of the terrorists was whimpering – there would be a short silence, then a little surprised cry like a child being slapped by an invisible hand, then the level whimpering again. Stears could hear it over the whine and rattle of the Chinook in flight. It hung in the air like the heavy tobacco of the relaxing troops. One of them jabbed his thumb toward the noise and made a quick joking comment to his neighbor. The neighbor took the cigarette from his mouth, laughed perfunctorily, and stretched.

Stears moved and looked at the man. He was in shock, the eyes glazed, the face childish. Probably he was belly-shot. It seemed to Stears that he should think of him now only as simple suffering humanity – but he didn't much feel it. Perhaps he would have if he had been alone with him. The other terrorists – few of them wounded, had surrendered – were manacled to the bulwark rail of the Chinook. A few, chiefly the youngest ones, had the look of bantam, unstable defiance that he had seen on skinny teenagers spreadeagled on a squad car. Most looked scared and sullen. But he carried in his head the scene of the massacre – old faded images of Belsen, of My Lai, now suddenly in technicolor, dripping, and with the sounds of terror – and he looked at the terrorists for some searing confirmation, for the faces of the damned or the appalled, and found nothing of the kind – *A failed op . . . It's going to be tough . . . I'm scared. . . .* His mind told him, *Their history made these people,* but he didn't feel it. Each helicopter carried about half unwounded Berbians, a quarter wounded, and the rest, terrorists. He made a quick calculation. The terrorists seemed too few. He wondered. He had been put on a Chinook early. Just before takeoff, the twin engines rising, he had thought that he heard a long burst of gunfire from outside. Well, probably. It shocked him that he merely shrugged.

They landed at the barracks of the King's Own Light Infantry, outside al-Tabek. They flew over the city. It was pockmarked by random fires. It was 3:00 A.M.

The terrorists' wrists were shackled to their ankles. They moved like crabs. It was a hundred meters to the barracks buildings. One terrorist blundered from the line. A Berbian sergeant redirected him with a kick to the head, as to a football. The wounded moved as they could.

Henry Peckham was there. So was everybody. Stears quickly saw that every functioning element to the status quo had representatives in those harshly lit halls, and that chains of command were as tangled as old rope. The King's Own was in charge: but police clustered in stolid groups; senior officers of other brigades fondled their swagger sticks and puffed their chests; competent, astonished young U.S. Marines, from the base or a ship offshore, followed their officers in inconspicuous formations; and some young Berbian fighter pilots had even put on flying suits for the show. But the CIA was in its glory. He recognized several, each reflecting a quiet wisdom, an arcane depth, that made all around look like the supernumeraries of a burlesque. Henry Peckham, chief of the CIA's Covert Operations, al-Tabek – and since the foldup of the intellegence networks its effective operational head – seemed at once shrouded in mystery and glowing with a genial fire; from his pedestal of error he surveyed his victory. He greeted Stears askance. Stears realized suddenly what Cy Bennett had wanted him to guess: that his report would contradict earlier ones by Peckham. He realized as quickly – it was like the dropping of a coin – that he could have more weight than Peckham, and that it was a question, mainly, of finding a lever for its use.

Burlesque stopped in the corridors. He was led into a hall, perhaps a mess hall, stripped of all furniture except a stage with a stiff chair facing television lights at one end and an arrangement of barbed wire like a cattle pen or an enlarged and vicious boxing ring covering most of the middle. It was empty. He blinked. The light was as harsh, almost, as the flare.

He heard a jingling susurration. The prisoners were driven in, hobbled, doubled over, craning up their necks like idiot children. But at the entrance to the pen, armorers released their wrist shackles. It was effective. They had been made pitiful to themselves. Now they could look dangerous for the show. The Libyan air crew, in uniform, was placed alone at the front corner of the pen. The pen seemed to have been nicely calculated. It was filled to compression. There was a small continuing panic at its outer edges of barbed wire. In the Kingdom of Berbia, he had no doubt, the Escobedo ruling was not widely enforced.

Cy Bennett joined him. Around the stage, people began to congregate; technicians, journalists, Western and Arab, a group of older Muslim clergy, anxious North Africans in suits, more officers, more police. He found it easy to place by expression the shades of Berbian opinion: grim triumph, surprise, suspicion, relief. The television lamps came on. Five meters away, he could feel their heat. A door opened behind the stage.

Yamadi came in alone. Under the lights, he seemed not only alone but at an infinite distance from everybody else. He was extremely small. Under black hair, his face was white. He licked his lips obsessively. Blinded, he stood still a moment. Close by, a police officer unobtrusively snapped his fingers. Yamadi jolted into action. He climbed into the chair. His eyes darted around the room at the level of the knees. He was as silent as the room. All at once, without raising his head, without drawing in his breath, but as though his shallow breathing had spontaneously turned to expressionless speech, he began. "My name is Abdul Yamadi. My name by birth is Hussein Kebbaj. I am a member of the Habbash faction of the PLO. I am a participant in an inhuman conspiracy against the Berbian state and against its people. I make this confession of my free will."

Power was like a telescope; Stears was looking at Yamadi, now, through it other end. How was it possible that the intense presence, the contained threat, the ravenous energy like that of a sleek and busy rat had changed, in hours, into the quintessential convict, skin grainy from slumgullion, breath sour from fear? He heard the stretched voice, saw the chalky face, barely recognizing the stuff of old nightmares. And the brain that had held the nightmares seemed as canceled as the gloss of Yamadi's skin. He wondered, with curiosity, what had happened to Khamal. He found himself glossing over the likelihood that it was better unasked. Within himself he suddenly felt power like a rich dessert.

Yamadi was thorough; he neither stumbled nor stopped

376

– an administrator's last thin pride. Stears saw positive unease on CIA faces – this was really too much for a public circus. No surprises in general: the growing ache of the splintered PLO for a base to call their own; the attraction of one far from the Israeli army; the increased militancy, in this regard, of the Habbash faction; the speculative encouragement, though not outright aid, by Arafat; the joint fingering of Berbia, the American anchor in the Mahgreb by Russia and al-Fatah, the logistical cooperation of Ghadaffi; the plan of disinformation. The plan, it seemed, had not been the KGB's. Indeed, Stears had doubted that himself. It had a wildness, an edge of lunacy, the polarity of a myth that he did not associate with the Kremlin – how could atheists so perfectly encompass blasphemy? Yamadi's voice, it seemed, agreed. When he spoke of Ibrahim/Shamak it was with disparagement.

Stears watched the audience. The Western press hung on to suspicion longest. But Yamadi's testimony was too flat, too much of it easy to prove or disprove to be doubted. He saw a fair-haired girl, well dressed, obviously American, grimace petulantly and cross out some earlier pages of her notebook – a gift unreasonably taken back. The terrorists, for the most part, watched sullenly. It surprised, even shocked him, to see so little hatred or anger except when a television lens brought forth a galvanic spasm of defiance. How many terrorists the Berbians needed to break, he did not know, and they certainly had enough. The problem remaining was to disseminate the confessions, the testimony, the news, to the streets while the streets still had human ears to listen. That was a matter for the Berbians – and not an easy one – but he was willing to assume that they could do it.

What mattered was not here, would not be said here by Yamadi, had not even been developed. Yamadi had alluded, a few minutes before the show, to a source of information in the Agency. It was – this was all that was yet known – an extra-Agency source, some kind of

American dissident. "Ibrahim," apparently, had been in America and had had contact with him. The Berbians had taken an obvious pleasure in keeping exclusive rights over Yamadi until his public confession. The CIA had not had access to him yet. But the obscure word was out – Cy Bennett had murmured it to Stears: perhaps that, now that he thought about it, accounted for the sudden unease on CIA faces. But for him it was a vindication, at least in part. The trail was running. The guesses, the terrors, the accidents, the pains, the luck, the contradictions, seemed to be gradually arranging themselves into an ordered whole – and separating themselves from him.

The show was over. He knew that every hole and corner of these sprawling buildings would now be given over to interrogations, that the air would be steeped in bullying and fear. He wanted badly to leave. What was left anyway, was a counterintelligence matter, wholly outside his skills. But there was nowhere to go. Al-Tabek was a battlefied. And Cy Bennett beckoned to him, grinned, and said, "Come see a friend of yours."

"Boris" Verkhelsky sat in an armchair. There was a Marine guard with him. Cy Bennett closed the door behind Stears. The Marine guard sat in the corner, a respectful stenographer with a gun. Boris's chair was near the desk. He gave the impression of receiving Stears. He looked a little tired. A distressing day. He looked at Stears and nodded slowly, not rising; his eyes again were clear and gray, stripped of the fatal fat of overconfidence. He said factually, "They trained you better than I thought. Congratulations."

Stears said, "You should not have said 'terminated his cover.' It made no sense until I thought about it."

"Was that it? Still, it was quick of you. But you would not have gotten so far with a Russian operation. Don't delude yourself. We never had control of this."

Stears said, "I noticed." Both were silent.

Boris said, "You have not come to debrief me?"

"No, no, I'm not counterintelligence." He added, "Just

a visit," and had an absurd vision of bringing flowers. Perhaps the nurse in the corner would have objected.

Boris as though of a changed vacation, said, "I suppose I shall be going to Virginia."

"Virginia's nice. Even Langley. Stay off the expressways at five o'clock."

Boris, politely, gave a little bitter smile. Stears remembered his manners.

"Would you like some coffee?"

"That would be nice."

Stears said, with finality, "I'll have it sent." He turned to the door. Boris said, "I'm sorry we had to rough you up."

Stears nodded.

"We only did it while you were an Italian."

"Yes," said Stears. "That's the usual way."

Cy Bennett said, "This is your man? No mistakes?"

Stears said, "Oh yes." But he had not recognized Hajji until then. The steel door, the bucket on the floor, the mean light overhead bisecting the space between the upper and the lower bunk with shadow, the prison pajamas, the quick look of fear, suggested an anonymous and shuffling fate. But he knew the voice. The flabby face lost some fear.

"Oh, Mr. Stears – do you know, I had begun to think it might be you."

Cy Bennett said, "I'll leave you with him. The Berbians have worked him over pretty good. But you can talk about his business connections. That's your field. Maybe motives too." He shut the door. It clanged. Hajji sat up painfully.

Stears said, "Why? Mr. Melouf. Why? I have asked myself and I have no answer."

The pajamas were too small. Belly and pubic hair swelled from the front of them. Darkening bruises lay like clouds on Hajji's checks. He seemed in internal pain. But his voice was surprisingly firm.

He said, "I told you, Mr. Stears, in a nicer place than this. But you would not listen."

He made himself remember the ship, the beating, Khamal, the guns. He said without warmth, "You made your ships available to transport weapons for the PLO to use in your own country?"

"Effectively, Mr. Stears, yes."

"So that they could murder women and children for a trick?"

"No, Mr. Stears, not for that. You know that yourself."

And he did. And nothing had appalled him so much as this. Hajji was Geneva. Hajji was Cannes. Hajji had given Marie-Sophie flowers one day. Waiting for Hajji, he had read the *Figaro* over salted almonds. Over Hajji's affairs, his mind had moved secure and warm. His own terrors had been in alien places, outside the walls, in a slum that he had blundered into and would never see again. But suddenly he felt a crack, as though the filthy bucket could stain the sapphire lake, as though fists and whimpers would be as familiar to his ear as laughter, as though the flies from those brown corpses could knock against his windowpane.

"I helped the Baath. I did not want to. I saw the King weaken. I saw every bandit and malcontent in Berbia wave a Russian gun. I waited for America's strong shoulder, Mr. Stears. I saw the Shah fall. I thought, 'Ah, now they will see. Now they will value their friends.' I saw the Brothers of Islam begin to lead the people, just as such men did in Teheran. I saw men like myself killed and kidnapped. And I knew that Berbia would fall. Then the Baath came to me and offered a compromise. They said, 'Which do you want, Algeria or Iran? Help us and it will be Algeria. You will still have a place here.' And I turned once more to America. I made an appointment with your ambassador – I was rich enough for that. I did not tell him about my contact with the Baath because he might have told the King. But I told him what I feared. And he thanked me very politely and said there was no 'organic instability' in Berbia, that the American people valued their Berbian alliance and that I should have confidence in the investment environment of my country. He liked 'organic instability.' He used it three times.

"So I began to help the Baath – I and many men like me. Of course, the demands increased. I had expected that. We began to be asked for more than money – I for my ships, my friend Khannafi, whom you say you know, for his warehouses and his name. And the Baath begins to change: once it had at least been Berbia, now it was Russia and the PLO. But you know all that. I do not have to tell you. Now we were not just businessmen paying a tax to the next government – now we were almost terrorists ourselves.

"And then the Americans came back. Your base. Your advisers. Your Marines. When the house was rotten, you moved back in. You play with us, Mr. Stears. You said, 'Come with us. Be like us. Leave your old ways behind. We will protect you.' And we did, for America looked very fine and strong. With you behind us what did we have to fear? And then you lost a little war in Asia and suddenly the world looked different to you. Maybe you might get hurt. We saw your allies set upon while you turned your backs. You made it the most important thing in the world for your enemies to destroy us, and then you walked away. The dollars we used now for our trade turned to trash. And although you had become very cowardly, you were also very pure and suddenly we were a corrupt and reactionary society that was not sweet-smelling enough for you to help. Do you know all that too, Mr. Stears?

"And then you changed your mind again. Maybe weakness was not safe for you after all. And you send back your fleets and you dust off your policies. But it is not very safe to be your servant anymore. Whoever takes your hand this time will certainly be destroyed the next time you turn away. And some of us no longer can take your hand. I wanted only to be your friend, Mr. Stears. I wanted to be like you. But to survive while you slept I became your enemy and then you came back in your own sweet time and there is Melouf, that fat treacherous Arab man, and now it suits you to destroy me. You will have lunch again in Geneva, Mr. Stears. I do not think I shall. But to answer your first question, Mr. Stears, no, I did not know what those weapons were for or even what they were. Very often, Mr. Stears, they were simply to kill and kidnap people who did not support the Baath. I told you this at the Amphytrion, Mr. Stears. Does it sound different here?"

"Yes," said Stears. He looked at the broken face and the bulging body forced into obscenity. He looked, but pity seemed as futile here as in an operating room, and besides, he feared the contagion now more than he pitied Melouf. He thought vaguely, *I won't let this be forgotten*, but he said; "But it is not the point. I have come for a number of details. We do not have much time."

24

He nibbled on spongy toast spread with a bituminous, salty substance and pondered the dissipations of first-class travel. Pan Am's martini, though, was better. Their sturgeons were poor sickly creatures, but Pan Am understood gin. Three hours out, the cabin was filling with discarded shoes, crumpled paper, torn plastic wrappings, and abandoned headsets – an expensive but particularly sluttish amusement park in the sky. But he felt a sense of intense well-being. The sun came in behind his shoulder. The seat next to him was empty. The ice in his cocktail gleamed. He waited with confidence for his canned and tepid soup and his thawed and sticky duck. He had only to smile and the stewardess would smile back. It was beyond imagination that she would beat him, kill him, or torture the man behind.

The summons glowed in the breast pocket of his suit. A summons from the National Intelligence Advisory Board itself deserved a better environment than a ready-made summer suit salvaged from a half-looted French haberdashery in al-Tabek. Besides, he'd freeze in Washington. But the summons had been urgent, personal, and unspecific, equally. It had come thirty-six hours after Yamadi's circus, barely more than a day after his later CIA examination would have started its analysis at Langley. He was to report to an address in Georgetown – evidently a safe house so esoteric that no one in the Company in al-Tabek had heard of it. He had no idea what arcane, resolving scrap of information he might be supposed to have that required so majestic a reception. Perhaps they wanted to thank him. Peckham's expression had suggested even that. He had given him the decoded message with galled disbelief. It had been an expression that had made Wop glow.

He liked Georgetown. He supposed he did. The cab struggled up M Street, turned right on Wisconsin Avenue. He had time to observe. Clean, small shopfronts. Things in them, teakwood furniture, ironstone plates, that looked nice and not grotesquely dear – there really were suppliers in the world besides Hermès, though he'd have welcomed Hermès now as a lifelong friend. And American girls had the behinds for jeans. And yet, carrying what he did, coming from where he came from, he felt uneasy, unsupported, and finally irritable. The adults did not seem to be in charge here. He had long suspected his country of being depressing in its earnestness and childish in its joys. There was a girl with a shopping bag, skin wholesome as bread, in a corduroy shooting coat, workman's red bandanna tied askance, hips with no trace of the ice cream she ate. She was darling, but he was depraved enough to miss the adult, made faces and hard diamonds of the Avenue George V. And beside Marie-Sophie she was a childish joke. "Milk-fed scaloppine" caught his eye. Well, they had them in Geneva too, and you didn't have to get them from the "Meat Boutique." His country's lambishness and his own response depressed him equally. But did the butcher really have to wear a bowler hat?

His destination was on the heights off Wisconsin, near Dumbarton Oaks – still Georgetown, but there was no playfulness here. It was a curving, descending street of Edwardian town houses, strict, brick, and proprietorial, gleaming brass doorknobs behind embellished railings. Over the lower roofs one saw the Potomac and the Monument floating below in the autumn air. Grand and gentle, the Cathedral hung above. The Company showed taste. He became aware of himself, face still scratched, bruises receding, standing in late October in a crumpled white suit. But a black manservant answered his knock and did not look twice.

The safe house was done up for a funeral.

His nose detected it first. The air was heavy with flowers. He first guessed wildly at some fictitious dinner party or dance. But there were at least a dozen separate arrangements in the room, all different, a bizarre re-creation of real and personal feelings, and the butler moved softly as though near a sickbed. In the living room, a fire was lit – an old person's provision on a day that was not cold. A retriever with a graying muzzle wheezed at him from the hearth. What a touch! It was a large blue room that should have gently smelled of roses, ending at French windows. The things in it were connected by a common thread of taste, intensely, unmistakably private. There were two portraits of the same woman, thirty years apart, the earlier a good de Lazslo. In silver and leather frames a man recurred, alone, with friends, in scenes of fine New England masculinity – fly rods, setter, and canoes. The Company showed a sense of humor, if somewhat macabre. It was an imitation of personal life so perfect it was sinister. There was another portrait of the man, this one with John Kennedy. His memory stirred. He vaguely remembered those long, equine features. Once spoken of as the next attorney general. Allman. Nelson Allman. Aldrytch. All from an archive, then. Was the man dead? He took a chair by a table with a pretty paperweight and a pair of silver scissors. The butler left. The retriever closed its eyes. He waited.

The man in the pictures stood in the door. Wop blinked. He had dozed off in the warm room. His opening eyes saw a ghost of the pictures, a ghost with fallen cheeks, skin like rice paper, a suit hung loosely from his shoulders. The retriever thumped its tail, twice. The man entered the room, Wop rose clumsily from his chair. The

385

man was now standing in front of a small table, and he reached behind him to a silver cigarette box, a gesture automatic and sure. Wop said, and found his tone was full of excuse, "This is a real house. It's yours. You're Nelson Aldrytch. Someone has died."

Aldrytch stood in the middle of the room. He looked at Wop with short, impersonal, cautious hesitation, as at the envelope of a telegram. "My wife. It was expected, but not quite so soon." That, the personal, was mechanical, but then he slightly smiled and said, "I am a member of the National Intelligence Advisory Board. That is your highest level of direction below the President. Do you wish me to prove that I am?"

Stears shook his head. Told, he remembered that it was so. The NIAB was as small as it was remote.

Aldrytch still examined him. He said, "You do not look like your father."

Wop automatically replied, "My mother was Italian."

Aldrytch moved slowly to a chair and sat down to face him. "Indeed she was. I was at their wedding. No reason you should know that. I never saw him after the war."

Stears said quietly, flatly, "Because he spent the war in Vichy France. A man like you would have considered my father a traitor. We had very few friends after the war. I do remember that."

Aldrytch nodded slowly. "Partly. Yes." His eyes left Stears and looked bleakly at the wall. "It's odd," he said.

Stears suddenly became aware that he was talking to a man in pain, as if of cancer. He wondered if his host, among the condoling flowers, was dying too. But Aldrytch quickly and dismissively shook his head and said, "You evidently did very well in Berbia. I had no idea you were with the Agency. But Giovanni Williston Stears could only have been you. You seem to have been rather a hero."

So to be thanked was part of it after all. But it was like being thanked in ice.

He said, "Thank you. I had two pieces of very good luck. That helped."

Aldrytch was not listening. "You had some contact with McNaughton, I believe?"

"Yes," Stears said. And continued into the silence, "I worked parallel to him. He was an extraordinary professional. I had an enormous—" He stopped, respecting the interruption.

Aldrytch was saying, "He was my sergeant in the war. I took him into OSS. I recommended him for his commission."

Stears had the fleeting impression that Aldrytch had grinned at him. He smiled in return. Aldrytch's face was frozen. Stears said, "I see."

Aldrytch went on. "I gather it was your opinion that he was compromised by a higher source than his agent. The wording of the report suggests that this opinion was adopted rather early by you."

Stears said, surprised, "I thought that was obvious by now. Yamadi told us they had a source. We know now that McNaughton's death was directly related to this operation. That he was killed in the knowledge of who he was. Even if we don't know exactly how."

"Yamadi told us they had a source. Their internal security was surprisingly bad, but it was good enough for Yamadi to know of the source only in general terms. That has yielded us a short list of suspects, each of whom is now under full surveillance and will be arrested if he runs. The source, of course, will assume this to be so and he will be very cautious. None of the suspects, besides, have any cleared access to highly classified data. He will be a middleman, a control. But I did not ask you what was obvious. I asked you what you thought. Perhaps you can answer me."

It was imperious, but only by habit and in words. There was a thin, controlled pleading under it – a disciplined patient asking for morphine. Clearly, the man was sick.

Stears answered, "Yes, sir, I did think so. I thought so on the ship. The KGB man made a slip of the tongue in

English. He said that Donnelly's cover had been 'terminated' through the agent. He could not have known through the agent that Donnelly was McNaughton, and he had no way of knowing that McNaughton had been killed. He also displayed reactions to data that should have been meaningless to him unless he had deep information on McNaughton's operation. He should really not have interrogated me in English. He was over-confident, I think. Would you like this in greater detail?" *This is what it must be about*, Stears thought. *He wants every detail of that.* He pushed his memory into recollection of Boris and the cabin. His body ached in sympathy. But Aldrytch perhaps needed his support, needed it perhaps to buttress a theory as unpopular in the Agency as his own had been. Hence the tenseness. Hence an interview that must surely be irregular. In its irregularity he, the outsider, felt an alliance.

"No," said Aldrytch. "Not for the present. Something else. Do you believe that McNaughton's cover was penetrated for the purpose of terminating him? I will make myself clear. Is it your opinion that they wished to identify and avoid a source of surveillance, or did they intend to eliminate it? I said 'opinion.' I am aware that that is all that you can give, but you have a feel for this operation, these people. That is why I brought you here."

It wasn't only the voice, this time, the queer mixture of authority and hope, but the question itself was, not irrelevant, but out of shape – a piece of the wrong jigsaw puzzle. He strongly felt a need for caution and he said, "I am not counterintelligence, sir."

And Aldrytch tapped the arm of his chair with fingers that had seemed to be gripping it and said, "But I asked you."

"The KGB would have known that a CIA surveillance of Arab expatriates was in place in Paris – they would have guessed it even if they didn't know. Whether the PLO knew it too, I couldn't begin to guess. The KGB

388

would have known that this surveillance somewhat endangered the *Lyusi* plan, and they would have increased their efforts to uncover it, with or without telling Habbash. If they had uncovered it early they might well have simply stayed clear of Donnelly, or they might have tried to pass him some false information, or something like that. The KGB would have had no reason to kill him and I doubt that they would have allowed the PLO to. But that didn't happen, sir, not unless we assume an extraordinary lack of communication between the KGB and their clients. McNaughton was uncovered well after he infiltrated Massoun, the Arab, into *Lyusi*. By that time, the pressure to terminate him must have been strong. By then he had particular advantages over a replacement agent in following these people. That's when termination must look attractive. When he went to Berbia and opportunity was added, it would have been almost certain. There was the ambience of *Lyusi* too, sir. McNaughton was exposed to unusually bloody men. But I must ask you to take note that this is not my field."

Aldrytch said, "Cover names and real names are not filed together. When I gave them Donnelly I did not know that it was McNaughton. Two days later, I was able to give them McNaughton. I did not think about the name. It was a time of some stress. I remembered that night. It should have made no difference, of course. I am responsible for them all. But it made a difference."

The man in the white suit had looked wrong, not like the other callers since the funeral. He had arrived by taxi. Probably not, then, a Washington person. Just possibly, he was a friend from the Southern states. No doubt it would still be warm there; visitors from the Crimea sometimes came in foolishly light clothing to Moscow in late fall. He certainly did not look like FBI or the Opposition. The man in the house across the street picked up the radiotelephone. Then he put it down again. It would take only a couple of minutes for the

Bulgarian to get in place. The second gunman, upstairs, was in place now. He did not want to give a false alarm. He could just see the subject and the visitor through the window. Not well, but it would have to do. On the whole, it had been thought that the death of the subject's wife would not affect his actions. His telephone conversations had been clean. He adjusted the earphones of the laser microphone. It was a sophisticated little device, American, trained on the glass of Aldrytch's window, and designed to pick up the vibrations of the glass and reconstruct them into conversation. It did not work very well; it worked only when the speaker faced in certain directions. It told him now that the two were talking, which he did not need to be told, but the words were indistinguishable. For now the laser was the best that they could do. Aldrytch, after all, was a government functionary with the highest clearance. His house was not especially secured, but to bug it clumsily would be foolish. To bug it expertly had not yet been possible.

Wop nodded. The words at first had no meaning – Aldrytch must be referring to some procedure he did not know. He smiled as he nodded. His stomach knew it before his head. As he began to think, his stomach was already cold. Then Aldrytch's words became meaningless, flying without order through a buzzing in the room. Then he saw that Aldrytch looked shocked, as though he had fallen where he had been screwing his courage up to jump. Then Aldrytch slumped in his chair, his chin on his thin chest. And Wop, without even thinking why, was above all afraid. He said, carefully, as though rashness might bring consequences he couldn't guess at, "You compromised him? You were the leak?"

Aldrytch looked at him.

"Why am I here? Why me?"

Aldrytch looked at him still, frozen. He formed the words, "The two of you, you boxed me in." But he had fallen, not jumped, and another expression came into his

390

eyes, of justification and appeal. He said, "I couldn't have left her. I couldn't until she died. They told me," and the fragment of jargon stamped through pity, "that they would employ disinformation procedures if I doubled so that maximum guilt would be established. I couldn't be in prison with her dying. She was frightened. I couldn't have killed myself. It wasn't possible."

Stears said, "What else was there? Was that all? How much else?" His mind skidded. He did not know what, in that instant, to do. Run to the telephone? Shout? He did not move.

In Aldrytch's eyes the look of appeal grew. It stripped him of authority, of grace. "It wasn't my choice. And it began with an act of conscience. That's the irony." Far away, in another world, came the bell, the butler's steps, then voice, the door again closing. The retriever yawned, stretched, and padded after the butler's voice. Aldrytch went on, his fineness ebbing with each word as though the distinguished suit were changing to a dirty dressing gown.

No callers had been refused before. This couple was of the same profile as the rest, elderly, ruling class. Then the man in the white suit was special. That could not be ignored. A decision was required. The man across the street cursed his assignment. High stakes and bad data. To eliminate the subject would not only remove him from all future use; it would point a crimson finger at him. Better to arrange an accident. But that took time, and better anything than that the subject should confess. It would not take long. The telephone was monitored; the line could be cut at will, the house rushed. They would know of any appointment made. But a face-to-face confession was also a danger, and the man in the white suit looked bad. His instincts warned him.

The laser still produced a garbled murmur. He picked up the microphone and this time pressed the button. The Bulgarian acknowledged. The man across the street said quickly, "Get into position. If either moves toward the telephone, take him and then the other. Otherwise wait."

The Bulgarian acknowledged.

Aldrytch said, "You have to understand. It was 1974. After Watergate. After Vietnam. All we had left was conscience. Don't you remember that? Loyalty was the whore of knaves. Patriotism belonged to fools and scoundrels. Our institutions were packed with lies. We had acted in the world like a drunken policeman. Everything that was decent, everything that pulled us through, was in the conscience of individual, lonely men. I didn't come to that easily, you know. I gave my own son. He died in sixty-eight, in Tet, an infantry lieutenant. I began to think of what he died for, what they all had died for. And then came Angola. They'd have sent them in, Ford and Kissinger, enough to get us stuck, enough to send for more. Back to the butcher's shop. No debate, no high purpose, no flags, no gladness, just the American kids who survived the last one being stuffed through a meat grinder in a back room. I could stop it by leaking it, I knew that.

"I knew Snead. I thought he was a good young man. I knew his magazine. There were young people then who were looking at the world in a new way. They began with the individual. When you do that, everything looks different. They were teaching us to think. I thought he was one of those. So I told him and it was in the press and then in Congress and Angola never happened. He taped me, of course. My voice. And he got me back and asked me other things – always things that I could tell myself shouldn't have been secret after all. Well, you'll have it all in writing. He was very clever. Even the threats were barely noticeable at first. It was always just a little easier to go on than to say no. I didn't even know when I was trapped. Well, it's all in the packet. Take it straight to Langley. Snead's one of the suspects, as a matter of fact. They were closing in on him already. There was a young man at the House Armed Services Committee that the FBI was watching, Salfield was his name, I think. Just before they were going to pick him up, he and his wife were hit by a truck on the highway. Both killed. It was too neat, and then the driver had a heart attack that day. KGB's done that too often. Salfield had been meeting with a girl who lives with Snead. So it began to add up. They'll have him tonight. But you see, I wasn't a traitor. No more than if I'd kept my mouth shut and let them do something I knew was wrong. I followed my conscience. I had to do that. It led me to hell. I know what I am. I know what I have done. But I wasn't a traitor. You must understand that."

Stears watched in silence the distinguishable face, heard the pleading, puzzled voice. An unlucky, noble man in a cruel heap. And one who had repented. Who would destroy himself in reparation, who had balked only at destroying the woman he loved in her last extremity. There but for the grace of God. It could happen to anyone. He looked at Aldrytch with boiling anger. He saw Hajji, the successful, the wise, the bruised face and the bucket in the cell. He saw the bodies crawling in the bloody dust and the terrorists lighting cigarettes. He heard McNaughton's gravelly voice and saw the clear blue eyes. He saw a catacomb of cells and fists and boots, a world of vomit, blood, and anger. It spilled over the delicate, airy room, over the delicate, fine dilemma. The puzzled pain on Aldrytch's face seemed as false as makeup, as Witham's smile. He thought that he was being unfair. Weren't such dilemmas treated with respect?

But he said, "I understand. McNaughton wasn't worth your conscience. And you're going to be caught anyway, aren't you? It's just a question of time. This is more graceful."

There had been a German shepherd at the house next door. It had found the scented meat at the edge of the wood. Yesterday morning, the Bulgarian had thrown the body, still with hamburger in its jaws, deeper into the wood. The subject had a dog, too, but it was ancient and barely left the house. He had not been able to poison it. He did not think it would be a problem. There were no more dogs.

These houses of the ruling class had deep gardens ending in trees. Behind these houses were no more houses, but a long, steepening slope, heavily wooded and overgrown, leading down into Rock Creek Park. The gardens were all walled along the sides. Most of them were open at the back, the limitless background of woods being part of the design, protected by wire fences discreetly invisible in the growth. The German shepherd had made his way under one of these. The Bulgarian, with wire cutters, had made another. It could be opened and closed at will. It would pass a cursory inspection. The Bulgarian had spent two and a half days now in the wood. The weather had been pleasant.

At the radio signal, the Bulgarian opened the fence and crawled through it. He left it open for a quick withdrawal. He was now in Aldrytch's garden, still well hidden in the trees. He could see the French windows of the living room and one of the figures inside. He could still advance another twenty yards and be in adequate cover. He was dressed as a gardener. His rifle with its silencer was roughly wrapped in burlap, a gardener's miscellaneous implement. Under his coat, he carried a silenced automatic.

Invisible to him, in the house across the street from Aldrytch's, a colleague sat near the window. The house had been bought three years ago as a general precaution, as the occasional residence of a West Coast developer with interests in the capital. The neighborhood was used to seeing it periodically occupied and periodically empty. There were two more colleagues, who would probably not be needed, in a telephone van farther up the street.

The plan was crude but it would work. The subject spent much of his time in the living room and invariably received there. The garden and the house opposite, between them, had an excellent field of fire into the room. There would be a sound of broken glass and nothing more. The man in the garden would walk quickly through the French windows to ascertain death.

If this were not possible, if the subject had to be eliminated where he could not be taken through a window, the man in the garden would enter the house through the French windows, find the subject, and kill him. The telephone would be cut at the moment of entry. If the subject ran from the house, he would be shot from the house opposite as he opened the door. The gunmen would evacuate through the backs of the houses. Unless they were picked up instantly, which was not very likely, they would have an excellent chance of disappearing. The Bulgarian embassy would help. If things became extremely complicated, if several people were in the house, the reinforcements in the van could be called in. This would not be desirable.

The Bulgarian crept forward. The figure he could see was the subject. He was in a chair, profiled. It was a difficult shot, but by no means impossible. He unwrapped the rifle, reserving the burlap. He steaded the rifle and relaxed. The subject raised his head. He could see the subject's features through the telescopic sight.

Aldrytch raised his head. His eyes were shocked. But as the shock in them cleared, his face returned neither to pleading nor to strained authority, but to the face in the photographs, composed and sure. In his present health, it made his skin seem transparent.

He said, "You are entirely correct. I wanted to be right without risk. And I did not send for Williston Stears's boy to make excuses." He looked for a moment at the fire and added, "Was he a good father?"

Surprised, Wop thought and said, "He was always

entertaining. I always knew that I was loved. He was not reliable. I always knew that I could depend only on myself. I never found it all that difficult."

"I felt so superior to him after the war. He had been more successful than I at Yale. I was obviously one of the successes after the war. I remember forty-six. It was so obvious that I was in the front rank of a victorious nation. It was clear and it was true. And Williston was a second-rate poet in a disgraced and half-criminal exile. *What a cowardly mess,* I thought. That came back to haunt me when I knew what I had become. I would have turned myself in quite soon. When I discovered what I had done to Michael I began to pray for Milly's death. That's terrible, isn't it? I don't think I would have let them use me again. But when I saw your name on the dispatch, when I saw it was you who had realized how it had happened, I had to do it quickly. I couldn't hide while Williston's boy came closer and closer. Even if it wasn't you, it would have been your doing. It was like a nightmare, a nemesis. I had to cut it free." He looked into the fire again, but Wop did not interrupt. Aldrytch said, "I said he was second-rate, not third. I have most of what he published. He really did no less well than the rest of us. Why did he have to go to France?"

"He didn't like to have things asked of him. I don't think he liked reality much. There was very little reality in Vichy France. And my mother's uncle was mixed up with Ciano, you know. I think her loyalties were a little mixed."

Aldrytch slowly nodded. "And you? You're not a career officer, are you?"

"No. I'm an investment counselor. I found a niche in the Arab market a few years ago. I've been very success-ful. I enjoy it."

He had a sense, now, that the interview, which had become no less appalling but at least more human with the change in Aldrytch, was taking on the quality of a conversation on a railway platform, not false, exactly, but artificially prolonged. And he did not know where his fear came from, but it grew.

Aldrytch said, "You obviously have a talent for intelligence work. You should consider it, I think. I have made sure that the suggestion will be made that you join the Agency as a career officer. It will be forgotten that it came from me."

"It will also," said Wop, "be refused."

"You say so now, but you will think about it. This gets into the blood. You soon will be my parting gift. Are you married?"

"Very soon."

"American?"

"No. Moroccan. But you could say that she is French."

"Then you are a little like your father after all. You must not like to be at home. Are you happy?"

He saw Wop stiffen and said quietly, "Forgive me. But you are the last person I shall talk to and I should like to know."

In Aldrytch's voice there was no drama left, nor appeal. The sunny, flowered room with the autumn woods behind took on a quality unreal and without substance, an inadequate frame for finality. He wondered if this was what had made him afraid. He thought. Untruth in his answer looked suddenly ugly, a malicious levity.

He said, "Five days ago, they were about to kill me. I had time to think about it. I realized that I had loved the world and that it was worth anything that one could give it. I was glad to have lived. That doesn't answer your question. I can't answer it. I'm sorry."

Aldrytch said, "It's good enough. I had forgotten how people felt. Thank you." He was silent, an old man looking into the fire. Then he said, "Well. No reason to wait. What I have for you is very detailed. It will undo such damage as can be undone."

He looked into the fire again a moment before he rose. He went toward the French windows. Stears, on an impulse of salute or of formality, rose also and stood. The farther third of the room was somewhat divided from the rest by a sofa placed across the room. In the far corner, on the same wall as the fireplace, was a walnut secretaire placed in the angle of the longer wall and the wall toward the garden and deep enough so that anyone standing or sitting at it would be framed in the right-hand corner of the French windows. Aldrytch bent to open one of the secretaire's lower drawers. It was nearly empty. There was a manila envelope, clearly visible against the darker wood. By it was a glint of dull metal. A gun. Stears realized. It was a service revolver. He saw it with a sudden shock, a queasiness, as an unwilling voyeur. Aldrytch tuned to him and spoke. The envelope was in his hand and his back was to the French windows. "This is a record of my dealings with Snead, both as to substance and method, from early 1976 until ten days ago. Some, like poor Michael, is irreparable, some can be cauterized, some may even give the Agency an opportunity for a counteroffensive. Much of it is from memory, but I can assure you that my memory is excellent. Take it, please, and go now."

The subject rose from his chair. The man in the house tensed and put the binoculars back over his eyes. The visitor had also risen; if he had moved toward the telephone he would have ordered the strike then and there. This was nonspecific. He cursed the assignment again. There was not much but luck between him and taking the subject unnecessarily or letting him talk. The latter would never be forgiven. The former would be harder to prove. He hoped he had convinced his superiors that an "accident" was imperative. He hoped it would take no more than two days.

The subject went to the far end of the room. He knew there was a desk there but it was out of the line of sight. He could just see the subject's back. He calculated: the subject would be framed in the corner of the glass doors, a good target for the Bulgarian. The subject bent. He must be getting something from the desk. It could be anything, it could also be it. He raised the microphone. He stopped. The subject had turned and was facing his visitor, himself, and the window with the laser trained upon it. Quickly, the man in the house snugged the earphones again. Possibly, luck was his. The subject seemed to be about to speak.

The words were buzzing, denatured, flat. He missed a few. He did not hear "Snead" until it had already gone past. But he had the substance. He considered a second. No, there was no chance that he was wrong. He pressed the microphone. "Take them," he said. "Both. Now."

Aldrytch stepped toward him. Stears's apprehension, more irrational than ever, was now such that he would have liked to bolt from the room. He found it hard to look Aldrytch in the face. He looked beyond him to the woods. There was no wind. The leaves were still. He saw one bush quiver. He saw a sudden wink, as of a tiny heliograph. And suddenly time changed gear; the moment froze. His fear came roaring out of its hole like a bear. A synapse deep within him, a synapse born during the last two weeks, clicked; the entire scenario became clear as crystal in the flick of an eye. He yelled, "Jump! Down!" and moved first himself, throwing himself forward and to the ground.

Aldrytch moved too. He was catapulted, spinning, against the secretaire. There was a thud as he hit it. There was a slap of the envelope hurled to the floor. There was the mild tinkle of broken glass. Nothing more. That was wrong. He heard a long, shuddering breath from Aldrytch. The sofa was between him and the garden. For a moment he was safe. He moved. He moved his head toward the closed door. No glass this time. Just the concussion of a hammer by his ear, the parquet dissolving a foot from his head, the splinters in his skin. He froze, bewildered, then knew. He was under two fires.

He scuttled like a crab. The leg of a chair disintegrated as he scuttled past. But he was under the window now. He was whining to himself.

The sofa did not quite block his view. Aldrytch was lying against the secretaire, his neck slack, his chest sodden, one hand lying limply by the open drawer. He might still be alive, but he did not seem to move or breathe.

A gardener was coming up the lawn. Stears even thought "gardener" for a second – a stolid, small, Eastern European peasant with a pencil mustache and a cast-off hacking coat, cheap labor for a Georgetown garden. Evidently, he had left the gun behind. Wop had a moment of obscure hope. Then, as the man came near the house, he reached unhurriedly into his worn-out coat. He was looking at the man's face. The man looked at Stears with dull satisfaction. He opened the French windows and walked through. The silenced automatic was in his hand. Wop pressed against the wall. The man looked at Aldrytch's body and at the envelope in passing. The living came first. He walked past Aldrytch to the sofa. He raised the automatic. Wop burrowed at the wall and shut his eyes. The gun was not silenced after all. The noise was terrific. He twitched at it. He lay still. He heard a terrible breathing. He was wounded then. It did not hurt. He waited for the finishing shot. There was none. He opened his eyes.

The gardener had gone. But the gardener's hand stretched out from behind the sofa, on the floor. The whistling breathing behind the sofa faltered and stopped. Aldrytch had toppled over, was lying on the floor. Something glinted in his lap. Stears scuttled forward toward the sofa. In Aldrytch's lap was the service revolver. The floor behind him erupted in splinters and he threw himself behind the sofa finding himself on top of the gardener. The gardener was wet. A hole the size of a fist appeared in the sofa. The envelope was at arm's length. He rolled for it, then swam across the floor.

Aldrytch was certainly dead. He guessed that at the very end of the room he would be back in the line of sight, so he rose to his feet like a sprinter and pitched himself through the open window, staggered, and rolled into a flowerbed. There was no shot. Magazine empty, perhaps. He had not counted.

He ran down the edge of the lawn. He was safe from that rifle now. The thought of others was more a pressing terror than a conscious thought. He was in the overgrowth and trees. A wire fence caged him in. He stumbled down the fence. He found a new-cut gap.

And then the ground steepened. He was falling as much as running now, the envelope clasped to his chest, his suit ripped by thorns, his ankle dully hurting. But as his hysteria seemed to mount, his heart was lightening. He had traveled to the head of the poisoned spring, and the spring was purified, and the spell was broken. He heard a police siren far behind him. He ran not from danger, for he now felt none, but out of the contagion of a plague. He saw a road of sorts below him with public picnic sites. He remembered, he must be in Rock Creek Park. A family sat at one: a father, pink-faced, with a windbreaker with "John Deere" written on the front; a woman in pants and box jacket, double-knit; two blond boys in sweaters. There was food wrapped in foil on the table. There was a yellow Winnebago behind. They looked at him, frozen, a man in a ruined ice-cream suit, bloody and wild-eyed, at once hobbling and crashing out of the wood, a legal envelope in his hand. He stood over them, leaning on the table. His ankle hurt damnably. The foil-wrapped food brought a sudden memory of Marie-Sophie's fish, a bridge to a real world. He was able to nod to them courteously. He said, "I hate to disturb you, but you must take me to the FBI. At once."

Epilogue

On the first day, the room had smelled of smoke; on the second, of distant tear gas; on the third, of his own habitation. The room was reached by a hidden staircase behind a garage controlled by the PLO. It had been used to store weapons. On the floor, there were the marks of crates, and, in the corner, now, a heap of bedding. There were no facilities. It had smelled sharply of gun metal and grease. That had comforted the engineer in him. It had no light and one window. He had stood by the corner of the window, almost for a whole day, his face pressed against the wall, seeing a wedge of street. Once he had seen the broken body of one of the Brothers of Islam, one of his own inner circle, dragged like a rag doll down the street by the mob. That had been in the first hours. After that, he had seen Brothers among the mobs that yelled for his own blood. Now that, also, was over. Now the streets were almost quiet, now the smell of tear gas had faded. Now the King's police searched methodically, block by block, at leisure. Hour by hour, Ibrahim had dissolved inside him. Ibrahim was gone. He did not know when he had finally died.

He had been brought here just in time. The PLO had snatched him away. It gave him, now, the afflatus of his own sublime gamble gone, some feeling of pride to be a part of a group skilled and daring enough to have done it. The first rumors of the confessions had come while he was the king of the al-Tabek slums. Though it had touched him icily, he had not even truly believed it himself. The first man he had heard speak of it had been hanged. But even later, as the rumors grew, he had easily bent them down. Ibrahim had grown within him. He had had a feeling of Ibrahim larger than himself, surrounding him like a black shield, stiffening him, of Ibrahim's power pouring through his eyes. It became more than rumors. Army helicopters, through loudspeakers, blared recordings at the streets. Leaflets fluttered down. On every side belief in him died, but his own presence could reignite it. He had moved faster and faster through the city.

Julia had given him strength. He would say, now, spent – like a child after a fever – that he had learned that she loved him. She, red-haired American, could not be seen with him in the crowd, but she had stayed close with the PLO/Baath cadres following behind. During these hours, they had spent perhaps three minutes together. The longest time uninterrupted had been a third of that.

It had been, of all places, in the back room of a cheap suitcase store. It had been when the rumors were first becoming inarguably dangerous. A Baath operative in the crowd had pulled him by his sleeve, three times, the agreed signal. He had made an excuse to the mob around him. There had been time for an inconclusive, momentary conference with his allies, whose growing fear had infected him. It was Julia who had saved him then. She had taken him aside by the hand and held his eyes with hers. She had taken his face in her hands. Ibrahim had grown again within him, fed from her eyes. She sealed it with a kiss, pulling his mouth down to hers. It came to him later that every carnality of his life before Julia was pale and remote beside Julia's kiss. He had carried the crowd another hour.

The time had come when one in the crowd shouted against him in his presence. The time had come when another – he recognized him, probably from the survivors at the tomb – had thrown a stone at him. The man had been kicked to the ground, but he had been

404

let live. The crowd would not be his for long. He was afraid.

Hands had grabbed him. The crowd had wavered between resisting and joining in. He had been pulled into a house. He had been pulled through it, out into the street behind. There was a van. The Mullah Ibrahim was gone.

The food and water they had left behind with him were almost gone. They were to come back when the streets were quieter, and magic him from the city. As yet they had not done so. He had the impression that the police had restored order with surprising efficiency. Perhaps there were cordons. It was true that he was safe here. But not forever.

He had failed. He was largely in ignorance. He did not precisely know the point of failure. He, Hussein Shamak the engineer, had never flinched from the hard truth that security was never certain, that *Lyusi* had specific points of risk, that there were dangers that Ibrahim, however perfectly realized, could not control. Nonetheless, he was honestly surprised. He had seen no indication of disaster. He had thought that he had won. In his time of weakness, at the tomb among the bodies, before Julia came, he had become aware of the possibility of failure from within himself. He had forgotten the danger from without.

Was he also at fault? He looked at it honestly, a devout Marxist before an implacable text. "Adventurism" was an ugly word. Adventurism was not only frivolity, the placing of personal impulse above the understanding of the proper pace of socialism's growth; but it was also the specific sin that could, in a given place, set socialism back indefinitely. *Lyusi* had done that, for sure. Was *Lyusi*, from the beginning, adventurism? In hindsight, yes.

But genius, too. Genius not only in Ibrahim's darker flights, but in scheme, in geometry, in form. The greatest force potentially serving the King had been the primitive religiosity of his people. The King, by self-indulgence,

405

had opened a crack in that force. Ibrahim, *Lyusi*, had entered that crack and had all but turned the King's potential strength into his downfall. *Lyusi* was superb. The sudden impulse for self-doubt passed. He had acted for History. Even Lenin, surely, would have forgiven him.

But Lenin was not here, and he had failed, and was frightened and alone. He longed for Julia. Surely she would find a way to come.

The PLO driver was named Youssof Mazdi. He was a serious young man who had briefly taught elementary school in Beirut. The American redhead beside him gave him the creeps. Among the committee, she had seemed like a rich girl in an American movie. In the cab, she had perhaps stopped pretending. She sat perfectly still with her eyes in her lap and seemed to be talking silently to herself. He would not have used her for anything. But perhaps she was specifically qualified for this task.

In the garage, he pulled aside a metal locker on rollers, full of tools. He showed her the door that led to Ibrahim's room. He said, "You understand? He is sure to be found here within three to four hours. The cordons are such that we may fail in getting him out of the city. If you find that he is in a state to resist interrogation if captured, we will risk it. Otherwise it ends here. That is clear?"

Julia said, "Of course it's clear."

She had her hand on the door handle, but he had to unlock it first.

He had filled her. She had made contact with him in Washington without much interest – the organizers, the couriers, were always just ordinary men. Meeting the trained operatives, the killers, always gave her a little beforehand thrill, a current in the back of the neck. It wasn't that she particularly admired them. Most of them were less skilled than she herself. But the killers had something, after they had done their work, that she could take from them in bed. She was not sure what it was. When she pictured it, it was like a mixture of fire, like a burning oil-derrick, and black, rushing water. Fire, but not quite light. That was something like it. It filled her lungs and let her breathe. Otherwise she felt dead. By morning she had usually taken it all, and the killers were just ordinary, flabby things. She supposed they got it back one day. She'd never tried twice.

This one had been different. It was like there was something bigger than him, around him, something that would have completely filled her, that was absolutely the thing she wanted, except that it wasn't completely there. It was an act, of course, the Ibrahim stuff; a frameup and quite a clever one. It had made her laugh. Even the real Shamak, the Egyptian who had thought it up and acted it out, wasn't bad for a commie. Commies were dull. But it wasn't just an act. Acts wouldn't fool her. Sometimes Ibrahim was really there. It came and went. She'd been to bed with Shamak lots of times now. Sometimes it was there and sometimes it wasn't. At first, when it wasn't, she'd thought of killing him. But he hadn't done his job yet and she couldn't.

Then she'd found she could put Ibrahim back into him, too. That was quite new. It excited her. It was like they'd had a baby they could pass between them. But it was complicated, because it made her despise him that she had to. She'd had to do it in that mess where they'd shot all the people. She'd had to do it in the crowd. She'd have enjoyed doing it just for fun and him doing it back to her, but she didn't like having to do it. She'd vaguely thought of killing him instead. But she'd begun to worry. If she did, she might lose Ibrahim forever. She wasn't sure what she'd do this time.

She'd climbed one flight of stairs. The stairs were narrow and almost dark. She could just hear the people living on either side. But this staircase had only one door. That was it, one more flight up. She checked her handbag. They'd told her there couldn't be any noise. So that would do nicely.

407

The room stank. Well, he'd been in it three days. He was by the window. He turned to her, open-mouthed. He had a stupid smile on his face, as though the sun were in his eyes. He said, "Darling!" She'd never liked that. But he was still in his mullah clothes. He looked like Ibrahim.

Then he was all over her, kissing her. She stepped back.

At his first touch, she knew that Ibrahim was dead. Not just not there completely, or waiting, but gone for good. She felt cheated. She felt cold. There was just an ordinary soft man around her, licking her like a poodle. She wanted to push him away, but the operational part of her mind told her that he was frightened already and would be easy to interrogate. She didn't have to weigh the situation.

This was obviously the best time. So, to distract him, she held his wet mouth with hers and used her free hand to reach inside her bag. He groaned when the knife went in and his head pulled back and his eyes met hers.

And she almost screamed. For his eyes were the same as her father's in the dream. She pulled out the knife and thrust it into his face to make them close. It bounced off bone and she pushed it through his neck. All expression left the eyes, then, but she didn't see that.

Sometime later, when the PLO driver reluctantly decided that he had better go upstairs and check, she was kneeling beside the body, stabbing it still. The driver was never able to forget that the point of the knife had by then become twisted and bent by the stone floor.

CHRISTOPHER HYDE

THE TENTH CRUSADE

'Historically there were nine crusades. We are the tenth.'

A wave of religious fervour sweeps America in the form of a fanatical right-wing group known as the 'Tenth Crusade'. Its aim is to topple the US Reagan government. Its recruitment methods are similar to those of the Moonies. Its implications are terrifying . . .

So when a former girlfriend of ex-Vietnam photographer, Philip Kirkland, becomes inextricably involved with the sect, he realises he must rescue her—and his country—before it is too late.

'A powerful thriller'

The Times

'The enveloping malevolence of the cult leaders is superbly drawn'

Standard

CORONET BOOKS

Also available from
Hodder and Stoughton paperbacks

CHRISTOPHER HYDE
☐ 39871 X The Tenth Crusade   £2.50

JAMES CARROLL
☐ 23183 1 Madonna Red   £2.25
☐ 38052 7 Prince of Peace   £3.50

RICHARD HUGO
☐ 38632 0 Last Judgement   £2.75

BARRY CHUBIN
☐ 37664 3 The Feet of a Snake   £1.95

ERIC CLARK
☐ 24271 X Black Gambit   £2.50
☐ 28439 0 Send in the Lions   £1.50

E. M. CORDER
☐ 24335 X The Deer Hunter   £1.95

All these books are available at your local bookshop or newsagent, or can be ordered direct from the publisher. Just tick the titles you want and fill in the form below.

Prices and availability subject to change without notice.

Hodder & Stoughton Paperbacks, P.O. Box 11, Falmouth, Cornwall.

Please send cheque or postal order, and allow the following for postage and packing:

U.K. – 55p for one book, plus 22p for the second book, and 14p for each additional book ordered up to a £1.75 maximum.

B.F.P.O. and EIRE – 55p for the first book, plus 22p for the second book, and 14p per copy for the next 7 books, 8p per book thereafter.

OTHER OVERSEAS CUSTOMERS – £1.00 for the first book, plus 25p per copy for each additional book.

Name ....

Address..

....